I0784392

LAURIE BOULDEN

Once Upon a Time in Fairy Land:

A Collection of Twisted and Retold Fairy Tales

By Laurie Boulden

Contents

Rumpelstiltskin 1

The Pied Piper 41

Beast 63

Sleeping Beauty's Potion.. 87

The Frog Curse 99

Wolf and the Girl with the Red Cloak 123

The Ugly Duckling 175

Curse of the Seven Swans... 219

The Fisherman's Tale 251

The Little Mermaid 273

The Princess and the Pea 291

About the Author.. 308

Get Hooked on Another Great Read! 309

Cinderella Spell: A Tale from Fairy Land Chapter 1 309

Rumpelstiltskin

(previously self-published as Creating Gold, now expanded and revised)
The origin of Rumpelstiltskin is German. Tales were told as early as the 16th century. It was in 1812 that the Brothers Grimm wrote it as part of their collection of household tales. In the original tellings, Rumpelstiltskin was some type of a goblin. In my retelling, he is something quite different. Happy reading!

Chapter 1

Sebastian Mornn, Chancellor to the king, observed the smoke-drenched common room of the Wayside Inn where he'd been forced to stop. Pouring rains continued beating against the slated roof, bringing more drenched, unwashed bodies into the crowded room. His favored jacket would have to be burned. Anger simmered beneath his quiet surface as he studied the denizens surrounding him.

A fly buzzed along a trail of rotten meat, landing on a heavy oak table. Air stirred and a heavy fist flattened the insect. Another man dropped his hand of cards in the center of the circle of players. Shouts rose as a queen of spade skid across the table. A large man tipped his chair and another player's arm swung into him. He fell back, his howl of anger disrupting the general cadence of the room. Laughter burst through the air.

Noise abated in a moment. The game continued and Sebastian frowned into his empty mug. He smoothed a crease from his black shirt as he waved to the buxom blonde for more drink. The flicker of fear in her eyes made him smirk. A pleasure it was, to have power.

"Aye, a talented lass for sure."

Another conversation nabbed his attention. He turned his gaze to a thin man lifting a glass of wine. His mode of dress suggested a pauper gentleman.

"Nothing compared to my daughter." A different man slapped the table, his grin wide. "The elder, mind you. Now there's a lass who'll turn flax to gold."

Narrowing his eyes, Sebastian assessed the braggart making a fool of himself. Nondescript, save for a decorated jacket inlaid with golden strands. The hair on his neck tickled. *What manner of man devised such tales of his kin?* Sebastian stroked his goatee. As night settled and fires were laid in the grates to ward off the chill, the king's Chancellor crafted a fine scheme to fill the dull winter months at the palace.

Chapter 2

Elizabeth Haddock stared at the card, causing her father to squeal boorishly. A symbol of the king's emblem had been etched in a silver plate. She turned it over, but there was nothing more. She looked at her father. "What does it mean?"

"It is an invite to the Palace a fortnight from today."

Shocked, Elizabeth flipped the card again. "Invited to the palace? Where does it say such a thing?"

"Not on the card." Her father, Benner Haddock, nabbed it from her. "The servant told me. A fortnight. From today. Caroline and I are invited to stay at the palace for a winter gathering."

Elizabeth looked over the dusty, old furniture against the walls of the morning room. And this was the nicest of their rooms. "Why would the king invite you to the palace?"

Her father shrugged. "Caroline is much sought after. She is a beauty, you know. Why shouldn't the king have heard of her?" He tucked the precious card in his pocket and grabbed Elizabeth by the hands. He began to twirl her around the room. "Your sister shall dance with royalty, my dear. She will dazzle him. I've always known it."

Elizabeth skipped her feet to keep up with her father as her mind whirled with danger. "But should you go? We aren't exactly in kilter with his usual ilk."

With a credulous cry, her father released her. Elizabeth stumbled backward, managing to catch her balance before falling to the threadbare carpet.

"Not go?" His eyes appeared to fill with horror. "Are you daft, child? Caroline not go to the king? She will captivate him. He will fall in love and marry her. Would you deny your sister the opportunity of happiness and wealth beyond imagining?"

"Of course not, Father." Elizabeth tucked her hair behind her ear. "But the king is not known for kindness toward young ladies."

He waved away her concern. "He is not likely to harm her with her father present."

Elizabeth opened her mouth for further protest, but an angry darkness hardened her father's face. Remaining silent, she stepped back and swallowed as he leaned closer.

"Disgrace and envy flow from your lips, daughter, and I will not have it. Depart from me, I want no more of your presence today." He pulled the card from his pocket and turned from her.

Elizabeth blinked tears from her eyes as she took the back set of stairs to her room. "I must warn Caro."

A tray laden with food arrived at her room before she finished dressing for supper. The kitchen worker offered a weak smile, placed the tray on a dresser near the window, and left her alone. Her heart grew heavy as she realized her father did not want to see her at the dining table.

Hours later, Elizabeth heard someone moving through the room beside hers. She rushed into the hallway and knocked on her sister's door. Caroline greeted her with a mocking grin and a shake of her head. Where Elizabeth was short and slender, Caroline stood tall and graceful. Her golden hair cascaded down her back as she pulled pins from the coiffure.

"Really, Lizzie." Her sister's gray eyes sparkled with teasing. "You told Father I should not meet the king? He supposes you to be jealous, but what is there to be jealous of?" She waved her hand. "His royal highness would never notice a little thing like you. How often have I told you, you lack presence?"

"But Caro, such a man." Elizabeth ignored the usual taunts and sat on the bed, leaning against one of the posters as she tucked one leg beneath her. Though less than two years older, Caroline's glance caused Elizabeth to feel like a scolded child. She faced downward and plucked at her dressing gown.

Caroline opened the double doors of her wardrobe. "Of course, I must go, silly girl. I will meet the king. We will dance, he and I." She rummaged through the gowns.

"You believe him to be an honorable man?"

Frowning, her sister sent her a sharp glance. "Honorable? He is our king. Why should I be concerned if he is honorable? Power suits me more than honor."

"He is not like the boys in town, Caro. You cannot toy with him as you do the others."

Head shaking, Caroline stepped away from her perusal and pulled Elizabeth to her feet. She guided her to the door with a firm hand against her elbow. Elizabeth sighed.

Caroline's eyes rebuked as sharply as her words. "You've a simple mind, my dear. When I am queen, I will invite you to the palace where you are sure to be a novelty."

"Don't go." Elizabeth tried one last time. For a moment, Caroline's eyes revealed doubt. But then she shook her head and ushered Elizabeth through the door.

"You will see, Lizzie. A great man is permitted to love. He is bound to marry someone, why not me?"

The door closed firmly, leaving Elizabeth alone in the dimly lit hallway. Heaviness tightened her chest and clogged her throat as she returned to her bedroom. Their minds were set, and one thing remained.

Entering her own room offered no comfort. A small fire burned in the grate, causing shadows to flicker against the walls. Her bed mirrored Caroline's, her dresser and stand elegantly gleaming, though she knew most of the clothes within were patched and worn. Sobbing, she sank to her knees beside the bed. Father had spoken frequently of the king's exploits with disdain. How could he agree to attend? Caroline she could understand, but Father? Tears dampened her cheek.

"God. I don't understand why I have such fear in my heart. Oh please, send someone to protect them. Let them not fall into danger. I shake at the thought of their going, though I know not why. Help them please, Lord. Protect them."

Cold seeped through her nightgown and she crawled beneath the covers of her bed. Prayers drifted through her mind until sleep claimed her.

~

The feel of smooth wood beneath his fingers gave Rumpelstiltskin a sense of accomplishment. Hours of sanding following days of carving were worth the effort.

"Rom."

He turned at the sound of his name being called. A moment later, his friend entered the workshop at the back of a barn. "What has you out and about, Olsome?"

"Searching for you. What's the prince doing in a worn-out barn?"

Rom lifted one brow. "The space was good enough for my grandfather."

"Your grandfather has a journey for you."

Rom stood. "For me?"

"Don't—"

Rom didn't wait to hear more. He thought of his grandfather and then allowed his mind to take him there.

Alforstiltzkin looked up from the ledger on his desk as Rom appeared. He frowned. "I would caution against your talent, but I think it may come in handy."

"Why is that?" Rom was used to being able to appear and disappear at will.

"Our High King has revealed someone in need. You are the means to help."

"My father approves?"

Grandfather's lip twitched. "The king recognizes the power that is greater than he. He will not keep you from this destiny."

Rom rubbed his hands together. "We are Guardians for our High King. I am excited to learn more."

Grandfather leaned back. "It will involve creating gold."

Rom sat to hear more.

Chapter 3

The last vestige of light turned the sky deep burgundy. Caroline paused at the window to stare across rolling hills dotted with trees. A loon called through the growing darkness. Excitement buzzed through her as she pulled the heavy curtains and faced her guestroom within the palace. Whinmoore Palace. She was really here. Though the housekeeper's servant who brought her to the room claimed it as one of the smallest, the room was larger than what she knew from home. Blue paper with gilded birds covered the top half of the walls. The bottom half was painted lighter blue. A large bed with dark wood posts took up most of the main room, though there was a straight-backed chair and round table near the window.

A second room held her clothes, most of those newly purchased. She also had her own indoor bathroom. What a lovely luxury. The maid promised to draw a bath for her in the mornings after breakfast. But for tonight… she twirled. Dinner, perhaps dancing.

A knock sounded at the door, pulling Caroline from exploring the opulent room. A small ladies maid entered. "Good evening, mum. I've been sent to help you prepare for this evening."

Caroline nodded and offered a tight smile. "I appreciate the attention."

The young maid helped her don a rose underlay with a crimson skirt and matching vest that buttoned up the front. The sleeves of the underlay ballooned at her upper arms and gathered with thick lace. The maid tugged on the back of the vest. "You look charming."

Caroline straightened her shoulders as she studied herself in the mirror. Her dark hair was piled on her head except for a long strand over her left shoulder that had been twisted into a curl. She'd thought the color of the gown too rich for a young woman, but with her dark hair and pale skin, she felt resplendent. Her green eyes shone. "You may fetch a lad to take me to the parlor where guests gather."

The maid bowed and left. Caroline pressed her hands against her belly. In a matter of moments, she would meet King Hewel. She was determined he would not forget her.

Another knock on the door and Caroline found herself looking up at a man more important than a palace servant.

"Forgive the intrusion." He bowed. "I am Chancellor Mornn. It would be my pleasure to escort you to our gathering."

She lowered her gaze. "Thank you. I appreciate your attention." Though she did not recognize him, his long blue jacket with gold buttons, as well as the thin circlet of gold on his head, marked him as one of great importance.

"I have been looking forward to tonight's party," he said as they walked the hallway.

"Is there something of significance?"

"I think the king has a plan. I would not wish to spoil it for him."

"Indeed, not." Caroline felt her heart swell within her.

Their chatter remained unimportant as he guided her through the labyrinth of halls and stairs until they reached a large room buzzing with people.

"Ah, my daughter." Her father called to her.

Chancellor Mornn bowed. "A pleasure, my lady."

Then he left her.

Father watched him leave. "Who was that?"

Caroline squeezed his hands. "Chancellor to the king. He personally led me from my chambers."

Father smiled as his chest puffed. "An honor."

Caroline gazed across the magnificent room. Chandeliers with crystal forms shone above the gathering like heavenly lights. "I shall have to write Lizzie."

"Don't waste time with that silly girl. You have more important things to attend." He took her hand for a moment. "Enjoy your night. Charm King Hewel. There is nothing else you need bother about."

Once he released her hand, he gave her a wide smile and then sauntered off.

"A glass of wine?" A servant offered, holding a silver tray with a goblet. His face was down. Caroline felt a burn of pleasure at the gesture of humbleness. She took the glass and moved away. More people entered. A palette of colors added to the festive atmosphere. Somewhere, a clock struck and the air itself seemed charged with excitement. A cord of trumpeters sounded. Caroline turned along with everyone else.

A set of oversized doors opened. Soldiers entered first, taking places at intermittent points along the walls. Then came half a dozen servants wearing gold uniforms, making them stand out from any others. An older woman with silver hair was carried in a litter. Most everyone's attention followed the king's mother, but Caroline was more interested in King Hewel. She longed for her first glimpse of him. The man did not disappoint. He entered, followed by Chancellor Mornn. Though the king was not as tall, his wide shoulders and thick chest made him appear larger. His dark hair was thick, with a slight curl. The tone of the metal in his crown seemed to have been chosen to complement his hair. His face tightened as he first peered through the crowd of people. Elizabeth's warning about him being a difficult man seeped into her mind, but she willed it away. There was more than romance involved here.

She watched as the chancellor introduced him to a sallow-faced girl with too many ruffles in her skirt. The two men followed by four of the servants wandered among the people, stopping to chat with some. Ignoring others. Caroline chatted with an older couple, although she kept her attention on the nearing pair. When they finally joined them, she turned.

Chancellor Mornn grinned. "Here is the beauty I escorted to our gathering. Miss Caroline, I believe."

Caroline dipped graciously, and then gazed up at King Hewel. His vivid blue eyes caused flutters within her stomach.

"A pleasure." He greeted.

Caroline tilted her head but said nothing.

King Hewel narrowed his gaze. "What?"

She waved her hand. "Some silly response."

His lips twitched with amusement. "I give you leave to speak your mind."

Caroline raised her chin. "You did not seem pleased when you first saw the crowd awaiting you."

He laughed. "I sent my mother with all the pomp she could desire so I might enter unobtrusively."

"You should not invite so many people if you do not care for a crowded room."

"Some events require pomp and ceremony, though I prefer more… intimate occasions."

Chancellor Mornn led him onward, and Caroline pressed her hand against her chest. She had done it. He would remember her.

~

Caroline sipped wine and flirted with a young man at her left elbow. Surreptitious glances toward the king revealed his attention. She waited until his eyes almost met her own, and then lowered her lashes and caused her cheeks to pinken. She lifted a silver fork to her lips, though she knew not what she tasted. Her attention fixed on the lush room with carved sconces and painted ceiling. The walls above the chair rails were a medley of colors subtly swirled together, perfect backdrop for paintings of plump nudes.

The king's table sat thirty patrons, and the din garbled her partner's words. She smiled prettily and nodded when she thought she should. Course after course was placed before her and removed by silent servants. Finally, the king's mother stood. The women placed their lap covers across the table. Caroline followed suit. She joined the line leading away from the dining hall and glanced back toward His Majesty. He lifted his glass and their eyes seemed to meet across the growing distance. Her heart skipped, but she allowed only a small smile to grace her face. She acknowledged him and turned forward.

The palace wormed its way into her heart. Dragging her fingers along a polished redwood rail, she envisioned herself dressed more splendidly than any woman currently present. She accepted the ornately carved chair one of the attendants indicated. With her back straight and crimson skirt settled about her legs, she knew the king's attention would be drawn to her the instant he entered the room. Voices of ladies twitted like birds. Though acquainted with a few, Caroline was intimate friends with no one. She sat, holding herself still, waiting for the gentlemen to join them. Not half an hour had passed when a servant opened the doors to the drawing room, allowing the men to enter.

The king walked the perimeter of the room, his hands clasped behind his back. He spoke a moment with men and women alike, and then moved forward once more. It was in this manner he arrived at Caroline's side. Looking up, she drank in the sight of him. Wide shoulders, square jaw, high forehead. Hard eyes the color of slate. She shivered. His hand stretched toward her, and she felt power in his touch.

"Dinner pleased you?" His voice murmured, this conversation for the two of them only.

"How could it not? Your chef is a master." Caroline felt her heart pound as his hand continued to hold hers.

"I hold quality in high regard."

"Your palace must be rife with masterpieces."

"Would you care to see some?"

The king offered a special tour. She had to quell the giddy excitement that bubbled in her veins. "But what of your other guests?"

He tucked her hand at his elbow and drew her across the room. Apparently, they did not matter. She floated beside him, barely taking note of the gilded rooms they passed, the marble floors they crossed, nor the carved stairs they climbed.

One painting, among a sea of his relatives caught her eye. The sad countenance of the woman leapt from the canvas.

"I, too, am moved by her." The king remained at her side.

"A talented artist, to capture such emotion." Caroline sounded awed.

"I relish talent. Craftsmen of quality are a rarity in these modern times."

Caroline studied the king. This close, she could see feathers of silver cascading from his temples. His hair waved around his ears and touched the collar of his dress shirt. The velvet vest pulled tight across his chest, and she doubted padding had been needed to adjust the fit. He stood a head taller than herself, allowing her eyes to rest on the golden medallion he wore around his neck. Lost in perusal, she hadn't realized he'd been talking. She looked up as a question registered.

"Are you?"

Caroline blinked. "Am I?"

"A master weaver?"

Her mouth widened with pleasure. "You do not require false modesty, do you, Sire?" At the shake of his head, she leaned closer. "I am known throughout my village."

"Who taught you?"

"My mother. Hers was a talent that could sparkle in twilight."

"Your father made an interesting claim. Caught the attention of Chancellor Mornn." The king led her into the hallway and up a flight of stairs. Caroline warmed to his particular attention. Dreams of living in the palace filled her mind.

They stopped at the first door to a wing of offices. She blushed when she saw the grand bed against the far wall. But then she noticed a mound of plant material and an old spinning wheel. She pointed. "What is plant debris doing inside the palace?"

"That is the flax you will spin into gold."

Caroline laughed, turning away. "Spin into gold? What an odd tease you are."

He stopped her with a firm hand on her arm. "Your father has claimed it is possible. You yourself claim to be talented."

"At weaving. With cotton or silk even. But this? How is such a thing to be achieved?"

The king's manner cooled. He distanced himself with arms crossed over his chest. "And yet, that is your task. You will spin the flax into gold by morning light, or you will die."

The king pushed her into the room. She stood in the bare space in the center of the bedroom as he offered a brief bow and closed the door. And clicked a lock. And a second lock. She stared, waiting. Surely, he meant to return. To joke at his clever humor? Silence dragged.

The walls offered no windows. She walked to the door and pulled. It refused to budge. Fear set in. She walked to the mound of flax and lifted a piece. The thin flat leaf was nearly as long as her arm. She looked at the spinning wheel. Was one piece even big enough to go through the machine? How would it work? Her chest began to quiver with sobs as she held the piece of leaf against the wood of the spindle, and then the wheel. Where was one to put it? Even if she could figure that, how could a plant become gold thread?

Despair overwhelmed her. She threw herself onto the bed with a howl.

"That's not going to help much, is it?"

Caroline screamed, rolled to the far side of the bed, and held a pillow to her chest.

A slender man, shorter than herself, stood near the door. His flamboyant yellow jacket and slacks lit the room with color. His eyes sparkled with mischief.

Though her heart still pounded, she found she could not fear him. Something about him set her at ease. She scooted closer, still clinging to the pillow.

"Why is maiden fair sobbing her heart upon the bed?" he asked with an elegant bow.

Caroline stood. She shuddered as she took a deep breath. "The king has set an impossible task. I will die when morning comes."

"Travesty." He pressed his hand to his heart, eyes widened with horror. "The king is a fool. What task has milady been charged with?"

Caroline pointed at the fresh mound of plant cuttings. More tears dripped down her cheeks.

"And the king wants?" His raised brows revealed his need and desire for more information.

"Gold. From that." She could barely say the words.

"Ah." The man nodded. He rubbed his hand over his chin. "A daring dream indeed. You are loved, dear girl, by powers great and true. For I have come."

"To help me?" Caroline wasn't sure how anyone could help.

"If that is your wish."

Caroline didn't hesitate. She released the pillow and crossed the room. She unclasped a silver necklace and placed it in his hand.

He took a step back, as though surprised. He looked at his hand and then at her face.

"I wish it." Caroline rushed. She grabbed a handful of flax, selected a wide piece, and handed it to him. The stranger stood for a moment, one hand holding the leaf and the other clasping her necklace.

With a shrug, he slipped the necklace into a front pocket and sat behind the wheel. He placed his feet on two boards near the floor. With a push, the wheel began to spin. He fed the flax through the guide, and then looked at her with his hand stretched out.

Caroline barely noticed. She watched the spokes blur as they spun. The machine seemed to shimmer. She startled when he stopped. "What are you doing?"

He gave her an odd glance. "I'm going to need more materials."

"But what has happened to the first?"

"Take a look for yourself." He nodded at the bobbin where the fiber was stored. Caroline stepped closer. Against the wood shaft of the spool lay a yarn the color of gold. She touched it, uncertain her eyes didn't deceive her. But the yarn felt smooth and metallic.

She didn't realize he'd crossed the room until he dumped a pile of leaves at her feet and sat down. Sweeping her skirts out of the way, she watched his legs begin to move and the wheel to spin. Joy surged through her. She danced across the bedroom, grabbing the pillow once more. With a contented sigh, she flopped onto the bed. Relief filled her. She was saved. Stretching, she imagined the king's surprise on the morrow. His delight. In her. Thoughts of grandeur and the sound of the wheel spinning around and around lulled her to sleep.

Pounding on the door woke her. She sat with a start in the dark, and then yelped as the door opened and slammed against the wall. Light poured into the chamber. With a gasp of fright, Caroline looked to the center of the room where the wheel sat. No sign of the slender man remained. She twisted around to look at the pile of flax, but only a few crumbs remained on the floor. The other wall was stacked with bobbins thick with golden thread. She raised triumphant eyes to the king and his chancellor.

~

Elizabeth flipped through the letters newly arrived. An invitation to a ball, but nothing from Father or Caro. She sighed. Could they not at least let her know they arrived safely?

She sat on the bench beneath the hall window. It was winter, so there were no leaves rustling on the trees. Gray skies gave everything a gloomy air. Was this to be her lot? Tucked away, only cared for by servants? "Please, God," she whispered as she pressed her hand against a windowpane. "Help Caro and help me."

A red bird fluttered to the ground a few feet from where she sat. Its vivid color shone like a beacon on the dull day. Watching it flip through dead leaves to forage for food gave Elizabeth hope.

~

That night, King Hewel celebrated. A grand hall had been transformed with tables and benches. To Caroline, it seemed hundreds made merry as minstrels sang and flautists played. She and her father sat beside the king, upon a raised dais. The chancellor and several princes ate with them. Caroline barely noticed the thick herbed lamb shank filling her plate. The king held her attention. His eyes enthralled her, their deep blue color warm and inviting. She could not resist accepting his hand as he stood.

"What part of the castle would you desire to see tonight?" His deep voice caused butterflies to flutter in her stomach.

"I do not have enough knowledge of the palace to make a choice, Sire."

"My name is Aaden." He lifted her hand to his lips.

Caroline debated if swooning would be a proper reaction, but she didn't want to miss a moment of her time with the king, with Aaden. He led her to an upper hall. They toured a set of rooms known for their color: peacock, amber, crimson, emerald, and jade. It wasn't until they had travelled up and down multiple sets of stairs that he opened one last door. Her breath caught in her throat when she saw the mound of greenery, twice the size of the previous night. She straggled to back away from the door, but he thrust her into the room.

"Serve me with your rare talent, and I will honor you exceedingly. Fail me, and you will die at morning's light."

She turned, grasping his arm with desperation. "Sire, it is too much, too soon. Aaden, I cannot."

He pulled her fingers from him. "You will. Or you die." He closed the door, and she heard locks engaging once more.

Caroline cried. Desperation overwhelmed her and she fell across the bed.

"Terrible sounds from such a lovely lady."

She sat up without a hiccup. The odd little man stood at the door. Today his coat and pants were green, set off by a white shirt and crafted tie. Several fingers were wrapped with thin strips of fabric, but Caroline did not care.

"You've come to help with the new challenge," she rushed to him, falling to her knees as she grasped his hands.

"If that is your wish."

She dug a leather pouch from a hidden pocket in her evening gown. She had lifted it from her father in case the need arose. She tossed it to the stranger. He bounced it once in his hand and then it disappeared.

Caroline flopped onto the soft bed with a sigh of contentment. The sound of spinning filled the room, and she allowed it to lull her to sleep.

~

"Here is your third challenge, my lady. Succeed this evening and I will make you my queen. Fail me and you die in the morning light."

She had expected it this time, but the sight of the tremendous mound of flax caused her heart to pound. She muffled her cries into the feathered pillow.

"My heart breaks for you, sweet lady. Is nary a night of peace your fate?"

Caroline rushed to his side, barely able to contain her excitement. "He has promised marriage. One final night, but I have nothing to offer you for your service."

"If you are to be queen, I am sure you could think of something."

Caroline couldn't help but think of the gorgeous gowns that would fill her closets. The dainty shoes that would cover her feet. And jewels. Mounds of jewels would make her rich beyond imagining. She cast a sly eye at her savior. There was nothing in her thoughts from which she would be willing to part.

"I have a sister," Caroline brightened. "She could be a great help for you. She is simple, but kindhearted. It is a perfect plan. I am certain she will adore you." Caroline didn't wait for his response. She picked up an armful of flax and dropped it by the spinning wheel. Exhausted by her night of dancing, she fell across the bed and slept.

Chapter 4

After days of quiet, the noise of a carriage in the lane grabbed Elizabeth's attention. She stood to peer through a window. "They've returned," she declared, clasping her hands and hurrying to the front of the house. A servant stood ready to open the door. Elizabeth waited, tugging at her hands. As the sound of a knock, she motioned to the servant. "Open, please."

But it wasn't her sister nor her father at the door. She frowned. "What…"

"Greetings, good lady. I carry a letter for Miss Elizabeth."

Though the young man was obviously a servant, he dressed more richly than herself. She rubbed a nervous hand on her simple muslin dress. "I am she."

"Perfect." He held an envelope embossed with gold toward her. "I am to await a response."

Elizabeth frowned as she walked away, turning the elegant missive over. When she reached the east sitting room, she sat at the narrow desk and used a letter opener to break the seal. There was only one page.

My dear Lizzie, though I have only been away these few weeks, I find I am missing your quiet presence more than I imagined. Please do not deny me the pleasure of your company even though I have come to this place against which you have strong objections.

The carriage will wait for your response. If you are agreeable, you will travel in the height of luxury to join me here. Yours, etc.

And that was it. Nothing about Father, nor how her visit to the king's court progressed. Her first inclination was to refuse. What purpose could she serve in a royal court? She closed her eyes. *I don't want to do this.*

But it is where you must head.

Such a strange letter. The fact remained, Caro called for her. Needed her. At least, Elizabeth hoped she needed her. Elizabeth rang the bell for the housekeeper.

The tall woman looked down her nose.

Elizabeth swallowed. "The servant from the carriage, let him know I will accompany him. I will need a trunk packed."

"Sir Haddock said nothing of you leaving us."

"Caroline wishes me to join them. Please make the necessary arrangements."

She nodded. "We shall."

Preparations took a few hours, but Elizabeth finally arranged a pillow at her back as she settled into the carriage. Though the carriage was not large, it held more creature comforts than she'd ever beheld. She could not feel a board beneath where she sat, yet no sagging in the cushions. The gentle rocking did not jar her or cause her to drop the book of poetry she carried.

She watched the familiar village and hillside give way to unfamiliar forests and farmlands. The sun moved towards its evening rest when they stopped.

After a knock on the door, the young man greeted her with a nod. "You will want to stay here for the night."

Elizabth gripped her pelisse as heat infused her cheeks. "I have no means…"

"Your room has already been requested. You will find a maid waiting for you. She will be your companion."

"Oh, I hadn't thought about that." She'd been traveling through her corner of the world since childhood. The need for a chaperone had never come up.

He said nothing but offered a hand to assist her descent.

~

Rumpelstiltskin chose a seat at a table outside the tavern. Olsome strode to join him. Rom's lips twitched as his friend tugged on the leather jerkin he'd had to put on. "You look like a real soldier of this land."

Olsome rolled his eyes. "I'd much rather be home planting fields." He sat across the table from Rom. "How goes the mission?"

Rom shrugged. "Still waiting to see where this adventure leads us."

Another carriage, more opulent than any they had yet seen, rolled to a stop within the gravel yard of the tavern. They both watched a well-dressed servant open the door. At first, Rom thought it was a child who climbed down, but when he saw her face, he realized she was an adult.

The diminutive young woman surprised him. Her gown was wrinkled from traveling and half of her dark hair fell out of its knot. Rom considered for a moment to make an opportunity to greet her, but then thoughts of his purpose pulled his attention away. Perhaps later, if God saw fit, their paths could cross again.

Olsome glanced at him, one of his eyebrows raised. "We do not often meet someone of your height." He paused. "A very pretty someone."

Rom watched the woman follow her servant into the tavern. He shook his head. "Tempting though she may be our purpose is not my own."

"Perhaps there will be a better time."

"By God's will."

~

The next morning, a maid sat across from Elizabeth as the journey continued. The woman had a knitting project on her lap and another spilling from the carpet bag on the seat beside her. Other than a simple good morning and an offer to help however she might, she seemed disinclined to converse. Elizabeth held her book in her hand and stared out the window.

They should reach the palace today. The clouds in the sky weren't the sort to bring rain. She must have dozed because the carriage stopping caused her to straighten in her seat. They were somewhere that did not resemble the open spaces she was used to. Through the window she saw a wall of dark rock.

"You missed the vista of the palace from afar," the maid said as she wrapped her projects to return to the carpet bag. "Not that it would help you find your way around." She shivered. "I am glad I do not have to stay here with you."

"Will you take the carriage back?"

"Heavens, no. I'll catch the post in the village."

The door opened and the servant arranged the steps for them. He nodded at the maid. "Your assistance has been appreciated." He handed her an envelope. Then he helped Elizabeth from the carriage.

Moments later, strangers surrounded her. Elizabeth stood to the side of a stone entrance to… she wasn't sure where. Her trunk sat beside her. People gave her a look, as though it wasn't a place to be waiting with her luggage. The young servant had disappeared, though he promised to return for her. She looked up at the stone exterior and shivered. It wasn't just the crowds that made her long for home. Something about the place pressed on her. She frowned. What had Caro gotten herself into?

~

"What do you mean you are getting married? You have been here less than a fortnight." Elizabeth sank to the bed, unable to stand. Caroline had demanded she come to the palace, but she did not look in need of help. Her sister grinned with a sly smile. Elizabeth did not care for the change she could see. Caroline stood with her head high, ignoring the servants setting up the guestroom and building a fire in the fireplace. She knocked over the coal pail as she swept to Elizabeth's side.

"Caroline," Elizabeth admonished as she tried to help the young servant. Caroline dragged her away, pulling her to the window.

"It's happening, Lizzie. I have succeeded where many fail."

"How? It doesn't make sense. Where is Father?"

"Hunting with the princes. He wants this as much as I do. King Hewel made up his mind quickly, as did I."

Elizabeth moved closer, quieting her voice. "They say he can be cruel."

Caroline offered a knowing look. "I will give him no cause to be." She gave the room a glance and smiled. "You will be comfortable, Lizzie. I will see you at dinner. Wear something colorful if you have it. I will send my seamstress, Christina, to you in the morning."

Elizabeth watched her sister exit the room. She bit her nail as worry flustered her stomach. In the letter, Caro longed for her company, yet now she raced away before Elizabeth was even settled in her chamber. What changed in the days that had passed?

~

Hours later, Elizabeth stared at the solid door that had just been slammed in her face, and then turned to face her sister. "What is going on?"

"It was supposed to be over." Caroline wailed.

"What was supposed to be over? And why is there a mound of plants in a bedroom?"

Caroline sobbed harder. She grabbed Lizzie's arm. "Help me! Please, you must."

Elizabeth felt her heart melt at her sister's despairing look. All was not well, as she'd feared. She shrugged her shoulders, confused. "Of course, I will help, but what is to be done? I do not understand."

"A pair of lovely ladies. I must have done something extraordinary to be blessed thusly. I am honored."

Elizabeth whirled around at the sound of a third person in the room. Near the door, although she would swear it had not opened, appeared a slender man. He stood much closer to her own diminutive height. High boots and buff pantaloons set off his navy jacket worn open at the front. He had a shock of red hair, and she could see freckles across his nose and cheeks. His eyes twinkled with laughter, and Elizabeth longed to laugh with him. She blinked, but he remained.

"This is…," Caroline frowned and waved her hand at him and then looked at her sister. "You said you would help. Help him. The king will spare us if the task is completed before dawn."

Elizabeth didn't understand the feelings rumbling through her heart. The man stepped closer. She could see flecks of green in his brown eyes.

"Elizabeth," Caroline jerked her around to face her. "Help him."

She shook her head, trying to clear it. "Help him do what?"

He walked around them and picked up a leaf of flax. "Turn this into gold."

She laughed, looking from the stranger to her sister and back again. Neither countenance changed, and her laughter faded into a nervous cough. "You are serious? But how is such a thing…"

He held his hand toward her as Caroline kissed her cheek. Her sister flopped onto the bed and turned away from them. Elizabeth could feel her forehead wrinkle as she returned her attention to the man. The hand he held to her had three fingers wrapped in cloths while the fourth boasted a nasty blister.

"Your fingers." Elizabeth gently took his hand and turned it palm up. She unwrapped one of the bandages and gasped at the red, weepy wound.

He tried to pull away, but she held tight. She gave him a hard glare. "Whatever you have been doing has not been good for you."

"It has been in service to another."

Elizabeth looked at the bed. "Caroline?"

He nodded.

Elizabeth shook her head. "I knew… I have something that may help." She pulled a small vial of salve from her handbag. "Works on dancing blisters, so it should help your wounds." Elizabeth led him to the chair beside the wheel. She knelt at his side and unwrapped each finger. Her lips tightened, but she tended his wounds as gently as she could.

She returned the vial to her bag and looked at the plants. "The flax did that?"

"Yes."

"Somehow you are able to turn it into gold? How is it even possible?"

"A gift."

"To be used by selfish people?" She glanced at her sister and then the locked door. "Why would you allow it to be this way?"

"Your sister's life was threatened."

"But now she sleeps."

"You may join her. I am able to complete the task on my own."

Her thoughts were not of sleep, nor of her sister. She stared at his eyes, drawn to their vibrant life. "I prefer helping you."

"Why?" His hoarse voice revealed he was as affected by her as she by him.

Their eyes held for a moment before he straightened, clearing his throat.

"We should begin if we want to complete the task by morning."

Elizabeth kept the pile of flax full as the stranger wove piece after piece into the ruts of the wheel. His feet turned the machine and in the blur of motion, bobbins filled with thread.

"Is this real gold?" Elizabeth placed another spool in the growing stack on the far wall.

"You must remember that with faith, nothing is impossible."

Elizabeth grunted. "A pity it goes to such a vile man."

"Gold will not change him. He will always hunger for more."

"As will Caroline?" She met his bright eyes over the whirl of the machine.

He agreed. Elizabeth felt sadness tug at her. "Why do you stay?"

"I cannot reveal that as yet." His lips twitched as his face brightened.

Her heart leapt at the sparkle in his eyes. She tugged at a wayward lock of her honey-colored hair and looked around. The pile of flax was gone. "That is all? The task is complete?" She reached for his hand. "What of your fingers? How did they fare?"

He managed to twist his hands, holding hers instead. Elizabeth felt him standing close to her, but she could not look up.

"Much better. A burden shared is a burden lifted." His breath fanned across her hairline.

"Caroline never helped?" Elizabeth wondered at the sound of her voice. He seemed to understand her, for he backed away a step, releasing her hands.

"She never thought to help. She's not cruel, just selfish."

Elizabeth could not refute his claim. She sighed.

"Take your rest. Morning will be here soon enough."

"Where will you sleep?" She found the courage to look at him. Already, his warm smile and dazzling eyes had worked their way into her heart.

A smile danced across his lips like a secret. "My bed is far from this place."

"You can leave, can't you? Without permission, just as you came?"

He pressed a finger to his lips. "Another secret I cannot share."

"Will I see you again?" She surprised herself by asking.

He held her hand once more. "Most definitely, if I please you."

Elizabeth nodded, unsure what to make of the stranger. A yawn grabbed her body.

With a laugh, he pushed her nearer her sister. "To bed."

~

The workings of God, the High King, should not surprise him. Rom stared at the bed. She was the reason he had been selected for this particular task. He wiggled his fingers. The salve she'd used cut through the soreness. He rubbed his chin, wishing he still had the goatee. How would things work out? Excitement stirred. He couldn't wait to find out.

~

Elizabeth was surprised she slept and woke feeling rested. There were no windows in the room, so she couldn't tell if dawn had come. A low fire in the fireplace provided enough light to see. Caroline still slept. Elizabeth thinned her lips as she stared at the spools stacked against the wall. There had to be hundreds of them. From the opulence she'd witnessed throughout the palace, why did the king need so much gold? An impossible question.

"Is it morning already?" Caroline asked as she stretched.

Elizabeth turned, hands on her hips. "How can I tell. How many times has the king done this to you? What on earth would make him believe you could weave flax into gold?"

Caroline fixed her hair as she sat on the edge of the bed. "Father said something on one of his trips."

"What would have happened if that man didn't appear? Do you even know his name?"

Caroline waved. "It's probably a secret. Does it matter? I'll be married and we'll never see him again."

"What if King Hewel decides he wants more gold?" Elizabeth asked, stepping closer.

Caroline dropped her hands on her lap and frowned. "He wouldn't do that, or maybe our strange little friend will always appear to help."

Elizabeth heard the lock and then the door opened. Caroline jumped to her feet. Any concern she'd been feeling faded from her face. She glided to the man standing there. Elizabeth crossed her arms and watched as Caroline cooed.

"King Hewel. Aaden."

The king reached for her hand. "I am pleased you have succeeded in this challenge yet again." He kissed her cheek. "I have arranged for your things to be moved to a more fitting suite of rooms. Preparations for our wedding will begin."

"I look forward to it." She gazed at him with adoration.

Elizabeth rolled her eyes.

The king either didn't see or chose to ignore her. "Would you like your sister to move with you?"

"Oh, no." Caroline placed her hand on his arm as she peered at her sister. "I fear my little sister is not used to so many people. Moving her deeper into the palace would be unpleasant for her."

He looked at her with concern. "There will be a ball to announce our engagement in a week's time. Will she attend?"

Caroline smiled. "If she has not begged me to send her home, I shall insist."

The two of them walked away, arm in arm.

Chapter 5

Caroline wanted to enjoy the amenities of her new rooms, but Lizzie's comments harped within her mind. She paced. What if the king needed more gold one day? It might not matter if she were his queen, or he could use it as an opportunity to be rid of her.

The little man had magical powers, but perhaps, there was a way to hold onto him. The dungeon was not a nice place, but she could make a space as comfortable as possible. But how could she capture him? He came and went in the room as he pleased, but was there a way to counter that ability? Who would know enough to help her?

She paused at a window. "Mrs. Joust." The old woman ran the herbalist shop in the village. Her knowledge went to more than herbs and medicines. She would have an idea. The thought brought hope. Caroline settled into her bed. She could claim she needed to go shopping for the ball. She had her plan for the morning.

~

"Names are very important," Mrs. Joust twisted a lid onto a bottle as she considered Caroline's dilemma. "What was his name?"

"He never said."

Mrs. Joust snapped her finger. "Of course, that has to be the secret. There are plenty of legends where having someone's name gives one control over that person."

"How do I find out his name?"

"Can't ask him. No reason to trust he'd tell you the truth anyway. Is there anyone else who's seen him?"

"My sister, Elizabeth."

"Did he treat her any differently than you?"

Caroline shrugged. "She helped him."

"Maybe he told her. Or you could ask her to find out for you."

"Oh, no. She would not approve of my plan."

Mrs. Joust was silent for a moment, and then her face brightened with a smile. "Accuse him of something horrific. Make her think he deserves whatever happens to him."

Caroline tapped her chin. "Bad enough he insisted on my sister as payment." She pressed a hand against her chest. "I had already given him what money and jewels I had." Her eyes brightened. "I could claim he has demanded my firstborn child as payment. Elizabeth would never stand for such a thing."

Mrs. Joust shook her head. "That is quite a story. Are you certain you can tell it well enough?"

"My talent is weaving. I may not be able to make gold, but I can weave a story not even Lizzie can deny is true."

Excitement with the plan made Caroline want to rush back to the palace, but she needed to gather supplies for the ball. Her sister would have nothing appropriate to wear. After saying farewell to Mrs. Joust, with a promise to return to tell her the outcome of all things, Caroline wandered further into the village. There wasn't time to have a dress made. She stopped at a clothier. She hadn't expected to find anything close to fitting Elizabeth's diminutive size, and yet, a silver gown caught her eye. Silver lame net covered a silver and white satin slip. The lines were simple with a tie beneath the chest and short sleeves edged with lace. It could have been made for a child. Still a bit long, but someone in the palace should be able to fit the hem correctly.

"I fear, I do not have the fabric to fit it to your size, my dear." A round woman with thick curly hair greeted her.

Caroline shook her head. "For my sister. She is quite small." She touched fabric that seemed to shimmer. "Have it delivered to the palace this afternoon."

"By who's authority?"

Caroline showed her the seal Chancellor Mornn had given her that morning.

The woman glowed. "My lady, of course. I shall deliver it myself."

~

Elizabeth stared out the window, longing to walk in the woods, not merely see them in the distance. "I should know better than to make promises with Caro. Where is that girl?" She muttered, but the window offered no answers.

Noise in the hallway drew her attention, and then her door burst open, and Caroline entered. Three women followed her, one of whom carried a dress in her arms.

"What are you doing?" Elizabeth asked in way of greeting.

"I found the perfect dress for you. For the ball."

Elizabeth frowned. "I do not need a new gown."

Caroline gave her one of those looks. "You have nothing good enough for a king's ball. Besides, I think you will approve of this one."

Elizabeth didn't want to like anything, but the shimmering silver in a simple form charmed her. "It is beautiful," she gasped.

Caroline looked pleased. "I thought you would like it."

"It will need to be taken up," the older woman spoke. She motioned for the girls to take measurements of Elizabeth.

Task complete, they whisked the dress away. Caroline took her hands. "I am pleased you like the gown. I have other things to do. Have you seen father?"

Elizabeth shook her head.

"Well, I will be sure he joins us for dinner. Tonight, will be simple and quiet. Everyone is preparing for tomorrow's ball."

Elizabeth did not mind simple and quiet.

~

The following evening, Elizabeth stood in front of a long mirror as a maid laced the gown. "It's still a bit long." The fabric trailed the floor. She touched the skirt.

"You look beautiful. Like a fairy." The girl sighed.

Elizabeth giggled. "I feel like a princess." But was it right? Though she'd been at the palace for days, she still felt uneasy. Caroline hoped the king would make an announcement. Why would she still desire to marry the man? The horrid things he'd required of her... Elizabeth shook her head.

"Is something wrong?" the maid asked with a nervous search.

"Oh no, this is perfect." Elizabeth turned around. "I'm not used to the grand scale of the palace. I'd much rather attend a small gathering at home."

The maid patted her arm. "This is a grand place, but you never know, you may find the one treasure of value amongst all the noise."

The words stayed with her, even much later in the evening when the press of people in the ballroom grew thick. Someone's elbow almost knocked her in the head. She'd arrived with Caroline and her father, but both had disappeared. Elizabeth ducked around a potted plant and sought a door into a quiet room. But she found herself outside instead. She could still hear the musicians, but this terrace had no lights. No people. She breathed in the quiet, smiling at the scent of jasmine in the air.

~

Rom flexed his fingers after removing the wraps. The salve Elizabeth used had them healing nicely. Thoughts of her brought a smile to his face. Tonight, was the ball. She would doubtless dance and find herself with a line of suiters. He sighed, even though the thought felt off.

She would not find much to appreciate in the press of a king's ball. He rubbed his chin. Perhaps he should attend. Seek her out.

Chapter 6

My lady, why do you hide in the dark?"

Elizabeth spun around with a gasp and then smiled at the man who joined her. "It's you."

He bowed with flourish, elegant sleeves falling from a velvety jacket of deep green. The fitted pants, delicate knot at his neck, and black leather shoes complimented his physique and Elizabeth felt herself fumble for confidence. The evening gown her sister had provided swept across the ground and she feared tripping at every step.

"An odd place to stand when attending a ball." He placed his hands in his pockets and leaned against a stone wall.

She grimaced. Beyond the open door, a cacophony of color milled throughout the opulent ballroom.

"A dainty such as yourself probably gets lost among so many." He nodded at the crowds they could see through open arches leading into the ballroom.

"I've been mistaken for a child more than once." Her sigh encapsulated frustration and embarrassment. "I admit, my pleasure is wandering in the gardens."

"But since we are here." He took a step closer, holding one hand to her.

She glanced at the doorway.

"We can dance on the terrace, if you like. Do you hear the music?"

Elizabeth placed her hand in his. "I do." Her forehead wrinkled. "I do not even know your name. I never thought to ask it of you the other night."

He bowed and kissed her hand. His warm lips sent shivers up her arm. "Rumpelstiltskin. Yes, I know. A mouthful."

She watched him smile as she tried repeating his name.

"Friends call me Rom. Come, they have started a waltz."

Laughter bubbled within her as he twirled her, one hand at her waist, the other firmly holding her hand. She enjoyed the movement of muscle beneath his shoulder where her other hand held him. Music seemed to swell around them as they stepped together across the empty terrace. Worry about her skirts faded as her senses filled with him.

"Ah, my dear Elizabeth," he whispered against her ear as they stilled. "I knew God sent me for a reason. It is you. I am here because of you."

Her hand lay against his chest, and she could feel his heart beating. Beating for her. "How is it even possible?"

He didn't answer with words. He kissed her. She fit perfectly against him. Never had she known such emotion. Her arms wrapped around him. Time halted, hovered above them, as they stood together beneath the full moon.

"Oh, my." She sighed as they parted.

"Lizzie," he spoke her name with laughter and joy.

She lay her head against his chest. His arms wrapped around her, and she could feel his cheek against the top of her head as his hand caressed her hair.

"Lizzie, Lizzie."

The sound of her name spoken with his accent sent shivers down her spine.

He continued. "Your sister will be queen. They will expect you to make a match with a count or a baron."

Backing away, she studied his face. A lock of wavy hair fluttered across his forehead. She knew in her heart she would find nothing better inside the ballroom. "I am content to remain here with you."

"Walk with me." He tucked her arm in his elbow. Steps leading from the terrace to the gardens were lit. More lights bobbled throughout the palace garden as a slight breeze fluttered the trees.

"Where is your home, Rom?" What could she learn about this man at her side?

"Beyond the mountain pass to the north."

"I have never travelled to the mountains."

"Summer is the best season. The alpine fields bloom with wildflowers. The air is as sweet as honey and butterflies dance upon the wind." He picked a dandelion that had gone to seed. With a light breath, feathery puffs floated around them.

She laughed. "Do forests not cover the mountains?"

"Not in the highest reaches."

His hand brushed hers, and she intertwined her fingers with his. "When do you return home?"

"When my purpose here is met."

"The king's gold?" She grimaced. "That is your purpose?"

The scent of lilacs curled around them. Rom reached for a bloom and placed it in her other hand.

"I came because of a request to protect. At first, it did not make sense. But now it has been made clear. I will return home when my heart's desire goes with me. For now, let us enjoy the garden, and perhaps another dance?"

Elizabeth tucked the bloom in a pocket and offered her hand to him. She fell in love twirling to the harmony of crickets and mating frogs. As the moon began to descend to the west, they returned to the castle and paused beside an empty door standing open. The ballroom sounded far away. Elizabeth rubbed a braided cord that lined his jacket. He lifted her hand and placed a gentle kiss in her palm. She hoped the joy in his face was mirrored in her own.

"I do not know when next we will meet," he said.

"Will you attend the wedding?"

"You may have need of me before then. Woods lay to the east, call for me there."

"The woods?"

He must have noticed her puzzled glance, for he laughed. "Trust me. If I do not come for you myself, look for me there."

Smiling, she shook her head. "Mystery upon mystery, but I will find you."

He lifted his hands to her face, drawing her close until their lips touched. His sweet kiss made her head swirl. He pulled away but remained close enough for his breath to stir tendrils of hair drooping at her temples. "I will leave you now, dear Lizzie. Dream of me."

She did just that.

Chapter 7

I t is the most horrid nightmare! Elizabeth, what am I to do?"

Elizabeth jumped, started from her daydream. Caroline raced across the library, to her side. Falling to her knees, she took Elizabeth's hands.

"We are done for. That horrid man." Tears poured from Caroline's red-rimmed eyes.

Elizabeth's heart twisted with fear. "What has the king done?"

"Isn't the king." Her sister sobbed, drawing shallow breaths. "It's him. That one who helped us." She released Elizabeth and scraped at tears pouring down her cheeks. "I offered compensation. He never said a word, so I assumed it would be enough. But he wants more."

Elizabeth pulled away with an exasperated sigh. "This has nothing to do with gold, Caro, he wants me…"

Caroline shook her head. "No, Elizabeth. He has demanded our first child. I must swear to it."

"What do you mean, first child?"

Caroline blushed and turned her head. "When the king and I… after we're married."

Elizabeth frowned. "No. Rom isn't like that."

Caroline's attention perked up. "Rom?"

"Rumpelstiltskin. But he isn't like that. He cares about me."

Caroline shook her head fiercely. "He doesn't care if you live or die." She grabbed Lizzie's hands again, squeezing painfully. "Neither of us. Without a promise, he will take the gold and the king will put us to death."

Elizabeth pulled her hands from her sister's grip. Something akin to anger began to simmer within her. "I don't believe you. I know him."

"Know him?" Caroline's voice lashed as she leapt to her feet. "How can you know him? I have seen more of him than you. He is a trickster and a liar."

"I don't believe you."

"Then let us meet with him together." Caroline looked down her nose. "Let him speak truth to us both. We will know who the liar is."

~

Elizabeth slammed the guest room door, having left Caroline in the library. How dare she speak thus? Blood had stained the fabric wrapped around Rom's fingers. Tricksters and liars didn't harm themselves in saving others. She paused in front of a gilded mirror. "But if not him, Caroline is the liar." Could she believe it of her sister? She nodded, though her chest clenched. She faced the window where a box garden and green field gave way to trees in the distance.

Elizabeth ran through the garden to a path leading into a wild, wooded area. "Rom?" she shouted into the bands of trees. He appeared from the shadows before she called a second time.

"Elizabeth. What has happened?"

She ran to him, wrapping her arms around his waist. His strength seeped through the cold as he held her. There was no need to even ask. She could sense he was honest and true. She snuggled closer with a sigh of contentment.

He murmured an endearment and kissed the top of her head. And then he tensed.

Elizabeth turned as her sister rustled into the open. She stepped out of his embrace. "Caroline? What are you doing here?" Elizabeth did not give her time to answer. "You lied, didn't you? But why--?"

Caroline's face hardened. She ignored Elizabeth and focused on Rom. "I realized that even once I am queen, I may have need of your particular skill. What if the king requires more gold? I need you to stay."

Rom pulled Elizabeth behind him, and she watched him face her sister. "This is not my home."

"No, it isn't." Caroline stepped closer. "But it will be your prison."

He laughed. "You have no power to keep such a one as me."

"I do if I know your name."

"Caroline, stop this." Elizabeth lunged forward.

"Rumpelstiltskin." Caroline spoke his name as a curse.

Elizabeth cried out as Rom fell to his knees with a shout of pain. "No!" She tried to touch him, but he pushed her away. His eyes darkened, and she felt lost.

"What is this?" She turned her accusation to her sister. "I do not understand."

"His name, dear sister." Caroline's smile chilled. She stroked his cheek. Elizabeth watched him strain, as though bound with heavy rope. "He is one whose name is precious. He came because the Great one called his name. He will remain because of me."

Elizabeth pushed her away. "You cannot do this. You must not! Release him."

"So I can die? You care that little for your own flesh and blood?"

"Your lies have brought you here. Rom has done nothing but try to help us."

"And he will continue to help me." Caroline motioned, and a pair of soldiers stepped forward. "Lock him away." She ordered.

Elizabeth watched, helpless, as they dragged Rom through the trees. He wouldn't even look at her. Fear pounded her heart, so recently light with love. She ran after them, determined to find a way to help.

Caroline snatched her arm, and Elizabeth yelped as sharp nails raked her skin. "Be careful. I can find another cell your size."

"Do not do this, Caroline. He is a good man. He doesn't deserve such treatment."

"What do you think the king will do with you, little sister?"

"Does it matter?" Elizabeth wrenched herself from her sister's grip. "I will not be like you, with your cold heart. Since when does gold matter more than life?"

"You don't understand."

"I don't want to." She ran after the guards and Rumpelstiltskin.

Chapter 8

Death clung to the air like icicles in the rafters. The king's dungeon was dim and cold. Its walls dripped with misery. Elizabeth saw the same guards turn a corner devoid of their prisoner. They paid her no heed as they quickened their pace toward their midday meal. She peeked around the edge of the wall. A lone door stood at the end of a short hallway. She ran, falling to her knees beside it.

"Rom," she called through the thick door. "Forgive me, I did not know. Please, my love. Forgive me!"

Something shuffled, and hope flared briefly. But silence reined.

"I am here. I will not leave you. We will find a way to break my sister's hold." Elizabeth sobbed, curling against the door. Shivers brought goose bumps to her arms, but she kept one hand pressed against the wood of the door. "I am here, my love."

She must have slept, for a strange howl startled her. She looked around. A single torch continued to provide light. She rested her head against the door with a sigh and pounded her hand against it.

"I am here with you, Rom." The dungeon remained eerily quiet. Tears pooled in her eyes, and she prayed for help.

"Sleeping in damp dungeons is not good for your health. You are supposed to be in your room."

Elizabeth cried out, and then her eyes widened as Rom knelt beside her. He wrapped a wool blanket over her shoulders. Confused, she looked at the locked door, and then at him. Her mouth hung open for a moment as she tried to determine if she slept.

He swept her up in his arms, carrying her with one hand behind her back and the other beneath her knees. She threw an arm around his shoulder. Dream or not, she found herself where she wanted to be. She nestled more comfortably against his chest and tried to stop a sob.

"Do not cry, dear Elizabeth." He nuzzled her neck, causing a shiver. "Your sister does not understand the nature of my people. I was led here by God."

She could feel his body shake and it took a moment to realize he laughed.

"Why would she suppose using my name would keep me here?"

"But you were in pain, so angry with me."

"A bit of dramatic flair." He had the grace to give her a sheepish look. "I'm afraid your sister's heart has turned to stone. I had to let her think she could capture me."

"Why are you still here? You should have escaped by now."

"I will not leave without you, my dear. You are my heart's desire."

"You might have gotten away if you had." The king's strong voice bounced against the stone walls of the hallway. He blocked their path, holding a long, thin sword pointed at them.

Rom set Elizabeth on her feet and pushed her behind him.

"Where is my gold?" King Hewel snarled, each word chilling.

Rom clicked his tongue. "You have grown too greedy, Sire."

"It is necessary for a king. The spools are gone. Where did you hide them?"

"Plants wither and die. That is what has happened to your gold spun from flax. Did you really suppose you could bend the nature of one thing into another?"

"Caroline says you have claimed her power. You stole the gold for your own purpose."

"What honor is there in a king who would attack an unarmed man?"

King Hewel's eyes traveled from head to foot as a sneer curled his lip. Elizabeth gripped Rom's sleeve.

"Am I to fear you, little man?"

"Give me a sword and we will see. If I lose, I restore your gold."

"If you lose? There is no if, boy. You'll be dead." He pointed his sword at Elizabeth. "Be sure she knows your secrets. I'll enjoy beating them out of her."

Elizabeth stiffened. "You'll not lay a hand on me, vile man."

The king's laughter echoed through the dungeon. "To the soldiers' field." He snagged Elizabeth, twisting his hand through her hair. She cried out, and stumbled as the king forced her forward. She didn't have to see Rom to know he followed. Fear eased, though the pain of her scalp caused tears in her eyes.

The soldiers' field spread like a green carpet over a slight hill. Early morning light bathed the area in its golden glow. Elizabeth remained on the ground where the king had pushed her. Clutching the blanket with trembling fingers, she watched Chancellor Mornn offer a rapier to Rom. "Please, Lord. Protect him. Let evil be defeated," she prayed as Rom and the king circled. Others hovered as well, but her focus remained on the battle.

Blades cracked against one another. King Hewel lunged forward. Rom skipped aside, his smaller stature providing quick bursts of movement. He eluded the king. Elizabeth watched the larger man roar with frustration. Metal against metal, over and over, until she covered her eyes. But the feel of the battle rumbled through the ground on which she sat. She peeked through her fingers, and then gasped as Rom went down. He rolled quickly and flew to his feet once more. His fluid motion added to the king's anger. His motions grew wild. One hand slipped behind his back. Something gleamed in the increasing light.

Elizabeth jumped to her feet. "Watch out, he has a dagger!"

Rom twisted as the king lunged. Elizabeth watched in horror as a line of blood appeared across Rom's upper arm. The smaller man danced aside. The king overstepped his bound and fell forward. He lay in the grass, face-down. Sunlight burst through the clouds and lit the field. Elizabeth stared, barely breathing. Rom's sword dropped to the ground. He knelt beside the fallen king. His head bow for a moment before he reached across and rolled him over.

She took a step closer. "Is he…"

Rom placed his hand on the King's neck. "He lives."

A guard knocked Rom away. "Get a flat."

Elizabeth sprinted to Rom. His good arm wrapped around her shoulders as they watched men lifted the king onto a board.

"What have you done? Is he dead?" Caroline's enraged scream flew across the field. To Elizabeth's surprise, she rushed past them and fell at the king's side.

"You should take your leave while their attention is elsewhere."

Elizabeth saw another soldier stand beside Rom. He handed him a leather satchel. "Here, my Lord. Two horses await outside the gate. Use the lower entrance. It is open and unguarded."

They shook hands. "Be well, Olsome." Rom slapped his arm. "Be swift in getting yourself removed from this place."

With a final glance of Caroline bending over the king, Elizabeth allowed Rom to lead her from the soldier's field. His fast pace quickened her breath, but her mind puzzled the words she'd heard.

"Why did he call you my Lord?" Elizabeth asked.

"Did I not mention I am a king's son?"

"A king's…?" she stumbled, but he kept her moving forward. "But he would have killed you."

"Even death would be worth it, having met you."

"But I could not bear it."

They came to an arched opening and paused. He pulled her close.

"I am thankful God pulled us through."

She looked up at him and his hand caressed her cheek. Love shone from his eyes.

"Ride home with me." His voice drew her closer. "Be my bride. We shall send word to your father once you are safe."

Joy rose through her, filling the dark, lonesome, fearful corners within her. Her answer must have shone in her eyes, because he kissed her. A short kiss filled with promise and a future together.

They rode toward the mountains.

40

The Pied Piper

(fairytale of the same name)

The tale of the pied piper may very well be based on real events as far in the past as the 13th century. An inscription on a house in Hamelin, Germany sets the date as 26 June. One-hundred-thirty children disappeared. They were last seen following a colorful piper into the hills. The Brothers Grimm wrote the story down in their 1816 German Legends collection of tales.

This retelling still involves peril to children. Be warned, if that is of concern to you. Otherwise, enjoy reading.

42

~

Wyrwhith Tavern bustled with customers as sunlight burst through the relentless cloud bank that had daunted travelers for a day and a half. A toddler wailed as a pair of siblings chased each other between tables.

"Watch your goings." A large man growled as the taller child knocked the table and beer splashed across worn wood. The boy offered a saucy grin before returning to the chase. Dale swiped a hand across his mouth, hiding the smile he was unable to prevent.

"I don't want to sit." A girl toward the front of the room yelled. She swiped her hand across the table to strike her mother.

Her father's hand connected with her cheek. "You'll not talk to your mother that way."

Dale could feel the buzz of unspent energy circling the room. Most were going on too little sleep. The accommodations couldn't hold all the people, so they'd spent the night curled up in corners or beneath tables.

Beams of light shone through the windows. The rain had ceased, but it would take time to clear the roads and prepare to resume travel. The children needed something now to draw their attention.

Music pulsed through his body. He lifted the worn tapestry carpetbag nestled on the stool beside him to his lap. Pushing the change of clothes aside, his fingers brushed against the flute. The wood instrument caused his fingers to tingle. Excitement built inside him. He grabbed a bar towel and tipped a bottle of oil. He rubbed the oil along the flute. His gaze wandered through the tavern's common room as he lifted the instrument to his lips.

With a deep breath, he blew through the end. Moving one finger to the first hole, the musical note rose. The cacophony of noise in the room dimmed. He placed a second finger and the tone rose even higher. He watched the room. The siblings who had been chasing one another froze in their steps and turned to watch him. The crying toddler silenced. All eyes turned to him. Dale stood and played a short melody, a series of notes that wound up and down, like a line of children skipping through the room. He continued to play as he stepped around the table. His fingers moved across the holes of the flute. A few children followed, their faces lit with wonder and fun. Parents offered tired smiles as the line of children increased. He moved to and fro among the tables. Light outside the main door beckoned. Music surrounded him. He danced through the doors. Mud splashed his shoes, but he didn't care.

Dale played through the streets, winding his way along alleys and across short rock fences. He played, and all around him children danced. They twirled. They sang. They ran in circles with joined hands. The music played on.

~

A rumble of voices drew Dale from slumber. He winced at the feel of hard earth beneath him. Where was he? He searched his memories, but the images were as hazy as a faint dusting of fog. He stretched and opened his eyes. Through the veil of green, he saw a baton swinging toward him. He swerved out of the way, but the wooden tool struck his shoulder. He rolled, howling with anger and pain. Half a dozen men reached for him.

"Hold!" He screamed out, snatching the baton as it swung again at his head.

He shook his head, trying to staunch the haze of pain and sleep. They were muttering and yelling incoherently. He heard the words 'children' and 'lost'.

"What has happened?" He tried to stand, but a large farmer knocked him down.

"Let him be." A woman's voice broke through the commotion.

Dale watched, amazed, as the disgruntled villagers lowered their arms. A figure draped in black approached.

"Where are they? What has he done with them?" The cries of the men gathered to attack him tore at his heart. He could hear desperation and despondency in their voices. What had happened?

The stranger lowered her cowl. Gleaming hair the color of moonlight streamed from her head. He could not see her face, but something about the hair tickled his memory.

"The children are not here. You have naught but speculation against him. Leave be. I will help as I may to recover those who have been lost." Her strong voice carried into the woods.

The group dispersed, seeming to fade into the waning shadows.

Dale breathed deeply to calm his racing heart. "How did you convince them to leave?" He pressed his hand against his injured shoulder. "I thought they meant to kill me." Dale struggled to his feet and then froze as the woman turned her face to him. Her features were of one that haunted his dreams. His nightmares. He drew a lock of her hair from beneath her cape, allowing it to drift through his fingers. "I remember you." Memories crashed into his awareness.

~

On a day when the sun shone in a blue sky and the air felt warm with summer's breath, two children raced along the bank of a river keeping eyes on a boat made from burnt wood and a bit of cloth. Dale looked from the feisty girl in front of him to the ship they had built.

"Run! We'll never catch our sail," she cried back to him, her voice a mixture of giggles and determination. Dale laughed as he increased his speed. The river was stealing their sailboat. He dodged tree roots and hurtled across crags as he chased after the vivid red ponytail of his best friend. They followed the river as far as they could, but the sailboat, freshly carved and hoisted, sped further and further from their reach. The growing tangle of brambles blocked their path and they had to turn aside.

Dale leaned his hands on his knees, breathing hard and laughing uncontrollably. She doubled over, her own laughter filling the woods.

Morgan. That was her name.

A bird perched on a tree nearby and squawked its displeasure at their disturbance. The odd creature gleamed in the afternoon sunlight streaming amongst the trees. Various shades of blue sparkled in its feathers.

"Have you seen anything like it?" Morgan took a step closer. The bird remained on its perch, beady eyes glaring at them both.

"From where do you suppose it is come?" Dale asked breathlessly.

Neither gave a thought to the sailboat, their full attention turning to the unusual bird. It fluttered a few trees away and turned back, gazing at them once more. The pair of children exchanged a look, and then gave chase.

The bird led them further and further from the river, deeper and deeper into the forest where trees stood closer together. Light dimmed and the branches around them grew gnarled and twisted. The bird kept them to a path they could traverse, until they broke through the brambles and entered a clearing.

The bird disappeared. Dale gaped as Morgan grabbed his hand. Clear blue sky shone above them, and a strange house stood on the far side of the clearing. Its windowpanes were bright blue. The hemispheres above the windows were purple. The walls were white. Its steep pitch roof overhung the walls and curved outward.

The bird had been enchanting, but this... He stepped closer, desiring to touch the rich colors they beheld. Morgan stayed at his side, her hand tightening on his. The wood door opened, and a woman stepped onto the porch, stilting their progress. Though her skin looked smooth, and her hair was the color of oak, something about her gave the impression of great age.

"My, my, my. What have we here? Have you come to visit old Meg?" She put one foot onto the upper step of her porch. And then the other one. "Meg's a lonely woman. She don't get to visit often." She moved to the next step.

"We're sorry. We didn't realize anyone lived here." Morgan found her voice first.

"Don't be sorry, child. How else am I to meet people, then if they come unawares?"

"You live here by yourself?" Dale asked.

Meg smiled. "As alone as one can be in the woods." She stepped to the ground and walked closer to the children. "What lovely hair you have child. That color is..."

The few moments of silence caused the hairs on his neck to bristle.

"Brilliant." The old woman continued. "Red as the autumn apple harvest." She moved closer. "And your eyes. Cerulean blue. I've not seen the like."

Dale shivered. The woman's attention seemed completely fixed on Morgan, yet he couldn't move. He wanted to. He wanted to pull Morgan back and run through the twisted and garbled trees until they found the river once more. He wanted to get away from the stranger named Meg. But he couldn't move. He could only watch as she moved closer and closer to Morgan.

"I had daughters once. Long ago, but they were never so sweet. Not a one bore colors as vivid as you."

He watched Morgan flinch as Meg reached for her hair. They should run, but neither seemed capable of going anywhere. Meg didn't just touch the silken red strands of Morgan's hair. She curled it around her hand and pulled.

Morgan began to scream as though she were in pain. He snatched at Meg's hand, but the old woman knocked him to the ground.

Her dark look held him to the ground. "Your turn comes soon enough, boy."

Before his eyes, Morgan's hair began to streak with white. She fell to her knees, struggling still. Dale curled his fingers into the dirt as he watched the bland door turn a brilliant shade of red. A streak of blue washed across a white wall. Finally, Morgan lay in the dirt as the witch panted with excitement. Morgan's hair had turned silvery white. She looked at him, and he could see her face had been bleached of color as well. She staggered back on her hands and knees as Meg released her. She looked as though she had been drained into a pale semblance of a girl.

The witch turned her attention to Dale. He saw Morgan stagger to her feet and run away. He reached for her, but she turned her back. The last he saw was the streak of her white hair disappearing into the shadow of the trees.

~

Morgan snatched her hand from his and drew her cloak around herself. She stared. He gulped. Her eyes were the same pale gray color he'd seen staring at him in the clearing so many years ago. He could see recognition in them.

"I left you," Morgan whispered.

Dale couldn't seem to find his words. He could only stare. Those memories, they had no place in his mind.

Morgan reached for him, but dropped her hand before her fingers touched his skin. "I thought she killed you." Her voice sounded full of wonder and pain. "You never returned. Your parents couldn't bear living in the village. They left." Her eyes filled with tears. "I never spoke... I didn't know how to explain."

Dale shook his head. "You're not a real memory." He backed away, his brows furrowing as he fought the onslaught of images that overlapped. "Your hair was red, like the door. I hated that door. I tried to paint over it once, but the red bled through. It wouldn't go away."

"You stayed there?" Morgan drew her cape close as she stared. "What did she do to you, Dale?"

"No." He put his hand up to stop her from stepping closer. "Mother lives in the woods. That's where I grew up. I've lived there my whole life. Without father. He died long before I could remember him."

"But you know that's not true. You know me, don't you?"

"But how? I don't understand." He pressed his hands to his eyes, trying to block the sunlight. Pain sliced his head as memories warred with one another.

He felt Morgan's hands touch his, drawing them from his face. "Let's not think on the past for now. Focus here. When did you arrive in the village?"

"Yesterday, midmorning. It was pouring rain and our coach pulled in to wait it out." He furrowed his brow, trying to think through the fog. "Or was it the day before?"

"The sun came out in the afternoon yesterday."

He nodded. "Then it was the day before. Yesterday, the children were restless. I started playing my flute to distract them."

"Your flute?"

"I'm a minstrel. The bar master paid me to play the night before. Yesterday I played for fun."

"The children were in the street. I heard them. I stood on the stoop and watched you lead them up the hill."

"But to help." His voice broke. "The children were tired of being locked inside because of the rain. I came back for my bag afterward." He kicked the carpet bag leaning against the tree. He'd used it as his pillow. "I don't know where the children went. I thought they went home."

But Morgan shook her head. "None of them returned down the hill. I heard the villagers. They waited. Your music faded, as though you led them further and further away."

"It doesn't make sense. I didn't do anything with the children. I would never hurt… I couldn't hurt them."

"It's the witch." Morgan's face became hard. "She did something to you. She has the children. We must find them."

Wordless questions caused the pain in his head to intensify, even as Morgan's touch calmed the anxious beating of his heart. He knew her, and that knowing threatened to topple his world. "We must seek the truth." A hoarse whisper was all he could manage.

~

"We wait until dark." Morgan sat on the ground a few feet from him. From Dale. He lived. Was it possible? She glanced toward him. With his head leaned against the tree, eyes closed, he looked older. Harder. Same blonde hair. Same blue eyes. She pulled on her hair that had been drained of color. Why her and not him? She swallowed. That wasn't fair. He lived, but at what cost? She closed her eyes. It would be a long day.

Hours later, Morgan tightened the cinch on her saddle as she took a quick glance at Dale preparing his mount. He didn't speak, just followed her directions like a child. She moved her horse to a log she could use to help mount the horse. She placed her foot in the stirrup and pulled herself up. Twilight settled over them as they moved to the village. Voices cried in the night.

"Stephanie," a woman called, but her voice cracked, as though she had been at it since dawn.

They road past another parent crouched in a doorway of the inn holding a stuffed toy. Morgan led the horses along a fence so they could pass without being seen. Within minutes, they were through the village following the road south.

"Am I responsible?" Dale's soft tone caused her to jump.

She could hear the catch in his voice. Despair. She gripped his hand. "We will find them. We'll make this right."

"Music is not an evil thing."

"No." Morgan turned her head at the shrill cry of an animal hiding in the dark. Shivers ran along her back. She turned once more to Dale. "No. The evil lies with the witch."

"I don't see how she can be considered evil." He pressed the heel of his hands against his eyes as his horse followed Morgan. "Mother is a lovely woman."

"She is not your mother." Morgan felt her throat tighten with emotion. "I remember your mother crying. I had to listen to her, nothing to ease my feel of guilt. I left you back there, abandoned you, my dearest friend." Morgan rested her head against the horse as sobs shook her body. Years weighed on her shoulders, yet here was Dale riding beside her on the empty road. She felt a hand on her back, rubbing in circles.

"I am sorry." She could barely breathe. The horse was stopped, and she found herself in his arms. "I was scared. I didn't understand what had happened. I thought she meant to kill us. And I left you there to die."

"But I am not dead." The air of his words brushed against her hair. He held her for a time. It was strangely familiar and oh so unusual. Hardly anyone dared touch the paleness she'd become. Did any remember the deep red color of her hair? The blue of her eyes? Crowded thoughts drew her away from Dale.

She returned to her horse. Morgan wiped her eyes. Now was the time to look forward, not think back. What had happened to the children? Could they find them in time to save them? Night crawled. The sound of hooves against the road mesmerized her, but she fought against the pull of sleep. Further they must go.

It wasn't until the eastern horizon began to lighten that Morgan allowed them to stop. Dale seemed pensive, an obedient child once more. He laid a blanket for her and one for himself further away. Morgan curled beneath her cloak. Her mind whirled as light crept into the forest. She forced her eyes closed. *God, lead us well, for I am filled with fear.* She repeated the prayer until merciful sleep pulled her free.

~

She'd been dreaming. When she opened her eyes, she'd find herself at home in the back field. She wasn't steps away from Dale. She opened her eyes. Trees, late afternoon gloom, and the sight of Dale studying his flute greeted her.

"Good morning." He smiled as he closed his carpet bag.

"We have fewer hours to evening."

He laughed, throwing his head back and allowing a rich, resonate laughter to fill the air. Morgan couldn't stop her responding smile.

"Yes, so it is, Morgan-girl. We should be going."

He folded the blankets as she stretched and traveled a little way to take care of business.

When they were ready, she allowed him to take the lead. As the horses moved with an easy gate, Morgan studied the man. He would be close to twenty-five, a year older than herself. Wide shoulders, but would he be reliable? Straight back, but would he be honest? That her heart wanting to trust him confused her. He had been more than ten years in the control of a witch. The manner of man he had grown into could not be of quality. And yet, she saw her childhood friend in him. She sighed. The horse plodded on as her mind battled with emotions.

~

Dale slowed his horse as they approached a village. There wasn't supposed to be anything along this path.

"Where are we?" Morgan asked as she came abreast.

Dale gripped the horse's lead. "I haven't been here before." He hadn't. But if that were true, how could this be the path home? They dismounted to pass through the city gates. The strangeness of the town made his blood run cold. How could he not know villages that the road home passed through?

The horses' hooves clomped on the cobblestone street. Morgan stood with him, for which he was grateful. The gray, quiet village ate at his heart. Gray dominated the landscape. Gray stones forming the wall, the streets, and some of the houses. He pulled his jacket tighter, such a chill in the air.

"You haven't been here before?" Morgan seemed to sense the strangeness of the town as well.

"I don't know this place and I don't understand. I know where I'm going, Morgan." Night had yet to fall, and they passed several villagers going about their business. The gray theme of the town passed into their clothing. No color, everything was dull.

"They're sad." Morgan stepped closer. He wrapped an arm around her, drawing warmth from her even as the village tried to drag it from them.

"Where are the children?" He looked for them. There should be signs that they had been playing in the street. Their things should be scattered about as children did. No swings hung from trees in the yard. No toys rested against the front stoop. House after house, street after street, the light of childhood lacked. Tears burned in his chest, though he fought to keep them at bay.

"Look." Morgan pointed at the schoolhouse. Boards had been set across windows, barring the front door. White paint peeled from the wood siding.

"I cannot remain in this place. Is it any wonder my mind chooses to forget it?" Leave now. Urgency filled him.

"Dale, wait." Morgan pulled on his coat, but he jerked away, gathering the reins and lifting himself onto the horse.

"I cannot linger in this place, Morgan." No children. No music. No joy. How could any of them remain? Why did his stomach burn? He pressed the side of the horse with his heal. Morgan's voice whipped through the air streaming past, but he dared not turn back.

For it hadn't always been this way. He was almost certain. Memories that weren't really memories, they were more like ghosts of children playing ball in the street. A little girl chasing her brother as she squealed for her tortured doll. How could he have images in his brain of a place he'd never been? He kicked his horse into a gallop and prayed for relief.

~

Morgan watched him go. She could hear the hooves of his horse picking up speed. The villagers mulling along the thoroughfare barely gave a glance in his direction. Barely glanced at her. She followed Dale at a sedate pace. How could the gray-clad villagers care so little about the world around them? The road turned uphill, leading away from the dour town into the woods. Gathering clouds deepened the shadows. She expected to see Dale around the corner, but there was no sign of him. Nor could she hear his horse. Morgan frowned, wrapped her cloak tighter against the drizzle starting to fall from the clouds, and plodded on.

Sometime later, she came upon him standing beside the path holding the leads.

He offered a sheepish grin. "I shouldn't have taken off like that."

She shrugged. "I don't think anyone noticed our coming or going."

"I found a shelter we can use. Rain is coming." A flash of lightning followed by thunder marked his words.

Morgan jumped from her mount and followed as the drizzle thickened to raindrops.

They sat beneath a lean-to with the horses lightly tethered to a branch.

"Where do we go from here?" Morgan asked as she stared into the driving rain. She could feel warmth emanating from Dale, but his quick abandon gave her pause. How well did she know him? Not at all. How far was she willing to trust him? She couldn't be certain.

"Across the river. The road leads through Chestershire, and then into the forest. Our home is there. My home."

"I don't recall it being so far."

He shrugged. "I cannot explain the memories. They are mixed up, like dreams in my head."

"We'll figure it out." Morgan placed her hand on his arm. She could feel tension harden his muscles. Could see his eyes darken.

The storm passed in the night and dawn greeted them with blue sky. The depression of the previous night seemed to have dissipated.

"What do we have for breakfast?" she asked.

Dale searched one of the bags and held up a loaf of bread. "I prefer to think it has raisins, and not something more unsavory."

"Too bad we've no cows around for milk." She sighed. "Is there anything other than water?"

"Apple cider." He tossed her a bag.

She tore off a piece of bread and tasted it. "Not a bad breakfast." She looked out from their shelter at the rain-washed path. "We did not get far yesterday. Will it be safe to travel this morning, or should we wait?"

"The trail leads on," he said as he shrugged. "Into the woods and to the foothills of the mountains. We are not likely to meet anyone."

Memory of the strange village from the previous day tightened her chest, but she wouldn't say anything about it. He'd probably already forgotten. "I'll need your help getting on the horse."

"I'm sure I can give you a hand." He grinned before finishing his bit of bread.

His good mood did not dissolve once they finished their meager breakfast and prepared to continue their journey. He bent, fingers entwined, to assist Morgan with her horse. Morgan lifted a leg, but then Dale straightened, and itched his head. She tilted her head.

He cleared his throat. "Sorry about that. Let's try it again."

She offered Dale an exasperating glance as he moved his hands once more, right when she was ready to step up.

He giggled. "It was an itch, couldn't be helped."

She wrinkled her nose. "Any more itches awaiting your attention?"

He wiggled as he pondered her words. "Nope. Feels like we are all good." Once more, he bent to provide her with the leverage she needed to mount her horse. And once more, his hands shifted out of the way. He laughed. "It is not I, but the world that moves beneath me." His blue eyes twinkled.

Morgan pressed her hands against her hips and tried to glare at him. "We will never reach our destination if the world continues to behave in such a way."

"I will not fail you this time, my lady." He offered a royal bow and set his hands to assist yet again. Morgan wrapped her hand around his collar. This time he allowed her foot to press against his linked hands and she lifted onto the horse.

He was soon mounted and ready to go. "Follow me."

She did, though her heart warred within her.

~

She wasn't too surprised when their path led them into another village. Dale at first paled, but then the sound of children playing brightened everything. They dismounted the horses to walk them through the gates. It was a small village with a winding road that followed the path of the river.

Dale pointed to where they could see the gate on the other side of town. "Straight through. We've no reason to linger here."

The children were curious about the pair of them and moved closer.

"This is life as it ought to be," Dale laughed as a gaggle of children ran around him and Morgan before chasing each other across the market. With a wide smile, he grabbed Morgan's hands and twirled her across the cobbled street. Morgan didn't notice her hood falling back, her attention held captive by Dale's bright eyes.

"Look at her hair!"

"She must be ancient."

"She doesn't look that old."

The murmurs of children playing in the streets cut through her pleasure. She slipped from Dale's arms and quickly lifted the cowl, covering her face with shadows.

"There is naught to fear." Dale drew her close although he spoke to the young ones.

"But where is her color?"

"Is she a witch?"

Dale's strong voice lifted with the sound of laughter. "She is a child of God, as we all are. There is no evil in her."

Morgan felt the warmth of his hand against her cheek. She looked at him, unable to hide the tears in her eyes.

"Why do you hide from them? You are beautiful."

"I am colorless."

"Does the moon lack color? Is there shame in the silvery light that brightens the darkness? The witch may have taken something from you, Morgan. But she did not take you."

His hand moved to her cloak. She stood with him in the middle of the street, in his arms, as he pulled the cover away from her. Her face heated, but it was the intense gleam of his eyes rather than embarrassment. His attention, in that moment, focused entirely on her, and Morgan knew she would offer her life to save his.

The sounds of the market drew them apart, although Dale kept hold of her hand. Morgan offered a sweet smile as she swung his arm back and forth.

"Ah, I smell roast mutton. Shall we stop for lunch?" Dale drew her to an inn across from the market. They joined a table with a farmer and his wife.

~

The smell of steak and mushroom pie lingered in the air. Morgan thought Dale would attack it with gusto, but he seemed more pensive, though an odd light burned in his eyes as he watched the children. The farmer tried to get him to talk, but he would not be distracted.

Morgan pressed her hand against his. "Eat. We need strength for the day. This is much better than the bread you still have in your bags."

Her touch drew his attention. He shook himself and bit into the pie. Moments later, he'd slipped back into watching, his foot tapping to some unseen music. With a sigh, Morgan finished her meal and stood. She thanked the farmer and his wife for sharing space with them, and then she glanced at Dale. "We should leave. You do not know if we will be able to reach your home before nightfall."

He pushed away from the table, eager to move.

They hadn't gone far when he pulled her into an alley. "Something is happening." He held his hands toward her. She laid her small ones on top of his and he wrapped his hands around them.

She shivered. There was no warmth in his fingers. "What is wrong?"

"Something is happening to me. I want to play my flute." He moved his fingers as though he were already creating a melody. "Follow me, Morgan. Stay with me. Even if I don't want you to."

Morgan drew her hands from his and placed them on his cheeks. "I won't leave you." Her promise came with a kiss. The warmth of his breath, and then her lips against his, drove the cold from him for a moment. He pulled her closer, deepening the kiss. Love for Dale burgeoned through the confusing memories and feelings that warred within her. Breathless, they parted. He rested his forehead against hers.

Morgan felt her chest tighten. "I won't ever leave you again."

"I must go." Dale spoke, his eyes swirling with an eerie light, and then he pushed her away and ran from the alley.

Though his abrupt departure startled her, Morgan spun around and followed. Doubts that had consumed her as they waited out the storm no longer mattered. Her heart chose to trust him. She went to follow him into the tavern, but he burst through the doors. He had removed his jacket. His white shirt open at the neck revealed a patch of dark hair upon his chest. He paid her no heed, though he sprinted past with his camel breaches tucked into his boots. He lifted his flute to his mouth and began to play.

Instantly, the street transformed. Children ran to join him, transfixed by the elegant notes weaving through the cool air. He played for them. Bowing to reveal his fingers dancing across the holes drilled through the wood. Chasing them. Running from them. He fell to the ground, and they piled upon him. His laughter filled the space between notes.

Morgan couldn't fathom what had come over him. He frolicked like a child, charming them and drawing them to him. She drove through the mass of bodies to help him rise, but his eyes showed no recognition. He ignored her hand, bouncing to his feet on his own. He continued to play. Children of all ages followed as he skipped along the main street. They passed the houses that opened to the fields and farms. Voices filled the air, jubilant in their sounds. Two small hands tugged her forward, bade her to join them.

Dale played through the streets, turning into a field, and leading them away. Is this what had happened in Wyrwhith? At least two dozen children followed the sound of the flute. She turned back, but the village was no longer in view. The children tugged against her hands. Two faces, one a boy of about six and the other a girl slightly younger, looked up at her as they pulled to get away. Mist chilled her feet, rising to engulf them. More and more children appeared in the mist. They milled aimlessly, staring at Dale. She could still hear the flute trilling through the fog. The little ones slipped from her hands. A young girl stood a few feet away. She looked at Dale, but she also glanced at her. Morgan's breath caught in her throat. Red hair like her own. The apron that had once been hers. No, it couldn't be…

"Angel?" Morgan fell to her knees beside the child. Freckles across her nose. Butterfly birthmark by her right ear. She grabbed Angel by the waist. The child's attention remained with Dale, her feet bouncing to the music. Others danced and ran around him. What had he done? What had he become? Morgan sobbed as her heart chilled. She turned back to Angel. How could she have forgotten? Lived so long without remembering her sister?

"Angel, look at me!" Her hands gripped the coarse fabric of Angel's dress. She shook her. "Wake up," her voice choked. "Father and Mother need you to come home. I need you. Angel, how could I have forgotten?""

The body beneath her hands strained, struggled to get away from her. Angel stared at Dale.

"No, Angel. You don't have to go. Be free of him. Come home with me. Angel, please. Wake up."

Angel blinked as she turned her face to Morgan. Her brows drew close. "Don't cry, Sissie."

Morgan couldn't stop the tears. "Angel."

"I have to go," she tried once more to pull away.

"You mustn't. Come home with me. To your family. We need you."

Her eyes looked sad. "This is where I belong."

"How can I save you?"

"You cannot. She is too powerful."

"The witch? There has to be a way to stop her."

"There's an old man on the river. He knows something." Angel began to cry. "At least I think... he's seen us."

Morgan wanted to pull her close, but Angel slipped away. The music stilled. Children stopped, grew silent. The fog lifted as an eerie quiet settled across the hill. When the mist had cleared, only two of them remained. Herself, and Dale.

"What have you done?" Morgan ran at him, fists flying against his chest. "You stole them. You stole all of them." She knocked the flute from his hand. He pushed her away to retrieve the instrument.

"What are you talking about?"

"The children were here. You led them here with your music. But there were others as well. My sister." She hit him again. He grabbed her hands.

"I don't know..."

"You." How could her body betray her? To want the feel of his hands on her? "Angel disappeared." She closed her eyes against the onslaught of memories. "They sent me to my grandparents, but many of the children in the village disappeared. How could I have forgotten for so long?"

"It wasn't me," Dale shook his head.

She twisted in his arms. "I saw you. I witnessed it myself. You can't say it wasn't you. Where are they? Where are the children? Where is Angel?"

"I don't know. The last thing I remember is being in the village." He looked around them at the hills dotted with large oak trees whose long branches swayed towards the ground. "Why are we here? This isn't the right path to home." He rubbed his head.

Morgan pushed against his chest. "No, you led them here to take them. Is that why you led me to the witch? To be rid of me?"

He rubbed his head. "I would never harm anyone. Not you, and certainly not children. I wouldn't. Couldn't."

"You did." Tears pained her throat and her hits against his chest weakened. "Where are they? They were here and now they are gone. The villagers will come for you. They will kill you."

"Then the children will be lost forever."

She jerked out of his arms. "Angel spoke of an old man by the river. We visit him first."

Dale didn't argue.

Morgan moved from him. "I will get the horses. You wait by the road." Would he be there, or would he run, the coward?

~

Dale paced at the side of the road. They had gone into the town. Had tavern food, though he didn't recall eating much. Children were playing in the alley. But what happened after? Why was Morgan furious with him? And Angel, her sister? He fought to remember. She'd been much younger. He remembered a toddler stumbling through the house. What had happened to her?

The sound of horses drew his attention. Morgan sat, back straight, face firm. Gone was the affection, the comradery. Here was a woman who had learnt pain. He mounted the horse without a word.

"We go to the river. The stable master had a vague notion of an old man who lives near the water." Morgan took the lead.

Dale followed, watching her. Tendrils of white waved through the air. She turned, and soon they were encompassed by trees. Eventually they came to a little hut a few yards from the flowing waters of a river.

Shack was a kind description of the old fisherman's house. Boards dried, beaten, and warped by weather and age formed the mishmash of walls that kept it from falling over. Barely. The old man rose from his rocker as he spied their arrival. He held a rod in his hand and looked as though he was about to take the boat onto the river.

He nodded and listened as Morgan explained their quest. "A witch, you say?"

Morgan nodded as she gripped the rein of the horse in her hand. "My sister said you could help us be rid of her. You've seen them. You can help us save the children."

He frowned, glancing past them into the woods that surrounded his home. "Are there children who need saving?"

"She stole them. We have been in three villages we know of. There are likely others."

The old man shook his head. "You will need to ask her the purpose for the children. That is a question I cannot answer."

"How do we free them from her power?" She watched as he moved closer to the edge of the river.

"Destroy the witch, of course." He leaned his rod against a tree and hooked a worm. "There is little else you can do."

"What of Dale?" She glanced at the silent man sitting on his horse beside her. "With the part he has played in this, will he be saved as well?"

The old man stared at her. His eyes were the color of pine needles. "Will you? Is there a way to regain what has been lost? You must wait and see."

"You waste time." Morgan snapped, and then covered her eyes. "I apologize. I did not mean to be rude. I weary of this journey."

"Three things you must look for. Three. One of them may be the means of destroying her. First, there is something precious to her that will need to be broken. Second, put her house to fire. But be warned, you will never regain what has been lost if you destroy it. Third, there is starlight glass. One who has been in the power of the witch must open it."

"What happens when we do?"

He shrugged. "Whatever must be done. That is the way of it."

The old man dropped his fishing gear into the boat and pushed the bow from the river's edge. He jumped in and went away.

Dale moved off his horse and stood beside her. "What's happened? Where is he going?"

Morgan stared at the disappearing boat. Had he been helpful? Three things that might work. She closed her eyes, putting the three items to memory.

"Morgan?"

She turned from him with a glare. "We waste time. Lead me to the witch's lair."

"Is there naught we can do?"

Morgan didn't bother with an answer. She raised her brows and waited for him to do what she had said. He was both man and boy and she could both love and hate him.

~

It took another day for them to find the witch's house. The woods turned cold. The chatter of birds silenced. The path narrowed with little chance to go any other way. When they crossed into the clearing, Morgan swallowed the lump in her throat. Much remained the same, except more parts of the house were now vibrant colors. She pushed her hands into her pockets to keep from touching her hair when she saw the red door.

"Do you remember when we came upon it the first time?" Morgan stepped closer to Dale.

He nodded. His face was tight with pain. "But I also remember playing in the garden as a boy."

"She planted those memories to make you stay. To do her bidding."

"Then it is time to be rid of them." He walked closer.

"You have returned, my son." An older woman moved across the porch.

Morgan shook. She remembered the feel of those hands. Her cold eyes. Morgan grabbed Dale's hand. His warmth chased away the chill of fear.

"Who have you brought home with you? Have you found yourself a young woman?"

"She is an old friend."

The witch came down the stairs.

"Old friend? I do not remember such a one as this."

Morgan pulled her hood down. "Mayhap you will now."

Dale squeezed her hand.

The witch gasped. "My goodness, I do remember you."

Morgan straightened. "We have come to stop you. To save the children."

"Are children in trouble?" The witch searched around the clearing and the side of the house that was in view. "Why do you come here?"

"You are the one who has them. You've used Dale to draw them from their homes."

"There are no children here, foolish girl." She lifted her hands. "My son is grown, as you can see."

Dale tugged Morgan's hand. "Why don't we go inside? Have tea and make some sense of things."

"Yes, do come in." The witch beckoned to them. "I have a fresh fruitcake cooling on the counter."

Morgan did not want to enter the house. But the old man's words compelled her. She would not find something precious to the witch outside. She allowed Dale to lead her up the steps, across the porch, and through the open door.

The house was bright and well-tended. She could smell the mixture of cinnamon and oranges in the air. There were a few knickknacks lying about, cases of books, fresh flowers and dry sprigs.

"Have you no compliment for me, my dear?" The witch stood in the kitchen smiling at her.

Morgan swallowed. "Um, it is a lovely house." For all its cute comfort, the house crawled with unseen menace. Morgan felt it like tiny spiders crawling across her skin.

The witch puzzled. "You did not expect my house to be pleasant?"

"No, ma'am, I did not."

"Things are not always as they seem." She pulled cups and saucers from a cupboard and placed them on a tray. "You think you know my son, and yet, how is that possible?"

Morgan's mind whirled. Something unseen worked within the walls of the house, trying to make her forget. She closed her eyes. The image of Angel strengthened her resolve. That memory remained strong, of holding her sister and then having her ripped from her arms. Pain and sadness were real. She opened her eyes.

"Tea?" The witch held a tea pot above a cup, poised to pour. It was a green tea pot that made Morgan feel ill to look upon.

Dale still held her hand. He tugged her toward the table. She pulled back, unbalancing him. He knocked into the witch, causing her to drop the pot. The sound of shattering pottery crashed through the room.

"What have you done?" the witch hissed.

"I am sorry," he said as he danced away from the spilled tea spreading across the tile floor. "I will clean it up."

"No. Leave it be." The witch's voice hardened. "Take your guest outside."

Had that been precious to her? Morgan wondered, but nothing seemed different. Dale tugged her toward the front door.

Morgan paused, glancing around. "Does your mother," calling her that left a bitter taste in her mouth. "Does she have a starlight glass?"

"Starlight?" Dale seemed confused for a moment, but then his face brightened. "Do you mean the lantern that can be used at night?"

"It could be." Morgan shrugged. "Where does she keep it?"

He looked at the stairs to the loft.

Morgan placed her hand on his arm. "Please, Dale. We need it."

It took little time for him to retrieve. The object looked like a spherical ball of glass held in a net.

"What are you doing?"

Dale started at the witch's tone. He flushed and swung around. Morgan tried to stop him, but his elbow struck a candle. Instead of snuffing out when it hit the floor, the flame lit the curtain and fire blazed to life.

"Not the house," Morgan rushed forward to pull the drapes from the window. She fell into the witch who had moved as well.

The house caught fire, as did the witch. Her morning gown burst into flame. Dale grabbed Morgan, lifting her off her feet. She buried her head in his shoulder as the cries of the old woman mingled with the roar of the fire. She felt a breath of air as they exited. Across the garden, he dropped to his knees. Morgan turned to look. The house was engulfed. How could it have spread so quickly? Dale groaned beside her. His hands covered his face as he bent forward. She placed a hand on his back. If the spell were broken, he would not grieve the woman he thought to be his mother. But his body shook, and he fell against her. She wrapped her arms around him. Was the witch not dead? They could no longer hear her cries. What about the children? Tears poured down her face. The colors of the house burned up with the flames and smoke. There would be no recovering that part of herself.

She leaned her head against his. "Where is the starlight glass?"

"What good is it to us?" His voice sounded husky.

"The old man at the river said three things could break the spell. Breaking something of hers. Burning the house. Or using the starlight glass."

"You told me nothing of this."

"I could not. You did not wish to see the children restored. Or the witch destroyed."

"You don't understand what I suffer." He dropped his head into his hands. "Knowing some things in my mind are real. Other thoughts are false. You have taken so much. How do I know you are not false as well?"

Morgan shook him. "Burning the house took from me any chance of restoring what the witch stole."

"What will the starlight do?"

"I don't know. Someone who has been in the witch's power must open it."

He offered her the sphere, but she shook her head. "You had more time within her power. You open it."

He removed the sphere from the net, holding it in his hand. Sparkles of sunlight danced on the ground beside them. Morgan wanted to touch it, and yet she sensed she should not.

"What do I with it?" Dale asked.

"Break it?"

He moved to the stone fence that closed in the garden. Morgan remained kneeling on the ground, watching. He raised his arm, looked at the smoldering remains of the house, and threw the starlight glass at the rock. Shattering glass pulsed through the garden. He remained transfixed. For a moment, nothing happened, then light arched out from the rocks followed by a thick mist. Dale fell.

"Dale," Morgan cried as she jumped to her feet and ran to his side. "Dale," she whispered his name, grabbing his hand as his body convulsed. His hand crushed hers, but she did not try to release him. She pressed her other hand against his forehead, brushing through his hair. She felt shadows brushing against her in the mist. His body relaxed, but he did not open his eyes. The fog around them began to swirl. She moved her hands to his chest, shaking him. "Dale." He did not respond. She leaned over him, holding him as the wind blew against her. Something slammed against her, and she knew no more.

~

"The boat, Morgan. The boat." Dale urgently cried.

Morgan shook herself. Something had just happened. Something important. The boat she had built with Dale bobbed on the water, further and further from shore. That didn't matter. She looked at her hands. Looked at Dale.

Dale watched her. "What is it?"

For a moment, the image of a man imposed itself over her childhood friend. Then a bird squawked. A strange bird with a beautiful blue tail.

"Have you seen the like?" Dale asked, but she placed her hand on his arm to prevent him from stepping closer to it. He turned to her.

Morgan felt cold slither against her skin as she peered at the bird. Bad things would happen if they followed it. She didn't know how she knew, but she felt certain of the truth. She turned her back on it. "Let us stay with the boat. I do not wish our labor to be in vain."

He grinned, a boyish charming grin. "As if anything with you would be labor. Come, the boat will put to shore somewhere. We follow the river."

This is what she wanted. Her heart lightened, as though a mysterious burden dissipated. Dale noticed something. He curled one of her red locks around his finger. Kissed her cheek somewhere near her mouth. They moved forward. Someday he wouldn't miss. She was certain of it.

Beast

(Based on the fairytale Beauty and the Beast)

Tales of a young woman marrying an animal groom that transforms into a handsome man have been around for centuries. A French collection of tales, called The Young American and tales of the Sea, is the first written account of *Beauty and the Beast*. Since that time, the story of the enchanted prince and the beguiled heroine has been taken onto the stage and movie screens (thanks to Disney). I've grown up hearing the story multiple times, which is probably where the retelling of such a tale comes from. Please, enjoy.

64

ONE

Once upon a time in a country much like England before machines ran on their own and smog poisoned the air, was the realm of Hwelsham. Birds flying over the land could see the curling river and the road that followed it, the forest that covered the hills, and the valleys between with small villages. Beyond the hills came flatlands, perfect for farming when the high sun cast off winter's cloak. Great manors controlled the farming lands, and the small villages that grew nearby provided workers.

Nimglen was such a manor. Thick stones piled on one another formed the main house which could easily sleep a party of four and twenty in their own rooms. Green moss and lichens grew along the mortar, giving it an abandoned air; and yet, the curtains moved, candlelight flickered from upper windows, and on a cold evening, wisps of gray smoke floated into the night sky, filling the nearby fields with the scent of applewood and old tobacco. Farmers worked the fields of Nimglen with pay regularly offered to them. Yet the master of the manor hadn't been seen in years. Perhaps, that is how the stories grew.

Just outside the region of Nimglen, too close to the woods to be good for farming, lay the village of Bakersfield. Rather than farming, a good portion of its welfare came from the bakers. As one would visit Smithville for ironworkers, and Seamsville for the finest in clothing, Bakersfield housed the best bakers of Hwelsham. On Fridays before market, the air shimmered with sweetbreads and pies baking in the ovens. Birds would laze in the trees, drunk on the scent of apples and spice.

In the village of Bakersfield, lived a father with three daughters. He was a good sort of man, neither rich nor poor, neither powerful nor slave to any other. Selwyn Orcroft wasn't a baker. He took the goods produced in the village and distributed them across Hwelsham depending on where requests were made. His daughters, being of an age to take care of themselves, sometimes made requests of him—to find on his travels such things as fabrics, tools, plants, and the like.

TWO

Gladra, the eldest of the three daughters, leaned against the kitchen doorway. "Looks like fine weather for the next week."

"Have you turned your interests to the skies?" Selwyn teased.

"I have many interests, no thanks to your influence." Gladra grinned, and then noticed Torsa, a few years younger than herself, reclining on a simple lounge near the window. Gladra recognized the gleam in her sister's eye. Torsa was up to something, usually trouble. She glanced back at Selwyn, reposing against the mantle as he smoked his pipe. The sweet tinge of Cavendish added to the comfortable room with its cheery yellow walls. Selwyn's wavy light brown hair needed a trim, but the late spring season kept him busy. "Will you be gone long?"

"Not more than usual."

Torsa perked up. "If you arrive in Wellsford by Saturday morn, you can shop the market."

He laughed. "Is it to be one of those journeys? I've goods to deliver across the valley."

"Would you father?" Ora, the youngest of them at thirteen, straightened from her place at the small table beside the window. With hair the same color as Selwyn but curlier, large blue eyes, and an easy smile, Ora would be the beauty of the three sisters. Torsa had a similar look to Ora, but Torsa cared more for books and learning, not taking the time to fix her hair or arrange her outfits to best suit the slender Orcroft visage. Gladra looked on her sisters with affection.

Selwyn nodded at Ora's question, and her cry of delight was sufficient for them all. He laughed. "What would you have?"

Ora dropped the needle she'd been holding above a crocheting pattern of an owl in a blue tree. "Do you think they would have a jeweler?"

Selwyn grinned. "Would you desire a diamond or a ruby?"

Ora blushed. "Nothing so grand. A gold pendant with a pretty chain, perhaps?"

He nodded, then used the end of his pipe to point at Gladra. "What for you, eldest?"

Pretty jewels had little use for her. With her father's strong facial features more so than her mother's, one would be hard-pressed to call Gladra pretty. Adornments wouldn't change anything. But there was something she desired. "If you are sure, a group of Elves forge in the lower hills. I hear they sell their wares at Wellsford. I long for a blade, a light silver blade. If you could."

"An Elven blade for my silver-haired elf?"

She nodded, not minding the reference to her silvery blond hair. Mother's hair had been like hers as well, if she remembered correctly.

Selwyn looked at Torsa. "This is your idea. What would you have?"

Torsa twirled a lock of her blond hair around her finger. "Now that I've thought about it, Father, I desire something altogether different. A rose, a beautifully blooming rose."

"From a flower vendor?"

She crinkled her nose. "Not from a vendor. Those roses would be cut and starting to wilt. No. It must be a fresh rose in perfect bloom."

Gladra gave her sister a puzzled look. Did she mean to plant the rose in their garden? Why did something strange seem to be at work with her request?

"A blossom for my bookworm?" Selwyn didn't seem bothered at all. He grinned, returning to smoking his pipe. He would try to find her the perfect rose.

Gladra looked at Torsa. The girl positively beamed with contentment. Odd.

THREE

Selwyn intended to return by the sixth day. On the seventh day, Gladra paced the halls of their modest house. The rose carpet that lined the hallway was already worn thin. The back kitchen had been cleaned. She'd tried to get Torsa and Ora to straighten their bedrooms on the second floor, but the chore wasn't likely to be accomplished anytime soon. When night settled without news, she reassured her sisters. Selwyn applied himself to obtaining their gifts. He'd be home or a note sent round by the following morning.

A note arrived just a few hours after the sun had risen from its slumber, but Gladra hadn't slipped into sleep until the wee hours of the night and so tripped getting out of bed at the sound of the bell. She heard Torsa and saw her holding the note with a gleeful look on her face. Gladra waited impatiently with her heart in her throat, longing to tear the note from her sister's hands. "What does it say?"

"Father asks me to join him."

Gladra frowned. "You? Where?

"Not that far." Torsa gave Gladra a look. "He stays at Nimglen."

"Nimglen?" Gladra wrapped her arms around herself. Why did even saying the name of the manor make her want to shake?

Torsa bounced on the balls of her feet. "I can go on my own and take the carriage. Perhaps Father has an injury."

Gladra hated herself for considering it. "It is too dangerous on your own. Why would he call for only you?" Gladra reached for the note.

Torsa crumpled it in her hand. "Nonsense. I've travelled beyond town on my own before. If I leave now, we'll be back before the sun begins to set."

"Bessie couldn't handle more than two of you in the carriage." Gladra didn't really want to travel. Considering the horse was a kind thought, wasn't it?

Torsa offered a comforting hug. "I'll go and bring Father back. It will be fine, you'll see."

FOUR

Except it wasn't. Selwyn returned, as promised, in the carriage late that afternoon. Gladra ran to help him, taking a rose he held out to her. He didn't say a word as he pulled himself down the two steps to the ground and shuffled to the house.

Poor Selwyn. His skin had turned ashen; his eyes swam with weariness and pain. His shoulders drooped with weight though he let his bag hit the floor beside the front doorway. The sword she requested lay within the bag. The end of the chain for Ora dangled from it. In Gladra's hand lay Torsa's blood red rose, still fresh and vibrant as the day it had been cut. He took it back from her, laid it upon a silver platter on the buffet in the dining room, and placed a glass over it. Gladra blinked, then faced outside the front door once more. The carriage was empty. How could that be? Where was Torsa?

He rubbed his eyes. "She is safe. Visiting for a while."

"Visiting who?" Gladra's throat hurt, and the question came out more like a squeak.

But Selwyn shook his head. "She is safe," he repeated, and refused to say more.

The house felt wrong. Dinner was upon the table, but none could eat. Selwyn did not speak, and Ora became weepy without knowing why. The rosemary potatoes were hard, and the lump of meat resembled something best left in the field. How was Gladra supposed to focus on cooking when her heart was so burdened? She battled sore thoughts as the evening progressed slowly. What if the three of them had joined Selwyn, instead of Torsa going alone? What then?

Earlier than necessary, she retired to her bedroom. From her bed, she watched a quarter moon hang outside the window facing toward the west. Facing toward Nimglen. Something tugged her in that direction. It had to be Torsa. Why else would she be drawn to a place she'd never seen? She closed her eyes and fell into an uneasy sleep riddled with shadows.

Why indeed. For what Gladra didn't know and couldn't imagine was that a curse lay upon Nimglen, and here finally was one who could break it. Not the girl who had come to stay at Nimglen, but a close relative. The curse reached for the close relative even as it reached for the one who had created the curse in the first place. One would destroy the other, it was just a matter of who.

FIVE

Cold stone beneath Gladra's bare feet startled her. She stood just inside a stone fence watching her father struggle to crawl over it. Over it? Why would he sneak into such a place? She looked around. The garden was not well-tended. Bushes closest to the massive manor were dead. Only those nearest the fence beckoned with blooms larger than her hands in colors like burgundy, crimson, and yellow. Selwyn gave a nervous glance at the house but walked the path around the roses until he stopped to make his choice.

Gladra saw movement from within the house. Though she cried out, the sound of her voice gave no pause to her father's actions. Nor did it cause the creature striding through the wasted, untended spoils of a dead garden to pause. He was a man bound up within a monster. Looking at them both made her dizzy, but that didn't explain how her heart lurched within her chest. The beast-man paused, its nostrils flaring as though searching for the scent of something it could not see, before continuing to move toward Selwyn.

Gladra found herself within the house. Selwyn sat on a chair, a glass of brandy in his shaking hand. The beast paced the marble floors, growling about something she couldn't quite grasp. Then Selwyn was leaning over the table, scrawling his note.

Time passed swiftly, the sun set and rose as Gladra stood for what only seemed like minutes. Suddenly, Torsa stood beside Selwyn. "Let me stay. It is my mess." Her younger sister's voice wobbled.

Gladra gave herself a shake. *What had happened? Was happening?* She looked at the beast man. He watched Torsa with hungry eyes. Not an evil look, but needy. Torsa snuck a few glances, but her attention focused on other things in the room. Gladra frowned. Why didn't Torsa seem surprised to be there?

"You tried, Father." Torsa murmured as she held his arm.

Gladra saw him tremble. His lower chin quivered. Then Torsa faced the beast.

"I will remain with you, but you must allow our father to return home. The children cannot survive without him. We have no mother."

Children? What children? Ora was thirteen already and Gladra almost twenty.

Spittle soaked the deep ridges that bordered its mouth, and its beady eyes traveled from Torsa to her father and back. His jaw lowered and a panting growl emanated from its mouth. Gladra felt her stomach quiver. The beast walked on two legs and dressed as a man. The white long sleeve shirt hung open to its chest revealing thick muscles covered with dark coarse hair. Its legs were draped in loose fitting trousers, but the bare feet were wolfish with long claws. The gentleman-like manner of the beast whispered where its wild nature roared.

Torsa paled but faced the beast. "I'll stay," she repeated, though no smile tempered her face this time.

Selwyn shook his head. "No. You return to the others. I can provide…"

"She stays." The beast spoke deep from his chest. Gladra wondered if she hadn't been in a dream could she have felt the sound of his voice moving through the floor.

Torsa crossed her arms. "Unharmed and unhindered. Promise my father that."

He looked at them both and nodded. "I promise. Unharmed and unhindered. She stays."

"For how long?" Selwyn whispered, the edge of fear evident in his voice.

"Until it is done," it grunted. "Take the rose. Its price is paid."

"Go Father, while light remains." She placed her hands on his arm.

"Torsa." He drew her close for a moment. His tears dampened her cheek, and he stepped away. His feet moved him across the marble squares, through the arched doorway, and then he disappeared. Gladra wanted to scream at him to turn back. He couldn't mean to leave Torsa with it. She looked at the beast, but it watched Torsa walk away. The beast man stood in the middle of the room, and Gladra snuffed away compassion for it. What right did it have to demand Torsa remain at Nimglen? Finally, it growled and sauntered in the opposite direction.

The vision faded and Gladra woke shaking. Tears dripped down her cheek. She was the eldest child. When Mother died, most of the responsibility for her two younger sisters fell to her shoulders. Anger stirred among the other emotions, ruining her sleep.

Making a decision spurred her to action. She dressed swiftly. A few minutes later, Gladra pressed the final button through the last hole of her leather vest that wrapped around her beige chemise. She pulled at the waist, adjusting the fit. The split skirt in green was full but allowed her to move more easily. Selwyn had taught her to fence, and she'd demonstrated a talent for it. A talent the beast would soon feel. She strapped the slim scabbard with her new elven blade to her side. The unusual weight at her hip unbalanced her walk. She tested drawing the sword and brandished it easily. Orange hues lit bits of clouds close to the eastern horizon as she walked from the house. Mist clung like ghosts to the edges of the village. Gladra swallowed fear as she saddled Bessie and took to the road.

Another saw her coming as a vision of doom. The witch, too far and weakened by the woman whose presence already snapped at the delicate weavings of the spell, sought a means to bring the interlude to an end. A permanent end.

SIX

The ride to Nimglen was slow in the fog. Gladra rubbed Bessie's side as she encouraged her to keep to the road. Even as daylight brightened, the fog remained their companion. Several hours passed before she made the turn toward the manor. Though she'd never seen the actual building, she knew where Nimglen was. There was the stone wall with roses peaking over the top. That must have been what drew Selwyn for Torsa's strange request.

Gladra moved Bessie close to the wall. "Stay still," she muttered to her horse and then lifted herself high enough to grasp the top of the wall. She wobbled and hugged the wall. Determined not to give way to fear, she pulled herself to where she could go over the top. Her sword jangled as she landed in a soft patch beside a tree.

Silence, like an expectant hush, surrounded her. The sky overhead was hazy. Gladra brushed dirt from her vest. Her skin tingled. Where was Torsa? Would she be alright? She stepped out from beneath the tree. The manor loomed to her left. It was so big. What of the beast that lived in it?

She did not have to wonder for long. Gladra felt her heart move in her chest once more as she glimpsed it. He lurched from a doorway at the side of the house. Fear shook her hands, and she gripped the handle of the sword. His eyes looked at her hand, and it snarled. Gladra barely had time to pull the sword from its holder. The beast had its own weapon. She stumbled through the first moves but managed to stay out of its way.

He growled at her. "This is not your place. Why have you trespassed?"

How dare he speak of trespass when her sister was held against her will? Blind fury gripped her, and she swung wildly with the blade.

He parried her attack, his blade ringing against hers. With height greater than her own he blocked her attempt to retreat. Chest heaving, Gladra held her sword toward him and kept the stone wall at her back.

"The time has come to kill the beast?" He snarled, swinging his thicker blade in an arc.

"I would free my sister."

"Free?" He lowered the sword with another snarl. "She came of her own volition and stays of her own free will. Torsa is no prisoner."

"Is she not?" Gladra raised her chin. "Then bring her to me, allow me to return with her to my father's house."

"She stays," the beast screamed.

Gladra refused to back away though her fingers shook, and the muscles of her arms ached with the effort it took to keep a grasp on the weapon. "That is what you call free?" Something other than fear stirred her. Though anger gave a red glow to his features, the eyes of the beast were not those of an animal. They were human.

He lowered his arm. "This fight is not yours."

"Not mine?" She actually took a step closer to him. "She is family, of my own flesh and blood. I will not leave her here to rot."

"Your sister chose, what right is it of yours to question that?" It spat.

Gladra moved closer still as fury burned within her. "The choice being our father or herself to remain as captive? What else could she do?"

Its eyes flared, and then of a sudden, the rage faded. "I weary of your meddling. Find you sister and speak with her yourself. But she remains until I release her." With a grunt, he spun on his heel and walked across the garden.

Gladra wasn't ready for him to walk away. She followed, her small footsteps prancing to keep up. She could almost touch the white shirt covering his back when he swerved around to face her once more. Gladra gasped as pain seared her side. Somehow, she'd been impaled on his sword. Horror darkened his features, but his eyes captured her attention as darkness swirled around her. "Your eyes," she gasped and then lost consciousness.

No one was around to hear the howl of the witch as she faced her failure in the crystal ball. The girl should have died, not release him even further from the curse. The sight of roses across the garden bursting into bloom hurt her eyes. She must hurry.

SEVEN

Gladra stretched an arm above her head, wondering as she sank into a soft mattress. She savored the unusual comfort, but then something within jarred her. They had no mattresses—she moved, and pain ripped through her side. She gasped. A sob sounded from the shadows. Someone pressed against the bed, grabbing hold of Gladra's hand. She turned her head and frowned at Torsa. "What are you doing here?"

"What were you thinking?" Torsa sobbed as she knelt beside Gladra.

Gladra offered a weak smile. "What happened?"

"You don't remember? It hurt you, tried to kill you. And then fever has raged for days. What would I have done if you…"

Gladra patted Torsa's hand, silencing her. "Not your fault. Not its fault either. His, I mean." She tried to take a breath and pain seared her side. She used shallower breaths.

Torsa brushed hair from Gladra's face. "How can you say that? The leather from your vest saved your life. It would have taken it."

"Where is he?"

"I haven't seen him." Torsa scowled. "Not for days. He brought something to break the fever. I waited to use it. I don't think it can be trusted. "

Gladra closed her eyes and breathed. "The medicine worked?"

"Or I waited long enough for the worst to pass, and it couldn't harm you."

Sleep pulled at her, but Gladra didn't mind. She dreamt of eyes, surprisingly human for a beast.

The last tendrils of the spell clung to Nimglen, feeding the black fever that kept the girl from connecting with the man. The witch was ever so close, another day or two and she could finish the matter. She touched the crystal ball and wove the black fever into the beast as well, even as she sickened the roses that had dared bloom. "You think you know despair?" She touched the figure that looked more man than beast. "Wait for me."

EIGHT

The following day, Gladra felt well enough to get up from the bed. She stretched to the left. The wound hurt, but not so much as to keep her down. She washed in cold water and dressed for the day.

Torsa grabbed her in the hallway. "Something is wrong." She kept hold of Gladra's hand and pulled her through the hallway to a room on the end. Heavy curtains had been pulled back, allowing light into the room. A man lay on the floor.

Gladra ran to his side, ignoring the pain in her side as she dropped to her knees. "What has happened to him?"

"I don't know." Torsa knelt beside Gladra.

Gladra pulled him gently over. It was him, but no longer a beastly form. He was deathly pale. She opened his shirt and laid her ear against his chest. She could discern a slight beat. "He lives." She looked at her sister with delight. "We must move him to a bed."

He was heavy. Much heavier than either of them could carry. They pulled him closer to the bed but were unable to lift him off the floor. "Hand me a pillow." Gladra raised his head, then set it upon the cushion.

Torsa moved to stand at the window. "The garden is dead."

"What?" Gladra ran to her side. They both looked at the man on the floor.

"This is my fault," Torsa blinked tears from her eyes. "I thought…"

Gladra placed her hand on Torsa's arm, encouraging her to continue, but her younger sister flushed and stared at the ground. "What did you do?" Unease caused her stomach to turn as Gladra waited for her sister to respond.

"I read about him in old tales." Her voice scratched with sobs. "He was ugly and mean and he'd been hiding here forever. I knew if Father crossed the garden he would be made to stay, if the beast still lived. I could switch places." She buried her face in her arms.

Gladra moved to the man. Her side ached, but the wound had been an accident. She touched his cold skin, smooth without the beastly mange.

What had happened to change him back? And why was he dying? "Why did you want to come here?"

"I'm sorry. It's my fault, isn't it?" Torsa whispered. She sat at the edge of the bed, by his feet. She wiped her nose with her sleeve. "His feet are dirty."

Muddy, as though he'd walked in the garden. Gladra wondered, and then she lifted one of his hands. "Dirt, and thorn pricks." She met her sister's glance. "He was searching for something."

"In the dead garden? But what?"

"A rose." She swept his long, obsidian hair from his face. "You needed a rose, but they were dead." His eyes didn't open, but breath moved through him still.

"Why is he not dead yet?"

Gladra looked up at her sister. "Because a rose survives."

"The one father brought home for me." Excitement stirred the air. Torsa jumped to her feet. "I will ride for it and bring it back."

Gladra shook her head. "I will go."

Torsa disagreed. "I am faster on a horse. Remain with him. He changed when he met you. I will return with the flower, and you can save him."

She ran from the room before Gladra could argue further. With a grunt of irritation, she pulled a cushion close to the makeshift bed on the floor. She wrapped her hands around his, praying warmth from her body would sustain him. "She will return, I promise." She chafed his hand, and held it close to her body. "Whatever ill plan she started with, she is sorry. Don't die. Wait for us. Don't die."

Afternoon light began to fade from the room. Gladra roused herself long enough to find candles and matches and pull together a platter of cold food and water for her supper. She dribbled water into his mouth and felt her heart leap with joy when he swallowed. But he did not wake. She tucked a blanket around his body, slumped across a chaise nearby, and continued to wait.

A rattle of breath and choking roused her in early morning. She ran to his side, turning him slightly and pounding on his back. "No, you don't." His coughing subsided and she lay him flat once more. She wrestled another pillow to elevate his head. "For being on death's door, you're not all light and feathery." She gasped as she released him. She kissed his forehead. "Do not die on me now, beastly man. Help will arrive soon."

The sun hadn't risen high into the sky when the sound of horse's hooves echoed from the courtyard. With a shout of glee, Gladra rushed to the window. Torsa had returned. She hurried to the strange man that had somehow touched her heart. "She is here with the rose," she caressed his face, searching for a sign that he would wake. "You will be well now."

Torsa laid her package on a dresser and pulled the edges of fabric away. "It lives. Look, Gladra."

In the dim light of the dingy room, the blood red rose drew her eye. "But he does not rouse."

"Lay it on his chest?" Torsa handed Gladra the flower. Gladra drew the blanket down and placed it on his bare skin. The deep color stood in stark contrast to his pallor, but he did not move.

"Try making a rose tea?" Torsa shrugged. "Will he drink?"

"He took water last night. We can try." Gladra carefully pulled two petals from the blooming rose. Their scent filled her nostrils. She went to the kitchen and lit one of the burners. She found an old cast iron tea pot, filled it with water, and set it in the fire. As steam rose from the opening, she placed the two petals into the pot.

"The flower fades, you must hurry." Torsa shouted as she grabbed the side of the doorway into the kitchen.

Gladra wasted no time. She removed the tea pot and placed it on a tray with three heavy mugs. They would all drink. She held the tray steady as they returned to the sickroom. The rose had withered against his chest. She removed it and poured three cups of tea. The color of the petals had tinged the water, and the smell wafted sweet and strong.

She lifted his head slightly and dripped tea into his mouth. A red drop slithered down his chin and onto the blanket. She poured more into his mouth. He drank. Drip by drip, she emptied the mug. When at last she finished, she stared expectantly, but he lay still.

"Here," Torsa handed her a second mug. Gladra sipped at it, its flavor rich and sweet. "Not you," Torsa admonished, "him. What if he needs more?"

But the man on the floor began to stir. Gladra held the cup to Torsa. She gripped his hand once more. A smile burst out of her as his eyes fluttered open. His hand in hers squeezed back. She blinked against the foolish tears that wanted to fall. Dark and unfocused though they were, she remembered his eyes.

Deep groans shook the house and Gladra gripped his hand. He struggled to sit up. She put an arm around his shoulder, "Here, lean on me."

He held his hand up, turning it back and forth. Gladra couldn't imagine how it must seem to be human once again. Then he grabbed her around the waist, bounding to his feet with a joyous cry. Gladra squealed, wrapping her arms around his neck as he twirled them. She could see Torsa laughing, her hand covering her mouth. He kissed her, a sweet touch of lips against hers, and Gladra forgot about her sister. Warm delight curled her toes even as embarrassment caused her to turn her head to the side.

Gladra blinked. She was back on the ground, world righted. Torsa pulled her away. "We should get cleaned up." She muttered something that sounded like nonsense. He was grinning, and Gladra felt butterflies invade her insides.

Torsa was still laughing as she pulled Gladra to the door. "My warrior sister tames the beast."

Gladra breathed easier as the stepped into the hallway and shut the door. "He is not a beast."

"Pretty close, all dark and sinewy." Torsa's eyebrows wiggled, and Gladra pushed her away with a laugh.

"Enough. I don't know what happened."

"I do. I believe it's called love." Torsa opened the door to the room she'd used. She tried to shut it just as quickly, but Gladra pushed through.

"What is this?" Throughout Torsa's bed chamber, boxes of treasures had been stacked. Gladra glared at her sister, but she received no response. "You were going to rob him? How could you? You know it is wrong to steal."

"I didn't know he was here. The stories were about a beast, an animal. And old, he shouldn't still live. I knew there would be—I mean, so much just waiting," she waved her arms weakly.

"You're not taking anything. You'll return it where it belongs." She stepped closer, her heart breaking at her sister's foolish greed. "How could you?"

"Father works hard, and there's three of us. How will we ever find good husbands? He can't afford to give us a season. We can't travel to any of those places we could meet eligible men. I just wanted to help." She hung her head. "I didn't think."

Gladra wrapped her arms around her little sister. What would he think of them? "We must tell him."

"I will take the blame."

"No. He cares for me. If he is angry, that will help." She took a step back and offered a wobbly smile. "Return these things." She left her sister. The day was still young, and even through the onslaught of emotions that had come throughout the morning, hunger gnawed. She returned to the kitchen.

The witch felt her heart thud even as she crossed the fields and entered the gate that should have been closed and locked. Age and death hovered just beyond her, eager to swoop in should she fail this final battle to regain her beast. She reached her hand out, nails latching onto the remnants of the curse, drawing what remained to herself. She prepared.

NINE

Breakfast was not her best effort. Gladra winced at the charred smell of ham that lingered around the iron stove. They wouldn't smell that in the dining area, would they? Slices of bread were a bit dark. Eggs mixed with ham, but both overdone. After carrying the platter to the table, she blushed when he stood to help, and his fingers brushed against her. She looked at him. He knew she felt something. Something inside her melted, coming alive. Something wonderful was making her want to grin like a fool and she had to bite the inside of her lip to keep from doing so.

"I'm starving." Torsa didn't seem to notice anything unusual and reached between them.

"Allow me." He served Torsa, giving her toast as well, which she gave a glance then raised a brow at Gladra. He next served Gladra and then himself.

The eggs had no flavor, but Gladra ate anyway to remove her eyes from him.

"I should share my story with you," he offered between bites.

"Not yet," Gladra sighed, laid her fork beside the plate, and began pulling at the tablecloth covering her lap. "We…I," she started again. "I must confess and beg your forgiveness."

"Forgiven."

She smiled at him. When had his face become dear to her? "It is not that easy. I intended to rob you."

He laughed. "Your sister, maybe."

Torsa blushed and lowered her face.

"You are forgiven as well." He spoke kindly to her, and Torsa lit up. He returned his attention to Gladra, and she suddenly felt as though she were twirling. "You came to defend her. I remember crossing blades with you. We'll have to do that again. You have talent."

"You don't understand." Gladra could remain seated no longer. She paced to the window. "We didn't come to help you. I mean, I wouldn't have hurt you, I just wanted Torsa home again. Safe, away from you."

"I understand. But am I as horrid as you thought? I was greedy enough to keep your sister here in hopes she would love me. I didn't care if she rummaged through the attics and the cellars, as long as she was willing to stay. Hope and despair plagued me day and night for she would have naught to do with me."

"Don't, please…" Gladra wanted him to stop.

"You were the first woman to stand up to me as though I were still a man. The swords didn't matter, you were magnificent."

"If you knew what Torsa did, why?"

"I don't care about her. She may take whatever she wants. Empty the manor, I will hire the coaches to return her to her home. If you will remain with me."

"As what?"

"Wife." He stood and stepped closer. "Confidant. Friend. Mother of our children." With each word he took a step closer. Gladra leaned against the wall.

"Am I interrupting something?" The flippant voice of her sister broke the trance. She closed her eyes thankfully.

"Yes." He growled but took a step back.

"I am not going to be able to leave the two of you alone, am I?" Torsa teased.

Gladra could feel her face flaming, but she sat and tried eating her eggs once more.

TEN

I sn't this a cozy little scene."

Gladra felt a cramp in her stomach and her body stiffened unnaturally. Her lungs labored to keep air moving in and out as prickles spread across her skin. She heard Torsa moan beside her but could not turn her head to look.

"Stop this!" The man growled, hurling himself to his feet, unaffected by what had just entered the room.

"What happened to my lovely beast?"

A woman moved into view. An older woman with gray streaks in her black hair stood close enough to touch him, but he backed away.

"I am not yours. Your curse is broken, let the devil take you and be gone," he snarled.

"Had you but begged me to end it, I might have. One of these days I would have given in to you." She shook her head and glared, spilling hatred toward Gladra and Torsa. "But not like this, it cannot end this way."

Gladra felt something new stir within herself. Although she'd not led a life in fear, she'd never felt courage. This man had brought something to her life that had been lacking, and something within herself woke to the knowledge this strange woman wasn't going to get to take him away from her.

The woman moved closer to Gladra and her sister. "I don't even remember what started it all." She waved her hands. "Someone wanted power over someone else. I was paid to place a curse on him, but not even I realized the benefits of tying my spell with a life force." She motioned and both sisters stood, still unable to do naught but what the witch required. She leaned between Gladra and Torsa, looking at him. "Do you realize the longer he lived, the longer I lived? And not just live, mind you, I stayed young." She held up her hands and moved them back and forth. "It stopped working, do you see the wrinkles?" She gave an ugly look at him. "Do you see what you've done to me?"

The witch's hand gripped the back of Gladra's neck, holding onto Torsa with the other. "Give me back my life, and I will spare theirs."

Gladra hurled herself from the wicked touch, kicking the strange woman away from them.

The woman rolled, then looked and screamed. "No! Not possible."

Gladra stood shaking, but she stood within her own power. "You had your life, now let him return to his."

The witch flew to her feet. "If this is to be my end, do you imagine I would let any of you live?"

"Gladra!" He pulled her to his side. She held onto the fabric of his shirt but refused to turn away.

"What a pretty picture you make." The witch scowled and waved her hand.

An Engling grew from a wisp of web on the floor. Gladra felt her heart skip a beat. Englings were nasty creatures from children's stories. Thin red hair dangled from their oval heads. They had dark beady eyes and bodies like small children, but wiry. If the tales were correct, a bite would send poison coursing through the body, death to follow. Gladra drew her sword, offering it to the man standing at her side.

But he shook his head, grabbing a knife from the table. "We do this together."

Gladra nodded, her body shaking but unwilling to give up easily. She grabbed a knife as well.

More creatures grew to join the first. Their chattering rose to a scream as they advanced. Gladra spun, pressing back-to-back with the man who was no longer a beast, using her sword to cut down any of the creatures that drew near enough. The elven blade sliced through the first one, deep burgundy blood smearing its silvery sheen. The creature lay dead on the floor. More rushed to take its place. The man pulled her away from blood spreading across the floor. One of the Englings had climbed onto a side table and another a nearby chair.

Rather than take flight, they fell inexplicably as a howling screech rushed through the room. He and Gladra spun as one to look. Torsa stood over the witch, the cast iron platter raised high in her arms, looking bewildered and sick. The witch lay crumpled at her feet.

Gladra gasped. "How?"

She lowered her arms but held the pan. "I was freed when you fought back. She paid me no heed and it was the only thing I could find to hit her with."

Gladra ran to her sister, helping her lay the platter on the table then taking her into her arms. He joined them, his hand warm on Gladra's back. They looked at the witch.

"What should we do with her?" Gladra wrapped an arm around his waist.

"The unbinding is taking its toll." He pointed at the witch's hair turning more and more gray. "We should leave Nimglen."

He did not need to urge them twice. They escaped through the front doors into a garden where roses were blooming once more. Torsa ran to the carriage, but he lifted Gladra and twirled with her in his arms, joy bursting from him. Gladra clung to him, laughing.

"I don't even know your Christian name." She pressed her hand against his heart.

"Tamor." He set her on the ground and covered her hand with his. "Tamor Nimglen." His eyes grew moist as he looked at her.

"Tamor." She repeated his name, and he kissed her. The beat of her heart matched his, but the kiss ended too quickly.

"Go to your sister," he whispered, his breath felt hot against her lips.

She pressed them against his cheek. "I love you." She whispered the words at his ear. The truth of it humbling and magical. She pulled away, but his hand lingered a moment at her waist. His eyes repeated her words back to her.

Sleeping Beauty's Potion

(Based on the fairytale Sleeping Beauty)

The origins of Sleeping Beauty come through German, French, and Norse traditions. Some of the earliest tellings are quite violent, including rape. The earliest renderings in print include the writings of Basile, Perrault, and the Grimm Brothers.

The telling here has a charming twist on the original. I'm sure you will enjoy reading as much as I enjoyed writing.

88

~

Flakes of snow drifted through the air, hanging suspended for a moment before falling to the hard earth. Rachel lifted her face, allowing the tiny crystals to sting her cheeks and melt into water. A hush settled across the glen, silent save for the sound of snow crunching beneath her feet. A few more steps, and the wall of roses stood before her. Even in the chill of winter, red blooms clung to thorny stems, thick leaves tipped with ice covered the twisted branches and brambles. For as long as she could remember, the hedge had stood, untouched, twisting thicker and higher.

She pulled the clippers from her pocket beneath her cloak as she made a selection. With her fingers curled beneath the flower, she cut the stem. One bloom once a year on the day her mother died. Using the clippers to strip the thorns, she then weaved the stem through her braid. Satisfied with her choice, Rachel skipped along the path that followed the hedge.

Snow made the dirt slick, and her foot slipped. With a gasp, she grabbed the bramble. Thorns sliced her hand as her feet flew out before her. She landed on her rump, with her stinging hand pressed into the wet snow. She bit her lip and wiped snow and blood across her brown jacket.

Cradling the injured hand against her chest, she wiped moisture from her eyes. Then paused. A section of the hedge seemed to have broken apart, providing a gap. She looked around, but no one else stood in the forest with her. She gathered her skirts and crouched beside the opening. She might just fit. She tugged her thick cloak as far down as it would go toward her fingertips, pulled the hood over her head. Gloves would be better, but she didn't want to waste time returning to the castle.

Rachel bent closer to the ground and crawled beneath the hedge. Roots knotted the ground, but it remained dry. The snow couldn't pass through the thick weave of branches and flowers. Something tugged at her back. She flattened herself against the ground and pushed forward. In a few moments, she cleared the hedge and slid into the hidden garden.

It wasn't snowing. Hadn't been snowing this side of the hedge. The sky overhead remained gray. Dead plants littered the garden and a stone path wound through, toward a massive house of similar color.

Rachel paused. Unlike the gentle hush of falling snow, this quiet held a hint of malice. Though the house resembled many found in the village, its curtains were tattered, and the back door was hanging on only one hinge. Nothing stirred. The upper windows were dark, looking like empty eyes staring down on her. She shivered. She should go back. This was not a place to play or wander. But what could be hidden inside? The roses had been there for an age, and no one ever spoke of a place hidden within. Were hers the first eyes to see?

She walked closer, stopping less than a stone's throw from the door. She tapped her foot. Her hand hurt, blood still seeping from the wound. At the least, she should find a cloth to bind it. With that thought, she moved onto the porch, pushed against the broken door, and stepped into the house.

The board beneath her foot creaked, and Rachel froze. Her heart pounded inside her chest. Nothing moved. There were no other sounds to be heard. The air smelled of old age. Windows provided enough light to see blanket-covered chairs, sofa, and a table. The hallway to the right led to the kitchens. The open back door revealed a vegetable garden filled with death. The ovens were cold and sink basin dry and rusting. She noticed nothing of interest, until she spied the stairs around a corner. Unremarkable in themselves, and yet, what may lie above? Someone had lived in the house. Could secrets be revealed in their bedrooms?

The house seemed to breathe with expectancy as she climbed. The steps turned and light dimmed. She slowed her pace as a long hallway came into view. The doors on either side were open, though most revealed nothing but darkness. All but one room. Toward the other end of the hallway, light spilled across the worn rug. Nothing moved, and still no sound. She crept closer, stopping before she stepped into the beam. She listened but heard nothing. Her hand ached. She should find something with which to bind it. But her feet refused to move backward. The need to know, to look for herself overwhelmed. She lifted one booted foot and broke through the beam of light. Nothing changed. She stepped forward. She stood close to the doorway. Just a peak. She leaned forward. The curtains over the windows on the far wall of the bedroom were pulled back, allowing light to fill the room. A bed with four posts was set against the side wall. Filmy white curtains were tied to the posts and draped between them.

Someone lay on the bed. Rachel could see their form through the curtain. She didn't remember moving, but somehow found herself standing beside the bed. She couldn't help it. She reached her hand out and pulled the curtain back.

Death lay upon the white covers. Rachel's hand stuck to the

curtain even as a scream built in her throat. The silence of the house pressed in on her and she couldn't break it. Fear choked her. The figure on the bed looked young, and yet her cheeks had sunken. Her skin pulled across a skeleton. Light hair fanned out around her. She wore a white dress with a green sash, all that remained of her arms and hands crossing her chest was gray skin pulled tight against bones.

Rachel wanted to run, but her body remained frozen.

"Too long I have waited for this."

The voice came from behind. She tried to turn and look, but something else happened. Air moved around the bed, a wind that began to swirl. Rachel found her voice as the remains on the bed blew away like dust. She screamed, trying to hold the bedpost, but the wind was too strong. It pulled her forward, toward the center of the bed where the other had lain. Darkness opened before her. She scrambled to get away, but magic overruled her. She fell into darkness and knew no more.

~

"Jackson," Allister hollered, but the hound bounded through the snow. He gave chase. Across the field, he watched Jackson pause, lower his nose to the ground, and then jump between the trees. "Jackson." The dog did not appear. With a growl of his own, Allister crossed the field. Cold seeped through the leather of his hessian boots. There was enough other mutts to get a replacement. Teach the animal to come when called.

He followed the paw prints into the woods. He didn't care for the feel of branches overhead, the cluster of trees and brush on either side of the slim path Jackson seemed to be following. If his workers could see him now, they wouldn't recognize their stalwart boss. Cold dripped beneath his collar. Where had the dog run off to? He tried calling again, but the trees stood silent, not even bothering to direct his way. Then he heard the whimper. Something had been found by the mangy mutt. Allister broke into a jog. The trail took a sharp turn and he nearly landed in the tall wall of brush that appeared.

Not brush. Red roses, a deep color nearly black, grew over the wall. But it wasn't a wall built of stone. The rose bush itself had grown tall and thick enough to form a wall. He looked to the right and to the left. The wall of rose continued for some length. Jackson sniffed at a branch not far to his right. The dog lifted a leg and left a stream of yellow in the snow. Allister shook his head. Looking down, he noticed footsteps. Not just his dog's prints. Another dainty foot had made an impression in the snow. A human foot. Someone else had been this way recently enough to still be visible in the freshly falling snow. He brushed at the accumulation of flakes on his shoulders. Bloody dog.

He followed the trail, stepping to the side. The smaller foot falls mingled with puppy paws meandered along the massive rose bush. It must belong to a woman with a light step. Jackson pounced across a patch where she had paused. And then she had run. He didn't find any traces of someone else. From what would she run? Or had it been for fun? Jackson stopped at another area. Mud showed through the snow, but there were also red splotches against the pristine white. Allister crouched.

He snapped his fingers at the dog panting beside him. "Jackson, sit." This time the dog obeyed, settling on its haunches at his side. The woman had been injured. He looked up. With the slick of mud, she must have slipped and grabbed onto the rose bush. Even from here he could see the wicked thorns tangled through the twisted branches and stems. A bit lower, he noticed the opening.

She couldn't be seriously injured, and he wasn't about to ruin more of his outfit. If the girl wanted to traipse through the bramble, so be it. He stood, but Jackson moved to the opening and turned to face him.

"No." The damn dog didn't obey. It disappeared beneath the rose bush.

Allister removed his jacket and laid it across a low branch. No point ruining everything he wore. The opening was not wide, but he managed to slip through without snagging his shoulders. The bush was not as wide as he had supposed, and he soon found himself nearing the other side. His shoulder stung, and he dropped to his belly with an oath. But it didn't stop. Something wrapped around his arm and tightened. He pulled against it, and then pain erupted. Instead of moving, he felt himself being dragged. Something else snaked around his other arm, more pain as thorns dug through his flesh. He cried out, struggling, making it worse, but he couldn't stop himself. A thorn tore across his cheek to his eyebrow as he was pulled from the thicket. Wet poured down his face. Agony washed through him as he was pressed against the bush. He gulped air in shallow bursts, fighting waves of darkness.

Something moved toward him. Someone. Flashes of light and dark danced before his eyes. The taste of blood filled his mouth as he tried to cry out. He spat. The bush held him tight. A woman stepped close enough he could feel her breath across his skin.

She gazed at him in silence until her hand moved toward him, but returned to her side before she touched him. "How did you get through?"

Her eyes were dark, slanted upward at the ends, giving her a foreign look. She seemed puzzled, and yet intrigued. Why did she not pull against the restraints to help free him?

"Who are you?" He sounded pale.

"I am the beauty that comes from death's sleep."

"Help me."

"Not I." She trailed a finger across his chest. White heat flared in its wake, and he hit his head against a thick branch. "None may enter, save those who will lay in my stead."

He gasped as the pain faded. "Who are you?"

"Do you believe in Faere Folk? Do their legends exist in the world as yet? When a child of the stars is borne, they will bring blessings to its chamber?"

"Are you one of the Faere folk?"

Her features darkened. "No. I am a child of the stars. I am one to whom they brought blessings. Or so they should have been."

"Hang a dream catcher in the windows to keep dark faeries from entering."

"Alas, my parents did not." She took a step back. "Am I not fair?" Her voice rose in a melody reminiscent of a songbird. "Is my voice not sweet?" She pressed her lips against his cheek. "Do I not smell sweet as honey on a midsummer breeze?"

His skin tingled with her touch, pain. "What curse did they bring you?"

Her lips thinned. "I was meant to sleep beginning on my eighteenth birthday. Until such a one as you," she waved her hand, "woke me."

She paced. Allister turned his head best he could. A vine from the rose bush had wrapped around his arm. With every movement, thorns pierced deeper into his skin. He closed his eyes.

"Mother wanted no such fate for me."

She had come closer, and he opened his eyes to find her a hands breadth away. "She found a way to curtail the curse. Circumvent its course, you might say. Such a price to pay."

"What price?"

"Have you noticed there are none to aid you? They were all taken, given over that I might be spared."

"Spared from sleep?"

Her eyebrows drew close. "Who knows what a Faere sleep entails? I may have been trapped for hundreds of years. Am I to wallow away my youth and beauty in such a way?" She shook her head. "It was not to be borne."

"So how have you broken the curse?"

"There is a potion. Others sleep in my stead. Time steals away their youth and beauty whilst I remain." She twirled.

"Remain here? Locked inside a gray world?"

Her lips pouted. "That would not be much of a life. I alone may pass through the wall and walk in the world. I live as I may until the beauty who sleeps for me has passed from this life." She snapped her fingers. "Or I make this world as I desire."

In an instant, the gray faded. Blue sky opened above them. The garden burst to life. Music poured from the house. People milled in senseless paths. The scene appeared vibrantly alive, and yet not real. As though it were a memory brought back.

"This isn't real, and you know it. Why else keep me here?"

"Are you that eager to meet death? It would not require much. All I have to do is pierce your neck with a thorn." She tilted her head, tapping a red painted fingernail against her lip.

~

Darkness weighed heavy, and yet something else pulled her. Something wet against her cheeks. Her forehead. Talons of sleep slipped away, and light pressed against her closed eyelids. Something warm rested across her chest, licking her face. With a grunt, she pushed herself up. The animal jumped from the bed. A dog? What was a dog doing in her chamber? She looked around. This wasn't her chamber. A white coverlet covered her. Curtains draped over the bed. Another body, drained of life, came to mind. With a cry of horror, Rachel jumped from the bed and staggered across the floor.

The dog barked, jumped against her, landing its two front paws on her thigh, and then pushing off to run across the room. It bounded over the bed and returned to her. A body had lain there, another girl. What had happened? Rachel shook her head. What was she doing?

Pain in her hand registered. She had come through the rose bush. But what had happened? She hadn't meant to fall asleep on the bed. Had intended to run, but something stopped her. Shivering, she raced from the room. The dog followed.

The house remained silent as she moved down the steps. Halfway through the kitchen, life broke out around her. Pans clattered. Fish simmered on the oven, flames sizzling. A large woman kneaded dough against a dirty cheese cloth. Rachel nearly jumped out of her skin. They weren't real. They were like ghosts. A small girl moved through her, and she didn't feel a thing. The back door remained open. She ran.

There were others outside. Gardeners pulling tomatoes from a plant that wasn't really there. A maid hung linen on the line between two trees. Rachel gulped against the sobs tightening her chest.

Through the blanket that waved in a breeze that had yet to reach her, Rachel saw two others further away. A man and a woman who were thick like humans were meant to be, not visceral. She halted a few yards from them. Her throat clenched.

The man was not standing. He was wrapped in the hedge, tangled with it. Blood dripped down his sleeves and across his chest. The bottom part of his face was covered in it. The other was a woman, taller than Rachel. And cold, like an evil wind across the moors.

"All I have to do is pierce you neck with a thorn."

"No," Rachel cried out.

The other woman whipped around and paled. "How? What are you doing?"

"Release him." Rachel pointed at the hurting man. The other woman ignored her, but the stems seemed to move. He cried out.

The woman grabbed Rachel by the shoulders. "I need you to sleep."

Rachel struggled, trying to shake off the fingers digging into her shoulders. The woman grabbed her hair as she pulled a vial from a pocket. Rachel clawed at the arm. She hit the glass away. Something shattered on a brick paver. The woman stopped with a hiss.

"What have you done?"

Rachel pushed again, but the woman held firm and began to change. The hair at her temples paled, growing longer moment by moment. Rachel stared in horror. Smooth skin at the corner of her eyes pulled, forming crow's feet. Fear pounded in her, and Rachel struggled harder. She began screaming as the woman's face thinned.

Then strong arms were pulling her away, wrapping her against a warm chest. Air beat against her back, but with sobs escaping, she wrapped her arms around the man. He held her. She felt his cheek against her own. The battering stopped, and stillness settled around them once more.

She was shaking. Rachel didn't want to move, but he staggered. She tightened her arms around him and pulled back enough to look at him. Blood covered one side of his face. The white shirt he wore was soaked with it.

"Lean on me," she urged, keeping her arms around him.

"How did you break the curse?"

"What curse?"

"Beauty's curse. She used a sleeping potion to keep others in her own fate. She said it would take a kiss to end it."

"A kiss?" Rachel blushed. Had this man kissed her? "Did you make it to the house?"

He shook his head. "I was trapped in the rose bush."

"Then how?" A dog barked, running a circle around them. Rachel raised her brows as she looked at the excited animal. "The dog? I remember now, he was licking my face when I woke."

The man laughed, then groaned in pain. "Jackson. He loves people. The Faere must not have spoken what type of male must be used to break the spell."

"Rescued by a mutt?" She shifted so they faced the wall of roses. How were they to get through?

"He is a fine hound. He found you, your trail in the woods, that is. Must have known you were trouble."

"What?"

"In trouble." He laughed and winced with more pain.

She meant to respond, but the thick hedge of roses surrounding the house moved. Branches thicker than her wrist jerked as though something large and strong beat on them. With a screech, the hedge of roses tumbled into the earth. The hedge thinned until the wall had broken down to one remaining section. Jackson barked but remained at their side.

The man clung to her shoulders and shivered. "I am ready to leave this place."

"My home should not be far. We can tend to your wounds."

Flakes of snow began to fall around them. It was a strange world through which they moved. Snow fluttered through the air. The cloud-covered afternoon was brighter than the gray of the house. Had it been a house? With each step, Rachel became more and more uncertain of the events that had occurred. By the time they reached the castle at the edge of the village, she knew she had found the injured man, but how his injuries had been sustained, she could not say. Loss of blood had taken its toll. Though he moved his legs step by step as she pulled him along, his body felt cold, and he leaned more heavily.

"Gail, Martin, your help," she hollered as they drew within hearing distance. Familiar servants ran toward her. The older gentleman, Martin, grabbed the stranger before he could fall to the ground.

"What trouble have you found yourself today, little miss?"

She shook her head. "I do not know."

"Tisk." Gail pulled her away. "He's half alive. And what of you?"

"I am well, he needs help. Get him settled, a downstairs room, I think. I will fetch the doctor."

~

Pain stabbed his arm as he moved. With a groan, Allister shifted to consciousness. He hurt. His cheek throbbed. His arms pounded. What the blazes happened? Something cool touched his forehead.

"Sh."

He turned his head toward the soft voice. "At least my nurse is a pretty thing."

She frowned. "Don't fun, or I'll slap your arm."

"Please, no. they hurt as it is."

"Serves you right, getting tangled like that."

Like what? His mind had grown foggy. What had tangled him? Where?

A puzzled look crossed her face. She wasn't certain either. "It wasn't pleasant, whatever it was."

"Neither one of you remember, do you?" A woman stood inside the door to the room. Tall, with thick dark hair falling like a curtain, she wore a burgundy dress with a high collar. An underskirt of black peeked through. Something about her set him on edge. He pushed his elbows, ignoring the white-hot flare of pain, as he struggled to rise.

"Be still, boy." She waved her hand.

The young nurse pressed against his chest. Her touch was cool, unlike another's that had been like an iron.

"Move too much you will rip open the stiches. Doc worked hard patching you together." The woman smiled, though it did not warm her eyes.

"Do you know him?" The nurse looked from him to the woman.

"No." They spoke together. Allister leaned back. He clenched his fists and released. The motion hurt, but he did it again. Small steps to rebuilding his strength.

She smiled again, and the glint in her eyes put him on edge. "No, indeed. But something this important I had to see for myself." She moved closer to the bed.

The nurse took his hand.

The strange woman ignored her and leaned closer to him. "How did you break the spell? I sense nothing remarkable about you."

"Because it wasn't him."

Another woman entered the room. Older, gentler features with hair pulled into a loose bun and gray gown. He felt the nurse stiffen.

"Grandmother."

"Rachel, dear. I am pleased to see you well. Your young man looks more battered."

He squeezed her hand. Rachel. The name suited her.

The other woman huffed. "Your Goddaughter?"

"Granddaughter, actually. Turn your head, dear. Show Priscilla what you've tucked in your hair."

Rachel acquiesced. He looked. She wore a rose, its vibrant red standing out against her tawny hair.

"That is not…" Priscilla stammered.

"It is." The grandmother looked pleased. "Faere blood runs within her."

Priscilla shook her head. "Had she gone through the bush, Beauty would have used the potion. Her last victim had been sucked dry. She needed fresh youth."

"The sleep of death." He'd heard those words.

Priscilla whipped around. "You were there?"

"It matters not." The grandmother stepped between them. "The curse is broken, Beauty is destroyed. The hedge is all but gone. Now you must go."

Anger twisted Priscilla's face. "It won't last. Their first child, I'll find a way."

"Go. You've darkened the house long enough."

With a growl of frustration, Priscilla stomped from the room.

The grandmother walked to Rachel and patted her cheek. "That woman never could stand to lose. I don't know how you did it, but you did good." She turned to him. "And you, young man. You as well. A handsome man you are, with a bit more heart than you thought you had." Her eyes twinkled.

"Grandmother," Rachel blushed.

"Yes, well. All in good time. He must heal first." She kissed Rachel's head, patted his foot, and took her leave.

Quiet settled the room and he realized he still held her hand. He liked the feel of it. From the soft smile on her lips, she didn't seem to mind either.

The Frog Curse

(Based on the fairytale The Frog Prince)

The origins of the Frog Prince go back to the thirteenth century, in Germany. It did not always involve a kiss, though the Brothers Grimm wrote that in their version as a revision on the earlier story where a violent act resulted in breaking the spell.

The idea of kissing a frog is repugnant, and yet, metaphorically speaking, I think we've all kissed a few. Ponder that, as you enjoy this retelling.

Chapter 1

Catherine Le Guin stiffened her shoulders as her young suiter stood with his hat in his hands. The velveted rim would never be the same. But that wasn't where her attention should be. "I am sorry," he said, staring at the ground. "Meeting Anastasia changed everything."

Catherine blinked. "You told me your intentions at the start of the season. I never considered any other beau."

He twisted the hapless hat some more. "I hope you will forgive me."

Catherine drew in a shuddering breath. "Of course." The words came even though she wanted to beat on him. The heart wants what the heart wants. Which, in Coleman's case, was someone with a larger purse.

She watched him leave, then caught a glimpse of herself in the long, gilded mirror hanging from the picture rail. Her curls fell from ivory hair combs in preparation for the evening's dance. Her pale face made her gray eyes darker. She grimaced at her reflection. No point strapping herself into the gown prepared for tonight's entertainment.

She hurried back to her bedroom, flinging herself across the fourposter bed draped in lilac brocade. Tears she expected to flow did not. There was a tightness to her throat, and an ache in her chest. Perhaps an uneasy feel in her stomach region. And a blister on her right heel… she flopped over to stare at the canopy above the bed. Flowers danced across the fabric. She blinked. Even in early fall, the gardens had flowers and greenery to design bouquets. It was what her bedroom needed.

Her mind paused only a moment on what might have been. With a sigh, she put on the brown apron she used to protect her clothes from getting dirty in the garden.

~

"Kiss me."

Catherine jumped, but no one stood in the garden save herself. Odd thing to hear, to think. "That batty Anastasia steps out with your suitor, and you start hearing things among the flowers." Catherine muttered, digging her toe beneath a wilting dandelion.

"You are not alone, I am here." The voice ended with a gurgling croak.

Catherine held her breath. She heard something. Definitely, heard something. She twisted slowly, yet no one stood behind her. "What manner of joke is this?" She stomped her foot. Someone was playing games.

"No joke, dear lady. I have not laughed in ever so long. Years. Decades perhaps." The short speech ended in another croak.

Catherine followed the sound of the voice until she looked at the ground. A massive frog sat among the reeds of the pond a few steps in front of her.

"See, I am here. And I did request a kiss."

Catherine screamed. She scurried back, but the damp leaves offered no traction for her shoes, and she fell on her bottom. The thing leapt forward, landing a few feet from her. Her throat clogged and her eyes blurred with tears. "I am mad. My broken heart has been driven over the edge." She hadn't loved Coleman that much, had she?

The frog's face took on the human look of exasperation. "You are not mad. I am an unfortunate prince trapped in this ridiculous form."

"A what?" Her voice caught. She swallowed, closed her eyes, and counted to three. She peaked, but he remained, a lump of green. She cleared her throat. "A prince?"

"Yes, a prince, hard as that may be to comprehend. Bewitched prince, but royal none the less. Prince Adderbatt."

"Adder-" She shook her head. "That is not a name with whom I am familiar."

The creature sighed. "I do not know if my kingdom still stands. How long have I been locked by this enchantment?"

"Who? Why would they do such a horrible deed?"

It hopped closer. "A witch." He lowered his head. "I deserved something, I suppose, for toying with her. She was young and beautiful and I a spoiled prince."

Catherine tucked her feet beneath her as it inched a smidge closer.

"I did not realize who she was." Prince Adderbatt continued. "I wanted to dance, to steal kisses. I wanted to know passion before I was to wed the woman chosen by my father."

Catherine frowned. "You toyed with her while you were engaged to another?"

The frog flopped on the ground. "Years, many years I have had to contemplate the errors of my way. I would beg her forgiveness if I could, but I do not know where to find her."

"Witch's curses can be broken." She tried to scoot further away.

"That is my dilemma. As the lowest of servants, I may have had a chance. But this? In the body of a slimy frog? What fool would kiss me?"

"Not fall in love, just kiss?" Her stomach turned at the thought of pressing her lips against the moist skin of a frog.

"The witch said a kiss. Not even my own mother would give me time to explain. She beat me with a broom and forced me to leave the castle."

The story was ridiculous. She should run. The thing would never catch up, never find her again. But his eyes were sad. His mouth turned down, as if knowing she longed to flee. Her chest warmed. The poor thing… prince… trapped so long. "What if it has been too long? What if breaking the spell now results in old age, or death?"

The creature sighed. "I would much rather die a man than live as this forsaken creature. The beasts know I am not as I appear. Humans turn from me in disgust. There has been no companion, no friend." Something blinked over his eyes as he gulped, throat bulging slightly. "She left me utterly alone in her bitterness."

"You are a pitiful creature. I wish our paths had not crossed this day." Before she could lose her nerve, or talk herself out of it, Catherine leaned forward and kissed the oversized frog on the top of its head.

The green creature stared at her with eyes turning blue. "You kissed me." He seemed surprised.

Odd. The air around them wavered and broiled.

The skin across his face pulled and paled. The frog truly was human. He, a prince.

For a moment, Catherine basked in her action. She saved him. Her lips tingled. Or was it her face? Indeed, her whole body tingled like someone scraped a fork across her skin. "What's happening?" There was something strange with her arm. It looked long and thin, stretching out, turning a horrid shade of green, like early grass.

"Sorry love. You should have run. Bad luck, meeting here today and listening to my story." He had grown quite a bit, or was she that much smaller? His lips pressed into a frown. "You did it from the goodness of your heart. No filling you with ale, spinning tales of romance, or offering huge sums of recompense."

She croaked, an odd deep sound that rattled through her chest. Horror shook her. She croaked like a frog.

"You'll get your voice, you will." He reassured her with a pat to her head. "Took me a bit of time to adjust." He stood, stretched his hands above his head, and pushed up onto the balls of his feet. "Oh, that feels marvelous." He had become a fully human man wearing britches, a white shirt with lace cuffs and a fancy collar covered by a crimson jerkin with a row of golden buttons.

"Why am I…" Her words rolled through a garbled gurgle. The skin at her throat pushed out.

He clapped his hands. "Quick learner. Your parents must be proud. Now what did you ask? Why?"

She nodded. He twisted his upper body to the left and then to the right. Bent at the waist. "Why. Right. You would want to know that. Seems this curse has been in play for quite some time. I met a man with a talking frog. Can you imagine? A talking frog?" He shrugged and grinned. "I guess maybe you can." He rubbed his chin. "Hm, we shared a few drinks. I got a bit carried away and kissed myself a frog. I'm sure she'd have kissed me properly when the spell broke. But I was the frog and she'd already made that mistake."

Catherine's mind whirled. Her body felt the way it should, only scrunched, trapped in a tiny box. How had she gone from wallowing in misery over Coleman's betrayal to being bewitched in the body of a frog? "You knew this would happen?"

"Don't cry, love. I'm only a man after all. You're a pretty little thing. Won't take you long to convince another to give you a peck."

"How could you? What harm have I done you?"

"None. This was never about revenge. At first, with the original prince perhaps, but since then, it's about getting out and moving on."

"I could never do this to another. There must be a different way to break the curse."

"Leave it for another," he scoffed. "Take care of you for now, like I took care of me. Let a different bloke figure it out."

"You have to help me."

"I would, really, I think I would." He scrunched his brows. "Kind as you are, but I've been trapped ever so long. I want to stretch my legs. Find home. Recover what I lost."

Sobs turned to froggish noises. "You can't leave me like this, not alone. Take me where you met the others. Help me find them."

Prince Adderbatt frowned, arms crossing his chest. His chin stuck out a bit. "It's not fair, you ask too much."

"I am not. Think how you felt at first. Didn't you want someone to help you?"

The man ran his hands through his hair. "I suppose I'd be heading that direction on my own. Might as well carry you with me. I'll even help you find a nice lad. Get past this and we can go our separate ways."

He caught her around the middle. Catherine flapped arms and legs. She was falling.

"Take it easy, lady. I'll find a box or something to carry you. Settle down."

She closed her eyes and scrunched her body as tight as she could.

Chapter 2

It took the better part of an evening for Prince Adderbatt to find a basket for her. He added a layer of grass pulled from a nearby field before plopping her into it. Her gasp caused him to frown as he lifted the basket with her in it. "This is deuced uncomfortable. I need a wagon to pull you."

"How big am I?" Catherine couldn't figure it out. Everything felt tight and squished.

"Took both hands to hold you, not touching."

She shuddered at the thought. The basket swayed, causing her head to spin. "Will you walk all night?"

"I am too excited not to keep going." He said as he gave the basket a little wiggle. "I have no idea how long it has been since I stretched my legs."

Catherine wanted nothing more than to stretch her own, but she could not. She curled up and tried to sleep despite constant shifting, tilting, and swaying.

~

"Look at this," Prince Adderbatt declared, causing Catherine to gurgle as he dropped the basket on something.

She'd been dreaming about a lovely ball and twirling with a crowd of dancers. It was odd. She'd never been to an assembly so crowded, nor seen gowns with ridiculously wide skirts. "Where are we?" She peered over the top of the basket. Her froggish eyes noticed a fly crawling on the wall. Everything else seemed gray.

"I finally stopped. We are at an inn in Walingford."

"Does that mean we are close to your destination?"

He shrugged as he pulled off his jacket. "I am unfamiliar with this road. We shall enquire about directions."

She slid back into the basket. How long was she doomed to this fate?

The door latch unhooked. Catherine pushed herself high enough to see. "Prince Adderbatt, where are you going?" He stood in the open doorway. Thoughts of being alone with herself scared her.

He grinned. "Call me Andy. I cannot ask directions if I remain here."

She gulped. "You will come back?"

"Of course. You worry too much." His grin widened.

Catherine didn't trust him, but what choice did she have?"

~

Dreams washed through her in the dark of night. A woman with green eyes watched a tall man dance with another woman. She followed their progress as the light in her gaze dimmed to bleakness. Catherine wanted to cry, but frogs didn't do things like that. The scene faded. The tall man accepted a drink from a boy as the woman with the green eyes watched from a distance. Pain etched the tall man's face.

She wanted to turn away or wake up in her own room. Catherine did neither. The man fell to his knees. Though he cried mercy, the woman crouched beside him and laughed. In another moment, she lifted a massive frog in her arms and twirled around the room with him. Then Catherine was being twirled, cold hands keeping her captive. The cry that rose in her throat couldn't be heard, but it didn't keep her from screaming.

Sunlight streaked across the basket, and she awoke with a loud croak.

"None of that," Andy growled, striking the side of the basket.

Another croak escaped as she wobbled. "What's wrong with you?"

He rubbed his head. "Nothing. I'd forgotten the aftereffects of too much ale."

"What are we going to do today?"

He winced. "Aren't you full of questions this morning. I'm going to eat breakfast."

"I'm hungry." She felt hollow.

"I've been told they have a salted ham with eggs that is decent."

Normally, she would have enjoyed such a breakfast, but her froggy body didn't seem interested. "I have no teeth. How would I eat such things?" Light from the window blazed. "What did you eat?"

He was silent a moment then tilted his head. "My memories of that experience fade. Perhaps I should put you in the garden and let you decide what will suit."

"No, I do not want to go outdoors." She rushed her protest. "Bring me something." She scrunched her body. "I feel safer here, with you." She wasn't completely truthful, but she knew he would most likely leave her in the garden, going on without her, if he could.

He chuckled. "Can't take you to breakfast, luv, not like this.

Should I find you a lad? Fastest way to clear you out of this mess."

"By putting someone else into it? No thank you." She warbled, her throat billowing out. "We return to the place where you were cursed."

Andy sighed. "If you insist, although I don't understand why you can't end things now."

He left the room before she could respond. She hopped from the basket onto the table. The window didn't seem too far. Her sense of distance proved false, and she landed on the floor. The rag rug scratched at her soft belly. She grunted. Then her eyes caught a scuttle of something tiny in a corner past the bed. She went after it without thinking.

Finding nothing else of substance, she plopped on the wood floor to wait. Andy returned sooner than she expected.

"Trying out your legs? What a good girl you are." He sounded jovial. He dumped something in the basket, grabbed her, and put her there as well. "Found something you should enjoy. You can search it out while we travel."

She had the sinking suspicion he meant to leave the premises without payment. She pawed through the lettuce as he wrangled the basket with other supplies. As long as he took her with him, what could she do?

Chapter 3

Catherine folded her legs beneath her and leaned over until her head rested against her arms. Days of travel, and now this, stuck in a dinky room on a narrow bed that smelled peculiar, even to her froggish nose, while Andy spent his time in the main room of the pub. Though he provided greens crawling with creatures and a bowl of water, how long had it been since they'd arrive? This wasn't where he'd met the others, and though she'd pleaded, he wasn't ready to move on.

The door burst open, swinging against the wall, and back again, hitting Andy in the head. Though the abrupt noise startled her, she couldn't stop a giggle.

"That's a good girl, keeping your spirits up." He rubbed his head with one hand and grabbed the basket with his other.

"Are you ready to leave?" Catherine glanced at the dark window. "Maybe we should wait for morning."

"You've been here too long, my girl. Soon you'll be thinking froggy thoughts and forget you were ever a lovely young lady."

He scooped her up with one hand and dropped her into the basket. "What are you doing?"

"Winning a bet, love. I have use of gold coin."

"A bet about me? But we decided it was better for me to remain a secret." She crawled across the bottom of the basket, causing it to wobble.

He slapped the side. "Be still. This is a better idea. I told you spending a few days among these clever folks would be to our benefit."

"Yours, not mine." She croaked.

"Tisk. What benefits me benefits you. We are happily tangled together. And there are gents for your choice. Big ones, small ones, smart ones, tall ones. Ale and your tears should convince the hardest of them to give you a kiss."

She heard the door slam. He was none too careful taking the stairs, rocking the basket this way and that, until Catherine flattened herself against the bottom and prayed it would be over soon. With a jolt, the basket came to rest on a table. Shadowy figures moved above her, but Catherine remained still.

"Blimy, that's a huge beast."

"Devil of the swamps, I'd say."

Something poked her. "Is it alive? You claimed it could talk. Said nothin' bout a dead frog."

"She's not dead. Not yet. Frightened, most likely. Give her a bit of room. Let me get her out of this thing."

With no other warning, the basket tilted over, and Catherine rolled onto the table. She gasped, hopped. There was nowhere to run. Nothing under which she could hide. Her body shook as she huddled.

"Look at those eyes. Mayhap she can speak."

Andy grinned. "Give her a kiss, she'll speak for you."

"No." Catherine glared at him.

One of the men straightened. "Odd noise for a frog. Sounded like a word."

Andy grinned. "You don't want a kiss?"

"Ask what happens, if he'll tell the truth." Catherine backed away from the hand reaching toward her.

"Those were words." Others around the table gasped.

"You heard her." Andy gleamed. "You all heard, she spoke, as I said she would. I'll take your coin."

Catherine simmered. "You win, now return me to the room. I don't like it here."

The others burst into laughter, but Andy pushed her into the basket. She struggled on her back, trying to right herself.

"Wait." A stranger's voice halted the revelry. "Let me see this creature."

Someone righted her. In the dim light of the pub, she couldn't see much more than the hand of the man tilting the basket toward himself.

"What happens if I give her a kiss?"

"No," Catherine hissed.

"Breaks the curse, of course." Andy hushed her with his hand.

She shook him off. "No, it doesn't. It passes it to another."

"Looks like your pet doesn't wish to play the same as you, sir."

"She'll find herself in the dirt, on her own after this," Andy growled.

The stranger smiled, rubbing his chin. "Let me take her off your hands. You've the look of a man who'd rather not be saddled with responsibility."

"He cannot." Catherine turned to Andy. "You promised to take me."

Andy shrugged. "He's as good a man as any I've seen."

"You don't know that," Catherine pleaded, but the stranger had his hand across the basket and lifted her from the table.

Andy raised his mug, offering a salute, and then he was gone. The cool evening breeze swept across her back.

Chapter 4

Catherine hunched inside the basket, pulling her arms closer to her body. "You got a smaller basket."

The stranger had said nothing the previous night, though he'd moved her to a different inn. He'd given her a second bed, arranging the covers in the middle allowing her sleep without falling.

As though she could sleep. How could she find the others who knew about the spell?

"It's the same basket."

"Is not." She gurgled. "It's smaller."

"I've been to breakfast and carried nothing with me in return. When could I have bought a smaller basket?"

"I'm pressed against the sides."

"You're bigger." He grunted as he lifted her. "And heavier."

Catherine pouted. Liar. "You did something."

"I would have if I could. I even offered to kiss you."

"Why did you take me from Andy… Prince Adderbatt?"

He laughed. "That man is not a prince. He would have dumped you in the field and been rid of you."

It was true, but the stranger wore on her nerves, and she wanted nothing to do with him.

He was tall and slender with a scruffy face. The frog eyes distorted color, making his skin sallow. A design in dark swirls twisted across his wrist. She peeked over the side. "What's that?" she pointed with her arm, then drew her arm back, hiding it beneath her body. She'd seen wrong. She wiggled it against her belly. Drummed her fingers. They felt like fingers, not the webbed toes to which she'd become accustomed. She drew her arm out again. Still green, but more like the arm of a girl, not a frog. She croaked and pulled it back under her body.

"What is it?" The stranger looked at her.

She gulped. Blinked back tears. "Nothing."

"Then why are you crying?" He sighed. "We'll get a larger basket."

"That's not it." She rolled to her side so he could see.

He set her on the ground and crouched beside her. He touched her human-looking hand, and she gripped her fingers around his.

"What's happening to me?"

"I don't know. Can you feel that?" He rubbed against her arm.

She nodded.

"What did Andy look like when you first saw him?"

"Like a frog. The way I look. Looked." Why was she crying? She should be glad.

"You don't look like a frog. You didn't last night and even less so now."

"I don't understand."

"Why did you want to remain with Andy?"

"He promised to take me to the ones who had the curse before him. I need to find the witch whose broken heart created the curse to start with."

"Broken heart? I doubt there will be any truth to that. She knew precisely the sort of man he was and what he'd do to be rid of the curse."

He straightened, and with a gasp, Catherine felt herself lifted into the air once more. She harrumphed. The man hadn't even bothered to tell her his name yet.

~

"Why are we stopping?" Catherine shook herself from sleep.

"There's someone I want to speak with."

She wrinkled her nose. "It smells weird."

The dim hallway with its worn red carpet did not feel safe. The room into which he carried her had webs swaying from the ceiling in a breeze coming through the cracked window. He didn't bother with a bed but placed her on the dresser.

"No need to worry. We shan't be here long."

"This place has an evil feel." She flattened herself in the bottom of the basket.

He lit a candle. "It's not a place you'd come on your own, but I have a purpose here. Once I finish, we leave."

Not that he gave her a choice, leaving her on the dresser and locking the door three times. She slept, until he returned. Hopefully it was he who twisted the locks and pushed through the door. Dusk left little glow coming through the windows and the candle had gone out.

"Here we are. Let me light another candle." His voice boomed into the room, as though to relieve her of any doubts.

"Oh my, your friend has a powerful spell upon her." The second voice was that of a woman of an older age. Catherine peeked over the edge as he lit the candle on the desk. An older woman looked at her with eyes of steel. Her gray hair was tied in a neat bun at the back of her neck. Her clothes were ordinary traveling clothes. What she could see of her shoes looked to be serviceable. But those eyes… Catherine wanted to hide from them. She wrapped her arms around herself and huddled beneath the thin cover.

He swept it off anyway, exposing her.

Catherine glared at them both. "Who are you?"

The woman cackled. "Mrs. Glarse will do. I admire a girl with spirit."

He rolled his eyes. "What about the spell?"

"It is an old spell. A hundred years or more, I'd say." Mrs. Glarse pulled on Catherine's arm and turned her hand over. "An unravelling spell. The weaver of this spell will be most distraught."

"But if it is that old, how do we know she yet lives?" Catherine perked up.

Mrs. Glarse released her. "It is the nature of the weave. The witch bought herself long life with a perpetuating spell. As long as this frog curse is passed from one victim to the next, she has succeeded. But you are managing to break it."

Catherine rubbed her hands together, hope flickering to life within her heart. "That is a good thing." The skin above her eyes puckered.

"A good thing?" Mrs. Glarse chortled. "Only if you manage to keep the witch from finding you until the spell has been completely unwound."

"Why?" Catherine shrunk at the old woman's ominous tone.

Mrs. Glarse peered at the man. "You managed an innocent, didn't you, Rorry." She returned her steel gaze on Catherine. "My dear girl, you are costing the weaver of this spell her life. As more and more of the threads that bind you break, the witch feels her power drain away. She must find and destroy you before the spell is completely undone."

Catherine looked at Rorry. That couldn't be true.

His lips thinned. "It is as I feared. She should have passed the spell when she had the chance."

"Not possible now." Mrs. Glarse sat on the edge of the grimy bed. "The spell is breaking. It cannot be passed. What is your name, girl?"

"Catherine," she grunted.

Mrs. Glarse nodded. "Catherine. Your goodness has been your downfall."

"No." Catherine shivered with fear, but a stronger sense of strength offered courage. "The one who made me good will provide what I need to win this battle." She gulped. "He must. I don't want to die."

The old woman shook her head. "Believe that if you wish. You can expect a battle indeed. Even with a champion such as this," she jerked her thumb at Rorry, "don't expect much success." She harrumphed, slapped her knees with her hands, and pulled herself to her feet. "A pleasure, Rorry. I look forward to hearing the outcome. If I should meet another little talking toad, I will know success has not been met."

They crossed the room and walked through the door but left it open.

"Leave her as soon as you can. What were you thinking, taking up with her in the first place?"

"The idiot she was with would have dumped her in the swamps. She'd be dead." Rorry replied.

"Hers is a death sentence no matter what. Her innocence attracts you. You should not have allowed it to sway you." There was a pause, and then the old woman continued. "You think you know the spell weaver."

"And it is long past time for our reunion."

"Be careful, Rorry."

No more was said. Catherine hunkered down as he reentered the room and closed the door. Why did he want to be reunited with the witch? Did he mean to help her or deliver her to the enemy?

"What now?" Catherine watched as he crossed the room, blowing out the candle on the desk, then the one beside her on the dresser. He stood at the window, watching night settle across the land.

"What do we do now, Rorry, if that is indeed your name?" He was silent and moody, not her type.

"We won't stay here. This isn't a good place for you."

"You think the witch will come?"

"How could she not? She will not be far. Look at how much you have changed."

Indeed, Catherine could now make out her legs as well as arms. She had feet and hands. Her skin remained green, no hair on her head. She gripped the edge of the blanket, felt better with it wrapped around her.

Rorry rubbed a hand through his hair. "Yet a few days and you will be released from this nightmare."

"Unless she finds me first?" Catherine gulped.

"I will keep watch."

Chapter 5

But on the first night, she woke to find him sleeping in the chair, head against the side rail, mouth hanging open. "Some watchmen you make," she grumbled, her voice croaking.

He straightened. "What?" His eyes looked weary, rimmed with red, as though he had passed most of the night watching for the shadows.

"Nothing." Shame caused her to lower her eyes. She heard him stretch, strange sounds emanating from his mouth.

"I could use a break from the fast of night. What of you, my green friend?"

"I am not--" she closed her mouth. He was teasing her.

"Not what, green?" He grinned. He took her by the chin and tilted her face. "No, still green, though a bit more flesh colored."

Catherine opened and closed her mouth at least three times. He left the room, but still, she could find no retort to satisfy the ache in her chest.

~

They traveled that day, him on the cushioned seat of a carriage while she rocked at his feet. She hid beneath the cover, but her body felt freer, as though the box in which she'd been trapped had grown. Maybe they could do it, continue moving and keep ahead of the witch. The carriage rumbled. Catherine pressed her hands against the larger basket to steady herself.

They stopped. Mutterings and grumblings she couldn't understand, and then he picked up her basket. "Lay down, before anyone sees you." Rorry pushed her head and threw a second blanket across the top of the basket. She heard him grunt as he lifted the basket. Lugging it from side to side as he walked made her stomach nauseous. They entered a room. He dropped the basket beside the door, not bothering to carry her to the bed.

"What are you doing?" She peaked from beneath the cover.

He frowned at her. "Going to find you something to wear." With that, he closed the door and left her in another strange room, still in the basket on the floor.

She used a choice word and sat up. Something changed. She looked down. The froggish body had a more human shape to it. She had legs, feet, and toes, although webbing still hooked her toes to each other. She had arms and a torso. She wrapped the blanket around her naked body. Her skin was still green, her body more child-sized than adult. She touched her head. Rather than smooth amphibian skin she felt short wisps of hair. Joy leapt through her. "The curse is almost gone."

The door opened and closed. "But we are stuck." Rorry tossed her a girl's dress. She managed to get it over her head with the blanket in place.

She wrapped the blanket around herself, feeling a chill in the air. "What do you mean, stuck?"

"I cannot travel with a green companion. Having to stay means the witch will find you all the faster."

"I will keep myself wrapped in the blanket. No one will see."

"You don't think they'll notice you growing bigger? Travelers in this region are more likely to kill an oddity before asking questions." Rorry shook his head. "No, further travel is not safe."

"So that's it? You'll leave me here and let the witch find me? You told that old woman it was long since time for a reunion. Is that what I am? Bait?"

He gave an exasperated sigh. "I'm hungry. Do you want real food or more bugs in your lettuce?"

"I'll go on my own." She stood, arms crossed, looking up at him, feeling like a young child threatening to run away.

He looked at her. "You are safer with me, and you know it. What do you want for dinner?"

She was hungry for real food, no longer drawn to froggy snacks lingering in the corners of the room. She shivered. "I'll try some stew, and maybe a pint of ale."

"Stay here. I'll bring it back to the room."

He left, and Catherine fumed. What right did he have to boss her around? She looked at the window. Night had settled. She pulled on the sash and heaved, the effort making her a bit dizzy. Fresh air caused the white curtains to wave. She dowsed the candle's light and returned to the window. They were on the upper floor, but a dormer brought the roof lower to the ground. A manageable jump, she surmised. "Especially for one who's been a frog these many days." The sound of her voice surprised her. There was no croaking or gulping. She gave a glance at the door which remained shut.

Rorry was right. Staying in one place wasn't safe for her. Leaving was her best choice, and if he refused to continue to travel with her, so be it. She would travel on her own. She pulled herself onto the bed and walked to the side table that sat in front of the window. She stepped onto it, crouching to take one last look at the door. Part of her wanted it to open, for him to keep her from leaving on her own. But what if his interest wasn't to her benefit? If this experience taught her anything, it was foolish to trust those she didn't really know. She crawled through the window.

Chapter 6

Leaving had been foolish. How soon could she turn around and not give him a victory? Crickets chirped as she crossed from the mud-thickened road to a grassy knoll leading to a small pond. Shadowed trees lingered across the glen, their branches swaying in a gentle breeze. The air held the warm musk of a summer's eve. Catherine pulled the blanket closer. Dampness clung to her skin. Was she still green?

There was a clatter of hooves in the distance, but Catherine remained off the road. The cicadas began their evening performance. Darkness had settled.

"What have we here?"

Catherine whirled around at the scraggly voice. Someone approached. Not Rorry with his quiet strength, but a woman that made her insides shiver.

"Taking an evening stroll this close to the swamps? Do you enjoy the feel of mud oozing through your toes?" She stepped closer.

Catherine shook her head but could not find her voice to reply.

"Are you her, my little frog princess? Are you the trouble that haunts my dreams?"

"Your trouble?" Something flared to life within her. The quiet reserve melted away and she wanted to stomp her foot. "I spent my eighteenth birthday as a frog."

"Funny thing, curses." The witch took a step closer. "They do go on. Who would have thought someone would have kissed that little--" The woman took a breath. "Kiss him she did, and my perfect little revenge took an unexpected twist."

"You shouldn't have done it anyway. Just because a man is rot…"

"What do you know about it?" The witch pressed close. Catherine stumbled away, but the old woman grabbed the front of the dress that had grown shorter and tighter than Catherine liked. "Look at you, a curse unbound. You still have the stink of swamp in you, and yet," she pulled a lank of hair, "the woman returns."

"Release me, I've done you no harm."

"No harm? Is my skin smooth as silk?" She pulled her closer, allowing Catherine to see the wrinkles cascading across her face. "No harm? Is my body the suppleness of womanhood?" She yanked her sleeve back.

"The fault is yours. You tied yourself to the curse." Catherine struggled to free herself. How strong had the witch been if her body was now weakened by age?

The witch snarled. "I am not the one to blame in all of this. You let some weak-bellied charmer talk you into kissing him."

Catherine gasped. "I'd rather have a kind heart that mistakenly trusts, then no heart at all."

Something, someone came running toward them. Catherine shrieked as a large body barreled into them, throwing all to the ground. She rolled from the witch's grasp.

Catherine gasped. "Rorry." How had he found them?

"Rodrick?" The witch seemed just as surprised. Her cackle echoed across the pond. "Is that you, dear boy? Grown into a man?" Her voice turned dark. "Is this your idea of revenge?"

Rorry jumped to his feet. "I tried to talk her into kissing me, but she wouldn't have it."

"What would you have done then?" The old woman's face twisted in a snarl. "Sacrifice yourself, all to get back at poor little me?"

"It's time to stop hurting people, destroying their lives."

Catherine stayed on the ground, turning from one to the other. She should run, but the play between the two held her captive.

The witch brushed dirt from her sleeve. "I expected my son to follow in my footsteps."

Rorry straightened. "I am not your son."

"Truly? Was it not I who raised you? Provided shelter, food, even affection when you craved it?"

"You stole me from my family." His fists clenched at his sides.

"Semantics boy." She waved her hand and then turned cold eyes on Catherine. "This one is more trouble than she is worth. We are well rid of her."

With the cold eyes of the witch fully on her once more, Catherine realized her mistake in remaining. She scurried back, but the aging witch was fast, stronger than most even in her weakened state. She nabbed Catherine's ankle, and Catherine could not shake her loose.

"Why did you follow us?" Catherine implored Rorry as she fought against the witch's grasp. "Do you mean to help her or to help me?"

"He'll wait until it's too late to decide," the witch cackled again as she stretched her other hand to grasp Catherine's throat.

Catherine fought against the weight pressing down on her, digging her nails into the witch's arm. A low growl emanated from the older woman, increasing in volume until the witch hurled herself away. The scent of burning flesh hovered a moment before wafting across the water. Catherine scrambled back. What had happened? Rorry offered a hand to pull her to her feet, and then he pushed her behind him.

"Go. Return to the village. Find our rooms and lock yourself in."

"Do you believe a locked door could separate us? Or have you used a little spell?" The witch stood, shaking her head as she rubbed her arms. "Foolish Rorry, there is no strength in dabbling."

"I have never desired your kind of strength."

"Of course not. You were too good for the life I offered." The witch rushed toward him. Too late, Catherine realized the gleam that caught her eye was a weapon. Rorry stepped into it.

With a cry, Catherine felt Rorry's body stiffen. She heard the sound of the knife being pulled from flesh. With her arms wrapped around his chest, she fell to the ground with him.

"Always a price for meddling," the witch's voice cracked as though pained by the turn of events. With the knife still grasped in her hand, she raised her arm. Catherine buried her head against Rorry, unable to flee, unable to protect herself or him from the blow to come. Her body stiffened, but just a swish of air moved across her skin. Time seemed to still. Finally, she peeked, sat up, and looked around. The witch was gone. Starlight gleamed across the pond. The insects began their chirping harmony once more. What had happened? She pulled away from Rorry. He moaned.

"Rorry," Catherine pressed against his chest until his painful cry made her jerk back.

He moved his hands to his side. "A flesh wound," he gasped, "not fatal I think."

She grabbed the blanket at her side, then realized her clothes had changed. She looked down. "My dress, the dress I wore when first I met Andy." What did it mean?

"The spell completely unwound." He tried to sit up, but she pushed his shoulder.

"Don't move, what if you do more harm?" She tore one of the petticoats free and handed the material to him. "Press this against the wound. We must stop the bleeding before we try returning to the village."

"Careful, Catherine, you sound like you might care."

"I don't wish you dead." Exasperating man.

"Nor do I wish death upon you." He closed his eyes and winced as he pressed the cloth against the wound. "Mayhap we should keep each other close for safety's sake."

He joked, didn't he? Such a thing wouldn't do. Not for her, and not for him. So why did her heart flutter at the thought?

Wolf and the Girl with the Red Cloak

This tale is based on the collection of stories well known as Little Red Riding Hood. There are both French and German roots to the original fairytale. The earliest publication may have been by Perrault, where innocence clashes with evil. Oral tellings of Red Riding Hood are much older, often more gruesome, and darker than we normally think of fairytales in our modern age. This twisting of the tale is also dark, a caution of the evils of greed, or perhaps the dangers of mental illness untreated.

This retelling involves peril and the use of spells to control and manipulate circumstances. It may send chills across your neck. It is best read by the fire with a warm mug of hot chocolate.

Chapter 1

Stay on the path," Sorsha Bostich reminded her daughter as she tightened the sash of her cloak.

Crissy cringed. "You tell me the same thing every time."

Sorsha pressed her hand against Crissy's cheek. "And every time you return safely. I am satisfied."

"I want to go," Sabine declared, peeking around the corner of the kitchen doorway.

Crissy wrinkled her nose at her younger sister. "You are too little. A wolf might gobble you up whole with his afternoon tea."

Sorsha frowned. "No need to fill her head with dark tales."

Crissy smiled at her eight-year-old sibling. "Stay home where you are safe. We will go in a few years."

Sorsha pressed a basket into Crissy's hands. "You best be going. The coin should be enough for a full basket of baked goods."

Crissy kissed her mother's cheek. "Thank you, mother. I will be back before the sun goes down. I may stop and visit Elinor." Crissy skipped through the back door. The midday sun shone brightly overhead, and a cool breeze blew across the garden.

Sabine ran to her side. "Will you bring a cake with cinnamon? Or hard candies? Do you have enough money for that?"

Crissy rolled her eyes. "I will see what fits in the basket."

Sabine twirled. "If you hurry, we can play in the garden. I will be a princess."

Crissy scoffed. "I am the real princess. Hurry back to your dolls before they all disappear."

Sabine scurried away. Crissy watched. Why had mother married another man? Why have another daughter? Life was better when it was just mother and Crissy. She glanced at the half-timber house. Her home. Stepfather and that sweet younger sister were not going to keep her from what was rightfully hers.

She started along the wooded trail. Once she went deep enough not to be seen, she turned aside. She'd already explored most areas but recently crossed a path she'd never noticed before. There hadn't been time that day to go further. Today was a new day. An extraordinary day. She remembered the way well.

She paused when she reached the narrow path. Perhaps an animal made the trail, and yet, something about it caused her skin to tingle. Beneath twisting oaks grew holly bushes and wild roses. For what did she wait? Curiosity drove her onward. Brambles pulled at her cloak, but not enough to stop her from following the dirt path. The branches thickened overhead until it seemed as though she walked within a tunnel. From without, birds called, and insects chatted. But within the tunnel, she was surrounded by a soft hush, as of a breath held before an exhale.

How long she walked, she could not say. It seemed to take hours and hours, and yet, no time at all. Enchantment hovered through the space. The path widened. She heard water running nearby. Something had to be around the bend of the trail. It did not disappoint.

From the tunnel, she stepped into a clearing. Rocks covered in moss dotted the hillside. Thin shafts of light moved like a breeze. There was a flatter area, some of it covered with wildflowers and tangled grasses. Beyond that stood a house wrapped in time's decay. It leaned precariously against a tree trunk.

A wolf's howl caused Crissy to jump. She had come far. Perhaps too far. Light barely reached through the clearing. All she could see beyond the doorway of the house were shadows. She nibbled on her upper lip. "I need to bring a torch."

The sound of her voice stirred the clearing. The tingle in the air should have caused fear. Crissy pressed her hand against her belly. Excitement fluttered. Somewhere inside the house, a lamp lit. She didn't consider running away, but instead moved up the stairs and stepped inside. Her attention was drawn to a dark oak table. A round cloth formed from twists of silk lay on the center of the oblong table. Upon it sat a leather-bound book.

Crissy wrapped the book in the cloth and placed it in the bottom of her basket. The lamp went out. She half expected the door to slam shut, swallowing her up inside the house. She ran toward the light outside.

Too much time had passed for Crissy to complete her errands. She turned onto the path heading home instead. She'd weave a tale of wolves in the woods, how she tossed food at them to get their attention from herself. Soon, she would be alone in her room, able to explore the book that had been given to her.

~

"You look pale, daughter." Sorsha felt Crissy's forehead.

Crissy almost told her about the book with its strange symbols and lettering. A part of her wanted to tell about the spells. But then *he* walked in.

"How are my girls?" Oleg Bostich's voice boomed as he entered the kitchen. He kissed Crissy on the top of her head, then gathered Sorsha close.

"Papa," Sabine cried as she ran to join them.

Crissy watched him lift her sister. Sabine giggled. Sorsha held his arm. Crissy felt something in her chest twist. It was wrong, but the view displeased her. She wouldn't tell anyone about the book. Instead, she'd hide it away. She somehow knew something within its pages would make the difference she desired.

Chapter 2

Time did not soften Crissy's thoughts towards the usurpers within her home. Sabine grew taller and more lovely. Mother doted on her sweet younger daughter. Crissy drew her red cloak around herself as they prepared to join the May Day festivities in the village.

Sabine skipped around her in the kitchen, soft blooms bouncing in her hair. "I cannot believe I was chosen to weave the May Pole." She stopped and glanced at Crissy. "Did you get to during your fourteenth year?"

She shook her head. "I preferred making a basket and filling it with flowers."

Sabine grinned. "Perhaps today someone will gift you with a basket. Master Johnathan perhaps? Or one of the Torr brothers."

Crissy blushed. Jedison Torr hinted he might try to kiss her as they danced around the May Pole. She shooed Sabine from the house. "Go on. You don't want to be late."

Sabine stood outside the house, gazing at it. Crissy frowned. "Is something wrong?"

She shook her head. "Wondering what it would be like to put flower boxes beneath the windows."

"It is not your place to make changes."

Sabine laughed. "It is as much mine as yours, silly. Of course, I can make changes." She turned and skipped toward the center of town.

"Too excited to wait for the rest of us?" Sorsha asked as she stepped up behind Crissy.

"I forgot something upstairs. Go on without me, I will catch up." She smiled at Sorsha and Oleg. The pair nodded and walked from the house. Crissy's smile faded away. Anger burned within. How dare Sabine think this house belonged to her? As though she had the right to what Crissy's father had provided. She flounced up the stairs and slammed her door. Something thudded in the small closet. She opened the door and saw the book lying on the floor. She picked it up and went to the window seat where morning light touched the bone-colored pages. She opened somewhere towards the middle, running her fingers over pictures and words. Pages turned, and then something caught her notice. Chills skimmed along her arms as Crissy studied the lines of a spell. She didn't want to kill Sabine, but this could be a way of removing her from the family. At least until Crissy had what she wanted. She settled her back against the wall and read.

~

The month of May passed far too quickly. Memories of weaving the May Pole faded. Something new would take its place. Sabine stood in front of Crissy. "You want me to come with you?"

Crissy chuckled. "I said once you were old enough. The time has come." She frowned. "Unless you no longer wish to join me."

"Of course, I do," Sabine giggled as she bounced.

"We'll take a basket and enjoy a picnic. I already have a loaf of bread for us." She swung the basket with one hand and linked arms with her sister. "We can stop in town for jam." They left through the kitchen door.

"Shouldn't we be heading that way?" Sabine asked, pausing on the path where it diverged. The path on the left would lead them away from the forest. The other path took them deeper among the trees.

"I prefer a short cut through the forest. Don't worry, it is early in the day. There are no wild creatures to worry about until after dark. We will return long before then."

Sabine nodded. "Then into the woods we go."

It was an easy walk. Sabine closed her eyes and enjoyed the feel of sunlight against her face as she skipped along the path. Crissy strode a few steps ahead. Sabine watched her sister's red cloak flutter through the air as though it was something alive. How many years had she wanted to join Crissy on one of her journeys? Crissy paused and looked back at her. Where Sabine was fair skinned with blonde hair and blue eyes, Crissy had an angular face and thick wavy dark hair. She sighed, oh to be as beautiful as Crissy.

"I have an adventure in mind," Crissy said. "Shall we be explorers? Are you brave, like the men of Spain who set across the ocean?"

Sabine peered around her sister. "Is that a path? Looks more like a trail used by deer."

"Or wolves?" Crissy's eyes widened. "We must be very brave." She chewed on her upper lip.

Sabine took her hand. "I am brave if you are." Though four years separated them in age, Sabine had grown almost as tall as Crissy.

Crissy smiled, and they stepped onto the path. It was as though the sun suddenly turned away from them. Cold crept through her. Crissy released her hand and forged ahead. Sabine took a breath. She needed to be brave, too. Or Crissy might never allow her to join her on a journey again. She followed her sister.

Nary a bird chirped, nor insect hummed through the trees. They'd walked a long time when Sabine slowed her steps. Light splashed across the weathered overhang of an ancient house. "Crissy," she whispered as the hush of the woods settled across her shoulders like a scratchy blanket.

Crissy turned on the path to face her. Sabine pointed. "Who would build a house this deep in the forest?"

Crissy's face brightened. "Grandmother's house." She skipped across a patch of moss.

Sabine shook her head. "We shouldn't be here." Though a chill touched the air, she felt flush, drawn and yet repelled by the Victorian shelter. With its sharp angled roof, the house fit between two great trees. Ornate lintels of deep blue hung beneath the gable, with matching spindles across the porch. Thin clapboards had faded to gray, and moss clung to cracked slate shingles. Present and yet abandoned. A relic of an older age.

Crissy didn't seem to notice. Her eyes shone when she grabbed Sabine's hand. "Grandmother lived here. Not right, that you would find it when she was my grandmother." She squeezed.

Sabine pulled her hand back. "What do you mean, your grandmother? We're sisters. She'd be my grandmother as well." She looked at the house. "And how do you know this is her place? I've never heard of it."

"My grandmother belongs to my father." Crissy tugged her closer to the porch. "Your father didn't have a mother anymore."

Sabine dug her heels into the soft dirt forming a path to the entrance. "Stop it, Crissy. You aren't funny."

But Crissy wouldn't let go. She tugged Sabine to the foot of the stairs. "My father was killed by bandits as he traveled home from a festival far away. Grandmother couldn't bear the news. She died right there, in front of mother and me. Mother dragged me away and we haven't been here since. She moved to town and met your father a year later."

"He's our father, Crissy." Sabine whispered. Her throat tightened. "I don't like this; I want to go home."

"Not yet." The normally calm and fearless Crissy pleaded, her eyes sad. "The house is here. Like I remember it, but older. I had a doll. A tiny thing with blonde hair and porcelain skin." Crissy's eyes filled with tears. Sabine gulped her own, but she couldn't walk away. Crissy pressed her hand. "Please, Sabine." Her voice was a whisper. "She should be there, if what I remember is true." A single tear dripped from her lashes and coursed down her cheek. "But I can't go in there. Grandmother… but you never knew Grandmother. The house holds no memories for you. Please, Sabine, if you've ever loved me. Please find my doll. At least try."

She didn't want to. Not one ounce of herself wanted to step onto the porch, let alone through the front door that gaped open. The afternoon remained bright, but the forest hid more shadows. She stepped onto the first riser. Her heart quickened, her mind begging her to run in the other direction. But she couldn't, not with Crissy urging her to the next step. Her feet moved, and she stood on the worn boards of the porch, watching dried and shriveled leaves brush across her shoes.

With the door open, she could see into the house. Large windows provided light, so she could make out a tall table, broken chair, and a stone fireplace against a far wall.

"Just a few more steps, Sabine. Please, for me? I promise I won't tease you anymore. You'll be braver than me."

She wasn't brave, but neither could she turn back.

Something changed as she crossed the threshold into the kitchen. The hairs on the back of her neck stood out. Her hand opened and she dropped the willow branch she'd been carrying all morning. Her body tingled, and then waves of pain rolled from her feet, up her legs, through her back, and over her head. She felt as though she bent double, yet she seemed unable to move. Unable to scream though her voice rattled in her throat. Her hands grew larger, longer. Indentations between her knuckles deepened. Her supple skin stretched, brownish spots appearing as its color faded. She stretched a wrinkling hand toward Crissy, but her mind started to gray. Her lips forgot the words pressing against her heart. Weakness pained her legs, and she fell to the stone floor.

~

Crissy held her breath as the air around her shimmered with the working of the spell. Her beautiful, younger sister had changed into an old woman. The force of falling to her feet rippled through heavy flesh. Deep wrinkles marred her face. She could barely see the old woman's eyes.

"Do be careful, Grandmother," Crissy hollered.

Sabine grinned as she waved a gnarled hand. "It's okay, dear. Tell your mother hello. So kind of you to visit."

Crissy walked up the steps and stood in front of the door. "I have a basket of food for you."

"Will you come in?" Sabine's voice wobbled, and she coughed. She still knelt on the floor.

"I mustn't. Just as you must never come out."

Sabine looked at her with faded, milky-blue eyes. Crissy blinked. She placed the basket on the threshold of the door and pushed it toward Sabine with her foot. "Goodbye, Grandmother." A sob scorched her throat.

She turned and hurried away.

Sabine's voice followed her. "Goodbye, dear. Oh, I wish I could remember her name."

Crissy ran. The forest enveloped her, and she wiped tears from her cheeks. An hour later, as bells rang through the village, she sat in the middle of the floor of her bedroom, legs crossed, eyes squeezed shut. It was done. *It isn't forever*, she told herself. When the house was hers, and all the things in it, Sabine would be released. Crissy continued to sit until the darkening day made her light a lantern.

The door of her room flew open, banging against the wall. "Have you seen your sister?" Sorsha cried. "She went into the village, but she is long overdue."

Crissy turned. Sorsha's lips were pale, and her hands clutched at a doll with blond hair and blue eyes. "She must be with one of her friends."

"But it is dark outside."

"Have you asked stepfather? Perhaps he should look for her."

The search continued, for days, then weeks, and into months. Crissy huffed as she turned the corner, heading for home after a visit to the village. Someone with a cart waved as he rolled past. Oiled wood peeked through a blanket covering most of the cart. She frowned.

Sorsha stood outside the side door wiping her cheek. Crissy gripped her basket. "What was that?"

Sorsha closed her eyes, then looked at her. "We sold the cabinets from the front room. The mayor has always admired them."

Crissy felt her heart thud. "You sold them? How could you?" She swept past her mother, racing up the steps to the sanctuary of her bedroom. She slammed the door and flung herself across the bed. Much later, she finally sat up and wiped angry tears from her cheeks. Sabine was gone. Why did they have to fixate on her? Her father had built those cherry oak cabinets. What right did Oleg have to sell them? None. A strangled scream burned her throat. Were they going to sell more of her things? All for the futile search for Sabine? She jerked the book from her closet. It fell from her hands and clattered on the beaten wood floor.

There was a soft knock on the door. Crissy dropped a blanket over the book as Sorsha entered. "Are you alright?" she asked.

Crissy blinked and nodded. "I dropped a box in the closet."

Sorsha placed her hands on Crissy's shoulders. "I know you did not want to lose the cabinets. I had hoped they would pick them up and be gone before you returned from town. But the chance of finding your sister..." Tears rolled down her cheeks. "Sabine is more valuable than the cabinets."

Crissy's throat tightened. "Father built them."

"Perhaps someday you can get them back. Wouldn't you rather Sabine return home?"

"She ran away from us," Crissy said as she let tears flow.

Sorsha wrapped her arms around her and pulled her close. "I don't know why she would do that. We must ask one day, when she is home." Sorsha's voice cracked. She released Crissy and wiped her face. "I will see you at dinner."

Crissy breathed once Sorsha left the room and closed the door behind her. She pulled her hair into a braid. When she lifted the blanket from off the book, the image of a wolf in the margins captured her attention. She sat to read.

Chapter 3

Old bones. Sabine lifted her hand to the beam of light streaming through the freshly washed windowpane. Through the glow of her wrinkled flesh, she could see veins and tendons. With a sigh, she dropped her arm and turned to the front door. How long had it been since she pulled the bench from the kitchen to the wall, offering a place to sit and watch through the open door. She hobbled to the worn bit of furniture and flopped down with a heave of frustration. She leaned her head against the moss-colored wall and bit her lip. She could feel her heart pounding in her chest. Her eyes drifted closed. Tired. But tiredness did not feel right.

Sabine jumped to her feet. A haze filled the air. She turned and saw the old woman asleep on the bench. Silver white hair, braided, fell across her shoulder. Sabine reached for her own blonde braid. She rubbed her hands along the length as she stared at the old woman. Sallow cheeks, thin yet wrinkled. Her skin seemed stretched. She wore a simple gray dress with a neat apron. Sabine looked down. It was the same apron she wore. She wiped the palms of her hands on it. Her feet were bare, and the weathered boards of the porch, heated by the afternoon sun, warmed her feet as she stepped through the door of the house.

The front needed to be swept, but the pull of birds fluttering through the garden drew her instead. She skipped down the steps and twirled, arms outstretched.

A person flashed across her vision. She slowed to a stop and let her arms drift down. It had been so long since she had seen anyone but the old woman who slept all the time, she could only stare.

His clothing was rough and well-worn with patched elbows and faded knees. The shirt was no longer white. She could see a brown vest beneath the jacket. Hair covered his jaw and chin, yet it was trimmed. The skin of his face and hands appeared tanned. This was a man who lived out of doors, in God's open lands. Why was he here?

From the look on his face, he was as puzzled as she. His blue eyes glanced from her to the house, and back to her.

"I am dreaming." The rumble of his voice pleased her ears.

She looked at the house. It stood as it had as long as she could remember. The blue accents had faded a bit, but she couldn't climb that high to paint them fresh. If she had fresh paint with which to accomplish the task. The house held a mixture of age and charm, but nothing particularly dreamy about it. "It isn't that great a place."

"No. I must have fallen asleep waiting for Graham to return."

"Then you have joined my dream? I've not known that to happen before."

"I'm dreaming you."

"But I was here before you arrived. Came from inside the house. How could I have been thinking and doing if I am merely a member of your dream?"

He stepped closer. "I don't know. This is the first time I've dreamt like this." He poked a finger at her arm.

She slapped him away. This wasn't a dream. Or if it was, it was her dream.

He frowned. "What do you do, if you are more than a dream."

"I live here with an old woman."

"Your grandmother?"

She shrugged. "I'm not sure. She sleeps whenever I am awake. The poor dear works herself too hard. And you? What do you do?"

"I hunt." He pulled the crossbow from his shoulder. "Not for pleasure, mind you. I see that look of disgust."

Sabine allowed her lip to remain curled in disdain.

"Wild animals can become dangerous."

"Is that why you are here?"

"But I'm not, I'm asleep. The land is open, no forest in which to hide."

He stood close enough that she raised her head to talk with him. His blue eyes shimmered and lips twitched. He was years older, though she doubted he was old. The hand she'd hit felt real enough.

Something tugged at her back, like a hand grabbed the cloth of her dress and yanked her toward the door. She stumbled a bit. "Guess it's time to go."

"Wait, no." he tried to grab her, but she moved backward, her arms cartwheeling. She should have fallen over, but something held her upright.

The woods, him, everything faded.

Sabine opened her eyes, air rattled in her chest as she drew a deep breath. She leaned forward, facing the door. The sun still shone. The trees swayed in whatever breeze moved them from above. Birds sang. But there was no man. No young woman. She pushed herself to her feet and felt pain radiate through her knees. The view outside was beautiful, but her heart thrummed with terror the closer she came to the door. She must never leave.

Chapter 4

Patrick woke with a start. The image of the woman and strange dream lingered in his mind. Late afternoon sun streamed through the edges of closed shutters. The time had come to hunt.

He tugged his leather vest over his shirt and used the toggle to fix it tight. His fingers slid along a tear formed by the claw of a wolf. By the Creator's grace, the beast hadn't torn him worse.

Someone pounded on the door a moment before it flew open. "Birds have taken flight over the trees."

Patrick gazed past the man at the late afternoon. "The turning of the year causes many of them to swarm south."

"Or wolves are lurking. I've paid you to rid us of them. Send the foul beasts back to hell."

Patrick frowned. "They are no more of hell than you or I. So long as they haven't attacked a human, I will capture and take them beyond the settled lands."

"I paid you to kill."

Patrick tightened his fists. "You paid to rid them from your farm." He motioned to the waning day. "Time wastes."

It wasn't that he refused to kill, but the creatures were majestic. It was only after they got a scent for human blood and flesh that there was no other recourse. The beasts attacking the farm went after pigs and chickens, no signs they traveled close to the cottage.

He swung his crossbow into place on his shoulder and slid a dagger into a holder on his thigh. A howl carried across the land as he sauntered into a field heavy with barley. He headed toward a thicket of trees at the top of a hill.

From the snarling he heard whipping around him, at least two creatures were trapped. The first trap held a young male with ears back and teeth snapping at the wooden cage. The animal fought. Its pelt was thick graying brown and well-formed muscles rippled as it tried to escape.

Patrick held his breath as he pulled a blanket from the crook of a branch. He removed the fleece and laid it on the trap, stepping back several feet before sucking breath into his body. The frenzy of the wolf continued for a moment, and then the scuffling quieted. Its snarls turned to yips. Then with a gurgle and a thud, there was silence.

He turned to the other trap several hundred feet away and repeated his actions. There were no other signs of wolves. Patrick frowned. acks were larger than two. He used ropes to pull the cages onto his wagon. The potion on the blankets would last long enough to get the beasts away from the farm and others in the community. He checked the other traps and freshened chicken carcasses used for bait. As he drove into the moonlight, thoughts of his strange dream mingled with the shadows.

Chapter 5

As the sun dipped behind the house, Crissy moved into the forest. In her hand she gripped a pouch holding Sabine's clothes, hairbrush, and a ratted long eared stuffed rabbit. She'd taken the things from her sister's bedroom. Two years, and they wanted it kept the same. She pushed memories of playing with Sabine as a baby, the way her blue eyes sparkled when Crissy swung her in circles. Their laughter across the yard. This was their fault, Mother and Oleg. Crissy just wanted to keep what was rightfully hers. What father had left for her. She swiped at tears on her cheeks. It wasn't fair that Sabine had to die, but what choice remained?

When it grew too dark, she opened her lantern. Her feet seemed to know the way, though her heart remained heavy with guilt and dread. Rustling among the brush let her know something drew close. Her breath tightened. Perhaps the wolves would kill her, and she could join her father. Shadows moved. A creature drew closer to her circle of light. It was smaller than she thought, thin, with silent paws. An intelligence gleamed from its yellow eyes. There were more. She could feel them around her. She clutched the package against her heart. It waited. Its direct gaze drew her in. It was beautiful. Awe dripped through the pain of what she needed to do. She tossed the pouch at its feet.

When they were gone, she followed. How could she not? But the snarls she heard weren't what she expected. Crissy doused the lantern, not wanting Sabine to see her from the ancient house. In the moonlight, Crissy saw wolves pacing along the edge of the clearing. Yet they could not step any closer. Their yips brought Sabine to a window. Crissy stepped behind a tree. The old woman gazed from within the house. Fearful. But the wolves could not draw any closer. Crissy closed her eyes. The spell on Sabine must be the stronger spell. Others would have to be sacrificed, strengthening the wolves until they could not be deterred.

Crissy gripped the lantern as she returned to the main path. She tripped on something, catching herself before she fell. The bag with Sabine's things lay in the dirt. She retrieved it and turned toward the village. She didn't have to go far when giggles sounded among the trees. She closed the lantern. Someone else had come.

Two lights showed a man and a woman in a passionate embrace. She recognized Jedison Torr. The sight of his bare back caused heat in her belly. He'd never kissed her like that. The opportunity seemed perfect. Neither one noticed when Crissy darted forward and stole his shirt. She raced back. It didn't take long for the wolf to find her. She tossed the shirt in its path. The desire to see what would happen next drew her to follow. Screams rent the melody of night in the forest. They were close enough to the village that someone would come. Crissy barely got a view of two beasts tearing into Jedison's chest. The girl just stood there screaming.

News of the attack blazed through the village the following day. Crissy smirked. It hadn't been an innocent walk through the woods in the moonlight. Sorsha refused to let Crissy leave the house. It wasn't until night had fallen when she was finally able to sneak away. She had the bag of Sabine's things. Once again, she dropped it for the wolf. Was it her imagination, or had the beast grown? The light from its eyes gleamed with evil intent. Had she done that to it? She followed, but the wolves could barely move into the clearing. Disappointment caused her shoulders to droop as she returned to her bedroom. She placed the bag of Sabine's things in her closet beneath a mound of clothes where it wasn't likely to be found by anyone else. She closed her eyes and breathed. More sacrifices would need to be made.

Chapter 6

"Grandmother, are you here?"

The muscles at the nape of Sabine's neck clenched. Why did she visit? Youth draped over the girl like a curse. She strangled her with it. The basket of food and goodies was appreciated, but the old had no use for youth.

She hobbled to the hall, resting her hand against the bench. The girl, supposedly her granddaughter, stood on the stairs. The young face brightened. Sabine wanted to slap the grin away. Her chest burned. What about the young woman caused such anguish?

"You look tired."

Sabine frowned. "I am old. You will know the sting of age as well."

"That is an awful thing to say Grandmother." The girl frowned. "You lived your life, is it not fair that I live mine as well?"

Had she lived a life? Sabine tried to recall. "I have no memory of my life. Not living it."

"Poor dear. It is a wretched fate, grandmother."

"Why are you here?"

The red cape the girl insisted on wearing billowed as she raised her arm. "I bring goods. Cans to store for the winter."

"Bring it around to the kitchen, my arms are too weary for such a task."

But the young woman shook her head. "You will not step through the doorway, and neither will I." She bent and placed the basket on the ground. She pushed it through the door with her foot.

Sabine put both hands across her belly. It was too close to the outside. Much too close.

"Come, Grandmother, let me see you take the basket."

"Devil take you, girl."

"I am sorry, Sabine. For all of this. But you do not have much longer to wait."

Of what did she speak? The girl was daft. Sabine shook her head.

The young woman watched for a moment, and then skipped away, going through the trees until she could see her no longer. Instead, Sabine stared at the basket. She shuffled a few steps closer. The air heated and her head spun. Every time. The girl tormented her. Could it be for a purpose? She took another step closer. Tears stuck to the back of her throat. Fear. Why such anguish? What could be beyond the door that caused such a feeling?

Chapter 7

What do you hunt?”

Patrick turned and found himself facing the young woman. His pulse quickened. How was it possible?

“You cannot be real.” He stroked her cheek.

Her eyes widened, and she pulled away. Her hand covered where he had touched her. She opened her mouth as if to speak but remained silent.

“You aren’t real, are you?” Patrick stared at her.

“I don’t know what I am. I walk in twilight.”

“Are these woods safe in the night?”

“I had thought so, but wolves have been here.”

“Wolves? How can you tell?”

She motioned him to follow. He allowed her to lead him through the side yard, circumventing a stone fence. When she stopped, she pointed at the ground. There were footsteps, at least two fully grown wolves tramped across the dampened earth. “They should not be this close to a settlement.” He looked at the house. “Is the old woman ill?” That could draw them.

The girl shook her head. “She is well enough, sleeps often.”

“Wolves can be dangerous. If they have tracked this close to your house, you would do well to remain inside. Or make your way to town until the pack moves on for winter.”

“I do not think we can go to town.”

“Is there one nearby?”

She tilted her head and looked at the forest. “Somewhere beyond. I think there is. Dover, perhaps? I lived there once, long ago.”

“If you are real, then mayhap I can come to help.”

“Help what?”

He waved, encompassing the clearing and the house. “This. You. The place that calls me in my dreams.”

A moment later, she was gone. The trees were gone. He lay beneath a starry sky where gentle bare hills rolled to the horizon. Just a dream. And yet, as he stood, stretching his arms over his head, he wondered if such a place could exist. "Dover." The name sounded natural enough. Perhaps it was time to move on.

Chapter 8

Grandmother's basket is ready, Crissy." Sorsha used a linen towel to cover the prepared meal.

Crissy finished rubbing oil into the maple chest. Its surface gleamed. The rose-banded China packed inside was intended for her wedding and the house she would start with her husband. *But I intend to keep this place.* She looked around the formal living room. The walls had been papered in yellow with vertical lines of ivy. Two formal chairs flanked the bay window with a sofa set across from them.

She replaced the lace runner across the chest as Sorsha stepped into the arched opening.

"Will you take the basket to Grandmother? Your father has not yet returned."

Crissy looked at the floor. The tightly woven rug had twisted vines across it. "He's looking for her, isn't he?"

"He still hopes to find her."

"What about me? I'm here, I didn't run away." She glanced at Sorsha as she blinked moisture from her eyes. *Why should it matter, he wasn't her real father.*

"He loves you, Crissy. Believe me. He just can't let Sabine go."

"It's been two years."

"When you have children of your own, you will understand." She lifted the basket. "Will you take the meal to Grandmother?"

"Yes, Mother."

"Wear your red cape, there's a chill in the air. And stay on the path. Stories are going around about wolf packs."

"You tell me the same thing every trip." She grabbed the handle of the basket.

"Be back before nightfall. We'll have dinner at eight."

"Yes, Mother."

"Tell Grandmother hello. Ask if she has needs."

Crissy kissed Mother's cheek. "This is not my first visit. I will see you at dinner come eight o'clock."

It wasn't her first visit. She'd been taking the paths into the woods for two years, though Sorsha and Oleg would say it had been forever. The main street through town had been paved with square bricks. Crissy hopped over the white ones, swinging the basket forward and backward. She passed the houses built with thin gardens between them, crossed over Macie's fence, and made her way to the wooded path. Blue sky peeked through the branches until the trees became twisted together and twilight settled along the path. Sometime later, after a sharp curve, Grandmother's house came into view. Candles burned in the windows, causing Crissy's mouth to twist. *Never did like the dark, did you?*

With quiet feet, she snuck up the stairs and across the porch. The front door stood open. Inside looked cheery. Two chairs were set by the thick kitchen table. The counter was clear of debris. A fire whipped in the fireplace. Crissy smiled. A quaint little home for an old woman. Only Sabine wasn't really old.

"Grandmother? Are you home?" Crissy called out.

Something thumped, words she couldn't understand, and then the bent old woman leaning on her cane moved into view.

"There you are," Crissy waved. "Thought maybe you went into town."

"Don't tease, little girl." Sabine narrowed her rheumy eyes. "You know I'll not step over that threshold. An evil world it is out there. Here I will stay, thank you very much."

"I'm not little anymore, Grandmother. I'm twenty now." Crissy swirled. "Don't I look grown up?"

"You look like trouble." Sabine inched closer. She breathed deeply and rubbed her back.

"Feeling old today?"

"As will you. Someday." She stared at something beyond Crissy's shoulder. "The world looks the same. I am the only one who aged."

"You enjoyed long life."

"Have I? I dream of my youth, at times chasing after you. I dream, and yet I remember nothing." She leaned against the door jam. "Not growing up. No beau. Marriage? Children? You are my granddaughter, there must be children. Why have I no memory of them?"

"Perhaps it is easier that way." She lifted the basket. "Here is food."

Sabine raised her skinny arm and reached for the handle. Her hand passed over the threshold of the door. Crissy watched the wrinkled flesh smooth, dark spots fading to creamy skin. She pushed the basket through the doorway and saw the hand turn old once more. Sabine staggered back with it.

"It's heavy today."

"Mother was expecting guests. There's chicken pie, apples from the orchard, and cobbler. I think she cut fall vegetables as well. Winter's coming, you'll have canned goods."

"Your mother is a good woman. Must be busy, never visits."

"I like coming, Grandmother. It is good to see you."

"Best run along. Night will be setting shortly. Beware of wolves. I've seen them strolling through the woods. Not safe, not for anyone."

"Don't worry, Grandmother," Crissy smirked, "they can't get in your home. Not yet anyhow." The old woman didn't hear the last few words. Crissy turned toward home but paused to peek at the side of the house. There were fresh prints in the dirt. The wolves came close. Her chest pounded. More sacrifices needed to be made. A shiver crossed her skin as she pondered who would be worth achieving her goals.

Chapter 9

The town existed. Patrick noticed the trees beyond. Somewhere in the woods could be a young woman living with her grandmother. Or his mind had taken a wrong turn.

People clustered in the street. The tones of their voices were hushed, and their shoulders seemed tight.

"Morning," he tipped his hat to an older gentleman crossing the road.

The man looked him up and down with a grunt. "There's no good in this morning."

Patrick was puzzled at the cold greeting. "I seek a room for hire."

The man pointed to a two-story structure further into town. "Gunthers has plenty of space. No one will want to remain after news spreads."

"News? Something bad has happened?"

"That it has." He tugged on his beard. "Never heard the like. An entire family gone. Murdered."

"Murdered?" Patrick folded his arms to ward off a chill. "Does a madman live here?"

"Not human. A pack of wolves turned ravenous. We've seen 'em, they been here a while. But this? Never imagined this sort of behavior."

"Wolves? How can you be sure?"

"It was them animals, right enough. Acting more like a devil than God's creatures."

"Walk with me to Gunthers. I may be able to help."

~

The next day, Crissy sat across the dining table from Oleg. Not quite tall, having a plump body, the man would have been considered jovial if circumstances hadn't taken his true daughter from him. In two years, he hadn't been able to forget, so though he smiled, sadness lingered in his eyes. His lips didn't rise quite as high as they might have.

"You look tired, Father." Though not hers by birth, he'd asked her to call him that, preferring Sabine to think of them as a real family.

He took a sip from the wine goblet. "Home is a good place to be. I am thankful to return to you."

People could easily be taken, death's touch cared little for young or old. But this house, the possessions within, these were the things for which she yearned. Things that belonged to her because they had been her father's. Some might try to take them from her, but they would not succeed. The book she had found reassured her.

"… Beckett homestead appears to be wolves."

Crissy's attention perked. She looked up from her soup bowl.

"The family was murdered, their bodies ripped…"

"Oleg," Sorsha admonished him with a glare.

But Crissy wanted more details. "The Beckett family? Who was killed?"

"The dinner table is not the place for such conversation." Sorsha rebuked them both.

"We will talk later this evening. The Mayor and the Kaughmans will join us."

"Whatever for?" Crissy couldn't remember a time when guests were brought in that late.

"Wolves have tasted blood. They will not stop until they are killed. We need to hire hunters."

Sorsha looked pale, but she remained calm. "Then this conversation may wait until our guests have arrived."

Alexander Fairmoore and Gunter Erhardt arrived first, followed by Eibella and Dietrich Kaughman. A stranger joined them, a man of indiscriminate height. Though his dark hair had been slicked and tied back and his beard trimmed, he reeked of wild. His clothes were pleasant enough, probably borrowed from Mayor Fairmoore, Crissy thought. She felt his eyes on her as she poured tea and prepared a tiny dish with jelly-printed cookies dusted with sugar. She narrowed her eyes at him, but he didn't even have the gall to appear embarrassed to be caught watching.

"Your guest?" Oleg shook hands with the mayor.

Mayor Fairmoore smiled broadly; his round cheeks puffed out. "An answer to prayer, you will see. Our Lord God prepares his response nary the words have left our lips."

"What?" Oleg looked at the man.

"Word of the packs has spread," the man's voice grated, "though I did not hear of tragedy until arriving in town this afternoon." He slapped the mayor's shoulder, as men were prone to do. "Met Fairmoore at the Inn. The public rooms were in an uproar."

"Terrible business." Dietrich shook his head.

"The family was slaughtered." Mayor Fairmoore looked at her.

Crissy gulped.

"Unpleasant business for a girl, are you sure you should be here?" The stranger asked.

Why should he care for her delicacy? Crissy handed a plate to the mayor and squared her shoulders. "More right than you to be here."

"Lass, I mean you no disrespect—"

"They are known to me. It is unpleasant to hear what has become of them, and I sorrow for the children. But I am of age, I will know what has happened and what is planned to deal with the problem."

"Crissy speaks truth." Oleg sighed. "Terrible things we must all face. What is your name, stranger, seeing you speak freely in my home?"

"I beg your pardon, sir." He offered a nod. "Patrick Slattery."

"You have the sound of the island in your speech."

"Aye, that is true, sir. The wilds of Iveragh. I'm a hunter. You are bound to get more of us as news of the attack spreads."

"We'll be grateful for your service, Mr. Slattery."

"Wolf is as I'm known."

Of course, he would be, Crissy thought with a frown.

Later that evening, moonlight splashed through the bedroom window. Crissy did not require a lantern to lace her boots, but she lit it and wrapped the silver case around the glass to block the light. With her room located at the back of the house, she easily slid over the windowsill and landed on the soft layer of mulch laid to winter the garden. Round footstones marked the path through the garden. The gate creaked as she pushed it open. The light of the full moon could not penetrate the woods. Crissy knelt beside a fallen log and lifted the lantern glaze, pulling away the silver lining. A soft glow encased her, and she could see the first pair of twisted tree trunks leading into the forest. She stepped around them. The rough track swept down a shallow ravine. She held the lantern aloft and pulled herself up to the far side. She took a few more steps through the underbrush and found one of the paths leading through the forest.

Crissy passed the trail she took to Sabine, skirting the heart of the woods for the western edge. Something moved to her left. Beyond the edge of light, a shadow followed her, matching step for step. More than one. She could hear their feet pattering across the uneven ground. She stopped, placed the lantern on the ground, and wrapped the silver lining around the glass. Darkness descended around her; her eyes could not yet decipher any of the ambient shine pouring down from the stars. She could hear movement, smell the musky pelts of wolves.

She stretched her hand out, and for a moment nothing happened. Then something nuzzled her hand. Amazing creatures. Lean, hard bodies were covered with thick, soft fur. Predators, cunning and deadly, yet they cared for their young, watched over them.

"You must be swift, my dears. Strengthen yourselves with human blood until you can break the threshold. Beware, hunters are come."

Beneath her hand, the body of the wolf tightened, and she felt its growl of understanding. She drew a small shirt from her pocket. Crissy gripped the shoulders and flapped it open and then laid it on the ground. She didn't think about the child, nor his brothers and sisters. She thought of Sabine. Her father had searched long for his daughter, imagine his shock at finding her ravished body deep in the woods. The wolves would break the spell surrounding the house and destroy Grandmother.

"What big eyes you have," Crissy imagined the wrinkled, rheumy orbs opening in fright.

"What big ears you have." Snarling and growling would be the last sounds she heard.

"And what big teeth you have." Screams would not linger. The wolves tore into the neck of their victims first, allowing blood loss to weaken their prey to the point of surrender.

Poor Sabine, such an end after two years of enchantment. Crissy's heart ached for a moment. But Sabine wasn't her blood. The new man, claiming to be her father, intended Sabine to inherit another man's toil. Her father had provided wealth and riches, not Sabine's. He had merely taken what belonged to another. Hatred burned, wrapped up in sorrow and anger. Sabine was a pawn. Look at the way he searched for her, and what he had sold to pay for it.

Crissy shook herself, drawing her mind to the woods and the surrounding night. Wolves had dispersed. She crumpled the blue shirt and shoved it into her pocket. Cherga Genbach filled the lines at the back of their garden with clothes. Seven sons and a girl. Prey, helpless against the power of the wolves. With the brief scent given to them, they would track to the family farm. Crissy slowed her steps, imagining. The pack would use the shadows, making their way around the house, searching for an opening, a weakness. A window left un-shuttered; a doorway cracked open to allow air to circulate. Silent and swift, they would move into the house, to the rooms where human warmth drew them. Take out the youngest first, the smallest, and then work their way to the adults, Cherga and her chunky husband. The smell of blood would soak into the wood, mixed with the pungent odor of wolf. Torn flesh, feast. Power would flow through them. How many more would need to be sacrificed before the spell surrounding Sabine could be broken?

Crissy quickened her pace. Time was essential. Another attack would draw more hunters. She uncovered the lantern and traced her steps toward home. A different noise captured her attention. Leaves crunching underfoot. Someone else moved nearby. Too close to her to put out the light, they would have seen her. She raised the lantern. "Show yourself."

"Not what I expected to find in the woods tonight."

Him. Wolf. She held her snarl inside. His hands should be dripping in wolf blood. How many of the majestic creatures had been slaughtered by them?

"I fear for my grandmother. I meant to stay the night with her, but I could not find her path. The darkness has twisted my way."

He moved closer. With his dark clothes, he hid well among the shadows. But where were his weapons?

He spoke, an edge of distrust in his tone. "You are alone in the dark? Perfect bait for the pack."

"I did not intend…"

"Yet here you are, folly of a young mind."

"Be my guide home. Surely the hunter can prevent himself from becoming prey?"

He laughed, a dry humorless noise. "I'm sure you could teach me a thing about predators and prey, Miss Bostich. What will tomorrow reveal to us?"

"I do not take your meaning, sir. I tire. Hunt your beasts." She peered at his empty hands. "Though I know not what you will do against them without arrow or sword."

"In due course. Their unusual behavior draws me."

"As you please. I mean to follow the trail home."

He backed away and disappeared into the night. Crissy didn't bother looking for him, she continued home. Shivers coursed her back as she imagined his eyes following her.

~

Wolf watched as Miss Bostich wound her way along the path leading out of the woods. Her dark hair and fair skin should have piqued his interest, but the lovely young woman caused his heart to clench. An aura of darkness surrounded her.

Somewhere ahead, snarls and a yelp drew his attention. More snarls and then a piercing cry sounded. After that, it was silent. Minutes passed before the usual sounds of night rose in volume. It did not take much longer to find something. A wolf lay on the path.

The animal's coat was a molten mix of gray, white, and black. Laying on its side, breath shallow and fast, it looked more to be pitied than feared. He slowed his steps, rustling leaves beneath his feet. The wolf shook its head but appeared unable to rise.

A mortal wound cut into its side. Wolf searched the nearby trees, but no other animals hid. Why had they not finished it off? The creature had sad eyes. Pained eyes. Where were the signs of rabid behavior? He touched her coat, well away from the wound. She whimpered.

"Are you not one of the wolf pack?" But this was no evil beast. He pulled his knife. Death would be upon her soon enough, but he could lessen the length of anguish to be endured.

After the deed had been accomplished, he resumed tracking the others.

Chapter 10

Crissy sat at the upper story window in the nook between bedrooms. A group of villagers lingered outside the General Store. She couldn't hear their whispered words, but frequent glances toward the woods suggested their topic of conversation revolved around the wolves. Mrs. Rhinebach, matron of the store, covered her mouth.

Crissy straightened as Wolf walked to the group. Being found by him during the night did not please. He was a tracker. Care must be taken until he could be dealt with. How could she obtain an article of his clothing? Beside him, Mayor Fairmoore pulled a watch from his vest. Others nodded. Reluctance to leave her solitude pulled at her, yet a plot was being concocted. She placed a ribbon in the book that had sat idle in her lap and headed for the stairs.

Wolf latched on to her almost as soon as she crossed the street. "You found your way home?"

She twirled to face him, putting a fake smile on her face. "Kind of you to inquire. I did not realize you were familiar with the Rhinebach's."

"My popularity grows. Another family has been butchered."

She nodded. "I heard. Horrifying, to think I was in the region as well."

"Your Grandmother should come to town if you fear her safety."

"She will not leave her home. I have never known her to step through the doorway."

"Will you take me to meet her? Perhaps I may convince her of the necessity."

Did he doubt there was a grandmother? Crissy tilted her head. "You may have charm, sir, but you have yet to convince me you are an honorable man. You, too, were in those woods last evening. Did you not cross paths with the wolves?"

"Only with you. I was distracted."

"Perhaps tonight you will be more successful. What is the plan? I saw several of the men confer with Mayor Fairmoore."

"We will meet at Luxley Hall this afternoon. Your father will be one of the men joining us."

"May I accompany him?"

"Plenty of curious ears." Wolf smiled, yet his eyes remained wary. "The ladies plan to prepare a meal, though I suspect more effort will go toward listening than cooking."

Females, especially those living in the village, were nosy to a fault. "I will see you this afternoon. What time did you say?"

"Two-of-the-clock."

They parted ways. Luxley Hall marked the center of town. The green square to the front was often used for festivals and many windows opened to it. Its large main room easily held everyone in the town. It was a grand building meant to impress both locals and strangers. Crissy headed away from it. Her father's house was infinitely better.

As the autumn sun lowered that afternoon, Oleg chose to take the carriage, allowing Sorsha and Crissy to ride in comfort, as well as to make room for a pair of black bird pies freshly baked. The main room of the hall was full when they arrived, people from the village and surrounding lands mulling in groups of various sizes. Crissy wandered aimlessly, staring at the floor as murmurings rose around her. Horror at the death of children. Lives lost. Torn asunder. The attack had been brutal. She shuddered thinking about it. The pack had gained strength.

Someone would have to be next. Plenty of farms surrounded the main village. How to choose a worthy sacrifice?

Wolf's voice carried across the crowd. Crissy cringed, though she could not hear what he said. How many wolf pelts had he carved from carcasses? Death stalked his steps. But a single victim would not be enough. Someday soon, he and her sister could feel the bite of fangs, the tear of claws. He was more deserving than Sabine. Another young life that would be cut short, but sister dearest stood between Crissy and security. It wasn't to be borne. She stood at a window and stared at the lawn that had turned brown by the cooling days.

"Doesn't seem fitting for the sun to shine on such a bleak afternoon." Wolf made his way to her side.

Crissy sighed. "Death is a natural part of our life here."

He shook his head in disagreement. "Wolves do not attack in this manner. Within walls? Dragging children from their beds?"

Crissy narrowed her eyes. *What implication did he wish to impart?* "You think something other than wolves did this? Some dark blight that hunts the night? Has your mind been turned by Gothic tales?"

"There is no doubt the animals killed the family. But it is not their instinct to behave in such a way."

"Dark dealings." Mayor Fairmoore joined them. "To live through such times is difficult to fathom."

His vest stretched across a wide belly. The dark hair at his temples had become peppered with gray. Crissy glanced beyond, where his wife, Eloise, stood with a brood of friends. Their voices supported the general hum throughout the room.

"It is a tragedy, sir." Crissy offered a weak smile. He was a good mayor, lived in town but his house had been built on the hill, far enough apart to give the appearance of separation. Elevation. The house included children. A grandmother. Maids and other servants. A massive household, many more victims than the Genbach's.

"We will meet at the smithy at dusk." Wolf was shaking hands.

Crissy returned her attention to the conversation that had been drifting around her. "Meet?" Wolf's dark eyes made her want to back away. He didn't trust her.

"It is past time to hunt these beasts." The mayor tucked his hands in his pockets. "At least thirty men will join us. We will take the woods tonight. Carcasses will foul the town center come morning. Wolf carcasses, not human."

Her smile came easily. Yes, into the woods. Would they think about protecting the streets and houses they left behind? The mayor would enter the front cubicle of his house and find bloody prints across the marble. No. His sacrifice would be needed as well. It needed to be all of them.

"Not a night to wander to Grandmother's house," Wolf admonished.

"Grandmother?" Mayor Fairmoore looked from one to the other, "Didn't she have an ancient looking place deep in the woods? Near the broken oak. I would think her long dead."

"Old, certainly, but not dead." Crissy reassured him. "Refuses to step from her home. Insane as a lark on dewberries, but she's harmless."

"Let us hope she does not draw the attention of the pack." Wolf stared at her. He couldn't know what she planned, but he suspected something.

"They seem intent on larger prey. Well, more numerous, anyway."

"Why is that do you suppose?"

She shrugged. Vile man. Someday he would know the truth. It would be her pleasure to enlighten him.

An hour later, Crissy knelt beside her bed and pulled the handle on the shallow trunk stored beneath the straps of the bed frame. She drew the locket from her neck and lifted the key from its compartment. A twist of metal, the click of a lock opening, and she raised the lid.

Daylight streaming through the window revealed the musty

leather-bound book. The secure chest proved a much better hiding spot than a shelf in the closet. Her fingers trailed over the cover. Ah, the power. Her flesh crawled with goose bumps, but she could no more turn from it than she could cut off her arm. She lifted the book from the chest. She cleared her mind and focused on the challenge. Get into Mayor Fairmoore's house unseen. This family hung no laundry in the garden. The task would be harder, more dangerous. But the reward—time to finish what was started four years ago. The villagers would hunt the wolves to the ground and destroy them. She needed the wolves to accomplish their ultimate purpose before that happened. Kill Sabine. Secure Christine's inheritance.

~

Wolf joined a group of men at a tall round table. Talk lingered on the woods, the wolves hiding among the trees. "What of places within the woods? Have houses been built? Carpenters, or loggers perhaps? Woodsmen?"

"Crissy Bostich heads into the woods frequently." A burly gray-haired man nodded, taking a swig of beer. "We all recognize that red cloak she wears. Caries a basket full of goodies, she's taking it to someone."

His slim cousin pointed around the table with the end of his pipe. "That old grandmother of theirs."

"An old woman?" Wolf leaned closer. "She lives in a Victorian house?"

"Not sure what kind of house it be. Never seen it." The man chewed on the pipe for a moment, then pointed it at him once more. "Nothing good in those trees."

"Hogwash. You've naught but a suspicious mind." The old man with a scar above his right eye turned to Wolf. "Think I saw it as a lad. Not sure how much could be left."

"Is there a map?"

He cackled. "A map?" He tapped his head with his finger. "This here's me map. I worked in those woods as a young man. The paths haven't changed much since then, I warrant."

"I have paper at my quarters. Could you show me the paths to take?" He tried not to let excitement buzz, but his fingers tingled. His feet longed to go.

Chapter 11

Crissy wrapped the red cloak around herself, securing it with a clasp around her neck. She drew the hood over her head. Speaking words from the book, she watched color seep away. A glance in the mirror revealed merely a shadow. Excitement flowed through her veins.

For late afternoon, the streets were empty. Fear kept people indoors, as though wood and metal could stop the beasts breaking through. They would have what they wanted. What she wanted.

Crissy walked to the tree-shaded edge of the street. A shadow moving in the open sunlight would draw unwanted attention. The glimmer would not stand up to careful watch. The lane turned, curving around the hill. The mayor's driveway, lined with oaks, took a more direct route to the top. She had walked it before, many times in fact. For parties. Dances. Midsummers Eve and Boxing Day. Two of the children were her age, unmarried yet. The others were younger. Sadness tugged at her heart, and yet, to offer such a sacrifice… they were lovely. Innocent.

The house on the hill appeared grand with its marble columns and wide yard. She skirted the front, knowing the kitchen door was most likely to be open and unwatched at this time.

There it was. The simple brown door and shadowy beyond. The smell of pies wafted through the air.

Crissy paused at the window just to be certain. Though trees and sky reflected in the glass, there was none of her. Pleasure rushed through her.

Eager to accomplish the task, she stepped into the house. The back stairs led to the maids' room with its short hallway, then the nanny's quarters. Nothing moved in the back of the house. Crissy pressed her ear against the wood of the nanny's door. Silence. She eased the door slightly open and peaked through. Her breath caught in her throat and her heart pounded. The nanny sat in the rocker by the window. Crissy froze, watched, expected movement, chaos. But all she heard was a rumbling noise. The nanny snored.

She pushed the door open enough to slip through. Across the

room, an open doorway led into the children's wing. It took little effort to cross the first bedroom, darting glances at the middle-aged woman cast across a chair with her jaw slacked open. The youngest pair of Fairmoore children were sleeping in their beds. One had discarded his shirt on the floor. Crissy picked it up and placed it in her pocket. She wanted more. Something belonging to the mayor.

She snuck through the room to the main hallway. It took two more doors before she found a large poster bed. The dainty nightgown laid across the spread would belong to Eloise Fairmoore. The delicate silk felt cool to the touch. Crissy twisted it into a ball and shoved it into the pocket as well. A tie lay discarded on a bureau. She added it to the growing collection.

Returning to the hallway, she heard footsteps on the stairs. Voices. She hurried to the children's wing of rooms, but a small dog trailed her.

"Cesar." Someone called for it.

The rascal had escaped its mistress to sniff at the edge of her cloak. Crissy paused at the door. Though the spell protected her from sight, opening and closing doors would be noticed. She kicked at the mutt with her booted foot. Rather than startling it away, the action seemed to entice it to play. With a yap, it jumped, bent the front two legs, and then pounced. Crissy swept her cape from its sharp little teeth, trying to push the dog further away without harm.

She rushed into the room, managed to close the door without letting the dog through. It scratched at the door, barking its displeasure. The boy in the first bed woke, sitting up and rubbing his eyes.

Crissy held her breath. Voices from the other side of the door yelled for the dog to cease its antics. Her heart stuck in her throat.

"What have you done, Jasper?" the older woman stepped through the other door. Crissy skirted them. The room was dim, shutters pulled to block the afternoon light probably to encourage sleep. Neither the boy nor his nanny seemed to notice her there. The woman moved to the boy's side as the hall door burst open. Crissy made it into the nanny's room before the dog could catch her. She continued on, retracing her steps. The voices faded as she made her way down the narrow stairs. Good thing no one rushed up from the kitchens.

But the lower rooms remained undisturbed by the commotion upstairs. She burst outside, picking up her skirts and running across the manicured garden to the protection of the line of trees. She gasped for breath, momentarily lightheaded. She threw the hood from her head as she leaned against the tree trunk. A glance to the side showed the house remained at peace.

She closed her eyes for a moment, drinking in the feel of victory.

A cool breeze caressed her cheek. When she opened her eyes once more, she looked to the right, down the hillside toward town. Wolf walked a path a way off. Perhaps something else could be won this day as well. She covered her head and took to the shadows, following him into the woods.

He was trying to find Grandmother's house. Crissy watched him turn the paper in his hand upside down, look from the drawing to the turn in the path, then back at the drawing. He turned the map sideways. With a frustrated grunt, he crumpled the paper in his hand and shoved it into his pocket. Was it suspicion that drove him? Concern for an elderly woman alone in the woods? Did he fear the big bad wolves would get her? Crissy hoped so. Fervently. He pulled something from the satchel hanging at his side.

Wolf turned aside, but Crissy continued along the smaller path. Though it was still afternoon, twilight hovered among the trees. She left the trail at the broken tree. A bolt of lightning, many years before, had breached the thick trunk of an oak. One side had fallen against another tree while the other side remained fixed in the ground, though the tree itself had long since died. Skirting the standing trunk, she found the indent leading to the culvert. She crouched and waited. Wind whipped the tops of the trees, and she could hear the rustle of leaves and branches dancing in the canopy. No birds chirped. No insects buzzed. The forest remained hushed with the feel of magic.

A wolf brushed against her. Crissy drew the articles of clothing from the inside of her cloak and laid them across a litter of leaves. A pup pounced on the boy's shirt, tiny teeth digging into the fabric with a growl. Crissy backed away. Others joined the youngster, muzzles digging through the articles. Two wolves snapped at each other, tearing the nightgown.

"Stay clear of the deep woods tonight. Men will be hunting you." Nothing reacted to her words, yet she knew she'd been heard. Tonight, blood would run in the town. Tomorrow would be Sabine's turn. She returned to Luxley Hall.

Chapter 12

Men who seemed brave in the protection of the day, drooped with the setting sun. The moon had yet to rise, so only stars were present to guide their way. They brought a variety of weapons with them: pitchforks, axes with sharp blades, a pike, and some brandished swords that had been dug out from the storehouses. These were their weapons against the beasts. Did they think metal would protect them? Could they be quick enough to avoid the natural tone of swiftness and cunning imparted to the wolves? Crissy hid her grin. It mattered not. The wolves were closer than the villagers realized. Men would travel the paths among the trees in darkness, quaking in their shoes, and all the while the attack would occur on the hill. She turned to look at the house fading from sight. How soon before the pitter of paws on the steps? Across the marble floor? Silent up the back stairs. Would the children scream? The little boy and girl? What of the older ones? Would they try to throw something? Protect themselves? Or offer themselves as the intended sacrifice should? She sighed. It would have to wait till morning to know.

"Crissy, Father wants you home. This is not a night to visit with friends."

She turned to Sorsha. "The hall will be safe enough. Marlee and Idabell are here. Most everyone. We should wait for them to return. "

Sorsha looked at the main building with gas lights already lit. The sign moved in an easy breeze. Though the light illuminated much of the street where they remained, the men stalking toward the dark forest disappeared into the night.

"They shouldn't go." Sorsha moaned, rubbing her forehead. "How long can these animals last? Better to hide here and wait for winter's sting."

Crissy laid her arm across her shoulders and offered a hug. "We may hope they go unnoticed. Besides, they are greater in number."

"The Gerbach's numbered eleven. Slaughtered. How is it none escaped?"

"We are left to worry and pray. We should join the others, among friends. We will learn of their fate together."

Her mother searched her face, touched her cheek. "When did you grow, my daughter? How did age creep upon you without my notice?"

"There were other things occupying your thoughts. Come." Crissy took her mother's hand and pulled her across the room.

Eloise and her eldest daughter, Mary, stood at a long table. Crissy paused. She hadn't thought about that possibility. She would need to find a way to send them home on an errand soon.

"It's horrifying." Idabell grabbed her arm and pulled her from Sorsha. "We rode to the Vinci's and tried to convince them to join us in town. You remember Heinrich? He's asked me to stand with him during the Christmas ball. What will I do if he's murdered? The devil curse those foul beasts."

"Dear." Crissy patted her hand. "You are fraught over nothing. Attacks have been to the north. And what's this, standing up with Heinrich? Did he not dip your braids in the ink well when we sat in the schoolhouse together?"

Idabell blushed and lowered her head. "He always was attracted to my golden hair." She sighed, her eyes taking a distant glaze. "I watched him this summer, out in the field. The way his shirt stuck to his muscles…"

Crissy laughed. "Enough. You will have me needing a fan. Romance for you. A lovely thought."

"And what of you? Any members of our noble town capturing your fancy?" Idabelle glanced around. "All the men have taken to the woods, but surely someone has your attention. Or do you prefer the stranger?"

"Stranger?" Who…no. her brows furrowed. "You cannot mean the hunter? He is an old man."

"He is not old. Marlee thinks him quite handsome."

She crinkled her nose. "His hands are drenched with the innocent blood of animals. He desires valor and renown."

"He is handsome, intelligent, and determined. I thought you would admire such qualities." Idabelle shook her head. "If not, we will find another who will suit you. Perhaps you should travel to London."

"I am pleased to remain here." Crissy pointed across the room. "I see Mrs. Fairmoore. I wonder if she has news."

The two girls crossed the hall. Candles burned against the walls, on the rough-hewn wood tables, and along the bar.

Mrs. Fairmoore twisted her hands. "The moon is just now rising. How will they find their way home? They must not remain in the woods for hours. The wolves will hunt them down."

"We've enough lights here to help them find their way."

Possibly, but Crissy could think of a better place. "What about your home? Light could be seen across the valley. You should have the windows lit."

Mrs. Fairmoore nodded. "Excellent idea, young lady. We'll remove the curtains, just to be safe. Mary, let us go home. We can set out the candlesticks we use at Christmastime."

"I will help," Sorsha offered, but Crissy grabbed her arm.

"You should stay. If there are any wounded when they return, they will have need of you."

Mrs. Fairmoore grasped Sorsha's hand. "Your daughter is right." She pressed her cheek against Sorsha's in a sign of farewell. "We must hurry. I don't want them out there longer than they need to be. Oh, this night feels foul."

Crissy breathed a sigh of relief as Mrs. Fairmoore and her daughter exited the hall. She took Sorsha's hand. "You should go home and rest. If they have need of you later, you will be ready."

She agreed. The large group of women began to disperse. They walked the quiet streets like ghosts. Crissy watched as the women turned by twos and threes into alleys and cross streets. She and Sorsha followed the curve to their house.

"I will sleep on the sofa." Sorsha declared, heading for the front room.

"Your bed will be of more comfort. Remain dressed, that you can easily rise if the need occurs."

"Very well." She gave in with a tired sigh. "But fetch Henley. She must wait with me."

With Sorsha settled, Crissy slipped through the side door as she pulled her red cloak about her. The moon had risen higher, and curiosity burned. To be so close… but she would have to remain unseen. She slipped into the shadows and made her way to the bottom of the Fairmoore's hill. The line of oaks rose before her. Remaining on the side facing away from the house, she moved from the first tree to the next and the one after that. The night had gone completely still. She moved closer yet and was rewarded with the sound of a strangled cry. High pitched. Could it be Mary? Short lived. A guttural snarl whispered through the cold autumn night. Moonlight shone strong, but there was naught to see. Her heart pounded in her chest. They were there, she could feel them, but there was no sound. The wolves must have arrived before Eloise and Mary returned, for the lights in the windows had yet to be lit. Perhaps the mayor would do it, reverence to the sacrifice that had been made.

Crissy withdrew to her home, content in the workings of the night.

Chapter 13

Are you lost? No one ever comes this way." Sabine crouched beside a blackberry bush. Her fingers were stained with purple. The woman paled, and Sabine jumped to her feet. "Are you well? Should I fetch water?"

"What has happened?" The stranger looked at the house, then returned her attention to Sabine.

"Naught that I am aware. Is there ill news from town?"

The pale woman clenched her throat. "Have you been to town?"

"Me? Gracious, no. My place is here. I'll not leave her."

"Her? The old woman? Grandmother?"

Sabine frowned. How did this strange woman know grandmother?

"I don't understand how this could be." She took a step closer.

Sabine didn't like the way the strange woman's eyes flickered. "Why are you here?"

She lifted the basket. "I bring food from Mother and Father. Do you know them?"

Sabine backed away. "Why should I know your parents? We have never met."

The stranger giggled and covered her mouth with her hand. She took a deep breath. "No, we haven't. Have we?"

Sabine watched as the other girl rushed into the woods. Odd. The man had been… friendlier? No, engaging. Handsome. But he hadn't been back in days. With a sigh, she returned to the house. The sound of a wolf's howl had her twisting to face the woods. Late autumn wind brushed against her, causing her skin to tingle.

~

Crissy jerked from sleep, shaking in her bed. A dream. Only a dream. An anxious chuckle tugged at her throat.

"Daughter, awake, we must flee." Sorsha burst into the room, causing the door to slam against the wall.

Crissy screamed. Sorsha paid no notice. She held on to the doorpost, her hand pressed against her mouth and tears streamed down her cheeks.

Crissy stared at her with wide eyes. "What?" She glanced at the window. Dawn barely touched the eastern sky.

"The wolves have attacked in town. We are not safe, not in this place. We will go to my sisters, across the river closer to London."

"Leave? Attack? What attack?" She sat up, the cloud of sleep not yet lifted from her mind. Sabine, she had been talking with Sabine.

"Mayor Fairmoore's family, the help, everyone. All of his children. And Eloise… we spoke with her last night." Mother's eyes looked huge. "We sent her home with Mary. They might have been spared had we not intervened."

"You know nothing of the sort." Crissy rubbed her cheeks. "The wolves attacked them inside their house?"

"The house on the hill. If the mayor is not safe, what about us? We will all be slaughtered, eaten by the devil's creatures."

"You make yourself overwrought, calm down." She crossed the room and took hold of her hands. "It must have been the lights in the windows. They drew the animals to them. The hunters in the woods sent the pack into the village."

Sorsha shook her head. "This place is cursed, there is no hope here. We must leave."

"What does Oleg say?" There was no way she was leaving. Sabine would finally meet her fate.

"He is with the mayor. You have never seen a man more changed."

Crissy could imagine the plump friendly demeanor would melt away. "We should go to the house."

"Absolutely not. Your father forbids. The sight…" She shook her head. "It is vile. The men could not walk the hallway without emptying their stomachs. No. You are to pack. We will leave before the noon hour."

She flopped back to the bed, arms crossed. Fear drove Sorsha, there would be no argument. Better to agree and take plans into her own hands. She closed her eyes, breathed deeply, then glanced at Sorsha without raising her head. "Fine. Allow me to pack in peace. I will alert our maid when my traveling box is prepared."

Sorsha gave a worried look through the glazed window. "Keep the shutters drawn. Our doom is near."

Sorsha was terrified. Crissy could see it in the paleness of her skin, deep circles beneath her eyes. The shivers along her arms. She wanted to draw her close. Reassure her their danger was nil. The urge to confess caused her own flesh to quiver, and her stomach turned. But Sorsha walked from the room, locked in her own torment, unaware. Crissy drew a shawl around her shoulders, but her hands continued to shake. What was this? This feeling of being torn? She had come too far, much too far. Blood taken. And more blood to be spilled. Sabine. And Wolf. She closed her eyes. Their deaths would release her from this ravening madness. She could forget, return to the age where innocence played among the trees. A sob cut her throat and she wiped tears from her cheeks.

She crossed to the wardrobe. She drew out the lower drawer and pulled at the board. In the tiny space beneath lay a red bag. She tugged it loose and held it against her belly. Her sister's things. Though her body trembled, she replaced the board and the drawer. The red cape floated around her as she adjusted the hook, not bothering to change from her night clothes. She shimmied the window and crawled from her room.

She had crossed the edge of the trees into the woods before she realized her feet were bare. Didn't matter. There was no going back. Crissy ran along the path. The air hummed with energy. Storms would rage across the valley ere night fell. An autumn storm that could end in snow. She made her way to the ravine where the wolves hid. Her heart pounded as her mind warred. Too late, much too late. It echoed in her head, even as she wondered at the new-found murmur to spare her sister. She couldn't love her. Couldn't care. Sabine had spent two years locked in enchantment. With a cry of frustration, she threw the bag. Everything stilled. She had done it. There was no going back. She had given Sabine to the wolves. She turned away.

Chapter 14

Crissy followed a different path to the village. Unlike the mad rush in, she walked calmly. Her mind cleared. No emotion raged within her. She felt… nothing. Victory was at hand and yet she felt empty. Void. It mattered not. Victory would be her comfort. A slight wind moved the air once she cleared the protection of the trees. Her nose wrinkled at the bitter smell. It smelled as though wood burned. Early for a fire, but the sting of cool could make it necessary. Another waft of smoke passed her. Wood burning, she was certain, but this was not a small fire. She broke into a run.

The town had erupted with frenzy. Buildings burst with fire; flames leapt from gaping windows. She stumbled into someone.

"What has happened?" Crissy clutched the jacket of a farmer.

"The mayor went mad. He managed to set four of the buildings on fire before they brought him down."

"Brought him down?"

The man pointed to something in the road. Crissy covered her mouth. The mayor's head had been bashed and his blood oozed into the dirt.

Home. Crissy skirted the body and ran.

Flames ate at the timber and through the shingled roof. The emptiness that had marked her journey out of the woods melted in an instant. Anguish took hold. A scream gurgled in her throat. She raced toward the building, but someone grabbed her around the waist. She struggled against the strong arms holding her, and she was lifted into the air, her feet kicking at nothing.

"No one is in the house. Your family is safe." That voice. His voice. His arms around her. She felt sick.

"Crissy," Sorsha cried, and then soft, familiar arms took hold of her. Another man, Oleg, his arms held her as well. Wolf released her. The other two gushed, speaking words that could not register. The house, her house. Her things. Burning in fire. Destroyed. All her plans frayed to nothing.

She grabbed at her parents. "The chest beneath my bed. I must… Sabine mustn't…" Fire roared behind her. There would be no going inside. No walking the hallways, running her fingers along the wooden banister. The book would be destroyed. Her hold on Sabine would be destroyed. She pushed away from her parents, staring at them, at the fire, at the stranger. She opened her mouth, but words refused to be spoken. She turned and ran.

"What have you done?" Sorsha's scream didn't stop Crissy.

This time she took the path to the ancient house. Sabine must not escape. They could never know what had happened. Rocks cut into her feet, but it didn't matter. Shadows were coming. She could feel them, sense them among the trees. She raced, her lungs on fire.

The clearing was as she remembered. Her labored breath the only noise. She looked at the house. The door stood open. The windows too. Light blue curtains moved in a breeze. The old woman shuffled past the doorway. Hysteria nearly bent Crissy double.

"Grandmother," her voice sounded weak. She fell to her knees and tried again. "Grandmother?"

Her call moved across the clearing. The old woman shuffled back to the doorway. Crissy stood. They stared at each other. Crissy dragged air into her body as she continued to look at what her sister had become. Bent with age, skin that looked like melting wax. Clear brown eyes. She had no trouble seeing them. Knowing that the old woman somehow knew.

Then those familiar eyes widened, the frail body staggered back. The hair on Crissy's nape stood. She turned, slowly moving her body. A wolf stood twenty feet from her. Its lips had curled back, its ears laid flat. Something she had yet to feel coursed through her body. They were magnificent. Larger, stronger, bold. Beautiful. Deadly. She felt fear. Saw death in their eyes. The bag in the beast's mouth dropped to the ground and rolled. Crissy suddenly realized her mistake. Two years in her wardrobe. Among her things. Her room. Her scent permeated and polluted, what should have drawn them to Sabine.

"Crissy."

She dared not take her eyes from the wolves, but she recognized Wolf's voice.

"Remain still." He moved into her periphery.

He was a dead man as well. Did he not realize? Her hope was the house. With Sabine, ironically. Perhaps the spell would hold. She moved her right foot backward, toe on the ground first, and then the heel. She shifted her weight to her right foot. Animal ears perked and settled once more.

"Crissy, don't."

His warning came too late. A flash of gray, and something hit her body. Not from the front, as she had expected, but from the side. She rolled to the ground, getting tangled in her red cape. The heavy material protected her for a moment. But the teeth could not be held back. Her arms were pinned beneath her. She screamed as pain tore through her shoulder. She rolled, but heavy bodies trapped her beneath them. They were trying for her neck, tearing at her face. Ribs cracked beneath the force of their attack. The coppery smell of blood thickened around her. She screamed until a blanket of darkness tore the life out of her.

~

Wolf chased after Crissy. The red cloak flew behind her like a bloody shadow. Madness quickened her pace and he struggled to keep close enough to mark her way. Then he recognized the curve of the path. This is what he had missed. She raced for her grandmother's house? What purpose would drive her in that direction? A cold shiver alerted him to danger.

The pack tracked them. Tracked her. He slowed, pulling his crossbow from its holster. He did not follow her into the clearing. He stopped with his back against a tree, able to watch Crissy and the scene about to play out.

He pulled an arrow into place and held his finger against the trigger. He watched. The old woman came to the door. He had dreamed of her. Of a young woman as well. He searched the windows but saw no sign of the girl.

His senses alerted him to the presence of wolves. He turned his focus. Shadows played among the trees, and he couldn't count their number. Three came toward her from behind. What? Something red dropped from the mouth of one of them. The animals were impressive, large, and robust. Deadlier than he had ever encountered.

Her body tensed for flight. Don't, that would bring them on her. He stepped from his position into the open. "Crissy, remain still." He slowed his motions, not wanting to startle any of the beasts. She moved her foot. No. Then he noticed the skulking fiend on the far side of the clearing. Crissy wouldn't have seen it, and yet, with her position between him and the wolf, he couldn't get a clean shot. Life be cursed, he ran, but the animal reached her first.

Her screams filled the quiet. He pulled the trigger, and managed to wound one of them, but rather than scaring it from its prey, it maddened its attack. Crissy writhed on the ground; darker crimson soaked into the red wool. His focus shifted as a wolf circled him. There wasn't time to load the arrow, but he wasn't as helpless as Crissy had been. He struck out with his weapon, the whimper of the injured animal brought little satisfaction as he was forced to the ground. He rolled onto his back, capturing the snarling jaws in his hands before a mortal wound could be placed. Claws tore at his chest, and he cried out. The jaws clenched together, and he felt fangs digging into his fingers. Weakness pulled at him.

Thunder shattered the woods, and a burst of light flew through the air. The creature fighting him froze. Its size diminished, and with a yelp of fear, it pulled away. Patrick's arms fell to his side. Pain radiated through his body, and he tensed for another attack. Something brushed against his head, and then cool hands touched his cheeks; ran across his forehead. He blinked. Could his eyes deceive him? The young woman of whom he had dreamt knelt beside him. He tried to draw breath to speak, but his chest erupted with pain. He gasped. She moved to his side. Wolf closed his eyes. He felt her spread his shirt, and then agony as she pressed something against his chest.

He gasped for breath, and she brushed a hand across his forehead.

"I am sorry." The same voice as in his dreams. "You are badly wounded. We must stop the flow of blood."

He swallowed. It hurt, but there was no death rattle yet. He forced his eyes open and lifted his hand to brush against her face. Though he left a smear of red across her cheek, she was real. His dream had come to life.

"Who are you?" His voice sounded rough. He covered her hand on his chest, tightened his muscles, and forced himself to sit up. Black swirls washed across his vision. He closed his eyes, drew a shallow breath, and waited for the wave of pain to pass. She gasped, wrapped an arm around his shoulders, and pulled him against her. Another wave of pain radiated through him, but he remained alert.

"Who are you?" Had she answered his questions?

"Sabine. Sabine Bostich."

Her voice sounded tight, hurt. "Are you injured?" He brushed his hand along her side.

She shook her head. "I am well." A sob contradicted her words. "Is she…"

He realized her attention was on Crissy. The red cape covered the body, though obviously stained with blood. "I fear it is so."

The woman, Sabine, cried. Her head pressed against his shoulder. He felt compelled to press his lips against her hair, though movement did not come easily. "You knew her?"

He felt her nod. "She is my sister."

Thunder rumbled overhead. "We should get into the house."

"No." Sabine stiffened. "I will not return to that place."

"But your grandmother, she can help with my wounds."

"There is none but I."

"But I saw…"

She moved enough for him to see her face. Sadness caused a sheen of tears in her eyes. "You saw me. Cursed to live in the memories of an old woman."

"I dreamt," he shook his head. It wasn't possible. "What has happened to the old woman?"

"I am free of her." She covered her mouth as tears coursed down her cheeks.

"Help me stand." None of it made sense. The wolves and their odd behavior. Crissy, mysterious and dark. Sabine and the old woman were the same person?

Darkness washed over him, and his legs threatened to buckle. Sabine's arm around his waist kept him up. The girl was strong. He looked down at her. Young woman.

Lightning flared, thunder followed, and then steady rain began to fall. "Can we not take refuge during the storm?"

She shook her head. He knew better than to ask a third time.

Chapter 15

Misery, thy name is Patrick. He swayed, but Sabine helped him remain upright. How far they had traveled he knew not. It took everything to place one foot in front of the other. Agony to be held against her, and yet without her support he would fall. Cold rain soaked them both, possibly numbing the edge from his pain. They made it through the woods onto the trail leading to town.

Rain poured heavily and he could feel her shiver. "We should be close now."

The rain would help put out the fires, but the scent of burnt carried through the air.

"Ho, a hand please." Sabine yelled. Wolf staggered. And then he felt another person lift his arm. They had arrived. He gratefully welcomed the darkness.

~

Sabine stood shivering in the rain as two men carried the injured stranger away. Billows of smoke wafted in the wind. She took a step closer. Crissy. A sob tore through her, but the pelt of cold rain washed any trace of tears from her face. What had her sister done? Why? Anguish burned inside. What was Sabine to do? Where should she go?

The buildings of Dover looked the same. Familiar faces drifted around her, like shadows from a distant dream. There were voices crying out, but she couldn't understand, her ears seemed filled with the roar of the storm. Someone grabbed her. Thick hands taking hold of her arms. That face—her heart had cried to see him once more, wrapped safe in his embrace. "Father." His name tore from her parched throat. She was home, time to let darkness drag her away for a short while.

~

"We thought fever would take you." Mother gripped Sabine's hand, as Father stood over her shoulder. His face shone with joy, though sadness rimmed his eyes.

Sabine accepted a drink of water and rested her head back on the pillow with a sigh. "How long was I gone?"

"Two years." Mother kissed her hand. "Your father never gave up hope."

Memories faded like shadows dispersed by the light of day. She had the impression of trees, a bench looking out the back door into a garden, and a red cape. "I don't remember what happened. It's as if I were lost in the woods."

"They found your sister in the woods." Tears welled in Mother's eyes. "They say she was the last victim of the wolves. More than a week has passed, and the animals remain hidden."

Oleg crouched beside them, one hand holding his wife, the other holding his daughter. "Let us go to London. Start fresh. I have contacts near London Bridge that can lead to a job. Salvage what we can from the ruins of the house."

"No." Sabine squeezed his hand, her heart thudding unpleasantly. "Nothing from the house. It is what Crissy wanted all along. Let her and that place rest together."

"But there may be treasures among the ruins." Sorsha said. She didn't understand.

Neither did Sabine, but she knew with certainty, the ruins needed to remain undisturbed. "Please, I beg. A fresh start in London. Take nothing from here with us, save each other."

They sensed her agitation, smoothing her forehead with a gentle touch. "As you wish." Oleg smiled as though he could deny her nothing. They needed each other, that was all. Tiredness wound through her body, and she drifted to sleep.

~

The hollow where grandmother's house had been, was cleared. Though the outline of gardens remained, no house stood, no blood marred the earth. Sabine stood in the middle, where the trees parted and allowed sunlight to float down. She twirled.

"You are much the way I first saw you, and yet different." Wolf's voice surrounded her, and she slowed to a stop.

"You're here."

He moved closer. "Our dreams want us together."

Sabine's cheeks flamed. Why would a man want an unschooled… what was she? On the verge of eighteen yet never having lived? She changed the subject. "How do your injuries heal?"

"Sore. But I survive thanks to you. I'm in London to recover at the hospital of St. Katherine."

"Father is moving us to London. Somewhere near the bridge, I think."

He stepped close enough to touch her, and the feel of his finger on her cheek caused her heart to flare. "I will be sure to find you before returning to Ireland."

She wanted him to. Something akin to hope bubbled within. She hadn't thought to ever smile again, and yet her lips twitched with genuine pleasure. His glance at her lips started a fire. He leaned in and kissed her. It didn't matter she was young, or that the mind of an old woman had aged her beyond her years. It mattered kissing him filled her with purpose. He would find her in London. Pursue her for his future. The promise shining in his eyes was that next time, their first time beyond dreams, would be more than either of them could hope for.

The Ugly Duckling

A Princess Fairytale

The Ugly Duckling was first written by Hans Christian Anderson way back in 1844. The tale written by Anderson tells about the woes of a bird who was thought to be one thing, and horribly mistreated because of it, but turns out he was a different bird altogether. This fairytale is nothing like that, and yet, something in it brings the idea of the Ugly Duckling to mind. It is a fun story involving a princess, a curse, a dragon, and a mysterious protector.

Happy reading.

Chapter 1

Soft light passed through the drawn brocade curtains of the queen's bedchamber to fall across the infant in her arms. Queen Stephanalia felt her chest tighten as she stared at the face of her daughter. "What happened? What's wrong with the princess?" She held her hours-old daughter close as she tried to push through the haze of tiredness brought on by giving birth.

Lady Beatrice, the queen's sister, hushed her. "It is your fault. You forgot to set wards against the dark faeries."

Stephanalia shook her head. "Of course, I set them," she protested, but doubts washed over her. She'd been sick for weeks.

Lady Beatrice brushed her hand against Stephanalia's forehead before touching the baby. "You mustn't let anyone know. She would be given over to the wilds if they knew about the curses." Her eyes filled with tears. "The king could order you killed."

Stephanalia wanted to thrust her sister away from the bed, but she was too weak. She blinked moisture from her eyes as she gazed at her daughter. She'd been perfect. She'd seen her. But now, the tiny face was marred by reddish blemishes and her features look to have been stretched. The pale blue eyes that watched her knew nothing of the ugliness laid upon her. Her mother's heart cried for what had been done, but it changed nothing of how she felt about her baby.

"Let me take her. You need sleep." Lady Beatrice wrapped her hands around the little bundle.

Stephanalia tried to twist away from her. "No. I want to hold her."

Lady Beatrice took her anyway. "There is naught for you to do but sleep."

The queen felt cold fill her as the princess was taken. Her eyes grew heavy. There should have been a way to fight against the curse, but a shadow rose in her mind, and she gave in to sleep.

Chapter 2

Sixteen years later

Light tumbled across wooden shelves, revealing a wealth of ancient tomes. A breeze of musty air wafted through the library, causing candlelight to flicker. Princess Derylla hunched lower in her seat, praying the curved wood divider would keep her from sight of the others. Voices disturbed the peace of pages scrawled with gall ink.

"She can never be queen. Who wants an ugly duckling for a ruler?"

She bit her lip as the cold voice reached across the shadowy library. Snickering laughs followed the derisive insult. The princess huddled behind the heavy wood desk. She twisted her pale hair around her hand and returned her attention to the open book laid before her. But the words swam. Her heart groaned. She had no more control over the way she looked than any of them. What right did they have to belittle her for things beyond her control?

Flickering sconces caused shadows to ripple across the page. Were more students entering? Or were the girls leaving?

A startled scream from a different part of the library caused her to jump. Something crashed to the floor. A scuffle ensued. Derylla slid from her chair and crouched on the floor. A high-pitched yelp, someone else hollering, and then heavy footsteps. Derylla could see nothing. Her heart hammered more loudly as the steps drew closer. Someone halted next to her hiding place. A burly hand yanked her from beneath the desk into the open. Strong arms lifted her to her feet. Foul breath blew next to her face. She twisted away. His arm tightened around her waist and pulled her against his thick-muscled body.

"Trouble, m'lady, and you be hurt." His voice rasped.

She gasped as the arm tightened and her feet left the floor. He carried her through the room. The knotted design of floor tiles seemed to bounce, causing her stomach to roll. Fear stole her breath. Her feet kicked the door as they passed into the outer hall. The pale afternoon sun lit stained-glass windows. Someone held the door. In a moment, the princess found herself outside.

An iron carriage waited. Another student railed against a captor, her skirts flailing. Derylla felt herself tossed. Light faded as she entered the carriage. She landed among a pile of bodies. Their arms and legs kicked against her, until they all managed to scramble out of the way. Panting breath and a brief glimpse of the prisoners, and then the door slammed shut, leaving them in darkness. Horses pulled forward. Derylla felt herself roll back. She cried out as a foot landed against her side.

Their prison lurched again. Her back hit the side of the wagon. She fell over onto someone else. Arms pushed her away. "Get off me, oaf." The sharp voice laced with fear cut nearly as sharply as the fist that pounded against her arm. Derylla backed as best she could, her legs tangling in her skirts. Someone else, to her left, pushed back.

"This is your fault." The tear-laden accusation hurled through the darkness.

Derylla started. "My fault? How?"

"I have no time for this." The young girl hissed. "The Quagger ball is two days hence."

The conveyance slowed. Everyone silenced. Derylla watched the door as the latch clicked. Low light filled the space. She saw five other students. Gayla's curls bounced as she glared. Rosetta and Gertrude looked equally hateful. Derylla did not recognize the two boys.

A shadow fell across the opening. Someone stood without. "Exit the carriage. Orderly and without fuss. Try to run and you'll discover what a brick against the back of your head feels like." A large man stood near the door. Another man held a rock in his beefy hand. The prisoners began to scoot. Derylla yelped as a hard heel pressed into her hand. Gayla gave her a haughty glare edged with fear. Hand throbbing, Derylla followed. She stumbled off the end of the cart. An unfamiliar hand caught her and pulled her to her feet. She jerked away from him. The third captor was slimmer than the other two. Dark hair fell in waves to his collar and a stubbly beard covered the bottom portion of his face. His eyes gleamed. But then a harsh grip on her chin drew her attention away from him.

A different man held her firmly. His olive skin marked him as a foreigner. The glint of evil shining in his sable-colored eyes made her stomach twist. She tried to pull away, but his grip tightened. "There was only supposed to be the one. Mind explaining why you brought six?" He kept Derylla's chin in his grasp as he glared at the other captors.

The larger man shrugged. "They were all in the library."

"You best find out who they are and what we can get for them."

Derylla tried to pull away, but his fingers tightened painfully.

"Going somewhere?" His grin was not friendly. He twisted her head from side to side. "I had not taken much stock in the rumors, but I see they told truth." The accent did not mask his snarl. The husky tone of his voice made him that much fiercer.

Derylla knew what he saw. Eyes too far apart. Crooked nose. Flat lips. Skin the color of wheat and hair barely a shade lighter. She knew what she was, but why did he care?

His lip curled. "Not sure the king will pay to have this one back. We will be lucky to be rid of her."

Derylla narrowed her eyes, anger mixing with fear. "Paid or not, your necks will still crack in the hangman's noose."

"Well now, the girl's got a bit of fire in her." His fist flew toward her face, but the other man stopped him, the sound of flesh against flesh loud in the clearing.

"We'll all be better off if she is unharmed. Do not allow her quick tongue to rile you."

The leader dropped his hand, but his eyes filled with malice. Derylla swallowed as he continued to stare at her. "Get the names of the others."

Derylla glanced at the scared group of students. Attending the same college as the princess was their only crime. She breathed in courage. "If I am your prize, let them go." Her voice sounded small, but the leader seemed surprised to hear it.

"Take care, my lady. No young whelp will protect you from a lashing if my heart is set upon it."

She looked at the outlaw. "I will stay if you release them."

His laugh chilled her. He pushed her away. "Like you have a choice." He pointed at the burly captor. "Did you get names?" At his nod, the man grinned, though there was nothing friendly or comforting about it. "Find an administrator at the university. Double the amount we discussed." He pushed Derylla from him and motioned to the others. "Return them to the wagon cart." His order rang with contempt.

Burly hands gripped her once more and she felt herself shoved backwards, stumbling over her feet. Someone caught her before she fell. The younger man steadied her. His smooth hand squeezing hers as he helped her into the cart. She glimpsed the other five huddled together at the front before the door closed. Derylla set herself in the back corner, using the two walls to steady herself as the vehicle lurched into motion once more.

Chapter 3

Hunger gnawed at her as night slid through the slats of the carriage. Chilling air kept goose bumps on her flesh even as the rocking motion of wheels bounced her between the sides of the corner. They continued on. She could hear the others talking softly, huddling together for warmth.

Rumbling of the wheels grew more pronounced as they left the main road. The vehicle lurched to the left, eliciting gasps from them all. They continued for some time across the uneven path. Princess Derylla bent closer to the floor, trying to protect herself from the abuse of ramming her shoulders into the walls of the carriage.

Movement slowed until the carriage stopped completely. It rocked from side to side as men jumped from their perch. Derylla listened as their boots scuffled rocks. The door screeched, though the dark night seemed barely lighter than the inside of their prison.

"There are six of you. And six of you will enter the house. If I have to go into the dark to find ye, you'll be a sorry lot."

A hand grasped her ankle and pulled her forward, her palm scraping against the wood floor. Derylla yelped and would have tumbled to the ground if a strong set of arms hadn't caught her. His breath wasn't rancid as the others, but she shoved him away, wrapping her arms around her body to control the shaking.

"This way, princess." He placed a hand against the back of her neck and pressed her in the direction he wanted to travel. She could not shake his firm grip, and the warmth of his flesh against hers eased the shivers of fear. Ridiculous. He was as much an enemy as the others. She lifted her skirt a bit and stomped across the ground. The darker shape of the house loomed before them. A slim light flickered, then grew as someone lit a lantern. Light spilled through the openings.

Derylla looked up. More than a house. An old keep. "Why have you brought us here?"

"Questions are not for you to be asking, princess. Stay quiet, and ill will not befall you."

"Stay quiet? You expect us to meekly accept our fate?"

"Princess, I beg you, for your sake. He will not hesitate to make your stay even more unpleasant. Guard your tongue. If not for yourself, then for the others."

"I tried to free them."

"Michaels' greed is too great for that. I will protect you as I can, but you must help."

"Protect?" Her hands fisted. "Your will is to receive a share of the ransom. What do you hope to gain by friending me? A stay of execution? No such fortune will befall you." Derylla fought the urge to cry. Tears would be a weakness that cost her. The shadowy figure at her side remained silent. They entered the building.

In a moment, the other five prisoners stumbled across the threshold, along with their jailors. Four men present. The tallest man, the olive-toned foreigner, carried a cane. Cold seeped through the room as he glanced at each of them, lingering on her, his gray eyes eerie. The others felt it as well, slipping closer together. The large, burly man who had carried her from the library cracked a mug against the wood table and lifted a jug. A brown liquid spilled into the cup. He downed it with relish. He poured a second. The third man, almost as wide as he was tall, pulled a seat near the window and sat. Wood creaked but held. Derylla glanced at the fourth. He seemed softer, and yet just as determined. His hair had been tied back, revealing a lean face with high cheeks. His eyes were dark, though she could not discern their color. One of his brows rose. She felt heat flush her face. She turned away.

"Two chambers are prepared. Ladies will take the room at the top of the first flight of stairs, gents you have the room at the second flight. I was not expecting a large catch, you will share what is available."

Derylla looked at the other girls. Share? Not likely. She faced her captor. "What of light? May we have a lantern? Or a candlestick?"

He moved swiftly, inches from her in barely a second. "Light I can grant you. But any thought of escape. Any attempt to attack us, and you will feel the brunt of my anger. I would delight to tear your flesh from your bones. From their bones." He looked at the other three girls.

She swallowed, hoping he would not see her tremble. "This will be resolved soon enough. No need to incur your wrath."

"You think you know things, my lady." His eyes sparked with knowledge. He took a step back. The distance did not ease her fear.

"I will take them." The kindest of them lit another lamp and held it aloft.

With a small grin, the leader dismissed her. Derylla spun on her heel and almost raced across the room. Her skin crawled.

The room he led them to was larger than expected, with slender windows through which none of them would fit. The moment he left, Gayla, Rosetta, and Gertrude pounced on the pile of covers and set a bed near the windows. A knock sounded on the door and the kind stranger opened it. He held an armful of blankets. He offered them to her, sliding a glance at the other three.

Derylla lowered her voice. "They are frightened."

"Did they behave better among the lecture halls of University?"

No. but she couldn't admit it. Not to him. Not here.

"Try to sleep, princess. You will need your strength." The door closed with a firm click, and then something slid over and locked into place.

Derylla pushed against the door, but it held fast. They were locked in the room.

Chapter 4

Derylla gasped as something sharp connected with her arm. She rolled onto her side and squinted through the pale light in the bedchamber. Rosetta stood beside her pallet.

"Are you mad?" She rubbed her arm. It hurt.

"It is your fault we are here." Rosetta's voice wobbled with emotion.

"How can it be my fault?" Anger surged, the unfairness of it. What gave her the right to judge? "I had no knowledge of their plan. I would gladly have warned you out of the library had I known."

"It is your fault." Rosetta's curls bounced as she swung her head. "This wouldn't have happened if you were as a princess ought to be."

"Will you call me ugly to my face?" Derylla jumped to her feet, felt her eyes burning. She no longer cared. "Do you really think I chose to look this way? That I somehow placed my own eyes too far apart, my lips too wide and narrow?"

"It is not merely your looks." Rosetta's foot pounded on the floor. "You traverse campus with no thought to bodyguards. Had they been present in the library, we would not be here."

"I have no idea what you think I have to do with it. I will gladly plead your case now and again, and if our captors choose to acquiesce, I will rejoice in your freedom. Until such a time, refrain from taking your fear and frustration out on me. I am not, nor ever will be, someone's punching post."

The lock slid and the great door creaked as it pushed open. Derylla whirled. The wide fellow grinned at them.

"Lively this morning, are ya? I reckon you can take it downstairs and put that fight into a decent meal. There are a few provisions in the kitchen."

"The kitchen?" Rosetta stepped forward. "Are you daft? Do you take us for maids? Scullers?"

"I'll take you farther than you want to go if you sass and make a fuss." He stepped through the door, one side of his lip curled up in a snarl.

Derylla stepped into his path, looking at Rosetta. "I am certain with the four of us we can manage a decent meal." She lowered her voice. "Do you want the likes of him, or the others, preparing your breakfast?"

"I am not stepping into the kitchen." Rosetta hissed, but then shifted her eyes toward the large man and back to Derylla.

"We will manage." Derylla spoke firmly. She faced each of the girls. Rosetta huffed but remained silent. Gertrude chewed her bottom lip as she glanced up from her place on the floor. Gayla crossed her arms but said nothing. Derylla returned her attention to their captor. "If you will allow us access to water to refresh ourselves, we will do our best to prepare a breakfast."

"Of course, you will. Do I look like I give you a choice?" He laughed, and spun through the doorway, leaving it open.

Derylla peaked into the hallway. The others stood close behind her. With little light available, she made her way across the fading carpet until she found a set of stairs. They curled around, going up into a tower, and down to the first floor.

"What of Nigel and Osgood? Do you think they are safe?" Gayla whispered.

Derylla didn't bother to respond. She followed the steps to the ground floor and paused. Someone bumped into her from behind.

"There is a bathing house beyond the kitchen gardens."

The girls gasped and several squeaked as the fourth captor turned into the room. Derylla couldn't be sure if she'd made a noise or not, though her chest beat rapidly.

"Go now, together. I primed the pump and drew water into the trough."

"Why?" What did he want? This man with deep eyes held secrets. Derylla shook herself mentally. He was one of them. Charming and alluring in a strange way, but still one of them. Hoping to profit. She raised her chin a notch. The slight widening of his grin revealed his attention. Her nostrils flared. How dare he?

"In which direction is the kitchen?" She kept her voice cold and emotionless.

"Through here." He leaned against the doorpost where they had to pass.

Derylla led the way. Ignoring him, or so she assured herself.

~

"This water is cold," Gertrude mumbled.

Derylla felt her skin shiver as she pressed her hands beneath the surface and lifted them to her face. It felt brisk. There was no soft towel to remove the droplets before they spoiled her gown. She looked down and grimaced. Sleeping in her gown had spoiled it. How long did they intend them to wear the same clothes?

She took her turn at the loo and led them to the kitchens. A basket with eggs sat on a counter. A loaf of bread was already starting to spoil. Something that looked like meat but smelled like the barn sat beside a cold stove. Derylla pressed her upper front teeth into her lower lip. How did one warm a cold stove?

"Are you going to turn it on?" Rosetta stepped up beside her.

"Do they really think we know such things?" Gertrude joined them.

"They are not a bright bunch. What do you suppose happens to them when they are caught? I am the king's only daughter."

The youngest girl looked confused for a moment, and then her eyes widened, and her mouth spread into a large round shape. "The gallows? Are we worth that much, they risk their lives?"

"I doubt the Michaels fellow considers anyone's neck of much value." Derylla turned to study the stove once more. "We need to get this working."

"I can help."

"Of course, you can. You probably let it go cold on purpose." She'd been waiting to hear his voice, and he did not disappoint. Derylla turned to face him.

He grinned, looking amused rather than annoyed. "Since I'd rather not settle for burnt eggs or raw meat for breakfast, this is more a help to myself than ingratiating with you."

Derylla breathed in, but the other girls responded before she could cut him down.

"Please, it will be worth taking the chill from the air even before breakfast is prepared."

She tried another tactic. "Where are the others? Osgood and Nigel? What have you done with them?"

"The choice was made to allow you first in the bathing room. Your friends remain locked in their room. Now, may I?" he asked as he stepped closer.

Derylla moved out of the way, setting herself at the counter beside the eggs. She found a bowl, managing to glance toward the stove four times before slamming the stoneware against the counter. The others looked at her, but she ignored them. She picked an egg from the basket and tapped it against the hard surface. She looked, but the egg remained intact. She tapped harder and felt a satisfying crack. She shook the egg above the bowl, but nothing happened. Nothing came out. She looked again. A sliver crossed the surface. She pressed against it, but it didn't budge. She tapped the egg once more on the counter. This time, the shell split open, wet goo running across her fingers. She jerked her hand to the bowl and felt her stomach flop as a glob of yellow slid out of the jagged opening. She scrunched her nose and looked at the bowl. It held raw egg with a piece of shell floating in it. She looked at the rest of the shell in her hand. Was it supposed to go into the bowl as well?

"There is a slop pan for the waste." His voice made her jump and she glared at him. He tilted his head toward the floor. "You don't want the shells. They have nothing for flavor and their crunch is unpleasant."

"You seem to know your way around the kitchen, I should leave you to it." She spun away, but his hand against her arm kept her from moving.

"Remain. The others will not invade this space until the meal is prepared. You are safe here, at least for now."

"You make no sense." Derylla hissed, stepping closer. "Are you enemy or are you friend?" She closed her eyes a moment, foolish question to ask. "What a question. You helped bring us here."

"A path may seem evil and yet stand for a different purpose."

"Who are you? A name."

He grinned but shook his head.

She frowned. "The gallows require no name. You will swing as easily without one at the end of a rope."

"Talk of gallows is unpleasant. Let us focus our attention on eggs."

He left after watching her crack a second egg, this time without adding shell to the mixture. Gone, to stay gone, she hoped. She moved the paddle a touch too hard, and egg slopped over the side of the bowl. He was confusing her on purpose. Irritating her. Challenging her. Helping her. Why? What did he hope to gain? His freedom. He knew they could not succeed. Then why attempt this dangerous plot at so high a price? She glanced toward the empty door. He was a buffer. No, foolishness.

An acrid smell reached her nostrils, and she turned to see smoke pouring from a pan. "Stir, Gertrude." She rushed to the stove, used her skirt to pull the cast iron pan from a burner, and moved the sausage-like meat, scraping at the burnt bottom.

"How am I supposed to know what to do?"

Derylla sighed. "We are trying our best."

A male voice interrupted. "Not good enough, if that is any indication."

Derylla jumped, swirled around. Michaels stared at the pan in her hand. Her wrist ached as he stood silent.

"You are a fool if you expect otherwise. We are ladies, not kitchen help." Rosetta's voice carried across the room. Michaels' eyes darkened as he turned in her direction.

Derylla scooted forward, both hands holding the heavy iron pan as she tried to set it back on the stove and intercept Michaels at the same time.

"Allow us time to finish, sir. It won't be the most elegant meal ever prepared, but it will satisfy."

He turned back to her with an evil gleam. "Do you know what will satisfy?" He wrapped his hand around both of hers. Derylla gasped as he tightened his grip, pushing her fingers painfully into the metal handle. He forced her to the stove, the pot clanging against a burner. She felt heat radiating from the belly of the stove. With a cry, she tried to yank her hands away, but he held her firm.

"Michaels."

The kind man pulled him away, and Derylla yanked her hands from the heat, wrapping them protectively in her skirt. She backed away from the stove.

Michaels roared, grabbing the younger man by the shirt, and slamming him into a wall. "You forget your place."

"I agreed for coin. What purpose is there to harm the girl? To harm any of them?"

"You want that ugly cow reigning over you? Wait, you are foreign. You don't care who leads in the castle."

Michaels moved closer to the other man and his voice dropped. Derylla couldn't hear. A moment later, he glared at her, causing shivers to run up her spine, and then walked out of the room. The other man… his dark look didn't instill fear. She crossed her arms protectively as he stepped closer.

"Are you badly hurt?"

She twisted slightly when he reached for her. "I am unharmed."

"Hurry with breakfast, and then remove yourselves from sight. I know not why he hates you, but he will harm you if he can."

He left, and once again Derylla felt tears gather in her eyes. Who was this man? This caring mercenary?

"If it were spring, we could find valerian root and add it to the pan. That would put an ache in their bellies." Rosetta grumbled as she stepped closer to the stove.

Gertrude thumped a bowl of lumpy dough onto the counter, Gayla close at her side. "Give them a well-done meal and they will think twice before asking us to cook the next meal." Gertrude gave a limp push to the wooden spoon.

Derylla shook her head. "Best we do not draw unwanted attention.

Do what we can to appease and wait for help to arrive."

"Is that what you have been taught? Appease the enemy? Wait to be rescued?"

"Mine is not the only life at risk. Stir, for pity's sake." Derylla pushed Gertrude out of the way and carried the mixture of eggs to the stove.

"You'll need a scoop of lard before setting the eggs in the hot pan."

His voice crawled over her like a wave. She closed her eyes, part of her wanting to dump the contents of her bowl into the pan without heeding his advice. Rotten man. She opened her eyes and scowled. "Where?"

His lip twitched, as though he read her thoughts. He motioned to the crock at the back of the stove. She looked at the bowl in her arms. He reached for the spoon, but she backed away a step. Hands held up, palms toward her, he slowly moved one hand forward and took hold of the spoon. Derylla watched as he scooped lard from the crock and dropped it into the pan. The fat sizzled and hissed, sending a woosh of steam into the air. She dumped the contents of her bowl into the pan and stepped back.

"That's one way to do it." He gave her a look she did not want to interpret. Amusement and something else flickered in his eyes. Cinnamon colored eyes.

She wrapped her arms tightly around the dirty bowl. He glanced from her to the pan with its bubbling contents, then back at her. "You should move the egg in the pan to keep them from burning." He gently pulled the bowl from her grip and held the spoon toward her.

With a huff, she snatched it from his fingers. "Be gone." He must have heard her, but he remained. "Why are you doing this?"

"I cannot reveal that to you, princess. I will protect you as I can, but Michaels' hatred toward you is strong."

"Why? I have done nothing to anger him or call such animosity upon myself." She moved the wooden spoon. Blobs of egg hardened. She scraped along the bottom, thankful nothing black rolled over.

"You are the daughter of kings. Their strength is within you, where he expected only weakness."

His words stirred her heart. He thought she was strong? She fought against the pull of attraction.

"What manner of man is your father? Were you thrown to the street? Is that why you have chosen a lawless path?"

The twinkle in his eye drew her. "No such tragedy, princess. I have lived a life of privilege. I pray you do not ask further of me. I can reveal no more."

She remained focused on the cooking eggs, but felt him move away, the kitchen somehow colder as he exited.

Chapter 5

Derylla stood silent in the opening to the dining hall, watching as the mound of breakfast food dwindled to crumbs. Her own meager fare sat heavy in her stomach. She swallowed, casting her eyes to the tapestry hanging on the wall. Faded colors hid the scene, but there appeared to be trees and an animal leaping over a ditch.

A door banged nearby, causing her to jump. The four men at the table froze. Michaels slowly lowered the mug of ale in his hand as a fifth man stumbled into the room. His breath pulled heavily at his chest. Derylla covered her nose as the scent of horse and unwashed body filled the air. The man bent over Michaels, whispering in his ear. He handed him an envelope. Fear soured her stomach further, but she straightened, mentally shaking herself. Cowering would do no good.

Michaels was educated enough to read, and his cold eyes as he glanced over the parchment at her caused shivers to crawl over her skin. He crumpled the paper, his eyes never leaving hers. Hatred burned in them. But why? Why hate her?

"Lock them in their room. I have preparations to make." He stood and left the room through a different hallway.

The large man lifted a hunk of sausage and tore a bite from it. The kind man rose and walked to her side. "It would be best for all of you to remain out of sight."

"What did the letter say?"

"I did not see it."

A ruckus ensued behind them. Derylla glanced around him. The newest man had grabbed something from the table and the large man had knocked him onto the floor. A plate crashed with him.

"Come on." He pressed a gentle hand against her shoulder and propelled her through the hallway to the kitchen. The other girls turned toward them as they entered. His hand was warm, and she shouldn't be thinking or noticing. She shrugged him off.

The pile of dishes in the sink hadn't moved.

"Don't worry about those. Let's get you to your room."

Derylla followed the others up the spiral staircase to the first landing. Before long, they were locked within their room once more.

"You said there was a letter? What did it say?" Gayla settled on a pile of blankets.

Derylla shrugged. "Michaels did not share. His look was not pleased. It could not have been good news."

"Our fathers will have followed the messenger. Even now, rescue is at hand." Rosetta rushed to the window.

"There is little doubt. The question is what will they do with us before they arrive?"

Three pairs of eyes glared at Derylla. She grimaced and sat on the floor, leaning against a wall. What did it benefit, not facing potential danger? She could not do it alone, but surely the four of them… nothing remained in the room that could be wielded as a weapon. Unless one threw a blanket over the enemy. And him? Would she fight him? Weariness tugged at her. She closed her eyes, leaning her head back.

The door slammed open, and she jerked to her feet. Time had passed. Light through the room looked different. She blinked as the other girls crowded closer to her. Michaels stood in the shadowy opening of the door.

"Get them to the roof." He ordered, then moved. The large man and the wiry drunk surged into the room.

The roof? Fear tugged at her, but Derylla moved with the others. Harsh hands pushed her through the stairwell door. She tripped on the first step, pain radiating through her knee.

"Get up."

Rough hands pulled her to her feet. She began to climb. The narrow steps curved along an outer wall of the keep. The eight of them spread out, the larger man unable to climb as quickly as the others. A hand over her mouth covered her gasp as she was drawn into a dark alcove. Derylla felt herself pressed against someone as she watched the others clamber up the stairs. She didn't need to hear the sound of his voice. Fear faded. She allowed a moment's weakness to lean into him. His hand moved from her mouth and his arms encased her.

"Follow me." He whispered as he released her and then found her hand. He slipped through a thin opening into blackness. Derylla felt a door swoosh closed behind her. She heard a hiss, and then a flicker of light broke the dark. They stood in a hallway.

"A secret passage?" Cobwebs and dirt caused her to shudder, but she kept hold of his hand. He lifted a lantern with his other.

Silence surrounded them as they walked. The passage seemed to angle downward.

"Why do you separate me from the others?"

"He means to kill you. The letter directed him to do so." He stopped, and Derylla bounced into his back. He turned and steadied her. "Soldiers have come. He meant to throw you from the roof before releasing the others."

"But why? What harm have I done?"

"He's been paid to rid the world of you, princess."

"Why? I am nothing. No one."

But suddenly she felt like someone. He pulled her close and touched his lips to hers. Warmth flooded her veins. Her mind faltered as he pulled away. She could only stare. His hand caressed her cheek, and she knew she could not bear harm coming to him.

"Stay here. I will find my way to the soldiers without you."

"No matter what may come, I could never abandon you." His voice sounded husky with emotion. Derylla pushed him away.

"The consequences are too great. Soldiers will take you. You will be imprisoned, most likely hung."

He kissed her once more, eliciting a squeak of surprise. "God will protect me." He pulled her forward.

She tried to stop him, but he refused to let go, his hand firmly gripping her own. Tears wet her cheeks by the time they exited the secret passage and made their way into the courtyard.

Chapter 6

Derylla paused in her traverse across her room to stare at the touch of light against the eastern horizon. Morning. The ache of her feet meant little to the confusion in her mind. Where was he? Were they treating him fairly? Why did she care? She covered her eyes for a moment and gritted her teeth. This was why he had behaved as he did. He wanted her to be confused. She opened her eyes once more and glared at the brightening sky.

"I shan't do it. I won't interfere." The room remained silent, though a faraway screech of an owl beyond the window beckoned dawn. "He deserves his fate, as they all do." Her voice broke no argument, but her mind faltered. He'd kissed her with no sign of revulsion in his expression. Kindness? Caring?

With a groan, she resumed pacing. He meant her to intercede. Every action, every word had pulled at her. Foolish, this desire to beg mercy of her father. She stopped at the mirror. How could he look upon her and not revile her image? Her own stomach flopped, twisting as it ever did. She pressed her hands against her cheeks. Her eyes remained fixed, too far from her nose. She dropped her hands to her sides.

His had been an act. There could be no other explanation. She sighed and turned from the gilded reflection. What of it? Even if he had lied, eloquently and masterfully, he made her feel what? Her feet resumed, following the edge of the carpet from the double doors of the closet to the picture window then a slight turn to the main bedroom door. Spin on her heel and back again.

She would do it. She would request of her father a show of pity. The kind criminal had earned it.

~

Breakfast hadn't been possible. Derylla barely managed a few sips of warmed chocolate and a glass of juice. She donned her white day dress with ivory trim. The light color made her own skin seem not quite as pale. The skirt flowed about her. Her nervous fingers twittered with the folds.

She stood before the door of the king's morning room. He would be perched behind the massive dark oak desk, papers and books piled around him. A dog would lounge on the floor at his feet, its tail thumping once it saw her. She took a breath and raised her hand to knock. He would grant her request. He should. Anyway. A mumbled grunt sounded from the other side of the door, and she pushed it open.

Light from windows on two walls provided the necessary means for paperwork. The king sat, much as she had envisioned. He had yet to don his royal robes, but his silver hair, high brows, and firm features marked him as one of importance. His dark eyes focused on her. She gulped.

"You are well this morning, daughter?" His voice filled the room.

Derylla smiled. He loved her, this she knew, even if she wasn't the son he needed or the beauty he would have desired. "I have recovered nicely."

He tapped a pile of papers at his elbow. "No fear these men will beleaguer you ever again. I am signing their death warrants."

Derylla pressed her hand against her throat. "That is the reason I seek you this morning. Doubtless, the captain of the guard told you I was saved by one of the men. He brought me to them, rather than allow their leader to take me to the roof."

He lifted the page in front of him. "The younger man with tawny hair. Refused to provide his name for the death warrant. But it matters not."

"Father, no." Derylla placed her hand against his arm to stop him from signing the document. "He saved my life. He protected me from harm. Surely that should spare his life!"

"He was every bit as guilty as the others. Any kindness was done for precisely this purpose."

"You are wrong. Please, I beg you this favor." Derylla didn't stop tears from flowing down her cheeks.

"I cannot." The king moved her hand. His quill marked the document, sealing the fate of the youngest kidnapper. Five men in total, condemned to death for crimes against the crown.

~

Derylla pulled her cloak close as she slumped through the shadows in the dungeon. She found him in a corner. His chains rattled as he turned in her direction.

"You shouldn't be here, Princess."

His voice sounded weary.

She pressed a leather bag of water into his hand. "Drink."

He accepted, draining the pouch. He dropped his hand to his lap with a sigh of contentment. He tilted his head in her direction. "I still will not reveal my name, Princess."

She had to smile at his tenacity. "But your family. Will they not wonder?" She broke a piece of bread with raisins and mince from the loaf hidden beneath her cloak. She held her hand close enough for him to reach for it.

He accepted the bread, and then pulled her hand to his lips, kissing the calloused skin of her palm. "I did as I ought to have done. I believe God will change my fate." He gave her a stern look. "Without your help."

Derylla, flustered by his touch, rubbed her hand against the rough fabric of her cloak. "You are a stubborn man."

"And you are a beautiful woman. In your heart, where time will never cause it to fade away."

She swallowed, trying to ease the thickening of her throat as she pulled another piece of bread and gave it to him. "Why continue your charade? The warrant has been signed." She looked at the package in the folds of her skirt, unable to face him. "I tried. For the kindness you showed, I tried to stay the king's hand, but he has signed your death warrant. Your acting has availed you nothing." She looked up once more. "I warned you it would not."

His low laugh brought bumps to her skin. "I did as I felt led to do."

"You will die. Why not explain yourself?"

"Your father may order death, but it is God who gives and takes. The story will not end here. Go, my lady. This is not a place for you. But be cautious. Michaels destroyed the letter before anyone could find it, but someone in the castle wishes you harm. Your enemies are not all residents among the chains."

She shivered as she placed the remaining bread within his grasp. "I will bring more water later."

"No."

She offered a tiny smile. "You are not the only stubborn one, sir."

Chapter 7

The halls filled with commotion, but Derylla couldn't focus. Two days remained and the prisoners would be executed. The gallows waited, a ready price to pay for their crime. Someone bumped into her. She looked up. A thin man had collapsed on the stone floor. Others mulled about him. Her mind cleared and she rushed to his side. The smell of charred flesh assaulted her nose. Skin along the right side of his face puckered, burnt layers looking more like the melting wax of a candle.

"Call the healer," she ordered. She pushed against his shoulder so he could lay flat. "Bring a blanket." She glanced at the growing crowd. Servants ran to do her bidding, but the others stood, staring in silence. She returned her attention to the injured man, placing her hand against his good cheek. His lips moved, but no sound elicited.

"What is this?" The king's voice charged through the hall. He stood over her.

"I know not. He is gravely wounded. Burned."

A hand reached to grab her arm. The man's mouth moved. "Dragon."

Her father crouched beside her. "What did he say?"

"Dragon. Beyond the vale." His body was gripped in a convulsion, arms and legs stiffening. His hand on her sleeve pulled and she heard the fabric rip. He tried to speak more, but his mouth gaped open. His eyes widened. She gripped his hand. His eyes glazed and light faded from them.

"Remove my daughter." The king pulled her to her feet and pushed her against a servant. She stared at the body of the dead man. "Go now."

She was pulled away.

~

Queen Stephanalia shivered as a shadow crossed her heart. With her daughter safely returned home, she should feel joy. Relief. Yet, her nerves twitched and hummed with unknown causes. The door of her sitting room banged against the wall, causing her to jump from her seat with a sharp cry. Hand against her throat, she turned to the young girl standing in the opening.

Curt words died on her lips as she took in the girl's paleness and wide, fearful eyes. "What has happened?" The queen adjusted her skirts, awaiting an answer.

It took a moment for her to respond. "The king requests that you attend him."

"Is something wrong?"

"A man has died. I am not sure what led him to such a state." The girl shivered.

"Death?" Too long she had expected it, feeling it nip at her heals. What had brought it to them? What dreaded doom must they face? "Is he in the throne room?"

She shook her head. "He awaits you in the library."

Queen Stephanalia hurried from the room. The door to the library was open when she arrived a few minutes later, panting for breath. She paused in the doorway, hand against her throat, willing her heart to settle.

King William rarely looked anything but put together, yet now he removed his crown, adding it to a large box. He must have heard her, for he turned. He stretched his hand to her.

Queen Stephanalia tightened her hold on a necklace at her throat. "My dear, what has happened? The servant said someone died." She moved closer.

He nodded. "Dragon's breath. Remove any jewelry or precious metals you may have. Take our daughter and flee."

Stephanalia felt her heart thud with fear. "Where do we go?" she asked as she pulled the clasp from her necklace. Gems sparkled in a flash of sunlight before she dropped them into the box.

"Be sure Derylla takes nothing that could draw the dragon's attention."

She nodded. "I will oversee her packing myself." She pulled away, but then grasped his arm. "What will you do?"

"We must find champions to battle the beast. I will be more at ease knowing you and Derylla are safely away."

She nodded. "We can travel to Carrath. That is a few days' ride from here."

The king closed his eyes for a moment. "Be quick in your preparations. I will find you within an hour to see you off." He squeezed her hand and released her.

Queen Stephanalia would have preferred a sign of affection, but she did not deserve it. She raced towards Derylla's room.

~

"You are not yet packed?" Derylla's mother swept into the room.

Derylla choked back tears. The smell of burnt flesh remained with her.

The queen opened a trunk at the foot of the bed. "We are leaving. Within the hour, if they can settle the carriages."

Derylla stopped pacing the length of the room. "Leaving? For where?"

"We'll go south to Carrath."

"But I can't leave, not now." She had to find a way to save him. Think. What good was a brain if it lacked substance when she needed it most?

"Your father has ordered it."

"Your king orders you." A deeper voice echoed the queen.

Derylla turned her attention as her father entered the room.

"Dragons have but one purpose. Seek treasure. If it is come to our land, it will make its way to the palace and the storehouses beneath us. It will come to destroy, Derylla."

"I will not run."

"You will do as you are bid. The word of the king is final. I must send men to fight the beast." He quickened his steps to the door. "You there," he waved at a pair of guards in the hall. "Bring the prisoners to the Great Hall."

The prisoners? Why would he want them? She moved to follow him, but someone grabbed her arm. She looked up at her mother.

"You heard the king."

"Priscilla will pack. Tell her where we go, she will know better than I what to bring." She pulled away and followed her father.

He used a side door close to the dais. The prisoners would be forced to walk the length of the room. Derylla hid herself behind a palm as the doors of the Great Hall were flung open. The men were brought in. Chains around their feet clacked louder than the patter of their bare feet across the marble.

The king stepped to his throne as the prisoners were forced to kneel before him. "A plague has come upon us. A dragon from the north. If you wish to save your neck from the hangman's noose, you will find the beast and destroy it."

Michaels' cackle echoed in the huge chamber. "A noose sounds like a kinder end than a dragon's kiss."

"Here there is no hope for you. The rope awaits day after tomorrow."

"I will go."

The king faced the youngest prisoner. Derylla shook her head. What folly did he plan? The king's voice did not sound pleased. "You endear my daughter to you. And now you would find a way to have your freedom.”

"God works in mysterious ways."

She watched as a soldier pulled him to his feet.

"I will join him. We all will." Michaels stood as well. The other three hesitated before rising beside him.

The king nodded. "Very well. Defeat the dragon. Bring me proof of your success. And then you will have your freedom from the noose. Betray me and I will hunt you to the ends of the earth."

Derylla recognized the gleam in Michaels' eyes. He meant to murder. "Father, no." She stepped from her hiding place.

His mouth tightened. "You disobey me, girl." He waved to guards on the dais. "Return my daughter to her chamber. Remain at the door. She is not to leave until the carriage is prepared."

"But you must not let them go together."

"Silence, girl." The king stood. Even through his beard she could see the snarl of his lips. "Will you tell the king his business? Do as I say, or you will feel the lash of the whip against your stubborn back."

"Go. I would not have you harmed on my account." Soft words of the prisoner caressed her skin. Derylla had no desire to upset her father further, but what was she to do about the stranger? She ran from the throne room. She could hear the clink of soldiers following close behind.

Chapter 8

Who will go with you, my lady? What do I pack?" The maid wrung her hands as Derylla separated her hair into three sections and twisted them around each other.

Derylla sat on the trunk that had been prepared. "Do not fret, Priscilla. Is the queen's trunk packed as well?"

The maid nodded.

Derylla finished braiding her hair and looped it around her head. "No jewels? Nothing to snag the dragon's attention?"

Priscilla nodded again.

"Good. Prepare the queen to journey to Abernathy, in Carrath. Get her settled in the carriage." Derylla finished braiding her hair and looped it around her head. "Let them think I am in the other carriage. By the time they realize I am not, I will have caught up with the dragon hunters."

"If you are to catch them, you will need something other than a dress. The wild is no place for soft fabric."

"Had I known this would be happening, I would have had the dressmaker prepare something more appropriate."

Priscilla bit her bottom lip, then seemed to make up her mind about something. "Wait here. I will return in a moment."

The slender girl flew through the doorway. A soldier peeked into the room. Derylla pulled at her skirt. No, the fabric would not survive travel through the brush. She checked the door. Priscilla had been with her for years, but could she be trusted with such a secret? What if she let the soldiers know? What if they kept her from going after them? Drat the man for refusing to tell her his name. The others would most likely kill him once they were far enough removed from the castle.

Priscilla slunk into the room with something draped over her arm. "They belong to Robbie, my brother. He won't mind, seeing how you be the princess and all." She offered them to Derylla.

A set of explorers. Derylla donned the unusual clothes. The pants were made of heavy weave interlocked with leather. She secured them at her waist with a belt. The shirt hung to her thighs, and a leather vest held it in place. She threw on her cloak to ward off the evening chill.

Priscilla chewed on her lower lip as she watched the soldiers lingering near the door. "They're still there."

"Then we put them to use. Ask them to take the luggage to the second carriage. I will remain inside. Send them for Mother's things next and then let them think I already went to the carriage."

Derylla settled at the window seat as the soldiers came into the room. She covered her lap with a quilt to keep them from noticing her strange garb. Priscilla followed them out, leaving Derylla alone in the room. She looked out the window. Daylight was starting to fade. She waited, allowing enough time for the soldiers to pack the carriage and head to the queen's quarters.

Night had come by the time she left the palace for the stables. No one stopped her as she selected a steed and wolf hound.

She knelt beside the hound, pressing a piece of fabric to its muzzle. "Find him."

The hound rumbled deep within its chest and took off into the dark. Derylla jumped onto her horse to follow.

The prisoners had taken the road from the castle into town. Though the hound traveled around a tavern twice, it soon found another trail following the main road away from the town. The hound led her north. Would they seek out the dragon? She hadn't expected it. Night closed around her as the light from town faded. Stars shone overhead and a gibbous moon lit the path. The hound remained closer, allowing her to track easily. A few more miles, and they took a smaller, unpaved road. She slowed her horse to a walk. The hound barked. It had found something.

"No!" She dropped to her knees beside the inert form of her friend. The wolf hound sat at his head. She turned him over, and then unbuttoned his jacket. She laid her head upon his chest. She could hear the beat of his heart. She closed her eyes against the swell of emotion. Moving her hand across his chest and abdomen, she found his wound. Blood turned her white shirt red as she wiped her hand and went to the saddle bags for supplies.

~

"How?"

"Sh. Don't speak." Derylla changed the dressing on his wound.

His eyes closed. "You do have a talent. You bring life from the grave."

"You speak nonsense." She reprimanded him gently. "God is the only one who gives and takes what is meant to be given and taken."

"I didn't think you believed in God."

"Of course, I do. I just didn't see how he could save you. Dragons never entered my thoughts."

He tried to laugh, but she could see pain in him. His hand touched hers. "I warned you. It would be spectacular."

"Go home." She huffed.

"You are the one going home, Princess." He glared at her. "I am going to hunt dragon."

"You said God saved you. You require time to rest and heal."

"I feel remarkably well." He stretched to prove it.

Derylla turned her head aside. "You can't hunt in the dark. You might as well sleep." Stubborn man.

~

Mists kissed the land as dawn brightened the sky. Derylla turned on her side and stretched her back. The ground was not the thick mattress of her bedchamber. She sighed. Small price to pay for helping him. She heard movement.

"What are you doing?" Derylla asked as he stood on shaky legs.

"Preparing for the quest."

"What will you do when you reach the others? Allow them to kill you properly?"

"I gave my word, and I will not yield." He stood in front of her, hands on his hips.

"Then I go with you."

"You return to the palace."

"I will not." She stomped her foot. "I move forward. With or without you."

They stood toe to toe, seething at each other. The wolf hound flipped his head back and forth.

"You are a stubborn woman."

"And you are a wounded man. There is no shame in accepting help."

With a grunt of frustration, he doused the fire and rolled his bed. Derylla prepared to leave, a tiny grin on her face and a lightness to her step. She pulled her horse to a rock where she could mount with ease.

As they journeyed, Derylla felt the horse tense beneath her. It wanted speed. But the young man walked beside her, and she refused to leave him unaided. "Give me a name to call you, even if you will not tell me the truth."

"Nolan." He winced, hand against his side.

She narrowed her eyes. "Are you bleeding?"

"No. Your stiches hold fast."

Mayhap they did, but he hurt. Willful man. "Ride with me"

"Wouldn't be proper."

"Wolf will prevent you from anything untoward. Nolan." She tried his name. Why did it matter that she was able to call him something? "At this rate, the beast will be killed, and honor given to our enemy."

"Honor will never go to that man. He has none to begin with."

He moved closer to the horse. He probably would not accept help for his own comfort, but his desire to accomplish the goal burned in his eyes.

She held her hand to him. Nolan accepted, placed his foot in the stirrup, and climbed behind her. He settled in place. She signaled the horse to move. Wolf followed.

With his head against her shoulder, she could tell he dozed. But his arm around her waist never slacked. She laced her fingers with his and held the reins with her other hand. No human being, save her parents, had been this close to her. He felt warm and solid, causing her stomach to flutter.

Hours passed. In the distance, mountains seemed to grow from the earth. A hint of fire wafted on the breeze. Derylla nudged Nolan. She felt his arm tighten as he straightened.

"How fairs your side?"

"I am well, your kindness is healing. This land is unfamiliar, where are we?"

"Are you not of the north?" Though she could not see him, his chest rumbled against her back as he spoke.

"I have never been this way. My home lies west."

West? To which country could he refer? "These are the Majestics. Some are solid granite. Others form a series of caves."

"A lair for a dragon, perhaps, that has traveled further than it should?"

She nodded. "Do you smell that?"

"Michaels and his crew may have camped nearby."

"They'd have walked half the night to get this far."

The wolf hound growled. Derylla pulled the horse to a stop. Nolan dropped to the ground, unharmed, she was glad to see. Derylla alighted and she moved the horse to a copse of trees. A sword slipped free of its scabbard as she tugged on the handle. "There is but one sword."

"That is all I require." He reached toward her.

"You?" She pulled away with a frown. "I brought the sword. I'll be using it."

"Your father freed me to kill the dragon. What do you think he will do if his only daughter is harmed in the process?"

"Doesn't matter what he thinks since he isn't here to dictate my actions."

"We can argue the finer points of diplomacy later, your highness." He tried to grab the hilt, but she skipped out of reach. Instead, she pointed the sharp end in his direction.

"You lost your weapon when you allowed yourself to be attacked by Michaels. I will hold the course for now."

"With a tongue as sharp as yours I don't suppose I'll have need for any other weapon."

She wanted to stick her tongue out at him. Insufferable. The ground shook and the seriousness of their predicament surfaced. Her smile swept away. They moved out from the protection of the trees to study the range of mountains closest to them.

He tapped her shoulder and pointed. A man lay sprawled across the grass. The large criminal. They sprinted across the distance. Nolan knelt to turn him over while Derylla searched the shadowy entrance into the caves. He returned to her side and shook his head. Understood. They continued forward without speaking. Light flickered and she looked down. Nolan had taken the dead man's sword. She raised her own, swiping it through the air. The balance felt good.

Nolan stayed her motion with a hand to her wrist. More bodies.

He pulled her aside and stood close enough for her to feel his breath on her cheek as he spoke.

"You remain here. I will enter the caves."

She shook her head. "God brought us together. There will be need for both of us."

"He will smell you first, not only girl, but royal. It is safer for you to remain here."

She placed her hand on his cheek. "I did not travel this far to remain safe."

He pointed at the bodies. "Not safe at all."

"If I can distract him, you can set the kill."

"Your father called you a stubborn woman, did he not?"

"I am not stubborn. I aim to do what is right. We go together."

They lost track of time within the darkness of the caves. Though firelight burned in the torches, the light did not reach far. Somewhere, a deep soft voice murmured with laughter. A red hue lit the cavern well enough to see the walls, the expanse of space. Though they could not yet see the beast, Derylla felt her blood turn cold. She pushed fear aside. Instead, she tapped Nolan's shoulder and pointed at an outcropping. He pointed at her, but she shook her head. He held up two fingers and distanced them apart. Yes, let the dragon move between them and they could attack on both sides. He pressed a hard kiss to her lips. *Why did he keep doing that*? But the beast was coming, and she could not linger her thoughts in that direction.

"You are of royal blood. I smell it in you." The sound of its voice was both pleasant and terrifying. With a deep rumbling, it spoke words she could understand. How did it learn language?

She gripped the sword tighter. "I am the daughter of kings."

"Daughter?" She could feel its movement through the rock beneath her feet. "Ah, daughter. What sweet savor you offer."

A great shadow moved against the wall. She raised her sword, but it laughed. Its voice chilled the heated room.

"You come against me with iron? Will you not offer yourself to me as a willing sacrifice?"

"Nay. I am here to destroy you. Why have you come?"

"The curses, my child." It hissed, voice pulling at her. "The curses. They draw me from slumber, wake me from dreams. You are bound by a curse."

"Me?" Derylla shook the veil of mesmerism from her mind. "I am no curse."

"Can you not see?" Its breath heated the air. "No. I suppose you cannot."

A brighter glow started in the center of the room. Gleams of light shone upward, to the ceiling of the cavern.

"Will you not look? See what it is that binds you."

Derylla found herself looking into a pool of water. So smooth and clear the water, it was as though she looked into a mirror. She stepped away.

Firey anger swept through her. "It is a lie," her voice reverberated from the rock as she screamed at the vile dragon.

"It is not my nature to lie. You are as you see."

"But my face is not lovely. I look nothing like that image."

"It is the curse that has made you as you appear."

"Curse? Who would put a curse upon me? Why?"

"Who can understand the human mind and what it conceives in its frailty?"

"You care naught for humans. Is that why you have come? You seek to destroy us?"

"I have no purpose to destroy. I was summoned. With you as my prey."

"But by whom?"

"Who will be in your stead?"

"My cousin is too young."

"But his mother is not. And your own mother's sin would prevent her from protecting you."

"Mother?" Derylla dropped her sword, the sound of it striking rock echoed through the vast space.

The dragon's voice drifted closer. "A moment of weakness, she has regretted for an age. But her sister refuses to release her. As she refuses to release you."

"Don't listen to him, Princess. Pick up your weapon!" Nolan's voice reverberated through the emptiness. Derylla shook her head. Dragon's breath washed over her. She reached for the sword. A dragon's scale sliced her hand. She ignored the heat and thrashed out. She felt it slide into flesh. The beast screamed. Something hit her, sending her flying through the air until her body slammed into hardness and she sank into oblivion.

~

Torches flickered throughout the cavern. The body of the beast sprawled across the room. Derylla sat slowly. Her body ached, and the wound on her hand burned. Nolan lifted his sword high and sliced talons from the dragon. He placed them in a leather pouch at his side. She used her sword to leverage herself to her feet. The room spun, but she refused to go down again.

"I've got you." She felt Nolan's arm around her.

"I must have hit my head pretty hard."

She led them back through the maze of caves. Each step seemed like a dream. It might have been days, or mere minutes. Dragon's breath had mesmerized her. How long had they waltzed with words? Even now, the curtain it had draped over her threatened to fall once more. Daylight became apparent, and her feet moved across the rock. Nolan kept pace with her.

Walking into the open seemed oddly bleached of color as they stepped out of the mountain. Derylla looked at the wound on her hand. She felt peculiar.

"Are dragons poisonous?" She held her hand to Nolan and knew no more.

Chapter 9

She woke in a soft bed, fire blazing. Clean covers draped over her body. Her hand and lower arm were wrapped in a bandage.

"You're awake, Miss?"

Derylla turned to Priscilla. "I believe I am."

Priscilla remained a few feet away from the bed.

"What is wrong?" Derylla recognized fear in her maid. "What has happened?"

But Priscilla ran from the room without a word. Derylla tried to sit up but felt too weak to accomplish it on her own. She began to pull at the wrapping around her arm.

"Leave it be." Her mother placed a hand over her own.

She looked up to see tears on her mother's cheeks. "What is it? What has happened?"

"You are changed."

"Am I so horrible now that all are to fear me?" She could hear her own fear. "Help me rise. What has happened? How did I return to the palace? What of my companion, Nolan? Where is he?"

Her mother fumbled, but Derylla managed to swing her legs off the bed.

"Who is Nolan?" Her mother smoothed her own gown before assisting Derylla with hers.

"The man who worked with me to destroy the dragon. The one who protected me from the kidnappers."

"Him? He is imprisoned, due to die on the morrow as he should. Nearly got you killed."

"He saved my life. More than once. Father promised to forgive him." She felt her strength returning.

"There was no proof. When the two of you were found, you were all but dead."

Derylla looked at her wrapped hand. "I must go to him. Speak with him."

"I forbid it."

Derylla stared at her mother. "See to your own sins before you condemn another."

Her mother reeled back as though slapped. Derylla found herself able to stand, and she walked from her bedchamber.

~

"Seems we've been here before, Princess." He accepted her water.

"What happened with the talons. I saw you take them from the dragon."

"The apothecary needed them to counter the dragon's poison. You would have died without them."

Tears pooled in her eyes and dripped down her cheeks. She shook her head. "Where is the apothecary? Why has he not spoken for you?"

"They think tis his work that has changed you."

"What has happened? Did the dragon…" she touched her cheeks but felt nothing but her usual soft skin. Nolan took her hands.

"You are as your heart has always been. The dragon's poison broke the curse."

"The curse." She sat up. "I must speak to mother. She will stop this." She offered a bright smile, kissed his cheek, and ran from the prison.

~

"How did you know?" Mother remained in the same spot as when Derylla left.

"The dragon revealed the truth. You must tell father, get him to release Nolan."

"I cannot! What would he think of me, allowing a curse to be brought upon his own daughter?"

"Nolan will die, even though he accomplished the challenge. I forgive you, mother. Please, spare his life. For me."

Sobs shook her mother, but she nodded. Sorrow gleamed in her eyes as she stood before Derylla. Though her mouth opened, no words were said. She ran from the room. Derylla waited.

Chapter 10

Queen Stephanalia thought her heart would break into tiny bits and pieces with each step she took down the long marble-floored hallway. "How am I to tell him? How can I not?" She muttered to herself as she walked. It might not have been as hard if her thoughts weren't filled with sweet Derylla's face. Sixteen years the child had suffered because of her mother. She wiped tears from her cheeks.

"You cannot reveal anything."

A voice hissed from a shadowed alcove. Lady Beatrice moved into the light. Any sense of sisterly affection had long since given over to fear. Even now, the sight of Beatrice' cold beauty made Stephanalia's stomach twist, and her chest tighten, locking her breath in her throat.

Stephanalia stopped. "I am going to the king with the truth." Her soft voice could not hide her tremors.

"What truth?" Beatrice glided closer. "You let your daughter be cursed? Allowed her to steep in a curse for years?"

Stephanalia could not deny her hand in Derylla's fate. In the excitement of being with child, the festivities, the lavish gifts—her head had been turned. Sickness had set upon her and her need to put up wards against ill omens had fallen to the wayside. The dark faerie had left her mark on the infant. Stephanalia allowed the mask to remain, claiming the child had been born to it. She glared at her sister. "I have allowed you to turn my head too often. Living in the palace, raising your son as a prince of the land… Derylla could have been killed."

"The girl is as foolish as her mother." Beatrice waved her hand in dismissal.

"She is not." Stephanalia stood straighter. "Derylla is smart and clever. And brave. She faced a dragon." She narrowed her eyes. "How is it a fire breather of the north comes this far south?"

"The people of this country do not desire the princess to rule over them. She is called the Ugly Duckling."

"They react to a curse. When Derylla is known, she will be loved for who she is. Her looks will not matter." She paused as the truth revealed itself. "Is that why you decided to kill her?"

Beatrice' dark eyes glittered with evil. "The king should have chosen me to be his bride. I would have given him a son. I would take my place as queen and the people would fear me with adoration." She drew a slim dagger from within her coat. "Once the king has fulfilled his widower mourning, I will show him how good a queen I make."

Stephanalia gasped, but a row of soldiers turned the corner.

"Protect the queen." The king declared.

Beatrice' dagger clattered as it struck the marble. She struggled against the men holding her fast until her arms were wrenched behind her back. She cried out in a pained voice.

Stephanalia stared at the king. *How long had he been near? What had he heard?* What he might or might not know no longer mattered, she could not bear the weight. "It is my fault. I knew a curse had been put upon Derylla shortly after she lay in her bassinette. Had I been willing to admit…" Tears choked her voice.

The king moved toward her. "But Beatrice convinced you to let us think our daughter had been born that way."

"I forgot to hang the wards. I did not protect her as I should. If you knew the truth, I would never be allowed close to my daughter."

"The wards were in place."

"They couldn't be. How else could…" she looked at her sister who struggled against soldiers.

"The dark faerie was invited."

The king spoke but Stephanalia kept her attention on her sister. She shook her head. "You wouldn't do such a thing." The tears in Stephanalia's eyes couldn't hide the hatred blazing in Beatrice.

"You are nothing." Beatrice snarled. "What use do we have for a worthless queen and her ugly daughter?"

The king turned a hard stare on Beatrice. "You hired a foreigner to kidnap the princess and kill her."

Beatrice tossed her head back in an act of defiance. "What does it matter? He failed."

"The dragon? Was that of your devise as well?" The king's voice drew softer.

"Curses have their use. I knew the dragon would be drawn to her."

"Beatrice! The dragon could have laid waste to our country. How could you risk such death and destruction?"

"If the land cannot be saved from the likes of Derylla, what better use than to fuel dragon fire?"

"Lady Beatrice Hongrove, you are convicted of crimes against the crown, for attempting to murder my daughter and my wife, for attempting to wreak havoc on the innocent people of our country. Your neck will be bound in a noose, and you will hang within the hour." The king looked to the captain of the guard. "Make it so."

Beatrice's screams echoed through the hallway until they faded as the soldiers drew her from the palace. Stephanalia held her arms round herself, her body shaking with fear and cold.

"Come." The king stood beside her.

"I am as much to blame as Beatrice. I have earned the same fate."

"Your actions have never come through hate nor greed. She caught you when you were alone at your weakest, made you believe her lies."

She finally looked at him, and the compassion in his eyes made her want to cry. "How can I face Derylla?"

"Do you doubt our daughter will forgive you?" He wrapped an arm around her shoulder.

Stephanalia rested her head against the strength of his chest. "The man who fought the dragon, will you release him now?"

He nodded. "She cares for him, but such a match cannot take place."

Stephanalia agreed. Derylla would be hurt, but wounds of a broken heart could heal. She closed her eyes, shuddering at the thought of Beatrice's body swinging from the end of a rope. She had to hope the wounds of a broken heart could heal.

The king took her hand and they walked together to the throne room.

Chapter 11

Silence filled Derylla's chamber in the wake of her mother's exit. Uncertainty gnawed at her, but she sat at her dressing table. She gulped and lifted her eyes to look in the mirror. She gasped at her image. It was the same, yet it seemed as though a warped mirror had been set to right. Her skin looked creamy. Her long hair was the color of autumn leaves. Her eyes were closer to each other, her lips full. She touched her nose. How she could look the same, and yet different. Feel the same, and yet different?

The image at the lake in the dragon's lair had been true. She touched her cheek, moving her head from one side to the other. Almost, she wished her other self to return. What would the people say now? How would they treat her? Only one man made her feel as though her looks hadn't mattered. Mother hadn't returned though several hours had passed. Derylla needed to know Nolan was safe. With a final glance at herself, she pulled away from the mirror to seek out the king.

~

"What has happened? Nolan is gone." Derylla raced into the council room. The sight of her mother dressed in black staring out a window gave her pause. She looked through the glass and covered her mouth. Aunt Beatrice swung from the gallows.

"Your mother swears she knew nothing of the plan to kill you and inherit the kingdom for her son." The King put his arm around Derylla's shoulder. "Is Nolan the man from the prison?"

She nodded. He pulled her away from the gristly sight. "I released him."

"Truly, Father?" The light of joy shone through her heart as she looked up at him.

"I pardoned his sentence." The king nodded. "He was taken to the edge of the kingdom and forbidden to return."

"Taken…forbidden… but why?"

"He trifled with your safety."

"I do not want him gone."

"You think you care for him, but it matters not. I have forged a contract with a neighboring country, a marriage contract."

"A marriage contract?" She stepped back, shocked.

"It was done long ago, child."

"Who is he?"

"Prince Valanon. By all accounts he is an honorable man. He will protect you, not allow you to be poisoned by dragons or kidnapped by ruffians."

"I know nothing about him. How can I be expected to marry a stranger?"

"Have faith. Give him a chance."

Night had fallen. Derylla returned to her room. The words of her father continued to echo in her mind. "Give him a chance?" Derylla pounded her pillow, damp with tears. "How can I?" Her heart longed for another.

Chapter 12

Days cooled. Leaves plummeted to the earth, leaving skeletal branches against the crisp blue sky. Word reached the palace of a convoy eight days out. The messenger presented a tiny box.

He bowed, head to the ground with hands raised. "For her highness, the princess."

Derylla unwrapped the gift. She removed the lid and a butterfly fluttered into the air. Her heart flared to life for a moment, but then settled once more into twilight.

Three nights passed, and another gift arrived. A single pendant on a slim cord glittered on a puff of cotton. The drop was precisely the color of dragon scale. The scar on her hand throbbed and she was loath to pick it up.

The third gift arrived the morning of the expected entourage. She unrolled the tapestry across her bed. City streets lead upward to a castle with high towers. A foreign flag stood proudly on its pole. She could almost hear the bustle of crowds in the marketplace and smell the golden sunshine. An odd longing beat in her chest.

A trumpeting fanfare announced the arrival of the expected guests. Derylla froze for a moment beside her bed and then raced to the window.

Banners passed beneath the gate. Grand horses clomped in rhythm on the cobbled walkway. Then a line of carriages rumbled by. A troop of her father's soldiers broke from the end. One of the foreign riders followed them into the stable.

Someone knocking at her door turned her attention away from the visiting royalty.

"You are summoned, my lady." A servant bowed after she opened the door.

Trepidation built as she walked the familiar hallways. She arrived at the throne room much too quickly.

"I wish to speak to my betrothed alone." A single figure draped in fur coats stood before the king.

Derylla watched from the doorway of the largest room of the

palace. What would the king do with such an odd request?

"That is not the way it is done."

"Please Sire, I am weary from many days of travel. Indulge me this one thing."

Derylla was shocked to see her father wave an attendant to open a meeting room. The prince beckoned her to follow as he entered. Holding herself stiff, she obeyed. She walked to a window and threw open the drapery. Light flooded the room. She heard the click of the door closing. "You insult my family with your actions, sir."

"I did not lie when I spoke of weariness. I do not have it in me for pomp and ceremony."

Her ears perked at the sound of his muffled voice. She could hear him remove the bulk of his outer garment.

"It will not do, Princess. You will have to turn around some time."

Her heart clamored to life at the sound of his voice. She whirled around.

"Nolan." She whispered his name, barely able to believe her eyes.

"Prince Valanon." He bowed.

"But how? Why?"

He stepped closer. "When I heard I was to be married, I chose to travel here to meet you. God allowed me to learn of the plot against you. But I am known to none. My warning would not have been heeded. I joined with the men and hoped I would be able to protect you from the worst of it."

"But you were captured. Why did you not reveal your true identity?"

"What proof did I have? I carried nothing with me. There was naught to do but trust God."

"And then the dragon happened."

"It would come for your family. I cherished your friendship and knew I would have to defeat the beast. And then you were too stubborn to go home, and I had to protect you myself."

"Protect me? Seems I recall finding you near death after Michaels stabbed you."

He smiled. "You had your own near-death experience."

They stood staring at one another, deeper emotions at play beneath the surface. Nolan took a step closer. Then another and another, until he could touch her cheek. "I would have died to protect you, to keep you from harm."

She smiled; joy barely able to describe the well of emotion awakening within her. "But then you would not be able to surprise me like this."

"Derylla," he said her name as a laugh.

She tugged him closer still, allowing his mouth to claim her own. His kiss curled her toes and love burst through her heart.

They returned hand in hand to the King's room.

"I accept Prince Valanon's offer." Derylla's voice resonated through the room. She never turned her eyes from him, and his smile washed all sorrows away.

Curse of the Seven Swans

Curse of the Seven Swans is loosely based on Hans Christian Anderson's fairytale "The Wild Swans". In Anderson's story, the evil queen curses her stepsons into becoming swans. Their sister learns she can save them by knitting each of them a shirt out of thistles. While she is making the shirts, she is unable to talk. Even without speech, a prince falls in love with her. They have a baby, but the baby disappears and there is blood on the princess' lips. Her prince believes she is innocent, but when a second child disappears the same way, the princess is thrown into jail and is going to be burned at the stake. Finally, all of the shirts have been knit, except one lacks an arm. As they prepare to execute her, her brothers, in the form of swans, arrive. She tosses the shirts on each of them, and they transform into princes (though the youngest still has a swan's wing). The princess is finally able to talk to her prince and plead her innocence.

Curse of the Seven Swans contains elements of the original tale: swans, inability to speak, and special shirts. Then there is so much more, starting with seven wicked brothers and an evil queen. How can Elspeth escape the curse and save the man she's falling in love with? This story contains dark elements, and yet, as the ending portrays, love overcomes darkness.

Chapter 1

Once, long ago, lived an evil queen with seven wicked sons. On a day when the sky was blue and a sweet breeze rolled across a small village, the evil queen noticed a gurgling baby. With blonde curly hair and dazzling blue eyes, the infant grabbed attention. The queen paused as she walked along the street lined with stores. She knelt, taking hold of a tiny hand. She glanced at the mother who stood anxiously hovering above them. The queen offered a narrow smile. "A beautiful child. Have the fairies blessed her?"

The mother swallowed and then shook her head, but the queen knew she lied. The baby had a special talent. Though she did not know what it could be, something within her recognized it would be great, wonderful beyond telling. She stood with a greedy heart. The mother offered a quick curtsy before hurrying away.

Late that night, the queen sent four soldiers into the village. Without a sound, they kidnapped the little girl. Wrapped in her floral blanket, the baby slept peacefully even as the soldiers carried her through the forest and far away from home.

~

Elspeth sat in the window in the tallest tower of the castle and gazed at the field leading to the forest. Beauty shimmered upon the day and her fingers itched to capture the scene. She went to the loom. Within an hour, the colors of sky, earth, tree, and bird shone through the tapestry she'd created. After tying the edges, Elspeth folded the tapestry and skipped through the castle to the chamber where she knew the queen greeted subjects of the kingdom.

The long hallway led to a longer chamber. Pillars of pale marble held the intricately detailed roof and ceiling. High windows allowed light to fill the space, except the far dais where the queen sat on a crimson throne. Elspeth stopped skipping, straightened her skirts, and used the tiny steps she had been taught to be most becoming for a princess.

The queen… Elspeth forced herself to think mother, nodded from her elevated position. Not for the first time, Elspeth wondered at the difference between them. The queen had dark straight hair surrounding a narrow, pale cold face. Elspeth's golden curls held with a blue ribbon which matched her eyes tumbled down her back.

Others awaited the queen's attention. Elspeth turned her head when the queen's dark eyes glinted cold. The light in the room dimmed.

"Daughter."

The cold voice made Elspeth turn around. She curtsied, though she felt wobbly.

"Queen… mother," Elspeth swallowed unfamiliar fear and then held up the tapestry. "I brought you a gift."

The queen motioned for an aide to retrieve it. She had him open so she could see. Elspeth felt joy as the queen's eyes brightened.

"This is remarkable. Why, I can almost feel the breeze in the meadow." She smiled at Elspeth. "Thank you, child. Where did you find it?"

She twisted her fingers. "I made it."

"You wove the tapestry? You are barely twelve years of age. This has the skill of an aged master."

Elspeth shrugged. "I watched by the large window facing the fields with the forest beyond. The light of the morning shone golden. I have been learning to weave, and when I beheld the beauty of the day, I felt a great desire to record it in the threads."

"This is your talent, then." The queen trailed her fingers over the silky threads. "I knew something great would come. Anything you desire to weave, we will provide the means."

"Thank you, mother." Warmth filled Elspeth. For the first time, the queen seemed genuinely interested in her.

Chapter 2

Ah, there you are, little flower."

Elspeth stood at her brother Raeborn's greeting. The twins, Breck and Neville, followed him. Crossing the room, the pair slumped in chairs. Elspeth folded her hands together and frowned at their weariness. "Are you not well?"

"I fear they are tired. It comes with age."

Elspeth tilted her head. "None of you are very old."

Raeborn sighed. "Tis true. I have surrendered my assignment to the warden. I am no longer able to serve as a soldier."

The queen flowed into the reception room followed by her other four sons. "Do not speak of these things. My heart breaks that you all must age and wear the brunt of life's ills."

Elspeth ran to Kingsley. "You are not ill, are you?"

His smile brightened his face. He removed a flower pinned to his royal blue vest and tucked it into Elspeth's hair. "I have been down with a fever, but I am better now."

A vision of a field of flowers came to Elspeth. White flowers covered in creamy threads that danced in the wind filled her sight.

The queen stepped beside her. "Has something come to you, daughter?"

"There are flowers that make threads. I could weave them into a fine fabric, so fine a wearer wouldn't see or feel it once they put it on." Elspeth grasped the queen's hand. "The threads will keep them from aging." She chewed on her fingernail. "I cannot tell where the field of flowers is to be found."

The queen quieted a moment and then clapped her hands. "We will borrow a spell. A small spell, mind you." She grinned at her sons. "You will become swans, beautiful, strong swans. You will be able to cross lands and oceans and scale peaks. With the sharpness of your eyes, you will notice the smallest detail, be it a mouse running to its burrow or strange flowers in a meadow. Find the field and bring the silken flowers to your sister."

All seven brothers eagerly took to the sky. Within a month, they had brought a bouquet of flowers. Their white feathers gleamed, and their long, graceful necks bobbed. As they delivered a flower to Elspeth, they assumed their normal bodies. But time and again, it wasn't the flower of her vision. She despaired if they would ever find it.

More than a year after the search had begun, Gavin, the youngest, presented her with the correct specimen. The bloom as large as her hand had long tendrils of thread-like substances. She touched a leaf. Threads covered it too. Elspeth's heart bubbled with excitement. "This is it."

Though Gavin was the slenderest of the brothers, they all slapped his shoulders and pushed him about. Laughter filled the room.

Chapter 3

Mounds of flowers in a dozen baskets rested in the room where Elspeth's loom waited. Once they realized the threads would be ruined if the flowers died before they had been removed, a company of servants worked for her. A lovely, sweet scent filled the room as she prepared the threads for spinning and then the loom. What came of it was a fabric, soft as air, strong as scales, and pale as the last light of sunset. Within two months, she sewed seven shirts from the fabric. She planned to fit each of her brothers once the basic shirts were prepared. Raeborn was much wider through the shoulders and chest than Gavin. But then, the magic of the flower worked on the shirts. When each of them put on a shirt, it fit into his shape and disappeared.

Raeborn twisted. "I know I put it on, but I can neither see nor feel it." He tugged at his side, and there it was. "Remarkable."

The others were astonished as well. Jarvis, Brennan, Kinglsey, Breck, Neville, and Gavin admired themselves and each other. "I feel stronger," Kingsley declared as he pulled on a cambric shirt covered in flowers.

"Can we still travel as swans?" Neville asked.

"Why would you want to? We won't need any more threads." Elspeth wondered. They ignored her.

"Think of the places we can go. Great riches we can find." Neville said as he rubbed his hands together. "I feel strength gathering." He looked at his brothers. "How can we make it even greater?"

Elspeth stared at them. "We are already wealthy, what need is there for more?"

Raeborn pointed at her. "You will be silent."

With that command, and to her horror, they discovered another element of the magical fabric she'd woven. She was unable to speak. She wanted to, and yet, she could not. Tears dripped down her face, but they didn't care. Kingsley finally grasped her across the shoulders and peered at the others. "Our sister has done a mighty deed for us. Let us not torment her in this way. It might be useful in some situations, but not here, not when it is only us. Release her tongue."

With a nod of agreement from Raeborn, Elspeth felt her throat open. She raced from the room. But with the making of the shirts and giving them to her brothers, she had given them power as well. Horrible power.

Chapter 4

"Why am I not allowed to speak?" Elspeth asked, tears dripping on her cheeks.

Jarvis shook his head. "Beauty and charm are all you require. They will find you... enchanting."

"Endearing," Neville agreed.

"Just a bit of fun," his twin, Breck teased.

Elspeth sulked. "Fun for whom? Not for me."

The queen tapped her hands with a fan. "Enough of that. Your brothers have your best interest at heart. Trust them."

She didn't, but there was naught she could do.

~

They arrived at a townhouse across from a walled garden. She paused on the steps of the carriage, drawn to the honey-colored lights and blue flames burning on candlesticks nearly as tall as herself.

"Come, little bird," Raeborn took her hand and led her to the ground before assisting the queen, Lady Gray, as she desired to be called outside her own kingdom.

They joined others meandering through the wide front door. Fashionable ladies wore gowns glittering with gems and shining threads. The younger swept through in pale shades of yellows, green, peach, and pink. Older patrons darkened the colors to rich burgundy and royal blues. Paintings of dogs on hunts and geese flying above the river graced the long hallway leading to a grand ballroom.

"Lord Gray," a large man boomed a greeting as they passed through the doorway.

Elspeth jumped, but Raeborn held her arm fast. "Sir Ellingworth," he replied, bowing. "A pleasure to see you once more. May I introduce my mother, the dowager Lady Gray."

Sir Ellingworth took her proffered hand and kissed her knuckles. "You look far too young to be a dowager." He turned slightly. "Who is this lovely lady?"

"Our sister," Raeborn introduced her. "I'm afraid she carries a malady from her youth. These fourteen years, she's been unable to speak."

"She is perfectly healthy in mind and body," Lady Gray assured him. "But a kind, gentle friend is what she needs. Can you think of such a darling to befriend out little bird?" Lady Gray gazed across the increasing gathering.

Sir Ellingsworth thought a moment, and then a wide grin brightened his face. "Indeed, a fine lady who will make an exquisite friend. Miss Haversham. Come, allow me to introduce you."

Raeborn took her arm, and they followed Sir Ellingsworth through a crowd. He then waved and nodded at a small group standing near one of the palm displays scattered across the room. Elspeth traced the long lines of a frond with her eyes until Raeborn jabbed her side. "Pay attention," he hissed.

Her focus shifted, even though she didn't want it to. Inside, she frowned, but her face showed all the proper details expected by her brother.

"We have a special case with us tonight, Miss Haversham," Mr. Ellingsworth motioned for the young lady to join their small group. "My friends have newly arrived from the continent. This is their dear sister, Miss Elspeth Gray. She is unable to utter a word, but in all other ways she is capable of interacting with us. Dancing, even?" he asked as he gazed at her brother.

Raeborn nodded and Ellingsworth's smile brightened even more. He returned his attention to Miss Haversham. "You were the first I considered. Kindness is part of your very nature. If anyone could successfully guide Miss Gray through this crowd, it would be you."

Miss Haversham laughed and took hold of Elspeth's hand. "I talk enough for the two of us. Do you know the dances? I can think of several young men who would prefer quiet as they dance. I think they try to remember the steps." She chuckled. "They need all the help they can get."

Miss Haversham tucked her arm around Elspeth, and they turned to her brother. "Shall I take her for a bit? Give you an opportunity to find partners for dancing?"

He nodded. "Only if you will save a dance for me, I insist."

She handed her card to Raeborn. Once he marked her card, the two girls wandered away.

~

The evening passed in a swirl of color and light. Drinks appeared when Elspeth felt parched. There was no lack of opportunities to dance. Not a word passed her lips and absolutely no one could feel the dread that filled her. Tired as she was, once they returned home, she went to her loom.

~

The next morning, Elspeth laid a fresh tapestry across the breakfast table.

"What is that?" Neville asked as he picked up one corner of it.

"Impressions from last night," Elspeth explained. Seven swans flew along the edge of the tapestry. She'd perfectly captured the grandness of the townhouse. Standing in front were three figures: Miss Haversham, her brother Nigel, and another gentleman, Mr. Scotts.

Neville tilted his head. "Why these three?"

Elspeth shrugged. "It is what came as I worked."

He tapped his chin and then waved for Raeborn to join them. "What do you think?"

Raeborn's eyes lit. "These are the ones we need to focus on. You have done well, little bird."

Concern swirled through her. "Focus on for what?" But none of her brothers deigned to answer.

Chapter 5

So it was, as the high season of town dwindled, the brothers and Elspeth traveled to Haversham House for a party. Miss Haversham greeted her warmly. "I am so glad you have come. Your brothers claim you've never attended a house party. I have determined to see you admired at every turn. I put deep thought into games and activities we can play." Miss Haversham drew Elspeth with her into the garden as she expounded on the delights they would encounter.

Nigel, Miss Haversham's brother, turned onto the path and bumped into them with a laugh. "Very deep thoughts, ladies." He took Elspeth's hand and pressed a kiss against her knuckles. "I look forward to knowing you better this senight." The warmth of his gaze and press of his hand brought a flush to Elspeth's cheeks. Elspeth frowned within herself, wanting to warn her friends against her brothers, but she couldn't do anything but stand with a silly smile on her face, appearing as eager as any other girl to be where she was, doing what she was doing. They both watched Nigel saunter to the end of the path and turn, taking him from sight.

Miss Haversham hugged Elspeth. "Nigel is the best man any lady could hope for. I would love to have you as a sister."

~

Though the week passed quickly, Elspeth found herself torn. Concern for her brothers and their plan had her insides twisting with fear and unease. Yet, she enjoyed her time among new friends. Enjoyed the warm glances from Nigel. But on their final day, everything darkened.

Elspeth flounced down the stairs holding her skirts to keep from tripping in her worn shoes. She blew hair from her face. Where was everyone? No maid attended to her after ringing the bell. She glanced into the breakfast room, but it was empty. No food at the buffets.

Her heart thudded in her chest as low humming drifted down the hallway along with a scent that caused chills to slither down her back. Humming grew louder as she stepped closer to the floral drawing room. It took a moment for her to realize what she saw as she stood in the doorway of the room.

Her brothers were the ones humming, tossing a wet towel smeared with red. How could their sizes have increased in one day? But then, the carnage littering the room caught her attention. Death. All were dead. Miss Haversham lay on the couch, blank eyes staring at the coffered ceiling. Blood soaked the bodice of her gown. Her brother lay beside her. Other guests of the house party sprawled throughout the room. Servants were there as well.

A scream passed her silence, and once it started, she couldn't stop, until Raeborn slammed his fist against her head and her mind fell blessedly into darkness.

Chapter 6

Elspeth stood in a tower staring across the beach. A wedge of swans swept by the window and disappeared behind rocks. Her heart thudded. Hunger gnawed inside her. They returned. Which meant she would soon be brought to a city. She closed her eyes but couldn't keep memories of bloody bodies strewn through parlors and morning rooms and ballrooms and bedrooms. The queen returned to her cold palace in the north but refused to allow Elspeth to go with her. Elspeth scowled as the brothers walked around a bend, pushing and shoving each other into the surf as they approached her prison. She flopped to the cold stone floor and waited. Though hunger and thirst gnawed at her due to their neglect since their last feasting, salty tears managed to burn tracks down her cheeks.

The brothers were thin, like reeds. Kingsley dropped beside her. Raeborn shook his head. "You look as narrow and needy as the rest of us. Have you no thought to take care of yourself, little bird?"

Elspeth glared. "The pantries are empty, the fires in the kitchen have gone cold. I have no means to leave this place since you locked me within."

Raeborn crouched in front of her. "I am sorry, pet. You ran, and we wasted time searching for you."

Kingsley laid his head in her lap. "We should not have left you for so long. Yet, here are you, safe and sound." He glanced at her face. "Did you make yourself a cloak? Is that why you live as we live?"

Raeborn laughed. "She lives because we have need of her. There is naught else that keeps her in this realm."

The twins moved to stand beside Raeborn. "Since we all hunger, allow us to prepare our next venture," Breck said as he tossed a bag of food to Elspeth.

Raeborn grinned. "Let us do what we need and be gone. Kingsley, send our little bird to her chamber to wash and change once she has eaten."

Kingsley pushed up and bowed. "As you wish."

Once the others had gone, Elspeth turned to Kingsley. "We don't have to do this."

Kinglsey touched her cheek. "Ah, little bird. Living is fun. Your talent has brought us long life and joy. Would you rob us?"

Elspeth ate, because the command from Raeborn forced her to.

~

Music swelled across the ballroom as Elspeth trudged the outer wall, trying to keep to the shadows where her brothers might not find her to force a dance on an unsuspecting eligible gentleman. Something caught her attention. Many people moved their hands as they spoke, but this looked different. The man didn't speak and yet his hands moved. The woman he stood with responded. Or she seemed to respond.

Elspeth backed up. Raeborn moved in her direction. She did not wish to go with him. She wanted to observe this strange phenomenon. Though she didn't understand why, she sensed great significance.

The couple moved further, and Elspeth kept pace with them from her shadowed trail. His hands moved as though they knew how to speak. Suddenly, Raeborn stood beside her, gripping her arm. If she'd been capable of speech, she would have cried out. He smiled pleasantly at her. "There you are little bird." He tucked her hand in his elbow. "Come. I have someone I want you to meet." He pulled her with him.

He brought her to a young man wearing a crimson waistcoat and striped cravat. "Ah, Lord Bendricht. May I present my sister, Miss Elspeth. She is a sweet girl, even if she is unable to speak."

Elspeth executed a perfect curtsy and allowed the young stranger to guide her toward the other dancers. A smile graced her lips even though she wanted to scream at him, making him run from her. Make them all run from her. But such was the nature of the curse, her countenance remained all that was pleasant. Tears that fed her breaking heart would never show through.

She enjoyed the dance instead. Thankfully, Raeborn or her other brothers were nowhere to be seen. She smiled politely then disappeared into the crowded ballroom. Her eyes sought the man using his hands to speak. Excitement made her giddy as she spied him across the way, close to a table with drinks and food.

Without her brothers nearby to stop her, she stepped close enough to be noticed. The couple glanced at her. With similar features and coloring, they had to be siblings. His hands were in front of him, and Elspeth grabbed hold of them.

"What are you doing?" The woman pulled against Elspeth.

Elspeth begged with her eyes as best she could, shaking her head while keeping hold of the young man's hands.

He lowered his arms, frowning at Elspeth. She lost her grip but then grabbed one of his hands again with both of hers. She peered from the man to the woman and then raised his hand and tapped it.

The woman rolled her eyes. "You expect us to believe you are deaf?" she jeered.

Elspeth blinked and shook her head. She then pointed at her mouth.

He pulled his hands free and waved them at the other woman.

She made a face. "You can't speak?"

Elspeth nodded, then pointed at the hands.

"What? Are you wondering what he's doing?" The woman asked. Elspeth nodded again, pointing at his hands and then touching her mouth.

He tapped her shoulder, held his hands in front of her, and then put fingers to his lips and drew them away. "Speech," he said, his voice odd, as though sounds weren't familiar to him.

Elspeth frowned. What did it mean? He repeated the motion with his hands, touching his lips and moving his hand down.

She blinked. Was he talking with his hands? She copied the movement he'd made, touching her lips and motioning with her hand. He beamed and Elspeth nearly forgot she needed to breathe.

The woman tapped her shoulder. "He uses sign language to speak. He's deaf. Even though he can say some things, a venue like this isn't conducive." She curled her lips. "Our peers don't like to be reminded of imperfections, although not one of them are perfect."

Elspeth tapped her chest and his hands until he grabbed hold with a chuckle. "Would you like to learn?" he asked in his strange voice.

Elspeth blinked. Could she? She nodded vigorously.

"I am Horatio, second son of the Earl of Gracen. This is my sister, Angel."

Elspeth absorbed what she could as they stood on the far side of a potted fern. Neville found her. "Here you are, little bird."

She jumped. If Neville knew what the siblings taught… she glanced at Horatio with wide eyes as she bit her lip before turning to smile at her brother.

Horatio placed a hand on Angel's arm.

Neville grinned. "I don't believe we've met."

Angel smiled. "Our pardon, sir. This young lady came to my aid after a most horrid dance partner. I have enquired for her name, but she has yet to respond."

"Relief," Raeborn exclaimed, pressing his hand to his chest. "I feared we had lost you in the press this evening."

Neville chuckled. "She has been assisting others, of course. They desire her name."

Raeborn's features eased into a pleasant smile. "I fear our sister is unable to speak. It has been so since she was a young child suffering from scarlet fever. I am Lord Gray." He bowed. "My sister is Miss Elspeth." He pulled her closer by tucking her arm into his.

"Horatio, second son of the Earl of Gracen," he introduced himself with a bow.

Angel grinned. "I am his sister, Angel. My brother is deaf, so it seems we have common ground." She curtsied.

Raeborn held her hand and kissed the air above her knuckles. "May I have your next dance?" He glanced at Horatio. "Perhaps you would like to dance with Elspeth? She has no promise for the next set."

Angel stepped closer. "Horatio is unable to dance, Lord Gray. I would be delighted to join you while they walk around the ballroom?"

Though he raised a brow, he nodded, releasing Elspeth. Horatio bowed again. "Thank you, Lord Hammond. I will keep you in sight."

Raeborn chuckled. "I have six brothers. We will be watching you." He turned to Elspeth. "Enjoy your walk, little bird."

~

Horatio noticed slight changes to Elspeth. Her eyes, eagerly attentive as they worked through an alphabet of sign language were now drawn blank and the serene smile on her face never wavered. The silence of the room meant nothing to him. He felt vibrations through the floor. Music and people moving could be felt.

There were brothers. He noticed them watching. Similar heights and similar coloring. They danced and enjoyed the entertainment of the evening, but kept note of Elspeth and his progress through the room. It was disconcerting in its oddness. Angel and Lord Gray found them as they completed a second turn.

Angel moved closer to them. "I have plans to visit shops in town tomorrow afternoon." She glanced at Elspeth. "Would you like to join me? A companion is greatly admired."

Lord Gray tilted his head. "She can offer no opinion or direction as you shop."

Angel smiled prettily. "In words, no. But companionship does not always require them. I would enjoy her company regardless."

Horatio noticed Elspeth watch Lord Gray to await his permission. Oddly, the girl was not able to form friendships on her own.

He gave a faint nod and Elspeth's smile warmed. Angel grasped her hand. "Splendid. I shall call at one. Will that suffice?"

Again, Elspeth sought permission before agreeing.

"Very good," Horatio said and then followed his sister. He could go with them in the carriage and teach Miss Elspeth more sign language.

Chapter 7

Weeks into the season, Elspeth learned the language of hands. Raeborn's command kept her voice silent, but didn't prevent her from speaking with her hands. After a particularly enjoyable evening, the desire to weave kept her awake through the night. Part of her dreaded the emergence of Lord Grace's image. The glow of his eyes warmed her. Angel's friendship gave her courage. The gift given by these new friends could save them.

Raeborn grinned as he held the tapestry in the light of a long window. "I knew."

Elspeth breathed. "Let them go. Darkness lurks behind the swans. Can you not see it?"

"Little bird," Raeborn said as he hugged her. "It is a greater thing we have here. That is not danger, but strength."

"Please," Elspeth whimpered as tears wet her eyes.

Raeborn kept hold of the tapestry. "You have marked our next party. It is their destiny, as it is ours. No more quarreling."

He left her standing in the morning room of their rented townhouse. Elspeth closed her eyes and sent a prayer, though she doubted the Almighty would respond favorably to one such as herself. And yet, perhaps the enemy of my enemy...

That evening, as music surrounded them, Elspeth stood with Horatio and Angel. Elspeth tugged on Angel's sleeve, checked that none of her brothers could see her, then started the conversation she'd never been able to have. Though her face remained serene with a gentle smile, her hands moved swiftly. "Raeborn and Kinglsey will invite you to a house party. Or convince you to hold one in their honor."

Horatio shrugged, then signed, "We have hosted many parties. It is not a hardship."

"Theirs is a gathering you want nothing to do with. They bring death."

Angel shook her head. "I hold doubts about your brothers, but if they were as bad as that—stories would surround them. You know how society desires rumors and gossip.”

“I have seen their carnage. More than I can bear, but I have no control over what they do, nor my role in their schemes.”

Horatio’s eyes darkened and he tapped Angel’s arm. “The fires. Paris, Budapest, Frankfurt, possibly even Edinburgh.”

Elspeth paled. “I know nothing of fires, but those cities are familiar.”

He stepped back. “What are you?”

Though her face revealed the pleasant smile and shining eyes of one enjoying the evening entertainment, her hands shook as she spelled a word she did not know. “Cursed.”

“We should go,” Horatio said to Angel, grabbing her arm.

Angel prevented him. “Wait. If not us, will they find another target?” She asked Elspeth.

“Yes.”

Angel frowned. “Is there naught we can do to stop them?”

“I am under their power. This language of hands is the first I've been able to step away from their expectations. If they should learn of it...”

Horatio grabbed hold of her hands a moment before Elspeth felt Raeborn behind her.

“The twins are besotted with another pair of twins,” he chuckled at the brothers walking with a pair of younger ladies.

“I understand their ardor,” Horatio said in his stilted voice.

Angel smiled at Raeborn. “Those would be the Gaylor girls. They are prized guests at our annual house party.”

“Did you say house party?” Kinglsey appeared beside them.

Horatio nodded. “At the end of the season, for a fortnight.”

Angel nodded. “We had nearly forty guests last year. A full house, but such a delight.”

“I’m sure Elspeth would adore attending a house party, but with seven brothers...” Raeborn shrugged with a grin. “It is not likely.”

Horatio signed something and Angel clapped. “You should all come. I will have details sent to your townhouse. He also asks if Miss Elspeth may join him, us, for a walk through the rose garden.”

At Raeborn’s nod, Horatio tucked Elspeth’s hand in the crook of his elbow. She didn’t dare try to communicate while she felt the attention of her brothers like weights pressing upon her shoulders.

Chapter 8

W hat can we do?" Angel asked softly after placing an order for ice treats. She and Elspeth sat on a bench beneath the shade of a willow as they watched carriages driven by dapper horsemen trudge the avenue. The gurgle of the river wandered behind them, and Elspeth took a moment to close her eyes and breathe. Then she suddenly knew.

"They each wear a shirt made from fair flowers in the northern mountains."

Angel frowned. "How did you manage to find flowers in the mountains?"

Elspeth swallowed and slowly moved her hands. "Our mother is an evil queen, and she turned them into swans. As birds, they have strength to travel whatever distance they require."

"Are they still able to take their bird shapes?"

"Yes," she signed. "But that is not what afforded them long lives."

Their waiter had no notion of the seriousness of their conversation. The two of them smiled warmly as he placed a lemon tree shaped ice before Elspeth and a green pear with a frozen mint leaf before Angel. Elspeth continued once he was gone. "The shirts cannot be seen once they have been put on. We must remove them."

Angel sighed, then pointed at the ices. "Let us enjoy our treat before they melt. Meanwhile, I shall ponder what we may do."

Their afternoon outing passed, and Angel returned Elspeth to the townhouse. Raeborn opened the door to the carriage before a servant stepped down. "Ladies," he greeted as he bowed. "Did you enjoy your afternoon?"

Elspeth smiled, accepting his assistance from the carriage.

Angel scooted closer. "Delightful. Will you attend the Bollingworth's ball this evening?"

Raeborn took Angel's hand and kissed it. "Indeed, that is our intent. Save me a dance?" He paused, then continued, "or dare I request two?"

Angel blushed and lowered her eyes, but her smile denoted pleasure. "I would not be adverse."

Elspeth clutched her hands tightly as she watched the exchange. Angel seemed genuinely pleased by Raeborn's attention. Did she doubt Elspeth's warning?

Raeborn turned as the carriage left. "Absolutely enchanting young lady."

Elspeth felt the tightness in her throat release. "She does not deserve what you intend."

Raeborn tucked Elspeth to his side. "I know this is difficult for you, but their sacrifice provides us with long life."

"Why can you not live one life, find love and have families. Grow old? You could end your days in peace and contentment."

He smirked. "That is not our destiny. Your skill and talent have given us more than a simple life." They entered the townhouse. "Now, no more of these silly questions. Your latest tapestry has shown us Lord Horatio and his sister are intended for us. We are their destiny."

~

The Bollingworth's Ball graced the evening outside town. The manor house glowed, along with gardens made of green hedges and flower borders. Elspeth rubbed her hands on the gossamer fabric of her gown as she searched for a dark corner after her brothers were occupied. Once settled, she peered through leaves of a plant at her brothers. Shimmers of gray in their hair. Faint sagging beneath their eyes which weren't quite as bright as they had been. Were they aging faster than usual?

"Do you see your brothers?" Horatio asked.

Elspeth jumped, then turned to him. The same silly grin on her face, but her hands moved. "They are dancing."

Horatio bent over her hand. "A lovely garden awaits in the moonlight." He guided her through an open set of French doors. They walked across a patio and then downstairs to reach the main path of the garden. A few couples skirted around them, then they were on their own, though muffled voices proved others weren't far. He found an alcove where they could see their hands well enough for a conversation. Elspeth sat on one end of a bench. Horatio joined her, leaving space for decorum. "Angel told me about the shirts your brothers wear. What if we remove them while they sleep?"

"They would wake before it could be done. One would easily alert the others." Her hands shook, grabbed hold of him. She tried to press through the curse, but tears would not show, nor words pass her lips. She returned to using her hands. "You must take your sister with you and go far away. Forget about us."

Horatio stopped her words. "There is no running from this." His strange voice still sounded beautiful to her. He touched her cheek. "I have a powder that can make them sleep without waking."

Her smile widened. "Long enough to rid them all their shirts? I can bring scissors to cut them open."

Horatio nodded. "There will be enough of us to remove them. Can they be burned in a fire?"

"Yes," she motioned, though the thought of what she had woven being destroyed knotted her stomach.

Horatio smiled. "We have a plan. But what happens once the shirts are gone?"

"I don't know. You may yet have to fight for your lives."

He straightened his shoulders. "A battle worth fighting if your freedom is won." He kissed her.

Elspeth closed her eyes at the unexpected contact. Sweet warmth flooded her insides. Though the kiss was brief, its memory lingered long after the night ended.

Chapter 9

When the carriage stopped at the end of a cobbled avenue, Elspeth starred at the front façade of a great country house. A central tower rose above the grand doorway boasting a portcullis. Towers on both the east and west sides of the house gave it elegant symmetry. Perhaps they hadn't exaggerated having more than forty guests for a party.

The door of the carriage opened as she gaped, but then her attention turned to Horatio. His smile and the warm glow of his eyes caused her stomach to flutter. He assisted her to the front garden, then bowed. "Welcome to Blickling House." His strange voice washed through her with pleasure, though she could only smile amiably and nod.

Raeborn jumped to the ground beside her. He clasped Horatio's shoulder. "This is a fine home you have invited us to. We are honored."

Angel joined them, wrapping her arm through Horatio's. "We are honored you've come. Did you have a pleasant journey?"

He grinned. "We barely noticed the hours, with such fine views and your enchanting valley."

Angel's cheeks colored. "I enjoy London, do not misunderstand, but my heart thrills to be home once more." She moved to Elspeth. "How about I show Elspeth to her room while my brother guides the rest of you to your guest suites?"

Raeborn paused but then shrugged his shoulders. "As you wish."

Another young man joined them. Angel introduced him. "This is our cousin, Ventnor. He and his friends have come down from university."

"We desired a country break before studies resume." He threw his arm across Horatio's shoulder. "I'm sure you are tired and hungry, having traveled so far. Let us help you get settled. Would you prefer a tray in your rooms or to join us in the dining hall?"

"I'm sure Elspeth should rest. It has been a long, tiring journey. The rest of us will join you." He turned to Elspeth. "You don't mind, do you little bird?"

Though a gentle smile appeared to agree with her brother, inside,

Elspeth trembled. It was their first night. The brothers couldn't mean to kill them so soon.

Angel wrapped her arm around Elspeth. "Come, we have left you standing here too long." Angel nodded at the gathering group. "I shall retire as well. We will see you in the morning."

Elspeth's angst eased as they walked away. Raeborn wanted Angel.

Through the entry, they passed a grand stairway curving to the second floor. They turned through several long hallways, including one lined with books. "The collection was left to a cousin, over a hundred years ago. He was more interested in the pages of the books than family, so the house and this wonderful collection fell to our grandfather."

Elspeth trailed her hands along a row of books and then turned to sign. "You have a lovely home. I fear none of you will be safe while my brothers are here."

Angel breathed. "I think we should put our plan into place tomorrow. I get the feeling they are eager to fulfill their purpose for being here." They moved up a narrow staircase. "This is the east wing. I thought you would enjoy the view from the tower."

"You should not be so kind to me, considering the trouble I have brought."

Angel hugged her. "A power greater than the curse brought you to us. Let us trust Him. Here is your room."

Through the raised panel door, they entered a charming room. Elspeth's eyes immediately were drawn to the canopy bed with a coat of arms painted on the headboard. Wooden dressers with elegantly shaped legs stood on either side of the bed. While a dainty desk beneath the window held a lantern already lit.

"Your dressing room is through there," Angel indicated another door, "and everything you'll need has been placed in the dresser."

Elspeth sat in a straight-backed chair. "The plan will work. It must."

Angel took hold of her hands. "Horatio will join us shortly. There is naught to fear."

"And here I am," Horatio tapped on the door. He checked behind him then slid into the room. His hands moved swiftly. "You're leaving us may have been good fortune, sister. The brothers did not linger in the dining room. If we are to do this, it must be tomorrow."

"You should all leave." Elspeth's hands shook.

"Too late for that, my dear. I could no more leave you than I could leave my sister." He walked across the room to the window. Elspeth joined him, allowing him to hold her in his arms. "Ventnor and Charles know.

Here's our plan."

Elspeth rested her head against his chest as she listened to his strange tone rather than move so he could communicate with his hands. Hope battled fear within her. Tomorrow would come.

Chapter 10

Pleasantries around the breakfast table did not still Elspeth's worries. Though her brothers were cordial enough, she recognized the hardness behind their smiles and teases.

Horatio caught attention as he signed to Angel. She smiled at the group. "Horatio says it is a warm morning if anyone would like to explore the gardens. We have billiards planned for later." She arched a brow. "How do you feel about friendly competition?"

Raeborn chuckled. "I'd be willing to wager for a kiss."

She lifted her head slightly. "A pert answer, sir. You'd have to put on quite a performance."

"Our little bird would enjoy a walk in the garden with our host," Neville said.

Elspeth nodded in agreement.

Ventnor stood. "Let them enjoy the garden. How would you other gentlemen like to see the hunters? The horses are a fine breed. We can meet back in the reception room for a drink before the billiards games."

Kingsley clapped his hands. "I love horses. Perhaps we can take a ride while we're here."

With that declaration, the group once again split. It wasn't until later, in the hall lined with books, Horatio motioned to a section near the grand piano. "Shakespear supposedly developed a character from one of the original owners of the house. Of course, we have several of his manuscripts."

Though he tried to distract her, Elspeth nearly shook with concern about what could be taking place elsewhere. "Do you think they've come back for drinks yet?"

"What is this?" Raeborn hissed.

Elspeth moved her hands behind her back. Though his unexpected presence caused her heart to thud with fear, the curse allowed her face to remain passive.

Raeborn stepped closer, eyes narrowing. "What were you doing with your hands, Elspeth?"

"I'm teaching her a game," Horatio said in his strange voice as he moved between them.

"Is this true?" Raeborn glared at Elspeth, whose face remained calm. He snarled at her. "I free you…" He stopped. Blinked. Shook his head. He took another step, but his face paled. He fell to his knees, then slumped on the floor.

Elspeth pressed her hand against her throat as she stared at Horatio. "He freed me," she whispered.

Horatio grabbed her hand as Angel ran into the room. "The others are down, but we cannot find Raeborn. Oh," Angel sputtered when she saw him on the ground.

Together, they rolled him onto his back. Horatio pulled Raeborn's shirt from buff pants. He tried to pull the shirt off, but Raeborn's heavy body wouldn't cooperate. Angel tapped his arm then signed. "Use these. Cut it off." She handed him scissors. Once they bared his chest, they glanced at Elspeth.

"There isn't a second shirt," Horatio said with his hands.

Elspeth knelt beside Horatio and his sister. She could just make out a faint glimmer. She pulled the fine fabric from his skin so they could cut it. Soon, Angel held a ball of fabric in her hands. "A fire is prepared in the room where the others fell asleep." She grabbed Elspeth's hand.

Elspeth kept her eyes on Raeborn as she exited, but he remained sleeping, his chest bare. She closed her eyes. When she looked again, the light around her seemed to have dimmed. She rubbed her eyes. It didn't change.

"In here," Angel led Elspeth into a sitting room. All her brothers slept. Five were lying on the floor beside each other. Neville snored slumped against the side of a chair. Other guests grabbed Neville's feet and chest and moved him to lay beside the five. Angel nodded at an older gentleman. "Cut their shirts open and then Elspeth will find the cursed fabric." She lifted her hand to show Raeborn's shirt. "You won't see it, but it is there."

One by one, Elspeth moved to each of her brothers and found the delicate fabric so it could be cut. She blinked as the light around her continued to dim as their shirts were taken. None of the other guests noticed. Only the fire held any brightness, its greedy flames eager to consume every thread she had woven with her sweat and blood.

Kingsley was last. He still resembled the happy young man who charmed her as a child. Yes, he'd committed the same atrocities as the rest of them, but still. She pressed her hand against his warm cheek.

Angel returned from flinging one of the shirts in the fire. "Hurry. They won't stay asleep much longer."

Elspeth pulled the fabric from his chest and sliced it. His blue eyes opened, and she stopped, inches from the edge of the collar.

Fury glazed his eyes. His arms moved and were suddenly white with feathers.

"No, stop him," Angel screamed, slamming her body across a wing. Several other guests rushed to assist holding him down.

Elspeth finished cutting, breathing hard at the glare of hatred in his eyes. They removed the shirt, and Angel ran to the fire, plunging it into the flames.

Kingsley roared, "What are you doing?" He staggard to his feet and backhanded Elspeth before Horatio could pull her away.

Elspeth remained in Horatio's arms. Light was nearly gone, save for golden flickers in the fireplace. She gripped Horatio's hand. "Has night fallen?"

"Elspeth?" Angel called.

There was a thud, gasps from others, and then silence. Peace flooded Elspeth and then darkness swept over her like a wave from the ocean. Everything ended.

~

Horatio felt Elspeth go limp in his arms. Kingsley had fallen as well, his pale skin turned ashen. Horatio laid Elspeth on a couch. Movement pulled his attention back around. Fear pressed against his chest, but it wasn't one of the brothers standing in their midst. A strange woman wearing a gray gown wrinkled her nose as she glanced at Kingsley and the other five brothers. As she moved, he could make out gossamer wings. He gasped but couldn't turn away as she drew closer. She touched his ears with her hands.

Instantly, a rush of sounds blew into his head. He squeezed his eyes shut, his hands against his ears at the onslaught.

She patted his shoulder. "It will pass, have no fear. A gift from the Maker for your service."

He heard her. HEARD her and understood. He shook his head.

"Horatio," Angel cried as she ran to him, grabbing his arm to pull him away from the fairy.

His heart thudded wildly in his chest as he looked at his sister. "I hear you."

The wonder of it overwhelmed him. He stared at the fairy. "How long will this last?" He laughed at the strange sounds he made with his voice. He touched his ears.

She shrugged. "It is the Maker's gift. I suppose as long as He wills it to last." She spread her arms and forced all of them to back away from the brothers.

Flames of fire roared, then shadow figures slipped into the room. Horatio pulled Angel to him, and they both turned their eyes away. Heat and smoke swirled around them and then they were gone. The twitter of a cardinal wafted through the open windows.

"There. That is done." The fairy clapped her hands, and everyone turned. Marveled. The bodies of the brothers were no longer in the room.

"Elspeth," Horatio cried out, then ran to the couch and flung himself to the ground beside her. He grasped her hand. "Elspeth?" He whispered her name. She remained still. He touched her warm cheek, then looked at the fairy. "What will happen to her?"

The fairy joined him, brushing her hand across Elspeth's forehead. "Her talent was gifted from the fairies. The fault is not hers, being taken by the evil queen and used by her sons. Still," she sighed, "great harm has come through her. It is a hard burden to carry." She tilted her head. "She may choose the quiet peace of death. Not into the flames as those who called themselves her brothers. The Maker offers grace."

Horatio pressed his head against Elspeth's arm. "Must she die?"

"If that is her choice, yes." The fairy smiled. "Or she may choose to continue this life. To love and wed. To grow old and die when the time comes."

After a moment, the fairy ordered them all from the room. "It is not yours to see the ways of shadow walking."

~

Elspeth came to her senses on the edge of a creek with water rushing over stones. She looked across a field at a quaint homestead. She was standing next to a fairy. "Where are we?" The whole scene felt weird, and yet so very normal.

"This is your home. Your real home, where you were born and blessed and stolen by the evil queen."

Truth settled through her with delight. "I am not the queen's daughter." She glanced at the fairy. "May I meet my real mother?"

The fairy shook her head with a sad smile. "You have lived too many lives to meet her in this world. I am sorry." She wrapped an arm over Elspeth's shoulders. "The path you were forced to take was not of your choosing. The burden of it has been a great weight. The Maker says you may come to Him to have rest with no burdens."

Elspeth closed her eyes. "I want that very much." Tears wet her cheeks.

The fairy hugged her. "He has another offer, if you like. Horatio loves you. You may choose to stay and live a full life with him. A life where you grow old and die. The end of which is still rest in the Maker's land."

Elspeth closed her eyes and felt the weight of the memories of her past. "Will I remember?"

The fairy grasped Elspeth's hands. "I have no power to remove memories from you. But I promise, love is stronger. Faith and goodness are stronger."

Elspeth drew a deep breath and released it. "Then I know which I will choose."

Chapter 11

Though quiet spread through the manor, Horatio found himself unable to settle. He crept to the parlor. Sound jarred his every step, making him long for silence. Peering from the corner of the doorway, he saw Elspeth alone on the couch lying as he had left her. The fairy was gone. Once again, he knelt beside her, grasping her hand. Tears choked him. "Have you made a choice?" He pressed a kiss against her skin. "Please don't leave me, unless you must because the evil was too much to bear." He stared at the ceiling. "Can she at least answer me once?"

Her hand moved against his and when he looked down, her eyes watched him. "Elspeth?" He pressed his lips to her hand, fear battling joy.

"Horatio."

The sound of her voice touched his heart. He felt her try to speak with her hands. He shook his head and held her tighter. "I can hear. The fairy said it is a gift."

She sighed and closed her eyes. "Do you love me?"

"With all my heart and all my being, until the end of my days."

"She said love is stronger than all the evil. Do you believe that?" She looked at him again.

He nodded. "Love is stronger. Faith and hope and joy are all stronger."

"Kiss me."

He did. Elspeth's strength returned.

~

Far away, the evil queen stared at the tapestry with seven white swans searching beyond the mountains. The swans were fading. Pain shot through her middle and she staggard, falling against a narrow redwood table. It crashed as she leapt forward, arm stretched toward the tapestry. With a cry, she pressed her hand upon the remaining bird, but it, too, faded. A scream rose from her throat.

Across the room, the fireplace burst into flames. Her screams didn't cease until a shadow that had come forth carried her away and the fire died to nothing. Darkness filled the castle.

~

Light surrounded Elspeth as she swirled through a field of wildflowers in the arms of her husband. Laughter danced in the air around them. Love shone from within. They would live one life, together, with happiness. Elspeth reached for a butterfly. The dainty creature paused a moment on her finger before fluttering away. She smiled. Love was indeed stronger.

The Fisherman's Tale

The Fisherman and His Wife was discovered by the Brothers Grimm and included in their collection of fairytales. This retelling of the magical fish story has a Spanish flare certain to delight readers. *The Fisherman's Tale* is a light-hearted, fun story that was born out of a plotting lesson for my students.

1-His Perfect Love

Blue of a calm sea spread to the horizon. Fishermen working their nets caused the boats to bob. Staven rolled the last of his line and dropped a few more fish into the damping tubs. The setting sun had yet to reach the tip of olive trees in the grove on the highest hilltop. He rubbed his hands together.

"It's early enough you can get a decent view of the procession," his brother, Bellon, said as he slapped his shoulder and laughed.

Staven was used to the ribbing. He didn't mind so much if it meant he could see the queen.

"Contrive to meet her," another fisherman joked as they turned the sails.

"Fall in love. Marry."

"Become king," Bellon interjected.

Staven slapped his brother. "I'm but a sweaty fish-man. She'd no sooner look at me than any of you."

"Find an ordinary local girl and get your mind off the queen."

He should. Staven knew he should and yet, he couldn't keep himself from climbing the narrow, cobbled street toward the upper avenue after helping deliver the full damping tubs to the market.

~

Queen Aurelia Josephine Isabella loved walking to mass on this sort of evening. Though the sun rose on the sea, colors from sunset in the west splashed across the water. The hues of gold turned rosy. Several stone houses along the upper avenue boasted doors in a similar shade. She'd known since she was a child she would one day be queen, just hadn't expected it before her twentieth birthday. For three years since, she'd kept the ritual of evening mass four times a week. It comforted her, like nothing else seemed to. Steep streets slithered down from the grand avenue to the beach and harbor. There were people, but she paid them no heed.

~

If she turned her head, she would see him. Staven leaned against an oak tree lining the grand avenue as he watched the procession. A boy in front of the procession held a cross almost as tall as himself. Behind him walked priests in their dull brown robes. The queen wore a red gown with tight-fitting sleeves. The decorations down the front must have taken someone many hours to embellish. For a gown that would be worn once. Staven shook his head, not wanting to think of the waste. Behind her, two ladies held the train of the queen's dress and a third carried her Bible. Guards followed them all. They paid attention to everyone along the street but needed only a moment to pass over Staven. He didn't matter. It hurt within his chest, and he opened his mouth to call to the queen, but no sound followed. The golden light of early evening embraced her, showing off highlights in her dark hair in a simple braid down her back. He longed to touch her hair, to feel her sweet kiss and watch her eyes light with joy in his presence.

The procession moved on and there was nothing for him in it. Unease and harder emotions swirled through him. He made his way to the harbor. It would be a night with a moon. He pulled one of the smaller fishing boats from its mooring, grabbed a pair of paddles, and pushed into the growing darkness. He didn't mind the wet seawater soaking his feet as he jumped into the boat. He belonged on the water, seeking fish. He had no place pining after a queen. If only she were an ordinary citizen. He sighed. Surely then she would notice him and grow to love him as he loved her. His arms strained as he rowed hard, unmindful of direction. Hopefully, the familiar sounds and smells of the sea would ease the gnawing hunger he couldn't seem to fill.

2- Meeting the Fish Who Talked

Staven leaned against the bow of the boat, adrift. He could barely feel the movement of waves, though the air itself tasted salty like the sea. Stars brightened in the east as dusk faded into the night. He had just noticed the moon peaking above the horizon when a silverish glimmer drew his eye to the water. At first, he thought the light of the moon glittered across the water along with the stars, but then, he realized the glimmer came from beneath the surface of the sea. It had to be some sort of fish. He slid off the bench and knelt to look over the side. There it was again. The creature swam so close. He slowly stretched his hand along the inside of the boat until he felt a fishing net. He kept his eyes on the animal as it glided beside him. He looped the net around his wrist and flung it into the water. The next moment, he had the fish and dropped the net on the bottom of the boat. He didn't have a tub prepared, so he grabbed a bucket, swooshed it full of water, and then placed the fish still caught in the net into the bucket. Though the thing darted back and forth, it could not escape. He waited for it to slow before removing the net.

"I don't recommend jumping out. The bottom of the boat isn't nearly as nice as the water," Staven chatted as he folded the net.

"Or you could release me back to the sea."

Staven fell back, heart thumping as he searched around for the source of the voice that had just spoken. No one was there. No other boat nearby. He peered over the edge of the bucket.

The most beautiful fish he'd ever seen stared at him. Its scaled body was silvery-white. Its fins flowed like silken fabric drifting through the water. In the dim light of night, Staven could see its eyes staring at him. Its mouth moved.

"Every fish knows a fate awaits should it be snared, but surely we can breach a different choice."

"You can talk," Staven proclaimed, then pressed his hand to his mouth. Had he gone mad?

Somehow, the creature rolled its eyes. "Enchantments that are not yours to know. Come, fellow, let us be good to one another. Render service for service."

Staven gulped. "What service could I give a fish?"

"Set me free, of course. It is far better to swim free in the sea than to grace someone's dinner plate."

"I…" Staven rubbed his chin. "I can see where you would prefer freedom. But if you won't provide a meal, what other service can you render to me?"

The fish moved as though it had wings. "I will grant you a wish."

"A wish? You mean, anything I want?" He studied the creature for a moment, then puckered his brows. "How do I know you can grant me my heart's desire?"

The fish rolled its eyes once more. "You have my word for it. What wish would you have granted?"

"For the queen to be an ordinary woman," he said before he thought through other possibilities.

"A queen? Is she an evil ruler you wish to dethrone?"

"Oh, no. She is good and kind. We are in love, but she could never be with one like me. Our stations in life are too far separated."

The fish ducked beneath the surface. Bubbles rose around it. Returning, it motioned with its head toward the sea. "Very well. I see no harm in what you have asked. Return me to the sea and I will grant your wish. Set to meet me here in one week to tell me if the granting has brought you the happiness you desire together."

"This is ludicrous," Staven muttered, but he couldn't see lopping the head off a talking fish. And for the chance for the queen to meet him and fall in love. "Very well." He grabbed the bucket, leaned over the side, and poured it out.

The creature, when it landed in the water, seemed to grow, its beauty nearly that of the queen herself. The sea shimmered, then it all went dark. It took time for his eyes to adjust to the dimness of the stars and rising moon. Had it worked? How would he possibly know?

~

Queen Aurelia stretched in her bed. She had an uncanny sense of being watched, and when she glanced to the left, two maids stood at the side of the bed staring at her. They were both frowning. "What is it? What has happened?" She sat up.

"I don't know who you are or how you got here, but you had best leave." The older of them said with a glare.

"Is something wrong with you? Of course you know me. I am your queen."

"The queen is away at her royal palace in Calais. The guards have been sent for. Remove yourself or they will do so by force."

"Do not be ridiculous. The trip to Calais is not for another two months."

"What is the meaning of this?" a masculine voice demanded as the doors of her bed chamber burst open.

Aurelia stood. "These two are up to no good. I want them removed from service immediately."

"Who are you?"

Aurelia crossed her arms and stared at the two servants. They said nothing. A guard stepped beside her and took hold of her arm.

Aurelia gasped. "You have no right to touch my person. Unhand me." What was going on? Could this be a grasp for power?

"Who are you?" he repeated.

She jerked her arm away, rubbing the spot. "I am Queen Aurelia Josephine Isabella. Whatever ridiculous charade is going on had best stop now. I am not amused."

He snapped his fingers. "Remove this girl from the queen's bedchamber."

Aurelia could do no more than sputter as two soldiers lifted her off her feet. "Please don't struggle, miss. I'd rather not hurt you." The kind voice of one of the soldiers caused her to stop struggling. Her head hurt. Her heart pounded with fear and confusion. What was going on? They couldn't possibly not recognize her. Perhaps she'd been transformed while she slept? An enchantment of sorts? But they passed a mirror, and she caught a glimpse of herself. Her pale face surrounded by dark hair falling out of its thick braid reflected in the mirror.

They were in the hall. Aurelia recognized one of her attendants. "Margarite, Margarite," she cried.

The woman turned and looked at them but gave no indication of recognizing her and turned away to continue her way. Aurelia felt her breath catch in her throat. Weakness assailed her and she would have fallen if the soldier did not grab hold of her. "What is happening?"

~

Benjamin felt the young woman tremble in his arms as he helped hold her up. Perhaps she had a fever? But she didn't seem overly hot.

"Take her to the dungeon," one of the guards declared as he snarled at her.

"No," Benjamin had the rank to counter what the guard said. "She is confused, possibly sick with something."

"You can't release her. That filth sullied the queen's chamber. It will take days to clean."

"And she is gone for two months. I will take this woman to my house. My sister and aunt are there and can watch her."

The guard glared. "If she steps foot in the castle, I will deliver her to the dungeons myself."

Benjamin took her. She'd become dazed and docile. He kept hold of her arm, not that it would be easy for her to run in bare feet while wearing a nightgown. He turned off the grand avenue onto a street lined with colorful houses built against each other. The row of houses belonged to captains and trusted members of the queen's court. He opened a burgundy door and motioned for the woman to enter the courtyard.

"Tia Sylvana tends the blooms," he explained as he waved at the tumble of bougainvillea flowers across an overhead trellis. He led her to the entry of the house. "I'll have Tia Sylvana take you to Mira's room. She's my sister. You should be able to find something of hers to put on."

"I do not need anything."

He raised an eyebrow. "No? You are wearing a nightgown, and your feet are bare."

As if just realizing the truth, her cheeks flamed with red as she wrapped her arms around herself. He almost laughed. The nightgown started at her throat and fell to her ankles. The thick material revealed nothing beneath.

"Are you home already?" an older woman asked as she came through an arched doorway. She stopped when she saw the stranger. "Who is this?"

"I am the queen," the woman whispered with something close to a sob.

"She is confused and disoriented. Take her to Mira's room and help her find something to wear. Hopefully some shoes will fit her."

Tia Sylvana walked close to Benjamin. "Does she really think she's a queen?" she muttered her question.

Benjamin shrugged. "She was found in the queen's bed. No one knows how she could have gotten there, or why."

"Strange. Is it safe to have her with us?"

Benjamin studied the trembling woman. A surge of protectiveness rose in his chest. "Something odd is at work." He needed to figure out what, and how to end it.

~

Aurelia wanted to hit something. Hard. She wanted to rant and scream and climb back into her bed until the nightmare ended. But they threw her out of her bed. Out of her castle. What would have happened if the soldier hadn't taken pity on her? She stood in his sister's room. What was her name? She tried to recall, but her head throbbed to the point of unsettling her stomach.

The small room with a window overlooked the hillside of homes cascading to the harbor. She couldn't see the castle from here. Perhaps that was for the best. A bed with a thin mattress on woven supports stood against one wall. Just a minute to lie down, close her eyes, and get the headache to cease. She drifted to sleep quickly.

~

"She is asleep on my bed?" Mira said with a frown.

"Maybe it will help." Benjamin hoped so.

"I will not sleep on the floor." Her nose scrunched with displeasure. "May I visit Sophia?"

Benjamin had no problem with their oldest sister watching over Mira for a few days. He gave his consent. It concerned him when Mira was able to obtain supplies for a short trip without disturbing the strange woman. Perhaps she was ill? He sent Tia Sylvana to check on her.

The old woman returned, gripping a handful of herbs. "She has a fever. What illness have you brought to our home?"

Benjamin tapped his foot. "Fix a cup of tea with feverfew and I'll try to get her to drink it."

When he entered his sister's bedroom, a breeze came through the open window. Afternoon light steamed through the room, but the woman didn't seem to notice. She still wore her night dress. Her skin had an unhealthy rosy hue, though the contrast with her dark hair and delicate features attracted his attention. He shook himself. This was not a woman for an attraction. He pulled the chair close to the bed and placed the tea on the nightstand. He lightly pressed against her shoulder and shook her. She turned toward him with a groan but didn't open her eyes.

"I'll need a name for you. Don't suppose we can call you Halva?"

"Aurelia," she said, her voice cracking.

He shook his head. "We are not giving you the same name as the queen."

"But I was named for her."

"Here, have a sip of tea." He held her head and pressed the cup against her lips. "So, you don't think you're the queen? Just named for her?"

"Me? A queen?" Her eyebrows pressed together as she peeked at him. She moaned and closed her eyes. "Oh, my head hurts."

Tia Sylvana scurried into the room. "I brought something that might help. Get her to drink all of the tea first." She pointed at the mostly full cup. "Then you can use the compress with lavender and rose. Wring the scented water out of the cloth and press it onto her forehead. It will cool her fever and help her rest."

"Hopefully, you heard that." He looked at Aurelia. Her dark eyes seemed familiar, but he couldn't think why. He helped her drink the tea.

She grimaced. "May I request sugar in the next cup, if there needs to be one?"

"We should have honey. That will help."

There wasn't much else talking. She drifted to sleep. The compress seemed to make her more comfortable. Benjamin surprised himself, not minding having to tend to the stranger. It's what God told them to do, and yet, as a soldier he spent more time barking orders and teaching his men to be fierce. He watched over her until the dinner bell rang.

3- Aurelia's New Life

Early morning light streamed through the window and Aurelia had to blink until her eyes adjusted. Her muscles ached, but she sat up and turned so she could put her feet on the floor. She didn't recognize the room, and yet, it didn't seem strange. A bowl of water waited on a little table with a scrunched-up cloth beside it. She leaned over to sniff the water. Pleasantly surprised by its scent, she dipped the cloth into the water and washed her arms and face. That felt good. Rummaging through a wardrobe, she found something to wear, a dark green overlay with ties on the front. She slipped it over her nightdress. But the shoes she selected were too large. She frowned. Why would the shoes in her closet not fit her? She tried a different pair, but the same result. Her foot slipped out.

She padded through the house in stocking feet. She felt a breeze moving through the hallway and made her way to a side door leading to a kitchen garden.

"Bless my heart, it is good to see you up and about."

Aurelia turned and saw an older woman on the other side of a bed of tomatoes. She finished dropping a few ripe specimens in her apron and came to greet her. Aurelia couldn't keep from smiling at the friendly face, but she had no idea who the woman was.

"I am sorry, I do not recognize you." Aurelia chewed on her bottom lip. "I am afraid I have few memories to recall."

"Bless me, child, of course you'd not recognize me. We've never met. My nephew brought you here. You've been very sick, and I worried it might be catching, but here you are, fully recovered. I'd say it is a sweet miracle. Perfect for such a beautiful day."

Aurelia grinned, uncertain how to respond.

"Follow me," the woman motioned to the doorway with her head. "Let me put these down. I see you found something to wear."

"But no shoes." Aurelia helped her unload the tomatoes into a basket. "None of them fit."

"Mira is not known for dainty feet."

"Mira?"

"Benjamin's sister. The room where you slept belongs to her."

"Oh." Aurelia pressed her hand against her abdomen. "Did I keep her from her bed? I am sorry. She should have had me move to the floor."

The woman patted her hand. "You were not sleeping on the floor, sick as you were. No. Our Mira went to stay with her sister. She has more freedom to enjoy there than she gets here with her older brother."

"He is not your brother?"

"Goodness, of course you don't know me, either. I am Tia Sylvana. My sister, bless her beautiful soul, passed on while they were still young. I came to help and never left."

"You are a good woman."

She smiled, her eyes glittering with humor. "I know a good thing when I have it." She motioned for Aurelia to sit on a stool beside the work bench. "Would you like tortilla Espanola? I'll add tomato since that is fresh from the garden."

Aurelia shrugged. "I am hungry. May I help?"

"Rest today. Once you are stronger, we will see what Benjamin plans to do with you."

She gulped. "Do with me?"

4- Second Meeting with the Magical Fish

From the back of the house, Tia Sylvana showed Aurelia the balcony overlooking the steep incline to the harbor. She saw crisscrossing streets over a narrow lane used by mules to pull goods up into the city. As she stood on the balcony, a man, about halfway down the hill, waved to her. She squinted for a better look at him. Could this be someone she knew? He stood too far to see any features clearly.

"Tia said you were up, but I didn't dare believe you would look this well after being so sick."

A deep voice drew her attention from behind. She turned. There was no problem seeing the features of this man. He wore tight hose with a long tunic beneath a studded brigantine. The knee boots were worn with a sheen of oil. Curly dark hair brushed the collar of his brigantine. His eyes were green. They stood looking at each other for a moment.

"You found her," Tia Sylvana's voice interrupted… whatever was happening. "Come to luncheon. Don't leave her standing outside."

Aurelia smiled as a faint blush darkened his cheeks. He held his hand to her. "Shall we?"

~

Staven waved his arms excitedly. There she stood, the woman who had been queen. It had been days since he'd seen her. He'd started to worry bad fortune had fallen upon her. But no, she seemed well. For a moment, their eyes met, and Staven felt joy burst in his heart. But then, she turned away. He could see a man behind her, but not well enough to identify him. Who was he? What was he doing with her? He marked the location of the house. He would find out.

Staven made his way to an ale house near the location where he'd seen the woman. The house boasted a periwinkle door with a crescent moon. Vines with flowers painted on the white stucco marked it from the neighboring house outlined in azure. Upon entering the pub, he heard his name called. He waved and crossed to join some friends. "Callen, Crest, and Hammond, Hola. Well met."

"Don't often see you in this part of town," Callen raised a flagon of ale.

"Delivered fresh fish on the crescent to Don Sanchez," Staven explained as he accepted a drink. "The flowers they painted on his house look real."

The others frowned. "Flowers? On the crescent?" They exchanged glances.

Hammond shook his head. "No, no, no. The house on the crescent with flowers? Did it have a blue balcony and bright door? That belongs to Captain Philipe. He's with the palace guard."

"Did you hear what happened last week?" Crest interrupted as he leaned over his mug of ale. "They found a strange woman sleeping in the queen's bed. Stafford would have put her in irons in the dungeon, but Philipe pulled rank and took her with him."

Staven gulped. "I am thankful she did not have to go to the dungeons." He looked out the window. Night was growing. "I think I shall enjoy an evening fishing. Skies look clear."

Callen cleared his throat. "May want to grab your delivery and find the right house first."

Crest shuddered. "Much rather stay here. I get enough time on the water during the day."

Staven slapped his shoulder. "Good thing I like a solitary expedition."

He finished his ale, but within the hour, he'd made his way to the harbor, unmoored his boat, and pushed it into the water, jumping in before his boots could get very wet. This time, he had a tub of water prepared.

He didn't really have a plan, but as the hour grew later, once again, he saw the sparkling shape of a large fish beneath the surface of the sea. He captured it with the net and carefully placed it in the tank.

It darted back and forth, its silken fins rolling like fabric he'd seen in a market filled with exotic goods from the East. The creature finally settled. Staven felt as though the creature glared. Then it seemed to recognize him, and the shimmering eyes became friendlier.

"Well met. You are a stranger from the past moon cycle. You could have leaned over the side of your boat. No purpose to go through this once more."

"I needed to speak with you."

"How is your fair love?"

"I fear someone has come between us."

"What of your love? Perhaps hers is not as real as you thought."

"No, our love is real and deep and strong. She does not remember. Someone else has drawn her, taken away my opportunity."

"I am sorry. Do not give up hope. Find a woman who's love will be true."

He shook his head. "She is the one I must have. There is none other for me. The look of a guard turned her head. I am a simple fisherman, what do I have to compare?"

"There is nothing to be done."

Staven tapped his chin. "If he were ugly… if the guard were to lose his strength and fierceness, surely she would turn from him and come to me."

The fish squished through the tub of water. "It is not a good thing to wish harm on another."

Staven pulled a long-bladed dagger from beside him. "If you cannot grant my simple request, there is no reason for me to keep you alive."

The eyes of the creature hardened. "Be careful what you choose."

"Grant my wish."

It sighed. "There will be consequences I cannot foresee."

Staven leaned in, hopeful. "But will you do it?"

"Release me, and you shall have your wish."

He narrowed his eyes. Perhaps threatening the creature hadn't been a wise idea. "How do I know you will?"

Bubbles blew from the tub. "I give my word."

Staven chose to believe him. He released the fish. Silver flashed across the sea, and it was gone.

In the distance, fire burst from one of the houses in the upper part of the village.

5- Fire and Death

Aurelia screamed as the door to her bed chamber burst open.

"Fire!" Benjamin shouted. He didn't wait for her to react but swept her into his arms.

"What happened?" She held on as he carried her into the hallway.

"I don't know. Fire seemed to come from nowhere. We must get out."

Aurelia felt the air moving over them as he shouldered through a side door leading to the kitchen garden. She gasped as she saw flames stretching through an upper window. "Where is Tia Sylvana?"

He set her on her feet. "There is a gate at the back of the garden that goes through to the street. Wait for us there."

Before she could respond, he was gone. Somewhere in the village, a bell clanked. She ran toward the gate, unmindful of her bare feet. A small crowd soon gathered, and they watched in horror as fire leapt into the house next door.

"Oh, dear God, please," murmured prayers floated around the group.

Aurelia focused on the back gate. They should be coming. He couldn't be gone.

A woman fell through the gate, her screams drawing everyone closer. Though her words were difficult to understand, Tia Sylvana's wild gestures toward the smoldering fire indicated something was very, very wrong.

Aurelia took hold of Tia Sylvana as she stared at the men around them. "You must go find Benjamin."

Why they obeyed her, she wasn't sure, but the contingency of soldiers moved. Sylvana sobbed on Aurelia's shoulder. "We were almost out when something fell on us. It must have been the ceiling. I've never been so scared in my life. He cried out. I know he's been injured, but he still got us from under the debris and found his way to the door. He collapsed again and I could not get him up."

"If he is injured, we need somewhere to take him." From the street she could see the palace and the surrounding structure. "Does the garrison have rooms?"

"I don't know," Sylvana sobbed. "I've never been there."

Aurelia held her close. "You live in the shadow of the palace, and you've never been?"

She hiccupped. "You have no shoes."

"I was sleeping." Aurelia shivered. "How did the fire happen?"

People with lanterns strove down Grand Avenue. "Are any injured?"

Tia Sylvana nodded. "Captain Philipe, but I don't know how bad."

"Is there a room in the garrison where we can take him? It is too far to go into the town."

"Follow me," a soldier said as he drew them to the long low building used by the guards. "A doctor will be heading this way. If he lives, there are beds to use."

Aurelia didn't go inside. She stood against the stone that still retained a touch of the sun's heat from the day. There was movement. People were coming up the hill. "Is he alive?" she asked the first person to arrive. Her heart thumped as he nodded.

"But it is not good. Part of his face and chest are burned."

Aurelia blinked at the unexpected feeling of tears in her eyes. She swallowed her fear. "Who is familiar with the gardens?"

"What are you thinking?"

"We need lavender to calm him. Helichrysum for healing. Pikes' bane can make him sleep."

The guard peered at her for a moment and then nodded. "I will see to it. There is a hearth in the central hall to heat water."

Aurelia was not prepared to look on fire yet, but she found someone else to go. Hours passed in a blur. Benjamin thrashed until they got him to drink enough bane to fall into a stupor. Nasty red puckered flesh covered the left side of his face and neck. His eye was swollen, there was no way to tell if it would be saved. The thick leather vest of the guard protected his chest from severe burns. She dabbed cooling water steeped with healing plants on his wounds, not allowing the cloth to stick to any of the burns.

Sylvana laid a hand on her shoulder. "You must rest. He is in the Lord's hands now."

"Where do we go? Your house is destroyed."

A kiss to her forehead surprised her. "A house can be rebuilt and the things within it replaced. What matters the most is safe."

Aurelia stood, wincing at the soreness of her bare feet. "Does Mira know? She will be worried when she hears about the fire."

Sylvana nodded. "I sent someone to his sisters to let them know." She placed her arm across Aurelia's shoulders. "We have a space down here. In the morning, we will find you shoes."

~

Staven couldn't help but stare at the gruesome wounds on the captain's face. His wish. The reality of it caused a sick feeling in the pit of his stomach. What had he done? On the lonely sea it didn't seem as horrible as this. A smell in the air of burnt flesh lingered.

"How is he?"

He turned, and his heart soared. She stood in the doorway. Her hair fell around her shoulders and dirt smudged her face. "I don't know," Staven stammered. "I came to see if there was anything I could do for you."

She frowned. "I am not the one in need of help."

Jealousy slashed him. The woman who had been queen focused on the soldier. He swallowed hard. "Something we can do for him?"

"Are you a fisherman?" she asked, motioning to the small, curved blade on his belt.

"I am."

"Could you bring seaweed grass? It is the only substance I know we can place on the burns and not fester the wounds."

"I will go now." He pressed his hand to his heart.

"Thank you." But her attention did not stay with him.

He left quickly. The quiet morning meant no breeze helped clear the air, so smoke drifted through the streets. He battled fury and fear of what he had caused. A row of houses smoldered. No one had died, thank God for that mercy, but only death could unite him and the queen. As long as Captain Philipe lived, her attention would focus on him. Her love would grow for him, not for Staven. He needed that fish. Needed another wish. Guilt tore at him, but his desire for her love would not be quenched.

More people than usual roamed through the harbor. Staven kept out of their way. He slipped the boat past the others. The cool sea water eased the heat of his anger. Someone from the shore shouted and waved at him, but he ignored them. If he crossed paths with the silver fish before reaching the seaweed fields, then the third wish was meant to be.

The shouting from afar increased, sounding like a warning. He looked across the harbor. There was a faint glimpse of something from the corner of his eye, and then smoldering debris showered over him. The force of it thrust his boat onto its side, ripped apart. He fell into the sea.

Disoriented, wallowing in the dark, Staven expected to die. The silver light surrounding him would lead him to the underworld. He wanted to cry against it, but all he could do was hover.

"Your love has not been good for you." The silver fish circled him, encasing him within its silken fins. "Can you relinquish your love for her or let it die with you?"

"Is there another choice but death?"

"There is always life. Let her go and perhaps love like you desire will find you."

Staven felt warmth surrounding him. "Yes, I wish to forget and release any feelings I've held for Queen Aurelia. I wish to release her." He closed his eyes. Death would be the only way. But then, a lightness encased him as though from inside out. He giggled, choaking on saltwater.

Hands grabbed him, dragging him onto a fishing boat. He heaved the water from his chest. His throat burned, but he was able to draw breath. He fell onto his back and stared at the blue sky.

"Were you trying to kill yourself?" A fellow fisherman jabbed his arm.

Staven breathed. "I don't know. I don't remember why I came out on the water." He looked around and noticed a blackened beam floating beside the boat. "What happened?"

"Fire along the upper crescent. You put yourself where the debris fell into the sea."

Staven slapped his chest. His lungs ached, but he was alive. "Thank you." He remained at the bottom of the boat as they returned to the harbor.

6- Restoration and Love

Your majesty, what are you doing?"

Aurelia rinsed her hands in a ceramic basin before she realized someone was speaking to her. "What did you say?" She frowned.

The young woman glanced around before lowering her eyes to the floor. She turned away without another word. Unexpected pain flared through Aurelia's head. She gasped, pressing against the wall to keep herself from falling. As soon as it started, the pain was gone. On it's heal came memories. Growing up in the palace. Her parents' death and ascension to the throne. Forgetfulness of who she was. The fire, and Captain Philipe.

The man appeared in the doorway. "Are you okay?"

She gasped. "You shouldn't be out of bed."

His eyebrows lifted. "I beg your pardon?"

She opened her mouth, but then realized the burns were gone. She rubbed her forehead. "You were injured."

He scoffed. "Not since learning to use a sword."

"I don't understand." Waves of dizziness engulfed her. She would have fallen if he hadn't caught her swiftly.

~

Queen Aurelia Josephine Isabella leaned against the stone wall of the balcony overlooking the rose garden. Three days of illness left her weak, but the fresh air felt better than the lingering stuffiness of her bedchamber. Something made her restless. Her heart thudded, longing for… she knew not what.

"My lady," one of her maids called from the doorway.

Aurelia turned. "Yes, Glenys?"

"The coaches with your trunks and household for Calais departed."

"Thank you." In a fortnight, she herself would take to the road for the long carriage ride.

Something moved in the garden, drawing her attention. One of the guards stopped and glanced at her. Without the usual metal hat, she noticed wavy dark hair that fell to his shoulders. His eyes appeared green. They stared at one another. It could have been moments or hours. He seemed to realize where he was and whom he looked upon, for he gave a stiff bow and hurried away from her. The restless feeling had stilled, and she no longer felt tired.

~

Somehow, he was lead with the guards on her trip to Spain. He held the door to a private dining room at the first inn. Again, they paused, just looking at each other.

Queen Aurelia tilted her head. "You should join me for supper. There is no joy found in eating alone."

He agreed. By the time they reached Calais, she'd asked him to be her king. He continued to agree.

272

The Little Mermaid

Hans Christian Anderson's *Little Mermaid* fairytale has become well-known through the efforts of Disney. How to twist such a beloved classic? What if the young mermaid were kidnapped, forced to live on land without memory of who she is or where she comes from? Forced to battle the weakening of her legs as she lives in an orphanage? Why would someone do such a thing? Well, you will have to read the story to find out. While this is intended to be a light-hearted read, there are elements of bullying among the orphan children.

Chapter 1: Lights in the Night

The first she saw of the strange light was a glow along the horizon after the sun had set and twilight diminished to night. Not a steady glow, as though candles had been set upon a pedestal. No, this light moved with shadows, distant dancing—unseen, unknown, imagined. Molly watched until her head touched the cold sill of her window. The dance of shadow and light carried into her dreams.

A harsh pinch jerked her awake. Molly turned, swinging her arm, but the offending orphan ran, laughter following in the wake of the pain she'd caused. Molly rubbed the spot as she pulled herself to her feet. Stiff legs threatened to buckle beneath her. She rubbed the thin muscles, hanging on to the window frame as she pulled each leg up and down. It hurt, made worse by sleeping at the window. But she couldn't help herself, something about the unusual lights called to her. Stars were too far away, too far above her to be anything other than cold and heartless. What she watched last night… those lights were within grasp.

She looked at her puny legs as she hooked the cold metal crutches on her arms and wrists. Long legs, and yet thin. Sixteen years old, but she wouldn't be noticed for a cute smile, the curves growing beneath her gray t-shirt, or the pretty blond curls down her back. Attention focused on her ill-formed legs, the uneasy gate that burned in her as she lumbered, right and then left, slow and steady with an uneven staccato caused by the crutches that kept her from falling on her face.

Except when the other girls in the orphanage played with the crutches in the night by loosening screws.

~

"Molly, over here." Tansy waved as Molly entered the breakfast room. Tansy wasn't a mean girl. She'd been directed by the head mistress, Mrs. Honeywell, to help, and help she would.

Molly sat with relief, turned her crutches over to Tansy, and accepted a tray of toast and sliced apples. She glanced at the other girls around the table. "Did anyone else notice the strange lights I could see from the window last night?"

The four girls seated at the table turned and looked at Molly. Perhaps not with any wish to answer, but Molly usually ate in silence and her unusual question garnered attention.

Tansy nodded. "I did see something. Is that why you were at the window so early?"

"I must have fallen asleep."

"What do you think it was?"

Molly shrugged. "All I could see were shadows moving. They were too far to see their forms."

"You two best not be telling ghost stories." Amira, a thicker, darker girl frowned at Tansy. "I'll be sure Mrs. Honeywell knows 'bout you."

Tansy scowled. "It's not a story. I saw it before I went to bed. Something was out there, far away, but not too far."

"Let's go see." Amira glared at Molly. "She can't make it to the edge of town, but we can."

Only they couldn't. Mrs. Honeywell and the other teachers refused to let them leave the house. They offered little sentiment and no reason to keep them from uncovering the mystery. Locks were engaged, alarms set on the outermost doors. Curiosity ate at the girls, and more than Molly jostled for a view from the window as night returned. Her left crutch was jerked aside, and Molly felt herself falling, unable to prevent the slap of hardwood floors against her backside. Metal cuffs bit into her wrists.

"That wasn't necessary." Someone put arms beneath Molly's armpits and pulled her up.

"Not enough room for those things."

Molly couldn't identify the nasty speaker through the tears in her eyes. She limped to her bed, unhooked the cuffs and placed the crutches beneath her bed. She rubbed the sores from her wrists and then lay back to sleep.

Still dark when she woke, Molly looked at the window. The others were gone. She pulled her crutches and slowly crossed the room. As in the previous night, light shone, and shadows moved. What would it be like to be free to dance? She leaned her head against the side of the window and watched until sunlight bleached the mystery from view. It didn't stop her from wondering.

Daylight brought an even greater mystery. An unknown person came to the orphanage. Molly couldn't see him. The others crowded around the doors and windows. All she could hear was a deep voice and a laugh. The stranger departed and Mrs. Honeywell joined them in the large living room.

"The lights you saw are no great mystery. A fair set up across the way. They have offered to sponsor your visit." She curled her nose. "An opportunity for pictures and fanfare, I dare say." She snorted. "Make nice with the orphans."

"We can go?" Tansy had the courage to ask.

Mrs. Honeywell shrugged. "If you wish. They will send a bus. Get on and you must stay until the bus returns."

Excitement weaved through the gaggle of girls. They tried to keep it contained, beneath the Honeywell glower, but at an upward tweak of one side of her lips, the girls squealed and took off to prepare. Mrs. Honeywell wasn't a bad sort, most girls liked the head mistress, and those who didn't likely thought so because they'd felt the working end of a switch against their backsides when warranted.

~

"You shouldn't go," Amira gave Molly a poke. "No one will want to remain with you."

Molly surprised herself, standing a bit taller to look Amira in the eye. "No one's responsible for me but me. Certainly not you."

"You know they'll make Tansy stick by you. It isn't fair for her."

"Why don't you volunteer before they do? Then you can run off and not have to worry about someone else forced to stay by my side."

Amira smiled, a cold smile that shimmered like ice in her eyes. "I think I will. Have fun, Molly."

~

The bus followed the main road toward the outskirts of town. But when Molly expected them to turn right, they turned to the left. She studied the image in her mind's eye. The lights had been further south, but they took to the north. As they turned the curve in the road, the fair spread on the green before them.

Amira offered her a hand down. Apparently, the bully of the orphanage intended to make the impression of being helpful before deserting Molly at the fair. Molly didn't care. She took a few steps. Amira remained nearby. The bus squeaked and bounced forward. The other girls sauntered away, drawn to the bells ringing across the field. Amira gave a look and then faced Molly, an unpleasant smile twisting her face.

"Stay here and you might be able to catch the bus when it comes back for us."

"I'm not worried."

Amira tossed her dark hair over her shoulder, turned her back on Molly, and walked away. Molly found herself standing alone near the edge of the main fairway. A path that appeared to look south started across from her. She gripped the hand bars on her crutches. She'd taken an extra pill that morning, a way to stave off pain. She'd feel it later, but now… she crossed the fairway and stopped where the path moved past a pair of trees. She turned and looked. No one noticed her. The noise of the fair bustled before her. Silence to her back. But it wasn't the silence of nothingness. Rather, silence of a held breath. Something waiting to happen. She looked over her shoulder at the path leading into the woods. Nothing unusual. No real reason she shouldn't be able to go a little distance. She maneuvered her crutches to turn and face the unknown. She crossed into the trees, the sounds of the fair swiftly fading. Birds sang, squirrels chattered and snarled their displeasure, air moved among the trees, creating a rustling sound. The path wasn't quite steady. Molly carefully watched her crutches as she moved forward. But for once the sound of their creaking was muted.

Chapter 2: The Lake Beyond the Trees

You are quite a way from where you belong."

Molly startled at the man who stepped from behind a tree. She might have fallen if he hadn't grabbed her arm to steady her, releasing her before she had time to get uncomfortable. "I don't think I've ever been where I belong."

The man was on the short side, though taller than Molly. He had curly hair that danced in a breeze and bright blue eyes glimmering with something she didn't recognize and yet somehow wanted.

"This is not the way to the fair."

Molly shook her head. "For the past two nights, I've seen lights dancing."

"The fair, of course." He waved at the path behind her. "You will find what you seek in that direction."

Molly tilted her head. "I know what I saw, and it wasn't where the fair is." She glanced at the man. "Where does this lead?"

"To the lake. Haven't your parents warned you not to talk with strangers?"

"I'm an orphan." She shook her crutches. "As you can see, if you meant harm, it wouldn't have mattered anyway. I've no hope of outrunning you."

"I'm not going to cause you harm." He paused, then nodded. "I'm Griffin. I'll walk you to the lake. You can see for yourself, there's nothing here. If you saw lights during the night, no one has stayed around."

"You're here."

He grinned. "So, I am. I help set up and take down at the fair. Since they don't need me between times, I choose to explore the woods. Far preferred to the crowds and noise."

They walked. He kept pace with her and chatted so freely, she felt none of the awkwardness that usually accompanied her around the orphanage. "How many places have you visited?"

"This is our eighth town. Another five before the season ends."

She frowned. "Thirteen? Isn't that considered unlucky?"

"Who's to say what luck is?"

They turned a bend in the road and Molly gasped at the shimmering water that spread before them. "I had no idea such a place existed so close to the orphanage."

From where she stood on the path, the lake seemed immense. Mountains framed the opposite shore. She couldn't see how far left or right the water went.

"Come on," he motioned with his head. "I'll take you to the dock."

The path continued across a green hill leading down to the water's edge. She could see the dock. It went yards and yards into the water. Her hands trembled, wondering what it would feel like to touch the lake.

But the unevenness of the hill was too great an obstacle for her to overcome with her crutches. "I cannot make it," Molly whispered as her crutches tore into her wrists.

"What if I carried you? I'll be a perfect gentleman. Consider me an older brother or uncle."

Molly sighed. "I can't. It wouldn't be proper."

"You've come all this way. Not going the final distance wouldn't be proper."

Molly chewed her lower lip. The greens and blues of the water sparkled as sunlight danced on its surface. The lake beckoned.

"Leave your crutches here. I'll come back for them." Griffin assured her.

"I shan't need them." Molly shook with excitement. "You won't leave me, will you?"

He smiled, and she could see no guile in his eyes. "I've come this far with you. No reason to leave you behind now."

"Miss Pritchard, what are you doing?"

Molly gasped at the voice of Mrs. Honeywell. Once again, Griffin prevented her from falling. She turned, then looked at the ground, unable to face the disappointment of the head mistress. "I wanted to see the water."

The older woman's voice remained hard and cold. "You were granted an opportunity to visit the fair. Not run away with a strange boy."

Griffin straightened. "A trip to the lake won't do her no harm."

"That is beside the point. If I cannot trust her with the permission that has been granted, the permission is removed." She turned her attention to Molly. "Wait on the bus."

Molly retrieved her crutches as she blinked tears from her eyes. "Yes, Mrs. Honeywell."

Chapter 3: Punished for Trying

Y ou nearly got me whipped," Amira hissed.

Molly remained at an upstairs window in the dorm room. The long afternoon on the bus waiting for everyone to return had been hot. Her head still ached from it. "I told her I gave you no choice."

"Thanks to you, we aren't even allowed to go to town on Sunday."

"Did you know there's a lake near where the fair is?"

Amira huffed. "What's that got to do with anything?"

"We should learn to swim. Or at least have a picnic and play in the water. Why won't they take us there?" Molly glanced at the other girl.

"I don't know. It's probably not real. "

"Of course it is. I saw it. It's beautiful."

"What do you know of beauty?" Amira wrinkled her nose as she motioned to Molly's legs. "You're a cripple."

Molly turned back to stare out the window. Memory of the lake burned in her mind. Never had she seen something shimmering with life. There had to be a way to get back to it. The next time Mrs. Honeywell left them on their own, Molly promised herself she'd walk, no matter how far.

~

Molly fell asleep leaning against a cold wall in the dark closet in Mrs. Honeywell's office. Though the head mistress didn't yell when she intercepted Molly's second attempt to walk to the lake, her cold glare and the tight tone of her voice caused fear to grip Molly's chest. The ache in her legs troubled her sleep, and a stranger's voice woke her.

"Where is my daughter?"

Molly jerked at the sound of a male voice booming in the head mistress' office. A sliver of light marked where the keyhole was in the door of the closet. Molly stared in that direction.

"Sir?" The responding voice, though muffled, held the tone of Mrs. Honeywell. "We are a home for orphaned girls. There is no reason to imagine your daughter is one of them."

"She was seen, though they said she walked with crutches."

Molly hobbled to her feet. He spoke of her? There were no others in the home with crutches. Her heart leapt. Was it possible?

"I am terribly sorry someone would lead you astray like this. We have no such girl here among us."

Mrs. Honeywell lied. But why? Though weakness assaulted her legs, she hobbled closer to the door. When she could no longer support herself without the use of her crutches, she sank to the floor. She could see little through the keyhole. Whomever stood in the office wore a thick sweater of variegated fur. She could see nothing else. Her father? She turned her thoughts to remembering, but naught but haze remained of her time before the orphanage. Even then, her earliest memories of the orphan home had faded. A symptom of her ailment, doctors assured.

Molly trembled, quashing the urge to cry out. There must be a reason Mrs. Honeywell refused to acknowledge her presence to the stranger. She chewed her bottom lip. She'd have to wait until after her punishment to find out.

~

The next morning, ignoring the growls of her stomach, she sat with the other girls awaiting permission to eat breakfast. After a long night on the cold, hard floor of the closet, she'd had to be carried first to the bathroom and then to the dining room, unable to manage even with her crutches.

"Miss Allen will see to you after breakfast."

Molly peered at the head mistress who gave permission to eat. Molly swallowed a bland spoonful of oatmeal. "Who was the man in your office yesterday?"

Mrs. Honeywell lifted one eyebrow. "I beg your pardon?"

"I heard a man's voice. It sounded as though he searched for someone."

"There were no visitors to the school yesterday, male or otherwise."

Molly frowned. "Of course, there was. I could see his sweater through the keyhole of the closet."

She scoffed. "You are mistaken. Speak no more of it."

Amira laughed. "Probably dreamt it."

Mrs. Honeywell fixed her gaze upon the other girl. "No one need speak of it."

All the girls returned their attention to breakfast. No need to risk punishment.

After breakfast, Mrs. Allen helped Molly into one of the bathing rooms.

"Pity she won't permit salts to be used in any of the baths. Would make a good difference, I'd wager," the young woman muttered as she lowered Molly into warm water.

"Do you think the big lake in the woods would be salt water? How close are we to the sea?"

"A lake in the woods?"

Molly grimaced as Miss Allen started bending her leg.

"I tried to visit. Mrs. Honeywell sent someone after me and locked me in the closet as punishment."

Miss Allen frowned. "You went alone? What if you had fallen? Or been attacked by wild animals or an evil man? You mustn't attempt such a thing on your own."

"Would you take me?" Molly asked, then gasped as a tight push on her leg caused pain. The ministrations were helping, it just took time.

"We'd have to get permission, but it is something to try."

Molly grimaced. "We'd have to do without permission. Maybe once she saw the results, Mrs. Honeywell would give us permission to visit again."

Miss Allen paused, studying Molly quietly. "If we were caught in an attempt, Mrs. Honeywell would punish you more grievously and remove me from this post."

They said no more, and Molly's heart fell. It would be foolish for Miss Allen to give aid.

The next morning, after breakfast, Miss Allen approached Molly with a straight back rolling chair. "As Mrs. Honeywell has gone to town for the better part of the day, today is a fine day for us to stroll through the woods."

Molly stared. "Are you sure?"

Miss Allen offered her arm so Molly could maneuver into the chair. The stiffness had abated, but she still hadn't regained her usual strength yet.

No one seemed interested in an outing, so the two of them took a path leading into the woods. Time passed as beams of light flickered through the overhead canopy. A breeze rolled dead leaves across the path. Miss Allen seemed competent pushing Molly, turning the chair around to pull over rough areas. For one area, Molly held onto Miss Allen's arm, and they stepped across a fallen tree trunk. She left Molly sitting on the other side of the trunk while she went back and moved the chair forward. Finally, shimmering blue could be seen in the distance. Excitement lurched within Molly. Almost, she felt as though she could leap from the chair and race to the edge of the water.

She thought they were going to make it, but a dark shadow lurched onto their path. "What are you doing?" Mrs. Honeywell glared at the two of them.

Elated emotions fell to the dirt ground. Miss Allen jerked the chair to a stop. Neither of them spoke.

Mrs. Honeywell's lips curled. "What, no excuses?"

"How did you know?" Miss Allen whispered.

"It is my duty to know." A cold smile pressed into Mrs. Honeywell's face.

The younger woman stood her ground. "Why do you fear the water?"

"I hold no fear," she scoffed. "This one will not dip a toe in the lake."

Tears pressed against Molly's eyes and caused her throat to tighten. "What is it to you?" She sobbed. She tried so hard never to cry, and yet at this moment, so close to the water that drew her, she couldn't stop. A large teardrop fell on her leg. The skin turned green, then faded to pale as the drop evaporated.

Chapter 4: The Siren's Song

A flicker of darkness in Mrs. Honeywell's eyes caused Molly's heart to beat faster. She could feel Miss Allen's grip on the chair shake. They backed up a step.

Mrs. Honeywell's lips tightened. "She is not going anywhere with you."

"How about with me?"

"Griffin," Molly gasped. "What are you doing here?"

He grinned as he glanced her way. "Told you, I prefer the woods."

"Miss Pritchard is returning to the orphanage."

"She is no orphan."

A large man approached them. Part of his size may have been the furs he wrapped around his broad shoulders and chest.

Molly sat up straighter in the chair. "You were in the office the other day."

"Hezebeth," he said as he turned toward her. Deep blue eyes overwhelmed his kind face. Sorrow shadowed them.

Molly shook her head. "I'm Molly. Molly Pritchard."

He faced Mrs. Honeywell once again. "What have you done to her?"

"I have done naught but provide shelter and substance for a poor orphaned child."

"You think I don't know my daughter?"" His voice thundered.

Her father? Molly tensed. She should know her father. She closed her eyes, but no memories broke through the gray cloud of her past.

Griffin lifted her into his arms as the large, older man moved in front of Mrs. Honeywell, blocking her view. She wrapped her arms around his neck trying to make no noise as he ran along the path to the lake. A screech of anger flew at them. Eyes wide, Molly watched as the head mistress took a different form. Wings unfurled. Her body forged into the shape of a bird of prey, though her face remained. Her hands and feet became claws of a great eagle. Breath stuck in her throat as Molly witnessed the transformation.

A sickeningly sweet sound whipped around them. Griffin stumbled. Molly screamed, and he seemed to recover. The man claiming to be her father spun, his furs falling away from his as he wielded a trident.

The siren's song faded as Mrs. Honeywell blocked the thrust of the weapon and attacked with one of her clawed feet. The man fell back, blood across his torso. He didn't seem to care as he swung the trident again.

Griffin reached the dock. The creature took to the air, claws extended as she reached to stop them. The horrible song filled the air around them. Molly screamed as Griffin fell to his knees. She rolled from him. The siren tried to catch her but wasn't quite close enough. Molly fell into the water.

Chapter 5: Breaking Through the Spells

The water drew her in, enveloping her. Sounds from above faded. The beat of her heart pulsed through her. Strength filled her. Her legs melded together, and a familiar motion sent her deeper under the water. At first, all around her was dark and murky, but then the strange world brightened. She stopped. Breath still moved through her, though water was everywhere. Shards of memory lay like broken bits of pottery in her mind. She looked at herself. Her legs were no longer feeble. They locked together allowing her to propel herself through the water, and yet she could still separate them. They were covered with sparkling green scales up to her belly button. She twisted to see her hair like seaweed falling over her shoulders and covering her torso. A sense of belonging filled her. Salt clung to the skin of her arms, forming intricate designs that were crystalline in nature. Blue shimmered all around her, along with variants of greens from the sea grasses swaying on the bottom to a herd of seahorses twirling around her as they travelled somewhere unknown.

Looking up, she noticed a hazy sun glowing beyond the water. What was happening up there? Questions flew through her mind, but a deeper anger caused her to swim for the surface. Her legs beat against the water, until, with great speed, she broke the surface and gracefully arched into the air. She twisted and then landed on the earth. No weakness assaulted her as she stood amongst them. Griffin lay on the dock with pain etched across his face from being caught by the siren's song. Miss Allen lay on the ground with a bloody wound slashed across her chest. The older man knelt, arms tense, muscles straining to pick up the trident that lay so close.

"Enough," Molly screamed as she slammed into Mrs. Honeywell.

The song of the older woman stopped.

"Hezebeth, no," her father cried to her.

Molly ignored him. She faced the siren. "Why? You took my memories, forced me to live a life that stole my legs. Why? What have I done to you?"

Mrs. Honeywell laughed. "You were but the prize. Too curious of other worlds to remain in your own." She reached to touch Molly's face, but Molly slapped her claw away. Mrs. Honeywell hissed. "I should tear your heart from your body."

"But why?"

"Because of me."

Molly glanced at her father. He crouched on the ground, wounds stretched from his torse around to his back. He pushed himself to his feet. "She ensnared my brother with her song. I forced him away from her."

"You stole him from me," she snarled. "I did not lure him. He chose to stay with me."

"Of his own free will?" Her father scoffed.

"I gave him everything he needed."

"Except the ability to choose for himself."

Mrs. Honeywell's eyes flared at Molly. "You were sweet revenge."

"Not anymore." Molly fisted her hands.

Mrs. Honeywell laughed. "What is to prevent me from taking you again? Keeping you hidden away until your legs wither and all these new memories fade?" Her voice took on a sing-song quality.

"Is that all you are?" Molly fought the snare of the siren's voice. "A harpy that imprisons?"

Mrs. Honeywell chuckled. "It is the nature of my being."

"What of the other girls? Are they truly orphans or more revenge?"

"Why would that matter to you?"

Anger burned through Molly. She took a step closer. "Because they deserve to be with their families. With people who love them, not being ruled over by you."

Wind whipped around them, and clouds covered the sky. Molly's words seemed to hang around them and the siren was silent.

Her father roared. Molly twisted out of the way as the trident sailed through the air, striking Mrs. Honeywell in the shoulder. Her scream rent the air like a thunderclap. Molly fell into the arms of her father. The noise faded, and in the silence, she looked. A body of ash lay on the earth. In a moment, a strong wind blew it away.

Molly shook. "What happened?"

Her father touched her face then pulled her close. "The power of the trident is our only weapon against the sirens. You distracted her."

Molly frowned as she noticed his chest. "Your wounds, they healed when she died?"

He laughed. "My daughter has healing power." He tugged on one of her braids and it broke away from her head. "Put this on the others to help their wounds."

Molly ran to Miss Allen who tried to pull herself up using the fallen over chair. Molly placed a hand on her shoulder. "Wait." She pressed what looked like a long strip of seaweed to cover the wound across Miss Allen's chest. Blood-stained clothes didn't change, but her breathing became more relaxed. Miss Allen placed her hand over the dressing. "I'll be fine. Go to Griffin."

But Griffin hadn't been wounded by the siren's claws. He shook his head and rubbed his hands through his hair. "I think I'd like to return to the water now."

Molly paused. "Are you one of us?"

He grinned. "Aye, lass. And many years we've been searching for you."

"What of the fair?"

"An excuse to be in the area." He continued to rub his head as though it pained him still.

Her father stepped up next to her. "I listened for sirens to guide us these four years. We've searched the seas for you."

"Does this lake lead to the ocean?"

Griffin grinned. "He brought it with him."

"Knowing you would be drawn to it if you were close." Tears fell from his eyes as he reached for her. Molly went into his embrace willingly. "Do you think I will recover my memories? I don't understand any of this." She touched the green scales covering her skin.

He smiled at her. "I don't know. But even if you are unable to have memories of your past, we can make new ones. Your family awaits your return."

"What of the orphanage? What will happen to the girls without Mrs. Honeywell? What if they have families they could return to?"

"I will see to it," Miss Allen said as she joined them. "She might have kept notes for where the others came from. It will be a starting place to finding their truths."

"Are you sure?" Her father frowned.

She nodded. "I have enough of the pills you gave me to be comfortable for at least a year. I will return before then."

"The lake will stay here?" Molly waved at the water.

Her father shook his head. "It will be drawn back when I leave. But the sea is not so very far from this place." He gripped Molly's hand. "Are you ready?" When she nodded, he squeezed her hand. "Just follow us."

There was no murky darkness this time when she entered the water. Warmth surrounded her with a gentle light. Her father kept hold of her hand, pulling her with him. Molly laughed as the sea rose up to greet them. The bitter years of pain and struggle were over. She was going home.

The Princess and the Pea

The Princess and the Pea is a short fairytale written by Hans Christian Anderson. It sparked an idea about the sweet pea plant. Missing baby princess, sweet pea plant that no longer blooms (now that would be a tragedy), and a jealous king who will do anything to keep his power- all elements for a newly twisted tale. This version called *The Princess and the Sweet Pea* is a delightful adventure.

The Princess and the Sweet Pea

Once upon a time, an old king and queen had a baby girl. Everybody was surprised, especially the old king's nephew. He expected to become king of their country when his uncle passed away. A little princess would ruin everything. The nephew did something very, very naughty. On a night dark as pitch, he scoured the woods until he found a fairy. Grabbing hold of her wings, he kept her from escaping. "I demand a wish," he told her.

She scowled. "I cannot kill, even though I see the desire for it in your eyes."

"Remove the princess far, far away, where she will never be found. That will be good enough for me."

The fairy shook her head. "I can make her plain as a barn and shy as a bird, but it will not change her nature. She is a princess by birth. If she is found, the spell will be broken, and you will reap the consequences."

"The only consequence I seek is to be king. Remove her from the palace. I doubt either of her parents will survive the grief."

She tried to deny him, but the pain of his hold forced her. "It is done, as you wish."

He pushed her away, an evil grin twisting his face.

The next morning, the royal crib was empty. Only an indent marked where the tiny princess slept. The palace was torn apart in the search for the baby, but no trace of her remained. No hope could be found. In the weeks, and months, and years that followed, first the queen, and then king succumbed to their broken hearts. Reginold Peagrove Allister Quincy gained the desire of his.

~

"Majesty," Captain Jacob Stowe bowed as he stood in the doorway of the king's sleeping chamber.

King Allister gripped the sheets of his bed. His hair stuck out around his head and his eyes looked just as wild. "I had a dream that the princess is still alive. She is out there, somewhere."

Jacob's heart leapt. "Is it possible she lives?" Though he was only six at her birth, he remembered the queen kneeling, baby in her arms. Dark curls around her baby face and shining blue eyes impressed him. He'd never forgotten her.

The king wiped sweat from his forehead. "The dream seemed real, vivid."

"Even if she is alive, would she know who she is? Whoever stole her away, if they didn't kill her, wouldn't have shared the truth of her birth with her."

He threw back the covers, stood, and paced across the bedroom. "You are right, of course. We must set a trap." He rubbed his hands together. "A test, I mean. Something that could alert us to her presence."

Jacob thought for a moment. "What about the sweet pea? They say the plant ceased to bloom when the princess disappeared. If she returns, could sweet pea blossoms be a sign?"

The king stopped, a look of shock on his face. His features darkened with anger, Jacob thought, but then he seemed the congenial ruler once more. "There have been no blooms since the baby left?"

Jacob shrugged. "Mother imports them for her birthday."

The king stopped at the dark window. "So, what do you think?"

"If she was to travel in our country, she would need to stop and rest. We could have sweet peas planted at all the inns. If any bloom, we will know where she is."

King Allister frowned. "There will be more than one girl."

"But of the right age? Proper features? If there is any question, we follow the possibilities to the next inn. Let the blooms be our guide."

The king was silent for a few minutes, then nodded. "It is a sound plan. I can think of none other idea that would suit our purpose better."

"Would you like me to speak with the chancellor? Have him set the plan into place?"

He shook his head. "Send him to me."

"How early?"

The king frowned. "Now. If I cannot sleep, there is no reason for him to sleep."

~

Not even an edict from the king could push Chancellor Corsairs any faster. King Allister barely held his anger in control once the older man stepped into the sitting area of the king's chamber. He waved for the guard to wait outside.

"Good heavens, what manner of emergency has you riled this early?"

"I dreamt Princess Adeline returned."

Corsairs laughed. "The princess? If she isn't dead, she is too far from here to be of any hurt to you.”

“Seemed real enough.”

“Have you grown a conscience?”

Allister’s frown deepened. “I took it more as a warning.”

“Even if she did come, no one would know her, and none would believe her.”

“Is it true, sweet peas have failed to bloom since the princess was taken?”

“Merely a coincidence, I’m sure.”

Allister snarled. “More likely something the fairy set up. I want sweet peas planted at each of the inns along every major roadway. They are to be tended with all the love and devotion the people had for the old king and his family.”

“To what purpose?”

“Captain Stowe will have the plants watched. If Princess Adeline shows up, even if she is disguised by the fairy’s curse, the plants will bloom. He will be notified.” Allister glared at Corsairs. “You must be prepared to arrive ahead of the captain and deal with the problem.”

Corsairs scoffed. “How am I to recognize her? I never even met her as a baby.”

Allister drew closer. “I don’t care if you kill every female close enough to her age to be her. Take care of the problem.”

“You want travelers murdered? Do you know what that will do to our country?”

“Repercussions can be managed after the deed is completed. I do not want Princess Adeline to survive.”

~

Addy Elizabeth Cole felt another bruise forming on her shoulder as the carriage bumped into a hole in the road.

“You’d think they traveled this path often enough to know how to miss the rockers,” an elderly passenger grumbled.

Addy grinned. “Thankful to be inside and not clinging to the back seat. Not sure I have enough grace for that.”

“And it was looking like rain, this morning.” Another passenger added.

“Very good to be out of the weather. I’ve thought my fingers might come off a time or two, trying to cling to those outside seats.” A woman with a Scottish accent rubbed her hands together.

At least the four women were pleasant enough company, Addy thought.

“Why are ye traveling on your own, child?” The Scottish passenger asked.

"It is the strangest thing. My mother died last month. I didn't know what was going to happen to me. I spent the night going through boxes in our attic. One of the boxes had papers, journals, and clothes. I read the journals and learned she was from the Kingdom of Is. I do not know how that could be possible. She never mentioned it before. I can't stand the mystery of it, so I had to come myself and find out."

Another rumble of the carriage caused them to rock. The Scottish woman's bag fell to the floor with a thud.

"Good heavens, did you fill it up with rocks?" Another passenger asked.

The woman chuckled. "I can hit hard enough to knock a man out. Never know what might happen on these roads."

Addy looked at her. "Seriously? You put rocks in your bag to hit with?"

She nodded. "When I'm traveling. Not like I do it every day."

Hm. At their next stop, Addy'd have to try it herself. There was something unsettling about traveling on her own from one country to another.

The carriage stopped for a moment.

"Are we at another rest stop?" Addy asked.

"'Tis the line. We've made our way to the Kingdom of Is."

A tingling sensation rolled across her skin. Good or ill will, she couldn't be certain, but something here was going to change her life.

Several hours later, they all groaned as the carriage turned onto a driveway. "Hackamore Inn." The driver's call alerted them to their destination for the day.

"I am ready for sleep. Don't think I have enough energy to eat any supper."

Addy helped the elderly passenger down the stairs. "Oh, do join us. A bowl of stew and a roll and you'll sleep through the night."

"Not even rocks in the mattress or this empty basket," she patted her tummy, "could keep me awake. I will be fine until morning."

"If you're sure," Addy said, then promised herself to save a roll, just in case.

The old woman's prediction was true. Addy, herself, barely managed the climb to the shared lodging after a bowl of stew. She yawned and collapsed onto an empty cot. She could change in the morning.

Sore muscles whined, but the scent of fresh baked bread and bacon pulled them all from the beds. Addy itched her head.

"Here, use some of this," the old woman handed her a bottle of oil.

Addy sniffed.

"Go on," the woman said with a wave of her hand. "It'll take care of the critters all these places have."

The driver hurried them through breakfast. It wasn't until they were leaving that Addy noticed the small pale blue and rose blooms in the garden. "Doesn't seem like the time of year for sweet peas."

The old woman turned to look. "Sweet peas? In Is? Those things haven't bloomed for ages." She frowned. "Maybe it's a primrose."

Addy shrugged. They looked like sweet peas, but she was too far inside the coach and in too much of a hurry to smell them to know for sure.

~

"She's going to need your help."

Captain Jacob jumped at the unexpected voice in his quarters. The woman who stepped from the shadows caused him to grip the hilt of his sword. Her hair was fair, and her pale skin sparkled. Her clothes brought to mind the forest with shades of greens and browns that seemed to shift and twirl. Effervescent wings twitched. On them, he could see what appeared to be bruises. He wasn't sure how, but he knew something, or someone, caused it. "Who needs help?" he asked once he found his voice.

"The princess. If he finds her, he will have her killed."

Jacob frowned. "He, who?"

She shrugged. "I cannot say. Who gained the most at the disappearance of the princess?"

"Disappearance? Most people think she was killed. Her parents did, and they died of broken hearts."

"She is not dead. I can tell you no more than that."

"Why tell me at all?"

"What happened was not by choice. You have already learned a sign to watch for. Be vigilant. Save the princess."

Doors banged in the hallway, drawing his attention for a moment. When he turned back, the fairy was gone. A heavy knock rattled his door. "What?" he hollered.

"Message arrived from the inn on the west road. Looks like Hackman… or maybe Hackson."

Jacob opened the door and grabbed the message. He looked at the smeared ink on the envelope. "Hackamore."

"Oh. I think that's the opposite direction we just sent Corsairs."

"Corsairs?"

"The king directed us to show him. Hackson is south. I'm pretty sure that's the direction he went."

An uneasy feeling in his gut tightened. "Hackamore is due east." He turned the envelope over. It was unopened. "Did he read the message? How did he know what business it pertains to?"

"The messenger gave the king a handful of flowers. Said they bloomed overnight."

Jacob ripped the missive open and read the short script. Something fell into his hand. He turned it over. "Is this a sweet pea bloom?"

"So, they do have a flowering plant?" The guard stepped back. "I have to send men to intercept Corsairs."

"No." On this, Jacob felt certain. "Let me go and see what I can learn. Do you really think this is because of the princess?"

The guard smiled. "It is a good sign if we are to find the princess."

An odd sign, Jacob thought. He folded the missive and placed it in his pocket. "Let me check. Make sure we are not party to fraud. I want to be certain before raising the king's hopes."

Once the guard had left, Jacob stared at his reflection as he tightened a strap on a bag he would carry. The fairy's question burned in his mind. Who benefited most from the disappearance of Princess Adeline? The king. King Allister was the only one to benefit once the baby was gone.

~

Three inns were quite enough. Addy resisted the urge to hug the old woman and the Scottish lady when the time came for her to leave the carriage. Porthe. She checked the name of the town against the page of a diary she'd torn out and brought with her. Looked the same.

An old farmer paused beside his wagon as the carriage disappeared around a curve in the road. He glanced at Addy. "Can I help you there, miss?"

Addy smiled. "I'm looking for Givney Manor. She said it's located in Porthe."

"Of course, of course. It's a long way to walk. Would you prefer a ride in the wagon?"

"I wouldn't want to be a bother."

"Not at all. I'll be heading past there myself to get home. Come on. It's not as comfortable as the post, but you can sit here and hold on. Dangle your feet if you've a care to."

Not as comfortable? The thought made her shiver, but she accepted the older man's hand to help her into the wagon. "Oh," she cried out and leaned to the side.

"Those are hard seeds, let me get them out of your way." He shoved the bag of peas behind a barrel of wine. He grabbed a sheep's pelt instead. "Here, this should sit more comfortably."

She smiled at him. "Thank you, it's perfect."

His eyes narrowed and he tilted his head. "You have a familiar look about you."

"I've never been here, but I think my mother might be a local. If that turns out to be true, I've no doubt this village is like all the others and news will travel faster than the wind."

He chuckled with her. "You aren't wrong, missy. Let's get you to Givney. There's a wrap you can use if you get a chill on the way." He pointed to a dark blanket.

They were soon on their way. Addy watched the rolling hills undulate while thickets of trees in the distance stayed still. They passed several roads leading to small cottages and fenced gardens. It wasn't quite half an hour later when the wagon stopped.

The old man came around and grinned at her. "There it is," he said as he pointed through the trees. "Bigger than most of the other houses here about, but they are good folks." He wagged a finger at her. "Don't you be causing them any trouble."

"I don't mean to. I just want the truth about my family."

He helped her down and handed her bag over. She impulsively kissed his cheek, causing him to turn red. "Thank you. I am glad I didn't have to make that walk." Then she turned and headed for the unknown. Givney Manor was larger than the cottage she'd grown up in. Was it possible this was her mother's family?

~

An old man held a round glass to his eye to study her as Addy stood beside an intricately carved table. She longed to rub her fingers against the dark wood and its pale frame. She tried to focus on the older gentleman. His hair was still thick, though more white than gray. He was probably tall, but he hadn't stood. He was also slender. The air of him suggested her mother.

"Clareann had no children." He plopped the glass in a cup beside him.

Addy clutched her bag to her chest. "Of course she did. She was my mother."

"She did not give birth to you, child. I'm not sure why she thought I wouldn't figure out the truth in eighteen years."

"My father died. He was from Savignac. It's why she never wanted to leave."

"Your father is dead." He agreed. "Both your mother and father. You're the princess. The one who disappeared and broke both their hearts."

She took a step back. "I am no princess."

"Of course, you are. And you aren't supposed to be here. It'll bring naught but trouble. You must leave. Go back. At least get out of Is."

"There is nothing in Savignac for me. Mother died."

"But you still have a house? Money to live by?"

"I belong here. Why can't I stay with you? Learn about my family?"

"We aren't family." He frowned at her. "Once they know you are here, they'll send someone."

Addy stiffened her shoulders. "Let them come."

He shook his head. "You'll not be invited to the palace for tea. They want to kill you." He grunted as he glanced through the dark window. "Too late to do anything tonight." With a sigh, he rang the bell.

A servant entered and the old man waved at Addy. "Take the girl to the blue bedroom. She's to be ready to depart an hour after sunrise in the morning."

He sat down and turned enough that Addy realized she'd been dismissed. The word princess rattled through her mind. How ridiculous that anyone would think she was a princess. She'd heard of the missing little girl. It wasn't her.

~

"There was me. The Crenshaws." Mrs. Buckle counted on her fingers. "Little Addy. She was darling."

"The Crenshaw's daughter?"

"Oh, no. From out past Woodsom, in the kingdom of Savignac. Said her mother died and she wanted to find her family." Mrs. Buckle ran her hand along the bushes of sweet peas. "Shame these haven't found blooms yet. It's been lovely seeing the flowers blooming at the other inns."

"Did someone leave your company before the stage arrived here?"

Captain Jacob, watching and listening from a table nearby as Chancellor Corsairs interviewed a passenger from the coach, didn't want anything more to be said. He grabbed a tankard of ale. "Corsairs," he yelled as he raised the mug, allowing it to spill across his shirt. "Bloody brilliant finding you here. That gel we seek didn't make the stage this far. She must still be at the inn in Dovershire."

Mrs. Buckle opened her mouth, but Jacob silenced her with a look. He forced a large smile as he draped his arm across Corsairs' shoulder.

Chancellor Corsairs glared at Jacob. "Captain, you have knowledge of her where abouts?"

Jacob chuckled. "What's to seduce...I mean deduce. You've followed the trail as well as myself. She hasn't made it here, so back we go." He frowned at the darkening window. "But not tonight. We'll go in the morning. First thing. Be sure we arrive before any chance of her taking a different coach."

"Hm." Corsairs allowed Jacob to lead him toward the public tavern.

"Let buy you a pint," Jacob offered as they found two empty seats at a long table.

Corsairs sniffed. "I'll allow two."

Jacob laughed as he waved a buxom wench to the table. "Two it is," he said loudly, then lowered his voice. "And a water for myself, same kind of mug." He flashed a coin, and the girl nodded.

As Corsairs chatted with an old man on his other side, Jacob managed to drop a few crystals into Corsairs' drink. He feigned a large yawn when he noticed the chancellor started to droop. "I'll be in the common sleeping room two floors up. Did you manage to secure a better room?"

Corsairs frowned. "Course I did. I'll see you in the morning. Might as well go together to find the girl."

"The princess," Jacob slapped Corsairs' back. "They'll honor us with a parade when we return the lost princess to the palace."

"She'd have to survive first," Corsairs said with a laugh, then waved as though he meant in jest.

Jacob didn't take the stairs to the upper sleeping hall once he saw Corsairs to his room. Instead, he turned the corner to find Mrs. Buckle's room.

"What do you mean, sir?" Mrs. Buckle hissed once she opened the door at his insistent knocking.

"I need to find the young woman. I think you called her Addy."

"But you didn't want the official from the palace to know?" She glared at him with narrow eyes.

"He is the king's man. I fear they seek to harm her, or worse."

"Why would they do that? She is a sweet young lady."

"She is the Princess Adeline. Rightful heir to the throne of our kingdom."

Mrs. Buckle gasped. "Can it be possible? The lost princess?"

He nodded. "You saw the sweet pea blossoms at the other inns."

"I thought maybe since we were near the border…"

But he shook his head. "No flowers have bloomed within our kingdom for eighteen years. Not since the princess disappeared."

"I heard her ask for a ride." She closed her eyes. Jacob could tell she remembered something. "Givney Manor. It's a plantation outside of Porthe."

Jacob grasped her hands. "Thank you."

"Be good to her."

He nodded. "I will protect her with my life."

~

Addy gasped as someone jerked her arm and pulled her from the bed. She staggered as she tried to steady her legs. "What are you doing?"

The muscular footman frowned. "You were given until an hour after dawn to leave. The maid couldn't get you to wake."

Rosy light shone through the window. "It's barely dawn now. Another hour wouldn't have hurt anything." Addy glared at the others.

The footman shrugged. "I obey my master. The cook has something for you in the kitchen. Then you'll be sent on your way."

"To where? I have nowhere to go."

He shrugged. "It matters not to me."

Addy quickly went through her morning ministration and then hurried to the kitchen. With her stomach grumbling, she didn't want to risk missing out on food.

A large woman pulled a tray of scones from an oven but paused when she noticed Addy standing in the doorway. "I heard the master talking to you last evening," she whispered, then dropped the pan on the table. "You're the princess, the one who disappeared all of them years ago."

Addy shook her head. "I am not a princess, I promise."

The cook failed to listen. She gathered scones, apples, a wedge of bacon and cheese and packed it all in a bag. She looped rope through the grommets and closed the bag before handing it to Addy. "I'll be praying you get safely away. Even if you never get to sit on the throne of Is, I'll gladly pray every night you are safe and well."

Addy gulped. "I don't even know where to go."

The cook pressed Addy's hand and then pushed her toward the kitchen doorway. "Through here, take the path across the gardens and the one that leads into the woods. Help will find you there."

The sky hadn't yet turned blue. White mist clung to the plants lining the paths. Addy blinked against the threat of tears. No good would come of them. She pushed open the gate at the back of the garden and continued to the trees. She could walk to where the traveling coach stopped. Return home, even though all that remained was a house. No one to make it home. She sighed. At least she could forget the nonsense of her being a princess.

The woods were dark, heavy with mist. She didn't see anyone until she knocked into another person. She screamed as someone gripped her shoulders.

~

"Princess," Jacob gasped. For a moment the thought of luck crossed his mind, but no, something greater worked.

The young woman with dark curly hair grimaced. "Why do people keep calling me princess? I am not royalty."

"Have you never seen a picture of Queen Merelda when she was young?"

"I don't know who that is." She crossed her arms over her chest.

Jacob stared at her until she looked down. She sighed. "My mother was Clareann. We lived our life in Savignac. I've never been to the Kingdom of Is and certainly didn't know her family—my family—lived here." She glanced at him, blue eyes flashing.

"I can't image how hard it's been to learn so many secrets. "

Addy blinked moisture from her eyes. "I'm going home."

"I think once you see the palace, you'll know where home is." She turned to leave, but he held onto her arm. "You aren't safe. You won't be safe until you go to the palace."

She shook her head. "I'm not who you think I am."

"Then we prove it by going to the palace and nothing happens. We make sure everyone knows and then they'll leave you alone. I'm afraid if we don't go, even if you return to your country, they will send someone after you."

She closed her eyes. Jacob could feel her tremble beneath his hand. "Let me protect you."

~

Addy pressed the heel of her hands against her eyes. If what Captain Stowe told her was true, her mother wasn't her mother. The woman who raised her kept her from her real parents, causing them to die from broken hearts. It couldn't be true. She didn't feel like a princess. She sat across from the captain and kept her head down.

"Are you familiar with sweet peas?"

She peeked toward him through curls that had fallen across her face. He held a bag. "I know what they are. It's my favorite flower."

"Even though they're small and delicate?"

"They're quite hardy, actually, with a scent that sparks the imagination."

He lifted a small plant from the bag. "The strangest thing happened in Is when the princess disappeared. Sweet peas stopped blooming."

"That can't be true. We've seen them at the inns."

"Here, hold this." He held the plant to her.

Addy took it without thinking. In a matter of moments, blossoms unfurled. Before long, the coach filled with the fresh scent of flowers.

"Only the inns where you stayed had blossoms."

She dropped the plant on the floor. "Why? That doesn't make sense."

"From what I've been able to glean, King Allister wasn't happy when you were born because it took the kingdom out of his hands. He caught a fairy."

"A bad fairy?"

"I think not. From the bruises on her wings, he hurt her to get his way. She caused you to disappear, with the woman who raised you. Then she caused a curse to fall on the flowers. I'm not sure why she chose the sweet pea."

"What happens if I go to the palace?"

"The curse is undone. King Allister is forced to turn the kingdom over to you. He could face execution for treason, having caused deaths and mayhem."

"Has he caused harm to the country?"

Jacob shrugged. "He forces taxes. Refuses funds to aid those who are sick or destitute."

"You think I can do better? Or will ending the curse somehow return my parents to me?"

"I don't think the fairies have that much power."

"I think we should stop at the crossroads and head toward Savignac."

"Could you really go back to your life without knowing for sure?"

Addy looked at the floor. The fallen plant gleamed with colors. Made the gray of the coach less dull. The country had been denied them for too long. Had been denied their rightful ruler for too long. She closed her eyes. A distant memory came to mind, of a golden bauble dangling overhead, glimmers of light sparkling from it. Laughter in the background. Loved. No matter what, she was loved. She opened her eyes and looked directly at Jacob. "Yes, let us return to the palace."

~

"How far are we?" Addy asked as they started walking along a trail near the river.

"A few days. We should keep to the woods and cut across fields as much as we can."

"No horses?" She grinned to let him know she teased.

He shrugged. "If we return to the inn, Corsairs might be there."

"Who is he?"

Sunlight dripped through the trees. A rabbit hopped from beneath a bush and watched them pass. Captain Stowe shook his head and then responded. "He is advisor to King Allister. Also assigned to search for you."

"But you don't want me to meet him?"

"I think it would be safer for you not to."

"I don't understand. Why is the king sending men after me? What am I to him?"

A pair of deer came through the trees to watch them pass. Jacob rubbed his hand over his face. "You are inherently a princess. Animals in the woods know it." He waved. "Sweet peas know it. People will meet you and know as well."

Addy shuddered. "It is a very strange circumstance to find myself in." She frowned. "My mother stole me away?"

"Doesn't seem as if she had a choice. Was she a loving mother?"

Addy nodded. "I always thought so. I have my own bedroom in our thatched cottage. The garden is at the back. Sweet peas grow on the wall." She glanced at the captain. "Our neighbors aways said they were jealous of the plants. How well they bloomed."

Their walk continued. Jacob talked about his family with two older brothers and one younger. His sister dying when sickness assailed their village. As the shadows lengthened, they found a barn. The cows were already penned. Addy rubbed her arms. "Don't suppose you have blankets in your satchel?"

"I'll find something. I have a meat pie we can split."

Abby brightened as she dug into her bag. "I forgot. The cook at Givney wrapped a meal for me." She opened a pouch and held a piece of bacon.

Jacob chuckled. "A three-course meal after walking in the woods and stowing away in a stranger's barn? Quite a feat."

They ate and then Jacob searched for blankets. As night settled with crickets singing and stars twinkling through a crack overhead, Addy cozied into her surprisingly comfortable bed and wondered what the new day would bring.

A cool morning gave way to a pleasant day. They had bread and cheese to break their fast. It wasn't a hard walk, but getting closer to the capital city of Is meant there were people. More and more people, and some of them stared at her. Addy rubbed her hand over her hair. "Why do people seem to be watching us?" she muttered to Jacob.

An old woman offered them pie. "Bless you, child. You remind me of our good queen."

"Me?" Addy gulped. "That's very kind of you to say."

"Here I thought you meant to betray the crown." Corsairs said as he stepped from the doorway of a public house.

The old woman scurried away as Jacob pushed Addy behind him. "If she is the lost princess, this is her home."

Corsairs shook his head. "The real princess is dead. Been dead for eighteen years."

"What about the sweet pea blossoms?" Jacob asked.

"I have no idea." Corsairs frowned. "Doesn't really matter, does it?"

"I think you are probably right," Addy scooted around her soldier. "Let us see the king, resolve this matter, and then I'll return home. I'm not even from Is."

Jacob squeezed her hand, then raised his voice. "But she is the missing princess."

People were noticing, drawing closer. Jacob turned to Addy. In a quiet voice he directed her. "Run. Let the people hide you." He faced Corsairs. "She belongs here."

Corsairs flinched. "Not anymore."

"Addy, now," Jacob pushed her into a group of peddlers from the market before reaching for Corsairs.

"What have you done?" Corsairs screamed, fighting Jacob's hold.

"She is the rightful heir to the Kingdom." He kept his arm locked around Corsair. "King Allister can't just kill his cousin."

Corsairs' eyes flared. "He's done much worse than that."

Pain tore through Jacob as Corsairs thrust a dagger into him.

Corsairs snarled, "Should have chosen your side better." He thrust with the dagger once more. "Yours is a wasteful death, but no worry. I will send her to you as quick as I may."

Jacob tried to hold Corsairs, but strength drained from his hands. He staggered, falling against the wall. The world around him dimmed as pain burned through him.

~

"I can't save your life." The fairy knelt beside him.

Jacob coughed, gripping his side as pain lanced through him. "The princess is safe. That is all that matters."

She pulled a sphere from a pocket. "I can send you back and let you reverse it all."

He understood quickly. "Stop him from taking her away."

"And hurting me." Her eyes darkened. She opened her hand. The sphere rested on her palm. Shadows swirled through the globe. "Take it," she told him.

Instantly, he stood in a wood. His side felt like fire, but he was standing and there was strength in him yet. He heard a cry.

"Release me."

"Not until I get what I want."

Jacob drew his sword as he hurried to a bend in the path. A younger King Allister gripped the wings of a fairy. "Unhand her," he bellowed.

"This is not your business. Be on your way."

"Protection of all who live within the borders of the Kingdom of Is is my business. Unhand her and face your consequences."

With a cry, King Allister did, drawing his sword and striking at Jacob. Jacob parried.

Allister laughed. "You're already wounded."

He pressed his free hand to his side. "Courtesy of you. Time to return the favor."

Allister thrust at him. Jacob knocked the blade to the side and pressed forward. Allister fell against him, Jacob's sword passing through his chest. There was a gurgling gasp. Allister's eyes burned with greed, then flickered, then faded to death. Jacob released his hold on the sword and watched them both fall to the ground. He staggered back.

"How did you know?"

The fairy drew his attention as shadows around him deepened. "You sent me. It's all undone."

Shadows gathered until all he saw was a path through the woods, a boy running toward him. And then suddenly, he was the boy, running and laughing as a butterfly danced ahead of him.

~

Once upon a time there was an old king and queen who had a beautiful baby girl. Princess Adeline was loved by all. When she was six, she crossed paths with an older boy practicing how to fight with a sword. She insisted he teach her. He wasn't always nice about it. Her backside stung more than once. But she didn't care. "Someday, I'm going to marry you." Adeline declared.

And she did. Together, they lived happily ever after as king and queen of the Kingdom of Is.

About the Author

Ah. Don't you love fairy tales? I sure do. Thank you for reading this collection. Be sure to make a review on Amazon and Goodreads.

Check out other great reads. Yes, I write fantasy, but I also have contemporary suspense, rom coms (think Hallmark Christmas), and Biblical fiction. You can explore these collections and more on Amazon.

Fantasy Fiction
Once Upon a Time in Fairy Land
Legends within the Dark Realm
Cinderella Spell: A Tale from Fairy Land
The Fruit of Her Hands Series:
Jewel of Jericho
Mistress of Moab
Pearl of Persia
Biblical Fiction
Flood: A Wife for Shem
Christmas Rom-Coms
Cookies, Cocoa, and Capers
Her Christmas Misfortune
A Jane Austen Christmas
Suspense-Full
The Cat from Camden Place
The Maxwell Murders
Hidden Gems

Get Hooked on Another Great Read!

Cinderella. Is she the sweet, mistreated, rags to riches story we've loved since childhood? Or is something not quite right with how the prince falls madly in love with her at the ball? Sounds a bit like a spell. But what would Cinderella need with a spell? Enjoy this introduction from Cinderella Spell: A Tale from Fairy Land.

Cinderella Spell: A Tale from Fairy Land Chapter 1

Cinderella's gray service gown swooshed as she crossed the wood-planked floor of the queen's sick chamber. Woven damask drapes lining the slim, long windows kept the room in shadows. Two iron-wrought candelabras fit with six candles cast a soft glow across the thick mattress piled high with fine linen and crafted blankets. Upon the bed, Queen Charlotte lay gaunt against a mountain of pillows. Her once-luxurious ebony hair hung limp, dampened by fever. Even with candlelight across her face, the vivid greens of square pillows and yellow bolster cushions couldn't bring color to her sick pallor.

Cinderella paused beside the bed and allowed a trickle of pleasure to bring a smile to her face before schooling her features. She cleared her throat loud enough to rouse the sick woman struggling before her.

The Queen's dull gray eyes blinked open and she offered a wan smile. "Cinderella? Why are you here?" Her raspy voice reached into the darkness.

Cinderella sat upon the edge of the bed and arranged her skirts. The dark cotton presented a sharp contrast to the cream-colored linen. Cinderella trailed her fingers across both materials before reaching for the queen's hand. "I have come for the key, my lady."

"Key?" The Queen's eyes closed with a sigh. "Rowley is the keeper of keys."

"Except Doorin's Key." Cinderella tilted her head, eager to see the Queen's reaction. "You have been its keeper, have you not?"

The sick woman gasped as she tried to free her hand from Cinderella's grip, but she was too weak. Cinderella kept hold of the queen's cold flesh as she pulled the silver chain that slipped beneath the queen's bedgown. But instead of the key, a silver heart dangled.

Anger burned within Cinderella. "Where is it?"

The Queen seemed to muster her strength. "Beyond your reach."

She tightened her hold on the Queen, but the sight of pain

twisting the queen's mouth did not please. "Give me what I want, and the sickness will end." She lowered her eyes, breathed patience, and forced her voice to a sweet and imploring umber. "You will be well once more."

"That door must never be opened. Why ask it of me?"

Cinderella scowled. "You have no knowledge of Doorin's secrets. How can you claim it should never be opened?" She paused until a thought brought a wicked smile to her face. She released the Queen's hand and sat straight. "With your death, the key passes to your son."

The Queen shook her head. "He is protected. The Faere Folk christened him."

Cinderella twisted her hair into a coil and brushed it through her hands over and over. Its dark color faded with each pass of her hand, until her head gleamed with golden hair. "Only until his twenty-first birthday. I have but to wait. I will make him fall in love with me." She grinned. The queen struggled to sit up, and Cinderella read fear in her eyes. "We will dance upon your grave." She stood. In place of the servant clothes she'd been wearing, she fussed with the ruffles of a pale blue silken fabric embroidered with silver thread ball gown. The queen's agitation lifted her spirits, and she giggled.

"No! He will never love you. His heart will belong to a woman of character and faith." Queen Charlotte's denial shuddered to silence as she fought to catch her breath.

Cinderella's laughter filled the chamber. She twirled, catching her image in a large mirror on the far wall. She was a picture of youth and health with bouncing blonde curls and a shapely figure. "Perhaps if you had lived to nurture and guide him as he grows." Cinderella turned from admiring herself in the mirror to gaze once more at the dying queen. She leaned over and placed her hand on the Queen's cheek. "But no." She rocked her head from side to side, taunting the Queen. "You have chosen death."

Queen Charlotte twisted away from her. "Be gone, witch! Darken my chamber no more."

Cinderella slipped into the shadows beyond the candle's glow, but her voice carried. "I will be patient, my lady. Just a while longer. Your son will come to love me, and I will spill his blood in the doorway of Doorin's room."

~

"Will, my gown!"

King William laughed at his queen's protest, then wrapped one arm around her waist and grabbed his son with his other arm. He growled and pulled the three of them backward into the snow. Cold embraced him, but the sound of Prince Robert's gleeful giggles warmed his heart.

Queen Charlotte pressed her slim hand against his chest. "You've ruined us." But the laughter in her voice belied her severity.

"Pull us up, Son," King William said. But the six-year-old pounced on his chest with ferocious growls.

"Now look, you've turned our boy into a bear," Queen Charlotte laughed as Prince Robert snapped at her fingers.

"I'll save you, my precious," King William wrapped both hands around his son and lifted him above them.

"No, you can't save her." A shadow lurked in his periphery. Though he chuckled at the dangling arms grasping cold air, the shadow moved closer, spreading across the snow. He got up and twirled. Prince Robert squealed and wrapped arms around his neck. Queen Charlotte clung to his side, her feet gliding above the snow. The shadow spun faster, wrapping around them like a snake. The joy of his family warred against the hiss of shadow.

King William lurched from his bed as the dream turned sour. Sweat clung to his skin even though the room was cool. "Charlotte," he muttered her name as he stretched his arm across the other side of the bed. She wasn't there. Hadn't been since she'd taken ill a day after their romp in the snow. "I must go to her." He raked his fingers through his hair. "Bartholomew," he hollered.

The tall, thin, silver-haired man entered from the servant's cove. "Sire, how may I assist you?"

King William gripped a post of the bed. "I must go to the queen."

He bowed. "Of course, Sire. Shall I have a bath drawn for you?"

"No, no. A dressing gown will do. I want to go now." He held his arms out, unmindful of the woolen weave of the fabric being wrapped onto him. Bartholomew buttoned the closure and tied the belt around his waist. He slipped his feet into leather slippers.

Torchmen waited in the hallway to lead the way to the queen's sick chamber. The palace remained quiet as they walked the halls. Something inside him twisted with pain as they reached Charlotte's room.

He blinked against the sting of incense permeating the air as he entered the chamber. Pain moved to his chest, clutching at the sight of her, pale and wan against the covers. Her dark hair shone with sweat, mirroring the shadows beneath her closed eyes.

How could this be? A week prior, she'd laughed, holding a hand toward him from her seat in the snow. His throat ached, catching what little breath he managed.

"My life, Lord," he prayed. "My life for hers." But his whispered words hit the ceiling and would go no further.

Her chest rose and fell. Mrs. Turney, Robert's old nurse, wrung a towel in a bowl of water and placed the towel across Charlotte's forehead. Her lips parted. William strode to her side. He dipped a smaller cloth in water and put it to her mouth. Precious drops wet her tongue, and the furrow between her brows calmed for a time.

"I am sorry, Majesty." Mrs. Turney's wrinkled face bore testament to her sorrow.

He managed a glimmer of a smile before looking down at his beloved wife. Her eyes shifted. The gray color that had held his attention since they first met at a dignitary's banquet had darkened. He wiped a stray hair from her face. The heat of her skin beneath his fingers put an ache in his belly. "How long are you letting this fever hold you?" He teased as her eyes met his.

She sighed. "Not much longer now."

He choked and turned to the nurse. "A fresh towel."

Charlotte tossed restlessly as her fever-ravished body refused to give up its heat. William pressed the new towel against her forehead, laying another on her chest. She did not calm. Her hand moved, and he took it in his own. She squeezed her fingers around his.

"What do you need?" William kept the tears at bay by sheer will. It was all he could do. Nothing seemed to work against the devilish fever claiming Charlotte's life.

"Promise me," she struggled to speak, but a familiar glint sparked in her gray eyes.

"Anything."

"Take a wife when I am gone."

William leaned closer. "Do not ask it of me."

"You must. For Robert." Her breath rasped between words. "You must. Protect him."

Her pallor turned ashen, and William noticed a drop on her cheek. His tear. Another dampened her face. Helplessness tore at his chest. He shook his head, refusing her request yet again.

Her thin hand brushed against his cheek. He dropped his head to her neck, overwhelmed in his sorrow.

"I am sorry, my love." Her voice managed a whisper, and then her body stilled.

He gathered her body to him and wept, praying death over them both.